THE EXECUTION OF
ROOKER FLYNN

LOCKE INSTITUTE TRILOGY

BOOK 3

A. R. WITHAM

Nepenthe House

For Brian Snyder,
Who Laughs.

TABLE OF CONTENTS

Fargil's Map

(Annotated by Jack Swift)

Lake

Clearing

Butte

Swamp

Buzzard

Vulture

Paradise Road

Hyena

Jackal

Once Upon a Time...

...there were two friends.

Rooker Flynn & Jack Swift attempted to escape the Locke Institute through the shiq tunnels with Copper Dave, Yenrab the Red Dwarf, Farah, Patch Picaroon, and her newborn child. The escape ended with their capture by Headmistress Gerba Whipmarples.

Finally in possession of all seven pieces of Nepenthe, Gerba used it to beat Jack half to death.

To save Jack's life, Rooker Flynn sacrificed the only thing he ever loved, the *Venture Brigand*. He surrendered the brass rings that bonded him with the ship. In exchange, he made the headmistress swear, under geas curse, not to kill or harm Jack.

In committing the only unselfish act of his life, Rooker Flynn gave Gerba Whipmarples no further reason to protect him.

She sentenced Rooker to be executed at dawn.

> Most of the book you hold in your hand takes place in the thirteen hours surrounding the execution of Rooker Flynn.

THE LOCKE INSTITUTE
KNOWN CRIMINALS

JACKAL

~~BOSS MAMBA~~
ROOKER FLYNN
JACK SWIFT
PATCH PICAROON
COPPER DAVE
BILLY PILGRIM

HYENA

~~BOSS WEST~~
~~RANSOM ADARE~~

VULTURE

~~BOSS LIGHTFINGERS~~
~~BARNEY BIALIK~~
YENRAB BIALIK

BUZZARD

~~BOSS HOOK~~
~~FANCY NAN~~
FARAH IBIS

Prologue

BERTH
= OF A =
PIRATE

Alone, alone, all, all alone,
Alone on a wide wide sea!
Samuel Taylor Coleridge

L OVE IS PURE IN the eyes of the young. There is nothing so bright as a child's love. It is whole, complete, boundless. A baby loves its mother with a single-minded zeal that cannot be found anywhere else in nature. A toddler's love for a puppy or a kitten can briefly outshine an adult's truest romance. Children experience love without the fear of being hurt. They remain blissfully ignorant of the truth that all things must end.

Pippin Winegrad's love was flawless.

Inside the sea cave of Thimble Tower, the dancing green of a million pixies encircled the mysterious ship in a swirling halo of eldritch romance. A colossal catamaran grander and more majestic than any craft he'd ever seen, she floated above the water on two long legs, a ship in the shape of a Λ. Pip stood at the very center of her. Below, the deck, her rounded belly, and her long legs that arched down to floating outriggers. Above, three long masts jutted skyward like arms, her tightly-furled sails like a woman's blouse, and at the very top sat her empty crow's nest, just waiting for someone to brave the climb.

Someone just like me.

Yes.

He heard the voice of the ship in his mind as if she were standing right behind him. He felt her melody in the brass rings she had offered him as a gift. He inhaled the scent of her timbers like a lady's perfume, the delicate ambrosia of elven majik. She spoke to his very soul.

Pip knew it was impossible. Ships do not speak, not even in stories. He was freezing, starving, and exhausted; his brain was as scrambled as an egg. The voice was only his imagination. Even so, it was the first voice Pip had heard since he'd been shipwrecked in the North Waste.

I can pretend, can't I?

Yes.

The boy giggled, then laughed. A tremulous joy washed over him like ocean waves, endless, loud, and powerful. He jumped, exuberant, and wrapped his arms and legs around the mainmast, hugging the ship like a mother.

Home.

The brass rings on his finger warmed. *Home.*

Hey! His akita pup barked. *Hey!*

Pip realized he had been hugging the mast forever. He blinked and shook his head. He was shipwrecked, freezing, starving, and in danger of becoming prey. He could not afford to daydream. Rooker needed him.

Rooker barked, spun in circles, and tried to catch the pixies that darted through the air. The little akita's fur was iced over, but Rooker didn't mind; the dog seemed to enjoy the catamaran as much as Pip. "Yeah? You think we found a home? Huh, Rooker? We got a home?" Rooker licked his face, agreeing with everything Pip said.

Pip thumped the dog's chest and took in his surroundings. The inside of Thimble Tower was dark and echoing, a huge sea cave two hundred feet tall. Pip could just make out old designs and painted colors on the ceiling of the great cave. It was clear this place had been used as a sheltered berth, a hidden harbor in the North Waste. Protected from the storms that raged outside, the water inside Thimble Tower was calm as a millpond, an ideal place to hide a ship.

"So why isn't anyone here?" Pip muttered. Judging from the dust on the deck, no one had been aboard in months. Years, maybe. Whatever had happened to the previous crew, it'd happened a long time ago. Plus, something else was wrong, something Pip couldn't put his finger on.

"Come on, boy." Pip moved for a better look at the sea cave.

Thimble Tower was almost completely enclosed. There was only one source of daylight, a single fissure two hundred feet high that opened to the Irridin Sea like a parting curtain, an invitation to a new world.

But the ship would never fit through it.

The catamaran was too wide to fit through the crack, half again as wide as the fissure. Pip blinked. He puzzled over it for a moment but couldn't make sense of it. "How did you get in here?"

There was no response from the ship.

"How did she get in here?"

Rooker cocked his head; the dog had no good answer either.

Pip walked up and down the rail as if changing his perspective could solve the riddle. No matter how he looked at it, the catamaran would not fit through the fissure. *It might as well be a ship in a bottle. We would need some kind of crazy majik to reach the sea.*

Yes, the ship agreed.

Rooker barked, tired of the puzzle. Pip's reverie broke as he realized it didn't matter. Even if he could get the ship out, he could never sail her by himself. It would take ten men to hoist the sails alone, to say nothing of steering, tacking, and jibing. Whatever fantasies he had of driving his new love out upon the open sea evaporated. She was trapped here just as much as he was, a gilded bird in a hidden cage.

Doesn't matter. She's mine.

Yes.

Pip adjusted his gigantic purple captain's hat and set himself to discovering something useful. The fore and aft lockers contained tools like adzes, riggers, mallets, boat hooks, marlinspikes, and roping palms, along with assorted longbows, crossbows, and pikes. A giant harpoon bow was mounted fore and aft. Every dozen yards a weapons barrel waited, filled with cutlasses and sabers. Pip strapped a cutlass to his waist and felt his step become a swagger. *Okay, now we're cookin'.*

He could find no food on deck and glanced toward the hidden darkness of the ladders that led below. He was suddenly nervous, although he could not explain why. Peering at the details of the woodwork of the doorframe, Pip spied a delicate wooden figurine of a bare-breasted woman. He kissed his fingers, touched her lips, and prayed for a bit of luck. Pip clapped one hand over one eye as Captain Roper Jon had taught him. He took a breath and descended belowdecks.

When he uncapped his eye, his pupil was already dilated. It was an old seafarer's trick, one that allowed pirates to move from sunlight to shadow without pause, an excellent defense against an ambush. Nothing waited for him below, no ghosts, no wraiths. Pip placed one hand on the bulkhead and listened. Nothing made a sound but the creak of the ship itself. He thumped Rooker. "Okay, boy." The akita padded down the dusty passageway, sniffing. Pip followed, embarrassed that his dog was braver than he was.

The galley had no food, not even moldy hardtack. All pots and pans were clean and bare. Every cabin was buttoned up and ship-shape as if awaiting the crew's return. There was no ship's log, no paperwork in the captain's cabin, and, even more strangely, no anchor anywhere on board. There were no skeletons, no bodies, no bloodstains... It was as if the crew had evaporated.

"Did they just abandon you, girl?"

The ship did not answer, remaining a mystery.

He came to the door at the end of a passage, placed a careful hand on the brass knob, and quietly turned it.

Flickering light danced on the ceiling of a round room. At the center, where a floor should be, a tremendous glass dome hung beneath the belly of the ship. The ripples on the ceiling were rays of light reflected from the water below.

Pip laughed, amazed. He circled the catwalk that ringed the dome. He could see the entire sea cave around him, a comprehensive view obstructed only by the ship's trim legs. It was the perfect lookout. Rooker sniffed at the big bowl and growled, not sure what to make of it. Pip eased over the side and slid into the glass bowl;

his butt made a squealing sound against the glass. At the bottom was a trapdoor, round and clear.

He found a clasp and slid it back. The trapdoor swung open and a mechanism caught, holding it open with a gentle klik. "Ha!" Pip laughed. *That's a good trick.*

"Hey, Rooker! Watch this!" Pip swan dove through the trap-door, dropped twenty feet, tucked into a roll, and flipped just before he hit. Cold water struck him and bubbles tickled past his face as he spun, weightless. Under water, he laughed.

Pip's head broke the surface. He tossed his hair back and saw Rooker pacing the trapdoor above, barking. *Hey! Hey!!*

"Stay there, boy! I'm okay!" Pip didn't want Rooker to jump down. Carrying the dog up the ship's leg had been difficult enough the first time; the beam was narrow and steep. It was the only part of the ship he didn't like: There was no good way to board her. *Who built this thing, crazy wizards?*

He scrambled onto a pontoon and climbed the ship's leg. Drip-ping, he walked back to the dome to find Rooker worried and barking. "It's okay, boy. I'm here. Let's get some food."

A few minutes later, Pip dangled his legs through the trapdoor, a cane pole in his hand, angling for the school of cod that circled directly beneath him. Pip giggled. *This is the best fishin' hole ever.*

They cooked the fish over a real cast-iron stove, drank fresh water from the pump, and slept in a real bed for the first time in forty days. Pip snuggled one arm around the dog and rested one hand on the ship's bulkhead, making sure they were both real.

Yes.

They lived like that for three days. When a lightning storm arrived outside, they stayed dry, protected by the walls and roof of Thimble Tower. Rooker ate as much fish as he could stomach and slept half the day away. Pip found a rope ball and spent the next morning on the ship's deck playing fetch with Rooker, the two laughing and barking. From dawn to dusk, Pip puzzled over the mystery of how the ship had entered the cave but came up with no answers. It didn't matter. They could survive here as long as they wanted.

When he finally solved the puzzle, it was because of the dog.

Pip was fishing from the glass dome when a shark rooked a tuna off his line. The beast was a white hammerhead, hunting the ice for easy prey. Pip's rod was dragged from his hand, fell, and sank into the depths. Pip hurled curses at the shark, but the thing had caught scent of Pip's leavings and wanted more. Rooker barked his own curses at the shark. Pip climbed out of the bowl and grabbed a new fishing pole from the catwalk, yelling at the shark. "That's our fish! You don't rook our fish, dumb shark!" Angry, Pip jumped back into the bowl.

He meant to slide but caught an ankle, tumbled head over heels to the bottom, and hit Rooker with one leg.

The dog yelped and fell through the trapdoor.

Rooker landed nearly on top of the hammerhead with a four-legged splash. The fish took off as Rooker struggled back to the surface. Pip was at the edge immediately. "No!"

Twenty feet below, his dog paddled in the freezing sea as the white hammerhead circled back to investigate.

Pip's heart caught in his throat. "Rooker!" He almost dove in but stopped himself at the last instant. *That hammerhead will have us both before we swim to either one of the outriggers.* If Pip dove in, they'd both die.

Rooker struggled to stay afloat and yelped; he could sense the shark closing in.

"I'm coming!" Pip scrambled up the bowl and grabbed a hunk of curled rope from the catwalk. He threw himself back into the dome and skidded down the glass so fast he nearly fell through the trapdoor. "I'm coming!"

He tied the rope off, but his knot was bad and he had to start again. Pip watched through the glass beneath his feet where the shark circled his dog, growing bolder with each pass. He knotted the rope, then realized he had no way to haul Rooker back up. Even if he could shimmy down the rope and grab Rooker, he wasn't strong enough to pull him up. And there was no good way to get a lasso around the dog. He threw the rope aside, hooked a leg inside the trapdoor, and lowered himself through the hole head first. Holding on with only his legs, Pip lowered himself as far as he dared. "Rooker! *Rooker!*"

It was too far. There was nothing he could do but watch as Rooker dog paddled, barking and pleading for him.

Down! I have to get down there!

He felt the brass rings warm against his finger and the ship suddenly lurched as if it had been hit by a rogue wave. Pip's stomach dropped out from under him but he did not fall, almost as if the ship wouldn't let him go.

Disoriented, Pip saw the cave wall move up. It rose, faster and faster. His only thought was *The ship is sinking. No, wha—*

Pip heard the ship's timbers creak all around him and watched, unbelieving, as the outriggers spread apart. The catamaran stretched its legs like a living thing, widening its stance. As the wood unbent and uncurled of its own volition, the belly of the ship descended toward the water. Pip hung from the trapdoor, dumbstruck. *It's going down.*

The belly dome lowered until Pip was only a few feet above the sea. As the hammerhead made one last pass, Pip snatched Rooker's rope collar and hauled him aboard. As the shark lunged, he slammed the trapdoor shut and held Rooker tight. "It's all right, boy. I'll never leave you. I won't. I'm here, Rooker. I'm here."

The dog licked his face.

Pip watched the hammerhead circle below him, close enough to touch. He glanced up at the strange and wonderful ship. *You saved him. I needed to go down and you went down.* "You really can hear me."

Yes, the timbers sighed.

Pip felt the tingle of the *wikk* inside the rings on his finger; he felt the boat listening to him, watching him, waiting for him. "What... what do you want from me?"

Free.

Pip felt the word like a gentle breeze through his soul. He wanted the same thing. He'd wanted it all his life. He rubbed dog slobber off his face. "You went down." Pip slung Rooker over his shoulder and climbed out of the bowl, the expression on his face hopeful. "Can you get up?"

Yes.

Pip ran above deck to discover now the sea cave walls were descending. The ship rose in the water, growing to her full height. Her belly dome lifted ten, fifteen, twenty feet above the sea. As her outriggers grew closer together, the ship got taller. Pip suddenly understood the puzzle of how she had come to the cave. *She can be wide and fat if she needs to be close to the water or tall and skinny if she needs to fit...* Pip eyed the giant fissure in the wall that led to the sea. *She must have been almost straight up and down to make it through that.*

Grinning, he placed his hand on the ship's deckwheel and stroked the smooth wood. "Get up, girl."

Pip felt the tingle in his brass rings as the ship's outriggers drew even closer together. He glanced at the dusty sails tucked into the spars above like bunting awaiting a long-forgotten parade. "Unfurl the mainsail."

Red silk billowed down like a red waterfall shimmering in the moonlight. Sails fluttered against themselves, luffing as they fell, then snapped into place at the boom, ready for service. Out of absolutely nowhere, a gust of wind filled the cave. It whirled within the stone walls that surrounded the ship, conjured from nothing. Hair riffling over his face, Pip watched as clouds of pixies were swept toward the sea, twisting like petite cyclones. At the very peak of all three topmasts, red pennants unfurled, whipping in the breeze, facing forward, ready to run.

Let's get out of here, girl.

Free.

Blood-red sails snapped taut and the ship darted forward like a hawk on the hunt. Rooker spun around the deck, barking, as the wind swelled to a pixie-streaked gale and the catamaran shot straight toward the exit of Thimble Tower.

Pip's eyes grew panicked as he realized she was still too wide to fit. "No. Nonono*no!*" The fissure rushed closer at an alarming speed. "Up! Get *up!*"

The outriggers drew toward each other until they almost touched. Pip watched, agog, as the ship stood nearly straight up, impossibly balanced on the water like a little girl on her tiptoes. Pip's heart thundered in his ears as the ship tilted to one side and threatened to keel over when a puff of wind lofted her upright and she passed through the fissure, balanced like a ballerina.

The majik ship emerged from her stone prison into a frostbitten sea, her sails a vibrant crimson against the pale white of the world. Catching the first real wind she had felt in half a century, she bent to it.

Pip screamed as the world tilted. The ship slowly toppled like a felled tree, certain to capsize. Rooker howled in terrified dismay. Pip grabbed the pup and held him tight.

The ship's legs stretched out against the fall and leaned into the turn. Using the momentum, she hissed a fast arc against the waves as the outriggers compensated for her shifting weight. Her sails billowed full as she hunkered down into a predatory stance and cut across the waves like a knife, leaving Thimble Rock behind.

Free.

Splashed with frozen seawater, Pip raised a shout to the white sky in a yawp of victory. Rooker joined him, howling in full throat.

Flying toward the edge of the world, Pip could feel the ship's song in his rings, in his ribs, in his gut, a joyous choir of angels liberated at last. Rooker propped his front paws up on the rail and snapped at the whistling air, tongue lolling out one side.

Free.

The next three days were the best of Pippin Winegrad's life.

A boy, his dog, and their ship, a perfect trio of adventurers skimming across the North Waste Sea. They had no objective, no tasks to complete, no purpose but their own pleasure. Pip twirled the brass rings on his finger and simply told the ship where to go. She listened best when he touched her deckwheel, but she could hear him from anywhere, even when he swam in the icy sea. Most days he just let her run, cruising lazy circles through the North Waste. She skated over the water, leaning into turns, dancing. Rooker spent most of his time down on the outriggers, barking and snapping at the sea spray, occasionally catching a flying fish. They ate together, traveled together, and slept under the stars together, three crimson pirates upon a white sea.

Whenever he wasn't at the wheel, Pip explored the ship. The wood was unlike anything he'd ever seen; it shifted colors from the darkest mahogany to lustrous cherry to a silvery white birch, all of it inscribed. Pip could not find a single seam or joint in the entire vessel. It was as if she had been carved from a single piece of wood, some colossal tree from another world.

Etched into her skin was a never-ending story told in carved tableaus, a tale of the moons and sun, the birth of Keymark, of satyrs, tidal waves, giants, curling winds, griffins, and dragons, all sculpted real as life.

As Pip examined the carvings, he came to a part of the story with a boy who looked remarkably like him.

He peered closer. The markings were still pale, as if they had been graven yesterday by an artist's hand. At the boy's side was a dog that looked like a tan akita with mismatched eyes. Behind the boy and the dog, three sails filled the breeze, each marked with the same sigil.

"Flin." Pip tilted his head and looked up at the riffling sails. "Is that your name? Flin?"

She sighed warmly, and Pip felt the majik purr within his rings. "Flin." Pip stared out at the sea, patting Rooker's head. "I like that name." He considered. "But you can't tell anyone your *real* name, girl. It gives them power over you." Pip didn't know much about majik, but he'd heard *that* warning from Roper Jon enough times. "We can't call you Flin. It's dangerous. You need a bandit handle." Rooker barked agreement. "See? Rooker knows. You want a nickname, Flin?"

It almost sounded as if the ship was laughing, the cry of gulls above. *Yes.*

"A good name. A *pirate* name. A name for treasure hunts and scalawags and rebels who cross the Irridin Sea with no one to stand in their way. An outlaw name. Not an outlaw. A *brigand*. The *Venture Brigand*." Pip grinned. "You like that?"

She laughed again. *Yes.*

Rooker barked and spun in a circle. "That's right!" Pip brandished his cutlass and ran to the foredeck. Rooker followed, barking happily. Pip could barely see through the thick white fog that hid them from the world, it was a blank piece of canvas, and he could see their future painted upon it. "They'll sing songs about the three of us! Long ones! Loud ones!"

Rooker jumped up and licked his face. Pip wrapped his arms around the dog and glanced up at the sails. Up to this moment in his life, his only companions had been a father with nothing to give, a brother who'd stabbed him in the back, and a pirate who'd taken him as a slave.

But now, joined by the dog and the ship, Pippin Winegrad had everything. Here he was, beloved and free, surrounded by the only thing he'd ever wanted.

A family.

Just before dawn on the third day, the ice storm came.

White clouds became sleet, sleet became fog, and fog became a whiteout. The only color in the world was the *Venture Brigand*'s red sails.

Pip and Rooker slept in the captain's bed, snuggled together under half a dozen blankets. Rooker stood up and barked. "Hush," grumbled Pip. "Come back to bed. It's cold."

Rooker padded up the stairs. Groaning, Pip cursed and followed the dog above deck, wishing he'd put on boots. Sleet and mist slathered the air; whiteness was all. Pip's eyes adjusted to the light to find Rooker at the prow, barking into the empty void. Pip thumped the dog's ribs. "Stop it. It's cold out h—"

Ahead, a slash of orange split the sky like a giant shark's fin.

Another sail.

Pip staggered backward and nearly fell, crashing into Rooker. He recognized the colors of the other ship; it was a Shaver vessel, his old pirate gang. Pip grabbed the deckrail and watched the sail come right for him. There was no time for either ship to turn. They were going to collide.

Pip sprang for the deckwheel. He spun it as hard as he could and screamed, "Starboard, go *starboard*!"

The *Venture Brigand* cut right hard, but her outrigger struck the Shaver ship. Wood squealed and snapped as the two ships traded splinters. Rooker barked madly, trying to frighten off all the noise. Pip heard several men scream in the other boat. Something hit the water with a splash. Pip jerked the wheel, only to discover two more sails ahead.

He'd driven straight into a Shaver convoy.

The pup whined, his ears flat, tail down, terrified. Pip rubbed his side, thumping him as they passed the second ship. "Hey. Hey, we're okay, boy. They won't get us. We're—"

Rooker snarled like a wolf, suddenly angry, and disappeared into the mist. Pip sprinted after him and found the akita leaning over the waist of the ship, barking at the water. "Stop. *Stop*. It's okay, boy. It's oka—"

A grapple hook was sunk into the outrigger. A rope trailed behind it.

Pip's head came up just in time to see the buccaneer emerge from the mist, climbing the *Venture Brigand*'s leg. He leapt onto the deck.

The Shaver was shoeless, tattooed, and bore a stiletto in his teeth. His body was caked in frost, his hair iced white. He charged Pip.

Rooker threw himself at the pirate, snarling like a wolverine. His sharp teeth sank into the man's forearm. He cried out and dropped the stiletto. As Rooker savaged the pirate, Pip grabbed a sword from the cutlass bucket. He charged to help, but the pirate slipped a blackjack from his belt and smashed the lead-weighted sap into the dog's head.

Rooker hit the deck, shrieking pain.

"Rooker!" Screaming, Pip charged. The pirate grabbed his stiletto. Pip nearly took his hand off with the sword. For a moment, they faced off, man and boy, circling. Pip reared back with the cutlass and swung. The pirate snatched his wrist and smashed his elbow into Pip's eye. Stunned, Pip hit the ground with the pirate on top of him.

Rooker threw himself at the man. He tore at the pirate's neck, savage sounds roaring from the dog's throat.

A sudden *yip* of pain and Rooker fell to the deck, whimpering.

"Rooker!" Pip screamed and bit the pirate's ear.

Something smashed into the side of his head. He hit the deck, not sure which way was up. Rooker lay beside him, the dog's mismatched eyes staring at him. Pip reached out for the pup. Then everything went dark.

When he woke, pirates occupied his ship.

Dozens of Shavers looted the lockers, scraggy freebooters exclaiming at their unexpected luck. Above, the *Brigand*'s silk sails hung dead slack, as if weeping. Not a puff of wind disturbed them. Most of the whiteout had gone, leaving a flat grey sky feathered with misty ghosts. The Shaver he had been fighting was nowhere in sight.

Gone, too, was his dog.

"Rooker?" Pip sat up and found a hairy fist on his chest.

"Stay down!" yelled an ugly Shaver. The pirate was almost on top of him; Pip smelled the reek of his rotten mouth.

"Where is he?" Pip snapped at him.

The pirate barked, "Cap'n Tanaka. Kid's up."

Muscled and thick, a figure loomed over him. His mustache was neatly braided to his jaw, his skin pale and marked with orange paint. Atop his head he wore Pip's favorite hat, the purple one with the feather. He grabbed Pip's shirt. "How'd ya do that?"

Pip looked past the captain, searching the deck. "Where's my dog?"

The captain dragged him closer. "There's no one else on board! How were ya *sailin'* her?"

"Where's my *dog*?!" Pip screamed in his face.

"Ya call me Captain Tanaka!" He threw Pip to the deck. "And I'm askin' the questions." The captain scratched under the purple hat and squinted at Pip. "How'd ya get yer hands on this beauty, eh? And why's she such a bitch?"

Pip ignored Tanaka, scanning the deck. He didn't see Rooker anywhere.

"She won't sail for my boys." Tanaka pointed at two pirates arguing at the deckwheel. Another fought the jib, trying to tack into the wind with no success. "Thirty years at sea between them and they can't catch a puff of wind. It's like trying to steer a brick tavern. But *you*—" Tanaka squinted at Pip. "*You* made her run like a jackrabbit. Shot right past us. If ol' Nix hadn't caught ya by the tail, ya'd be halfway to the Twist by now. All without a crew." He leaned in. "Now, how'd ya do that, boychick?"

"It's *my* ship." Pip straightened. "She listens to *me*."

Yes. He heard her timbers creak.

"O-ho, yer the only one that can pilot her, hah?" Tanaka spat. "We'll see about that."

Toughen up. Pip fingered his rings and pressed them into his palm. "Bring me my dog or I swear this ship is never going to move again."

Captain Tanaka scowled at him. He got to his feet and muttered to himself, angry, pacing back and forth. He traded a few words with the pirates who were unsuccessfully trying to make the *Brigand* heel. He turned back to Pip and a cunning smile crossed his lips. "Alright, boychick. Ya want yer dog? He's right over there." He pointed. Half a mile distant, Pip saw a trio of orange-sailed Shavers cruising the sea. Tanaka relaxed against the deckrail. "Them fellas liked him so much, they took him aboard. Wanted him for a ship dog." Pip saw the captain eye another pirate. "Ya want him, little Shaver?" He scratched his stubble with a dagger. "Go fetch him."

Rooker. Pip leapt to his feet and ran to the deckwheel. It spun easily in his hands, responsive to his touch. The air around him suddenly gusted and filled the *Brigand*'s sails tight. Pip's black hair twisted in the breeze as he cut hard a-port and angled for the distant ships.

"That one?"

The captain eyed the sails, impressed. "Aye, think so." Tanaka lit his pipe and puffed at the stem, watching him closely. "What's yer name, boychick?"

Pippin Winegrad wasn't about to give Tanaka his true name, but he'd never had an alias other than Pip. He felt the brass rings around his finger. "Flin."

"Flin." Tanaka nodded. "All right then."

When Pip came alongside the Shaver vessel, the crew seemed confused. They claimed they hadn't seen a dog, much less taken one on board. Tanaka hollered at them for being drunk on duty and demanded Pip describe the animal so they would remember it. Pip told them of Rooker's curled tail, the way he tilted his head, and his mismatched eyes. After some encouragement from the captain, one of the sailors blinked. "O yeah, *that* dog." He eyed Tanaka, grinning. "We didn't get him. I think the *Balconette* did. Right, Punch?"

"Yeah, yeah. Yer dog's over there. Over there."

Pip followed the next ship. When they didn't have Rooker, he sailed to the next. By that time, the Shaver convoy had met up with a twenty-ship flotilla of cartel ships looking to trade plunder. During two days of trading, Pip boarded nearly every single boat, searching for Rooker. According to the pirates, the dog had been traded for a gold ring, adopted by a woman, won in a card game. Shavers laughed when Pip boarded, and soon enough the cartel joined in. "Rooker!" They hollered back at him, mocking his high voice. "Rooker! Rooker!"

"Where's the dog?" one laughed.

"Don't worry, lad," said Captain Tanaka. "We'll find him. If yer piloting this ship, we'll find him."

After the trading flotilla broke up, he chased a rumor that Rooker was on the *Albatross*, then the *Rime*, then the *Ysteria Ray*. Pip never quit looking. Not after a dozen ships, not after thirty, hunting down ship after ship. Tanaka even attacked a few who he suspected of stealing the dog. But Rooker was always on the next ship. And the next. And the next.

Pip knew if only he looked hard enough, he would find him.

He believed it.

For as long as he could.

He never let the Shavers see him cry. He was too tough for that. But at night he would rock on his side, weeping an endless flood of raw pain that his only friend was gone.

His silent tears disappeared into the *Venture Brigand*'s wood, becoming part of her, along with the lost little boy's endless cries of mourning.

Shh.

She rocked him softly in the night, whispering comfort in his ear.

Shh. Shh.

And so Pip whispered to his ship, one night after another, a million thoughts and fears and hatreds piled on top of each other until the boy buried himself beneath an avalanche of words.

She listened to every one.

Rooker Flynn never told that story. Not to Jack, not to anyone. The secret of how his pirate name came to be. He wore an alias stitched together from memory: the ship that gave him freedom, and the dog that gave him friendship—the only two living creatures who ever loved him.

Pippin Winegrad died too that winter, although no one could tell you exactly when.

Only the *Venture Brigand* was left to mourn him.

By spring, Rooker Flynn refused to think upon the boy or the dog.

Neither brought him anything but pain.

PART 1

DAWN

= RAZOR'S =
EDGE

*I've had a hell of a lot of fun
and I've enjoyed every minute of it.*
Errol Flynn's Last Words

T HIS WAS NOT THE first time Rooker Flynn had been sentenced to death.

At sixteen, he'd robbed the Sultan of Thaj. His royal daughter, Shehzadi Ija, had the most stunning, scintillant, come-hither eyes Rooker had ever seen, and she kissed like a hungry snake. Wrapped in her embrace, he convinced Ija to flee with him to the sea, to sail away beneath the stars. But Rooker Flynn was sixteen and ill-equipped for dependable decisions. He and Ija got drunk on añejo and were discovered in bed by the sultanate guards. Bound and brought before her furious father, Rooker was ordered executed on the spot.

When granted a last meal, Rooker requested Ija.

Enraged, the sultan drew his blade to carry out the sentence himself. In a quick bit of half-drunken bravado, Rooker robbed him of his sword, his daughter, and his two fastest stallions. Together, Rooker and Ija fled the city astride the mounts and escaped into the night air. They rode together, free, their silhouettes cast upon the desert dunes, lovers illuminated by twin moonlight.

That night at the oasis, Gamilat and Anika were full in the sky, bright and majestic. They tumbled for a bit, the shehzadi and he, a game, or so he thought, until her knife was at his neck. Then her lips were on his and he found himself straining toward her despite the prick of blood at his throat. Her eyes were dark, her flesh was silk, her mouth was heaven. Lost in her embrace, Rooker had not seen the sultanate guards creeping up on them until it was too late. They were too many for him, and he barely escaped with his life. He was forced to abandon the princess and arrived at the *Venture Brigand* alone.

Captain Tandil boxed his ears in for his foolishness. Rooker took the beating, then flashed a wicked grin. During his time with the shehzadi, he had tickled a secret out of her: the hidden entrance to the royal counting house. Thus equipped, the pirate crew of the *Venture Brigand* robbed the sultan of his weight in gold.

But Rooker never had gotten his daughter.

"And I never got my last meal!" he shouted at the top of his lungs.

No one listened. No one was there to hear.

He was right back where he'd started. His first day at the Locke Institute. The same empty cell, the same bucket, the same mat. He could see the scorch marks from where he'd tried to burn the door so many months ago. This time, however, he was not facing something so insignificant as a prison sentence. This time was for keeps.

Late summer on Huánghūn offered no respite from the heat; the air was stifling inside his cell. He limped a path he'd worn clean in the stone floor of his cell, holding his broken ribs, another gift from the headmistress. He shouted again to no one at all. "I was guaranteed a last meal!"

His ribs stung from shouting and he winced. Sweat rolled freely down his neck and bare chest. Groaning, he attempted to remove his shirt. It took a few minutes of pain just to grip the hem and nearly half an hour to peel it off. He dragged it over the two broken ribs Gerba had given him during his failed escape attempt. The exercise was painful but distracted him from his imminent demise.

He felt no cooler with his shirt off and now had nothing to do with his hands. The shirt was covered in soot, burns, and globs of blood, so he picked it clean as he walked. A nervousness overtook him. He could almost feel it creeping across the room. His cell had no windows, so it was impossible to tell if sunrise had come, but after so many months in the Locke Institute, Rooker felt it in his bones. Dawn drew nigh.

Soon he would hang under the Great Bell of the Deep Blue South and dance his last jig.

"That order still stands!" Rooker yelled at the empty room. "It was a royal decree!" He stuck his finger under his eyepatch and scratched at the empty hole. It had been itching for hours and he was concerned it had gone maggoty. "For my last meal, I want strawberry cake! Mary *Kubrect's* strawberry cake!"

O, Mary. That girl could bake. Her fruit pies were palm-sized, golden-brown flaky crusts that hugged hot cinnamon apple jam. She made a butterscotch soufflé that disintegrated into sugar when it touched his mouth. But best of all were her cakes. Stuffed with cold, sweet buttercream, the little strawberry pastries were ringed with hardened sugar, a caramel cage made of tatted lace. The cakes were only the size of his thumb, but they exploded a sugary soft strawberry delight when they touched his tongue.

Mary's tongue had tasted of caramel too. She'd been a sweet girl.

She was dead, like most people he'd known. Her bakery gone, her genius gone, her strawberry cakes gone. Nearly everything he remembered from those early years at sea was gone, drowned, destroyed, or dead.

But even a condemned man could dream.

"Little Pip and his belly full of cake." Jasper's voice chuckled in the shadows of his cell. Rooker tried to ignore the voice. Here, at the end of all things, he was as alone as he had ever been, but his dead brother's ghost haunted him still.

Rooker heard the shift of Jasper's new coat, the creak of his wheelbarrow full of grain, the cruel whisper of his brother's voice from the dark. "You're gonna die this morning," it said. "You're gonna hang by that scrawny neck of yours until your face turns blue and your tongue puffs up and you're just like me. Dead and rotting in a grave."

Rooker thought of the way his brother had died, a knife in the eye. He touched his own empty socket. "Go away, Jasper."

"Strawberry cake," came his cold chuckle. "You always were good at lying to yourself, Pip. You're doing it right now. Telling yourself you're not alone." Rooker heard the voice edge closer, whispering from the pits of hell. "Your whole life was one big lie. I was gonna look after you. Dad was gonna sober up. You were brave enough, strong enough, loud enough. That they'd love you. That they'd write a song about you. All lies. Even your *name's* a lie."

Rooker's fingernails cut crescents into his palm.

"You die today, Pip. There's no time left for lies." He heard Jasper's shade move closer. "So I'll tell you the only truth that ever mattered." Jasper sucked in a cold breath. "No one ever loved you. Not me. Not dad. Not the sheik's daughter. No one. You were *always* going to die alone."

Rooker stood his ground. "Jack did."

Jasper's laugh was cruel. "Love you? He *used* you. Look at yourself, Pip. You're missing an eye, you've given away your ship, and you are about to be executed in his place. And where is he?" Jasper's cackle rattled inside his head. "He used you up. You forgot what Da taught us, Pip. You let yourself get soft." Jasper's whisper tickled his brain. "You let him win."

Rooker realized how tightly he had been clenching his fists when his fingernails pierced the skin. He inhaled sharply and looked at his palm to find it wet with blood. His nails had dug a furrow, a jagged line in his flesh, nearly identical to a scar he and Jack had once shared.

Rooker felt something pass through him—a warm breeze—and he felt like he was back at that campfire on Bounty. Jack's blue eyes watching him. Laughing with him.

Rooker discovered he was smiling, and here, on the dawn of his execution, he couldn't help but chuckle. "You wouldn't understand."

Jasper's voice was harsh, confused. The voice of a petulant child. "Understand what?"

Rooker thumbed his blood. "Brothers."

Silence from the shadows. When Rooker resumed pacing, Jasper did not come with him. Rooker reached the end of the short path, turned, and saw his shadow in the corner, just an angry child with a new coat. The shadow retreated, subsiding, fading away.

After a long pause, he heard one faint whisper. "I'll see you soon, Pip. I'll warm up a seat for you."

Then he was gone, never to return.

Rooker resumed his lonely march, his footsteps leading one by one to his looming death.

A shadow passed under the door.

"Hey?" Rooker leapt toward the shadow. A real person was on the other side of the door and he desperately needed someone to talk to that wasn't himself. "Hey! I'm *the* Captain Rooker Flynn! Sole survivor of the Battle of Barrel Strait! Savior of the Merman King! Hero of the Paladine Arch! And I deserve a last meal!" He leaned into the door. *"So give me some strawberry cake or I'm not going!"*

—*skissss*—

Something slid under the thick wooden door. A small flat device, metal and hard.

Rooker sucked air between his teeth.

A straight razor.

He eyed it laying there on the stone. The handle was inlaid with pearl and turquoise. "Now what do ya want me to do with that?"

No reply came from outside the cell.

Guess I'm not gettin' that conversation.

Rooker scooped the straight razor off the ground and flicked the blade open.

I hang this morning. The noose is waiting for me. They'll put it around my neck. A quick drop. My spine will snap. The bell will ring. He took a shuddering breath. *And when that happens, the bell will bring me—*

Rooker tried to silence the thought but succeeded only in gripping the razor tighter.

—*back. Only to kill me again. And again. And again. Thirteen death sentences, carried out back to back to back, dying over and over.*

He eyed the tool in his hand.

The razor would be quicker.

He flicked it with a thumb. Plenty sharp.

The razor said Gerba Whipmarples didn't care a tinker's dam whether he swung from the rope or slit his own throat. The result was all that mattered. The razor or the rope. One way or another, he would die this morning.

She doesn't care how I go.

As long as I go.

That, more than anything else, is what convinced him to shave. If Rooker Flynn was one thing, he was an ornery cuss, and if he hated everyone in the world, he hated Gerba Whipmarples most.

"No, ma'am." Rooker eyed his reflection in the razor's bright steel. "Yer not gettin' the last laugh."

He worked a coin of soap into a lather and rubbed suds over his chin. There was no mirror in his cell, so he started from the bottom of his neck and worked his way up. He felt the familiar bristle of the razor scrape across his throat.

He sang without thinking:

> *O, I got a gal who's always rotten*
> *Stuffs her shirt with a bale of cotton*
> *Six foot tall, eight feet of hair*
> *Poked holes in a barrel for her underwear.*
> *Don't know Liza, don't know me*
> *We got a ticket to the jamboree.*
> *A mule kicked her, she kicked right back*
> *Made her bed out of an old haystack*
> *Sung last weekend in a bass quartet*
> *You ain't seen nothin' like her yet.*

Don't know Liza, don't know me
We got a ticket to the jamboree.

Repeating the chorus, Rooker scraped the last of the stubble off his cheeks and shaped the hair on his chin to a rugged handsomeness. He always had liked a little scruff; it made him feel more of a man.

The razor bothered him, though. It *should* have made a metallic click against the brass rings on his finger, but his rings were gone, traded away for Jack's life. He had hoped their forgetting majik would make him unremember the rings when they left his finger, but no such luck. They were too much a part of him. For half his life he had worn the *Venture Brigand*'s rings like a faithful husband. The warmth of her, the assurance of her, right there in his hand. But now she was gone. He couldn't feel her in his heart anymore. All that was left was a hollow space and a groove worn into his finger over the long years.

He clicked open the razor and carved her name into the rock, her true name, the name he had taken as his own, *Flin*.

Rooker thumbed his naked finger and missed the feel of her rings the way an amputee misses a leg. *Goodbye, girl.*

Lonely, he looked for the shadow under the door, but the guard's boots were gone. There was no one left to talk to.

Rooker sat next to the wall, opening and closing the straight razor in his hands. He glanced at the crack through which he and Jack had talked on their first day at the Locke Institute so many months ago. The shape of the crack mirrored the cut on his palm, a little jagged crescent, an opening to Jack.

Rooker Flynn didn't want to be alone. "Hey?"

There was no response from the crack.

Rooker flicked open the blade. He pressed the metal to the stone and slowly scratched at it, making another mark, carving the name of the akita pup from so many years ago. The other name he had stolen for himself. Rooker. The thief.

"I know yer gonna bust me outta here, Jack." His voice was hoarse, quiet. "I know ya got somethin' up your sleeve. A bit of Toshan majik, right?"

Nothing. There was no one on the other side of the crack.

"Yeah. That's what I thought." Rooker lowered his head. "Still. We made a pretty good team, you and me." His thumb felt the emptiness where the rings used to be. "Woulda been nice, though. You and me and the *Brigand* makes three. All of us together. We woulda got that song sung about us, sure as yer born. Yeah." He wiped the shirt across his nose. "They would have remembered us then. Remembered us right."

He dug at the wall with the straight razor, carving into it, and made the symbol for the *Flin*. Then he carved the mark for Rooker over the top of it, combining the two. The condemned man cemented his legacy in Keymark the only way he could, by scratching his name into the stone wall of a prison cell.

He carved his signature for a long time, his face blank, impenetrable, a mask.

At long last, he finally spoke, his voice the ragged croak of a man at the foot of the gallows. "Forgive me if you can." Rooker stared at the crack in the wall. "Ya said that to me, ya remember?" There was no response from the nothing. "I never had *anyone* ask me to forgive 'em. Never. And I damn sure never asked for it. Never made any sense to me. It's weak. It's begging. But ya did it. Just like that. After I stabbed *you* in the back. Strangest thing I ever saw." He scratched at the stone. "I guess what I'm sayin' is... I don't know. I've never begged pardon, never said I'm sorry, never got on my knees." He shifted forward and knelt in front of the crack like a man at confession. "I guess what I'm sayin' is... forgive me if ya can."

A puff of breeze came from the crack, a breath of fresh air. *I do.*

Rooker exhaled a long breath. He nodded, smiling. "Yeah, I figured ya would." He straightened. "But I jest needed to say it. Before I go."

He looked at the carving he'd made above the crack.

His name. The one mark he would leave upon the world.

And joined with it, Jack's sigil.

"You and me." He stared at their paired names, and for a moment he imagined he stood side by side with Jack. Rooker folded the razor for good. "You and me."

A sharp *TOK* came from the door, then another, then another, the march of death. *TOK-TOK-TOK.*

Fear washed over Rooker like ice water.

This is it. They're taking me to the noose.

Desperate, he turned for the crack. "Hey, Jack—"

But no. Jack wasn't there. Of course he wasn't.

There was nothing behind the crack in the wall. No one was listening to him. Rooker was as alone as he'd always been.

The last *TOK* kicked the door and the boot stopped. "Razor," came a hard, male voice.

Rooker smoothed his fingers over his neck. *Time's up.*

He planted one palm on the markings he'd carved, leaving a bloody handprint upon his shared signature. And there it would remain, etched in stone until Keymark's final sunset.

"Razor," came the voice again.

Rooker ran his thumb along the edge, eyeing his wrists. *Last chance.*

The voice grew harsh. "If you don't send it through right now, five of us are going to come in with clubs and see how dead you are."

"Jest finishing my shave." Rooker's quick fingers worked at the hinge of the straight razor. "Gotta leave a good-looking corpse."

"Now."

Rooker felt the razor break free with a quiet snap. "Hang on, hang on." He slid the handle through the door. "There ya go. Quit yer bitchin'."

He palmed the razor between his fingers, hiding it. *If I go for his eyes—*

"And the blade."

Rooker sighed, defeated. "What blade?"

A boot kicked the door. "Blade!"

Rooker tossed the razor through the gap. After a moment, the door creaked open. A big acolyte cautiously looked inside to find a freshly shaved pirate buttoning up his crimson shirt, flicking off the lint. He turned, a wicked gleam in his eye.

"Now." He grinned. "About that cake."

A truncheon smashed Rooker's ribs. Dizzy with pain, he felt a pair of arms pin his hands together and tie them off at the wrists. He drew a long breath, waiting for the stars to stop spinning. As they did, he forced his back ramrod-straight, standing at his full height, chest out, ignoring the pain in his ribs. He didn't wait for them to force him. He ambled forward, prowling into the hall like he owned it. "Let's go see the hangman and hope he dies first."

Rooker Flynn forced a grin and kept his chin up.

If yer gonna die today, die well.

Chapter

2

A DANGEROUS MAN

Start where you are
Use what you have.
Do what you can.
Arthur Ashe

*I*F YOU'RE GOING TO *die today, die well.*

Jack Swift came awake with a start, eyes wide, fully alert. He shook his head to clear the cobwebs and wished he hadn't.

Bruises screamed on his neck. Half his face felt swollen and thick. One eye refused to open fully, and his hair was matted to his scalp with dried blood. But his mouth was the worst. He had no idea how many teeth Gerba Whipmarples had broken with Nepenthe, but his mouth was jagged glass. His tongue couldn't find a smooth tooth in the bunch and snagged on a new razor every time it moved. He felt as if he'd been turned into a shattered monster.

His body was no better than his face. It hurt to move, it hurt not to move. He drew in his limbs to try and sit up and heard something clink. His foot was chained to a stone bench. He dragged himself onto the seat and felt the bruises in his abdomen, the sting in his ribs. *She broke one.* He felt his chest with a shaky hand. *Or two.*

Trying to get his bearings, Jack took in the room through his one working eye. He knew this place. He'd never been here, but it had a reputation. Rooker Flynn, along with most of the cons on Huánghūn, had been sentenced in this room. The Inquisitor's Court.

"Excellent! You are at long last awake!" The voice was bright and familiar. One he knew too well. "Good morning, doktar."

Jack watched a shadow emerge from the hallway. The horn was distended in the torchlight, long and pointed like a spear. As it entered the chamber, he saw the chains of jewelry that dangled from it, the carvings that decorated the keratin. Gerba Whipmarples' powerful body was draped in the same blackened smock she had been wearing when she'd nearly beaten him to death. Her face was blackened with soot, highlighting the sea-green eyes that watched him.

Jack flinched at the sight of her. He couldn't help it. The monster had beaten him nearly to death with his own stick.

"Our *last* morning together, I am sad to confess." Her voice came in a birdsong lilt. "The end of our long and fortuitous acquaintance. And it has been *such* an exciting time we have spent together, Jack." Gerba Whipmarples smiled through smeared lipstick, a horror show.

The headmistress moved toward the window, her hands folded behind her back, and breathed deep the morning air. Jack smelled only the odor of sulfur wafting from Gerba's smock. "Winnifred." An acolyte emerged from the hallway, carrying something. "Please wash him."

The acolyte threw a bucket of water at Jack. He inadvertently released a shriek as the freezing water hit him like cold knives. Every cut on his body gaped pain, every bruise sang an agonized symphony. Another bucket of water hit him with a splash. *"Aih!"* Jack yelled through broken teeth. "Stop! Yu swore yu wun't hur' meh!"

Gerba laughed, a deep chortle Jack felt in his broken ribs. "The oath I swore prevents me from harming or killing you, doktar. I can certainly order you *washed*."

More pain as Winnifred went to work on him with a soapy sponge. She lathered him like a prized heifer, giving no thought to his comfort. Soot and blood came loose, dripping down his body in clumps. His hair broke into tangled wads as she scoured his head. Trying not to scream, Jack closed his eyes and gritted his shattered teeth, feeling them dig into his gums.

Gerba watched from the Inquisitor's chair. "When we first met, I must confess, I did not think much of you, Jack." She sighed. "Perhaps I had set my hopes too high. My first real Toshan, and the legendary Black Jack to boot... How could you possibly live up to my expectations?" She produced a mirror from beneath the desk and went to work cleaning up her face. "However. I will be the first to admit when I am wrong, and I *was* wrong." She delicately removed grime with a lace handkerchief. "You are a dangerous man, doktar. An ingenious man." Sea-green eyes gazed at him in the mirror, her head tilting. "I still have not been able to figure out one tiny mystery. How *did* you escape from Bounty?"

Jack eyed her through the soap. Leah and Memphis were likely aboard the *Venture Brigand*, but now Gerba owned the keys to the ship, Rooker's brass rings. If he kept his mouth shut, they still had a chance at escape. He wouldn't get them killed too. Jack forced one word through broken teeth. "Majik."

Gerba smiled. "Never reveal your secrets, ah?" She applied new lipstick and popped her lips. "If I had to make an educated guess, I would say you somehow stowed away on the *Hup Two*, which is the only thing that would explain why you are still on Huánghūn. You never actually escaped." She turned on him, looking for a reaction. Jack refused to give the headmistress anything but a poker face. After a moment, she nodded, satisfied that she was correct. "You could not escape the harbor in a single-manned boat. We would run you down. You needed your little band of merry men to help you escape. Not a difficult puzzle to solve. Am I right?"

Jack could hear the uncertainty in her voice. He said nothing.

"And you had a plan to get them out of the Institute. An escape through the shiq tunnels!" She clapped her hands. "Another impossible feat! I must admit, I am impressed. Using the Caged Eight to keep the shiq at bay. *Very* ingenious. Using one of my own tools against me." She held up her gloved hand and the seven pieces of Nepenthe came together in her fist. *Tak-a-tak-a-tak!* She smiled as blue majik illuminated her leathery hide. "Tit for tat, I suppose."

She put the mirror away, scooped something off the desk, and descended the steps toward him. "But I must admit, it is your latest death-defying escape that impresses me most. Forcing me to swear, under geas curse and pain of death, not to harm you. Your best escape yet. And your methods. *O.* That, I think, is what finally changed my mind about you, doktar. You did something of which I thought you were incapable. When all hope was lost, when you were finally caught, you played your last card: Mister Flynn."

"I din't—" He cut himself off; it hurt too much to talk.

She threw the towel at him. Jack threw up his hands, but his weary body did not react fast enough and it slapped against his face. "Yes, you are a very dangerous man, *doktar*... for all concerned." She came closer and loomed over him. He saw the rage carved into the wrinkles around her eyes and realized how much she wanted to kill him, how much she was restraining herself.

"You have maneuvered me into a position where I cannot injure you, much as you deserve it. If I so much as harm a hair on your head, the geas will kill me." Winnifred arrived at her side with an iron box. "Without the threat of punishment, training an animal is nearly impossible. And you have already proven so difficult to train." She gripped Nepenthe tight in her cornsilk glove and broke the bamboo staff into seven pieces, speaking one word for each. "Unruly, insolent, rebellious, ungovernable. Reckless. Selfish. Aggressive." She opened the iron box, thrust the pieces inside, and locked the lid. "A man like you has no place in a civilized society, Toshan." She produced a parchment with an official seal at the bottom. "To that end, I have signed Baronet Ket's offer to purchase you."

Jack's head snapped up. *What?*

Gerba's face hinted at a smile. "Originally, I turned him down. It was more profitable to kill you in the arena on Bounty, but you now have driven me to realize his coin is worth more than nine stone of skin and bone. Besides"—she patted the box containing Nepenthe—"there is nothing else you have left to offer me." She rolled up the parchment. "Lord Ket's ship will be here to pick you up this afternoon. That, of course, is why I ordered you washed." She leered at him, a smug expression on her face. "I would never sell a dirty animal."

Dripping, Jack glared at her. *Wasteka harridan.* He gritted broken teeth. *From prisoner to slave. And I thought I couldn't go any lower.*

"Once you are in the baronet's possession... Well." The headmistress spread her hands. "I cannot very well control what happens to you after that. And so"—she blew on her fingertips—"my Black Jack curse is lifted."

Jack swallowed the knot in his throat. *Well, this just got much worse.*

"Geas spells." Gerba flicked her thick fingers. "So easy to manipulate. Just like people. All you have to do is pay attention to the details." She turned. "Although I dare say you know a bit about manipulating people yourself."

Jack felt blood rise to his cheeks as he snapped. "Stop saying that." Through his bloody mouth, it came out 'stobsayntha.'

"O, Jack. Why lie now?" Gerba folded her hands over her smock. "The game is over. It is only sporting for me to admit defeat. As I begrudgingly admitted, you are a very dangerous man." She nodded, her eyes sharp. "From the first day I met you, you tried to manipulate me at every turn. You lied to me from our first conversation, played to my curiosity, played to my pride. Like a game of chess. Moving your pieces into position, countering mine. I did not realize it at first, but now that I have had the opportunity to observe you at length..." She moved closer. "Not a word comes out of your mouth before you calculate how much damage it can do. Watching you work is like watching a gifted musician, doktar. Like that Toshan fairy tale, what is it called? The Pied Piper. That's you." She tittered. "They all dance to your tune."

Some of that hit too close to home. *That's how she sees the world. How Rooker saw it. That's not me. I'm not like them. I'm not.* But even now, he looked for leverage. Something to use against her, some way to weasel out a win. He dropped his eyes, unable to meet hers. *That's not me.*

"That first Red Dwarf, the twin, what was his name? Yenrab backwards." Gerba tilted her head. *"Barney. That's it.* Barney Bialik. He was killed following *your* instructions, wasn't he?" Jack's chains rattled as he turned away on the bench. *Stop.* "After that, you somehow convinced his twin brother to follow you. All the prisoners who came through the shiq tunnels obeyed your orders, yes? Two of them nearly died defending you, and one is about to die in your place. And here you stand, unharmed." Gerba Whipmarples spread her hands. "I admit it. You outplayed me, doktar. All you had to do was sacrifice your rook."

The words hit Jack like a slap.

If you're going to die today, die well.

Air shot through his nose as he straightened.

I can save him. I can save all of them. If she hits me, this will all be over. The geas curse should kill her. His chains clinked as he stood. *Right after she kills me.* "Where'sh Rooker?"

"Awaiting his thirteen sentences of death." Gerba lifted her horn, imperious. "Loudly, I'm sure."

Closer. Jack limped a step toward her and twisted the towel into what the kids on the Walter Payton High swim team used to call a rat-tail. "An' Patch?"

"Is she your next most useful piece?" Gerba tilted her head. "Possibly that murderer Copper Dave could help you. Or the remaining Bialik twin. Perhaps even Farah Ibis?" She smiled. "I am afraid you are out of pawns. There is no one left on the board, Jack. It is just you and I."

"You and *me.*" Jack took his final step and snapped the wet corner of the towel into the center of her sea-green eyeball. The rat-tail stabbed her eye with a *pop* that hit like an animal bite.

She was on top of him in a heartbeat, eighteen hundred pounds of furious trol. Jack hit the floor, his bruises crying out in pain as he stared up in terror at the huge rhinoceros-like thing crouched atop him. Eyes blazing rage, Gerba reared back her fist to crush his skull into a bloody pulp.

Jack didn't flinch this time. *Do it!*

She stopped, looming over him like an angry mountain. Steam escaped her nostrils, her breath panting and savage.

Hit me!

Jack forced himself to press his nose to hers. He stared right into Gerba Whipmarples' one healthy eye and gave her Rooker Flynn's grin. "Yer *weak*."

Jack thrust out his chin, begging her.

Her furious snort blew Jack's hair back. He felt the dragonfire heat of her lungs on his face. Her eyes shrieked murder. She wanted to. But she wouldn't.

Jack punched her in the eye. She jerked away and knocked his hand aside. Reaching for her, Jack snatched her smock and felt himself lifted into the air as she stood. He clutched at the smock with white knuckles. Half the pocket ripped off in his hand as she tore herself out of his grip. He struck the ground and rolled to a crouch as she stepped away. *"Hit me!"*

Jack limped after her but the chain snapped tight around his leg; he was at the end of his leash.

They shared a hateful stare.

The room creaked as Gerba Whipmarples forced her mask back on. Her face changed, piece by piece, until the trol faded away and the headmistress took the reins once more. She opened her fists. "I believe I will allow Baronet Ket the honor." She removed the torn smock, pinched it between two fingers, and dropped it to the floor like a dead rat. Underneath, she wore black silk; a streamlined skirt and long bloused sleeves with a lace-veiled pillbox hat. Gerba Whipmarples was dressed for a funeral.

She straightened her skirt as her pleasant mask fell all the way back into place again. The only thing that betrayed the perfect picture of calm was her lipstick, still smeared on one side. "Now, doktar, it is nearly dawn. The work is great and the day is short. I have so much to finish today." She turned and walked toward the stairs. "And I am very happy to say none of it involves you."

Wait. Jack watched the headmistress stride to the exit. He moved after her but the chain drew taut. "Where are you going?" Through bloody teeth, it came out as 'weryugon?'

"As I said, it is dawn." Gerba touched her horn, bidding him goodbye. "And there is a hanging I must attend to. Good morning, doktar."

I have to be there. I have to. Panic ripped through Jack. *Think. She won't take me if she knows.* He forced his body to relax and collapsed to the bench. His whisper was just loud enough for her to hear. "Thank God."

The headmistress stopped. Turned.

"I beg your pardon?"

Jack waited. *Careful. She's not stupid.* "Goodbye, Gerba."

"No." She took a half-step toward him. "What was that?"

Don't. Jack took a breath and held it. *Don't say anything.*

Gerba's eye narrowed. "You thought I was going to force you to *watch* Mister Flynn's execution. As punishment." Jack closed his eyes, turning away from her. He felt a pit open in his stomach. *Please. Please.*

"What a *splendid* notion."

"No." Jack shook his head, mumbling through broken teeth. "Don't."

"Winnifred." Gerba straightened, grinning. "Unlock the doktar's chains."

Jack watched the acolyte undo his leg irons as Gerba draped her heavy arm over his shoulder. "Let me give you a word of advice, young man." Jack grimaced as she pulled him close. "When I was a little girl, Papa gave me my first pig. I named her Miss Purdy. I loved dear, sweet Miss Purdy with all my heart. Love. The world's oldest manipulator." Jack's chains fell to the floor and Gerba tightened her grip. "When butchering season came, I tried to run away with Purdy. I did not, however, get very far. Papa caught up with us. He made me slit her throat right there on the road. I cried for days." She took a breath. "My advice to you is the same advice my father gave me. If you plan to slaughter an animal, never become attached. Once you think of it as a pet, you are in for a rude awakening." She gripped him by the back of the neck and led him up the stairs. "In the end, every hog goes to slaughter. Let us consider this your final object lesson. Come see what happens when you get too close to a pig."

Jack ascended the stairs onto the rooftop of the Locke Institute to discover that dawn was no longer in its infancy. The sun was well into its ascension from the Irridin and threatened to spill over the wall onto Huánghūn. Atop the butte, acolytes, hammerdwarves, and attercops were abuzz with activity. Several white-robed acolytes ate breakfast at a table filled with varying kinds of fruit while others tended the hourglass, polishing the surface as the grains counted down to the morning announcements, and to the execution.

The plateau was littered with barrels of tools, mortar, trowels, adzes, and awls, indicating the recent work of dozens of men. A group of hammerdwarves conferred at a long table, poring over wide sheets of parchment that looked like building plans, arguing, and pointing at the Great Bell.

Now raised sixty feet in the air, the Agrat-ban-Haifa appeared otherworldly and commanding as a dragon. The pair of new support beams, made of stained Huánghūn jatoba trunks, held the bell aloft. The original stone dais still stood, dwarfed beneath the new tower. The old bell posts formed the base of a bamboo scaffold that rose between the new legs, a Z-shaped stairway that climbed into the bell itself. High above, dominating the island, the Agrat-ban-Haifa waited, freshly burnished with a dark bronze polish that made it feel like something corrupted, a perverted version of itself. Hammered into the interior of the bell, Jack saw Gerba's Caged Eight rune, her source of control over every spider on the island, gold on blackened bronze.

Attached to the bell mechanism was a fresh noose.

Jack felt his Adam's apple duck in his throat as he swallowed.

Gerba gestured to the hammerdwarf foreman. "Niko?" He turned. "Ma'am." She gestured at the bell. "Check the counterweight on the pull-arm again. We have never had a student make thirteen tolls before. Let us see if we can set a new record." Niko gestured to his apprentice and a team of dwarves hustled up the scaffold.

Jack watched them climb past the skirt of Tibetan prayer bells that hung around the rim of the Agrat-ban-Haifa and go to work greasing the lever. He turned to the headmistress. "Yur not *ashually* gonna to hang him fir-firteen times."

"You are correct. I do not believe Mister Flynn is adequate to the task." Gerba plucked up a blood orange mimosa. "But we shall do our best."

Despair and fury fought within Jack's chest like warring cats. "Doan—" He swallowed blood. "Don't do this. Ishn't killing him once enough to shatisfy you?"

"O, my dear Jack." She patted him on the cheek. "It is the *principle* of the thing."

Jack lunged at her.

Startled, Gerba backed away. "Winston!" she snapped. "Stop him!"

Winston landed in front of Jack. The big attercop hunched on its forelegs, fangs bared. Jack pivoted his back to the tool bench as three hairy arms shoved him and sent him sprawling. He stumbled backward into a stack of tool barrels, knocking them everywhere in a clattering shower of sawdust.

Jack hit the ground in a heap as barrels spilled all around him. Pain flashed through his body like strobe lights, his cuts and ribs screaming explosives. He retracted his arms, his head dizzy with the sound of screaming. For a moment, he thought it was his own voice.

But no. It was Gerba.

Her rhinoceros skin withered like a dying leaf, fading from honey-brown to grey. Her leathery hide deflated, the cracks growing deeper and wider. Dark circles appeared under her eyes as the headmistress aged decades in the span of a few moments. Her meaty fingers grew lank and bony as the geas majik devoured her body from the inside.

"Stop!" she shouted in shrill panic. *"Do not hurt him!"*

Winston froze. Jack moved behind one of the toppled barrels and shielded himself. Panting, he watched Gerba. The geas spell had paused at her command, as if pondering whether she had breached the pact. Jack had been hurt, but was she responsible or Winston? Gerba held her breath, signaling for Winston to back off. Jack watched with morbid fascination, hoping the curse would finish the job. In the end, the geas rendered its verdict. Slowly, Gerba's skin began to regenerate, restoring itself to a healthy golden brown as the curse slowly released its grip.

Gerba breathed heavily, one hand at her breast. She cleared her throat. "Winston. I want you to listen to me. Very. Very. Carefully." She pointed at Jack. "Do *not* hurt that man. I want you to keep him *away* from me." She took a shuddering breath. "And I want you to do it... *gently.*"

The spider crawled atop the remaining barrels and loomed over Jack. "Get up."

Covered in sawdust, Jack peeled a long ringslug off his face and threw it at Winston. "Make me."

Winston glanced at Gerba. She nodded. Jack tried to fight the spider as it lifted him to his feet, but there was nothing he could do to resist all those powerful legs. Carefully, Winston moved Jack away from Gerba, taking him to the edge of the precipice.

Jack looked down upon the assembly yard.

A thousand prisoners stared up from below, all of them silent, all of them waiting for the sun.

The prison riot started by Rooker Flynn had died a quick death. Trails of smoke rose from all four camps, smoldering cliques that carried Gerba's silent promise to burn them all if the revolt resumed. In the assembly yard, Jack saw outlaws he knew from Hyena, Jackal, Vulture, and Buzzard, all sagging and weary. They looked like they had not slept in days, a huddled mass of half-awake corpses. Attercops prowled the perimeter, watching for malcontents. Not one prisoner stepped a toe out of line. The revolution was over.

Two men who had trained alongside Jack in the Steel Trials, men who were deadly with swords in their hands, stood with the other prisoners, shoulders hunched, cowed. There was no fight left in them now. Jack spotted Yolanda Frost, the big razorback bruiser from Hyena, her eyes vacant. There was the orange hair of Billy Pilgrim, dressed in the tattered remains of his purple costume from the Steel Trials. The troubadour stared at the ground, holding his broken banjo, now mute.

Gerba's students were beaten.

"I do not know how you discipline the lower classes in your sphere, doktar, but here in Keymark, there is a natural order to things." She spread her hands as the sun's first rays touched the assembled men. "When you view your peers from this vantage, when you look down upon them from above, it changes your perspective. Now you see them the way *I* see them. Herded into little groups, just as they should be." She smiled. "Compliant.

Docile. Obedient. Waiting to be worked, fleeced, and devoured. Good. Little. Sheep."

Sunlight broke over the ridge, illuminating the haggard faces below. The headmistress turned. "Well." She smiled at Jack. "Time to give the animals what they want."

The headmistress moved to the edge of the cliff and spread her hands over the assembly. "Ladies and gentlemen, students of the Locke Institute. Welcome to a new day!" She paused as if she had been met with a round of applause. No one in the assembly made a sound. "Before your work assignments, I want to make a very special announcement. As you know, we have had a difficult few days here at the Institute. But I can assure you, what we all experienced was nothing more than a little... failure to communicate."

Some of the prisoners shifted on their feet. Others rubbed the bruises the attercops had given them. None looked at the headmistress. "Some of you—*many* of you—were led astray by lies. Lies told by a fellow student. Lies that put your health in jeopardy and made you act against your own best interests. As you know, I believe experiences like this are wasted unless we turn them into learning opportunities. I wonder what you have learned over the last few days." She rose to her full height, her horn held high. "Do we tolerate disobedience here at the Locke Institute?"

She raised her hands as if she expected a resounding 'no' from the prisoners. She didn't get one.

"Of course not!" she agreed. "There are only three simple rules at the Locke Institute. Obey your betters. Assemble at sunrise. Be inside by sundown. And when you follow these rules, you become productive men and women who serve their community, lift it up, make it better. So we will continue to dig in the mines! We will continue to fell timber! We will continue to harvest rice! For your only value *is* your labor."

She spread her hands.

"When you graduate from the Locke Institute, you will have learned to serve Keymark. Together, we can do great things! Graduation day *is* coming, and sooner than you think! But until we reach that glorious day when all of you are freed from your shackles, our eyes must remain fixed on our shared goal."

She took a deep breath.

"To that end, I have decided not to punish you." A murmur of surprise went through the crowd. Jack could hear it from a hundred feet up. "Instead, I have chosen to show mercy. Mercy! A lesson that can only be taught by example. Today, you will not be whipped, disciplined, or punished." Gerba's voice grew sharp. "Only *one* student was responsible for your disobedience. Only *one* student told you these lies. And only *he* will suffer for his crimes! You will not be punished for his actions. This morning, you will have a *healing*!"

The crowd's heads snapped up like dogs responding to a treat. Jack watched their eyes gleam at the thought of the healing *wikk*. They stared up at Gerba in rapt attention, drawing closer to the wall, beggars with their cups out.

Jack heard a thump and turned to watch a man's shape emerge from the stairwell. His heart caught in his throat as he saw the red shirt, the black hair, the eyepatch. Helplessness leached all hope from Jack as he saw the look in Rooker Flynn's one remaining eye.

Fear, that old wolf Jack knew so well, prowled within. Rooker's chest was up, his chin was out, but it was all for show. Every man fears death, and Rooker's haunted face saw it waiting for him atop the bell tower.

Unable to do anything but stare, Jack silently watched Rooker march to the scaffold. A flutter trembled inside his chest as tears welled in his eyes, and Jack knew from the bottom of his soul that part of him would die with Rooker Flynn.

Gerba's voice rang over the crowd. "Today, you shall learn my mercy!"

THE EXECUTION OF ROOKER FLYNN

Ask not for whom the bell tolls.
It tolls for thee.

John Donne

"**T**ODAY, YOU SHALL LEARN my mercy!"

Laugh or cry. You pick.

Rooker Flynn stepped onto the rooftop of the Locke Institute. Wind whipped his hair back as the sun touched his face. He closed his eyes as he felt the warm ocean breeze caress his skin and tousle his hair. He took a long breath of fresh air, sweet and perfect after so long in a cage. It felt so good, he almost smiled.

Might as well laugh.

Opening his eyes, he saw the crystal-clear water of the Irridin stretching to infinity. Above the water, dawn's baby blue sky was decorated with fluffy pink clouds that were in no hurry to get where they were going. The sun smiled over them all. It was a candy-colored morning, perfect in every way. *A good day for a long stroll.*

Rooker's fingers pulled at the knots binding his wrists. For the hundredth time, he wished for the razor blade. Locks were easy, ropes were easy, but unbinding a handcuff knot behind his back with no leverage at all was a tall order. Numb fingers fumbled at the rope, gaining no purchase.

"Move." The acolyte prodded him forward. Rooker took one stumbling step. His legs felt made of jelly. His heart pounded in his chest, making it hard to think.

Toughen up. He gritted his teeth. *Back straight. Chin up. Eyes up. Do it proper.*

His body tried to resist him, but he forced it to obey. Putting one foot in front of the other, he took a second step, then a third, a fourth, each a symphony of will. Rooker found his stride. *Come on, boys. Heel-toe, to-fro, off to the hangman's noose we go.*

He glanced up at the bell, now suspended high in the air on two big stilts, the tallest object on Huánghūn. *Damn, that's a steep climb.* A bamboo scaffold had been built between the two new legs. Switchback stairs snaked to the top, where the inside of the blackened bell seemed like a wide O, a mouth in the sky waiting to swallow him whole.

Rooker found he couldn't look at it. Instead, his eyes went to the creatures who occupied the rooftop.

They watched him with blank faces. The acolytes, the hammerdwarves, even a few eight-eyed attercops. He refused to let his eyes stay too long on any one of them, keeping his chin up like a king on his way to his coronation. They were beneath his notice. He could not, however, ignore Gerba Whipmarples.

Wearing black. That's a first. The headmistress stood at the edge of the cliff, delivering the standard propaganda that preceded a hanging with her signature lilt. He'd heard it all before, but he couldn't follow what she was saying; his mind was running too fast. As he stared at Gerba's little fascinator hat with a black veil that looked like a lace doily, Rooker couldn't help but laugh. *She looks like a two-ton funeral.*

"The student being expelled today will suffer for *all* your crimes, but make no mistake: Only he is to blame." Rooker was shoved to the edge of the precipice, on display for all to see. He raised his chest, refusing to look weak. From this height, the convicts looked like a single mass, a herd of animals. Hundreds of faces looked up at him. He saw white eyes, white teeth. Everything else was a shade of dirty brown. The prisoners shuffled, edging forward, jockeying for a better view. Rooker remembered what it was like to be one of them, hungry for a hanging. He knew exactly what the assembled convicts felt. That hunger. He knew how good it felt to watch another man die, if only to know it wasn't you. They watched him as wolves watched a sheep.

Put those tongues back in yer mouths, boys. I ain't done yet.

"You all know him!" Gerba's voice was loud and clear despite the wind. "The man responsible for your troubles! The one that fed you lies! Tricked you into open revolt! Put your lives at risk! All so he could abandon the Institute and all of you with it!" She turned to look at Rooker for the first time. "A man like that is less than an outlaw. He is an animal. And there is no place for animals in our society."

Rooker's one eye stabbed at her like a knife, a killing glare. Gerba responded with a smile as sweet as mint ice cream. She gestured at him like a carnival barker bringing a monkey to the stage. "Today, all of us are well served by the execution of Rooker Flynn!"

Rooker half-expected a cheer. Apparently so did Gerba, as she paused for a long moment. Nothing came. From here, Rooker could not read the prisoners' expressions, but their eyes were locked on him, silent. A pregnant moment followed. Gerba took a deep breath to begin speaking again, but a noise rose from below.

Sssss.

The hiss rose slowly, creeping up the wall. Through clenched teeth, the prisoners issued their judgement in a rising tide of seething contempt. Rooker couldn't see a single mouth moving. There was no way to tell which convicts made the sound, but the hiss came from everywhere below, hundreds of outlaws spitting their united hatred up at her like a nest of snakes.

Gerba took a half-step back, surprised at this act of defiance. Several acolytes glanced at each other, eyes nervous behind their niqabs. Around the perimeter of the assembly yard, the attercops seemed unsure what to do.

Billy Pilgrim's voice came first. The troubadour was easy to spot with his orange hair and purple rags. *"Booo!"* he sang in a performer's baritone, loud and long. Others joined him, shouting up at the wall. *"Boo! Boo! Booo!"* came their voices, building on each other like cresting waves. Many began slapping open palms against their thighs, adding another layer of condemnation to the din until the entire assembly rained voluminous contempt on Gerba Whipmarples and every lie she had ever told them.

Rooker felt a smile curl his lips.

"Keep talkin', sweetheart." He leaned toward Gerba. "I don't think they're buyin' it yet."

A scowl creased the headmistress' face. Unrestrained anger radiated from her eyes. Her expression twisted as the cultured mask she always wore slipped, revealing the monster beneath. "If he speaks again, gag him!" she snapped at one of Rooker's guards and thrust a brown finger past Rooker's head. "Take him to the gallows!"

The guards yanked Rooker away from the edge and he lost sight of the booing cacophony of convicts. The moment he was out of view, Rooker heaved into the guards and tried to break loose. He shoved his shoulder into one, knocking him back. Immediately he was hit several times, his broken ribs screaming in pain. Still he dug in his heels and refused to budge. One of the acolytes yanked his bound hands level with his shoulder blades and Rooker felt a stab of pain threaten to dislocate his shoulder.

"*Ahh!*" Rooker hissed as he was forced to the base of the scaffold. *Stop.*

He glared up the stairway to his death.

Gritting his teeth, Rooker shook off his fear. *Well, if we're going, let's go.*

He straightened his back and stepped up, refusing to let the acolyte force him along. *One.* He took another step. *Two.* He pounded his feet like he was trying to break the boards. *Three. Four.*

He turned at the next set of stairs and glanced above. It was a long way up to hell.

As he ascended, the crowd appeared once more. They roared protest, but it all seemed farther away now, a deadened drone of angry, impotent voices.

"Rooker!"

A shout below, not among the masses, but here, close, with him on the rooftop of the world. A familiar mess of blond hair broke from the acolytes and ran to the bottom of the scaffold, staring up at him with blue eyes.

Jack.

Rooker felt his chilled heart go warm. *He's here. He's here.* For his last moments on earth, on the path to meet his maker, here at the end of all things, his brother stood by him. Rooker's breath hitched. *With me to the end of the line. Even now.* A single tear threatened his remaining eye. Something more magic than majik fluttered through his soul, warm as the sun. *I am not alone.* His chin trembled as he whispered, "Jack."

The kid threw himself at the nearest pillar and wrapped his arms around it, wide eyes staring up at him, brimming tears. He looked a wreck, one eye swollen half-shut, his mouth bloody and broken. "Rooker! *Stop!*"

Acolytes sprinted for Jack, Winston right behind them. Gerba shouted "Gently!" but Rooker didn't hear her words. His eyes were locked on Jack, the sole point of light in a darkening universe.

He tried to conjure some fitting last words, but all he came up with was a crooked smile. "Ya comin' with me?"

"Clench your neck!" Jack shouted. "Tense it as hard as you can!" An acolyte arrived and grabbed at him. Jack kicked her away, his arms wrapped tight around the wood. "The bell can keep you going! Just stay alive!" Winston grabbed Jack and pried him from the pillar. Acolytes joined in and dragged him away. Jack strained against his captors, shouting, "Stay alive!"

Winston shoved Jack against a rail and webbed his hand to it, pinning him there. Another wad of webbing shut his mouth. Jack stared up at Rooker, his blue eyes pleading.

A low wind blew from the sea and filled the haunting emptiness between them.

There was nothing for it. This was the end. They would share no more words. There was nothing left to do now but laugh or cry.

"Don't worry, bubba." Rooker winked. "Dying's the last thing I'll do."

His guard shoved him forward.

Ascending further, Rooker felt his eye itch beneath his patch, but he had no way to scratch it. He rubbed it against his shoulder, feeling something wet on his shirt. Below, the sound of booing faded with the wind.

Suspended above the Institute wall, surrounded by nothing but air, Rooker felt his shirt riffle in the breeze. His hair blew back and he felt the sweat on his body turn cold. Above him, the black mouth of the bell ate half the sky, the Caged Eight inscribed in gold over a long crack.

Rooker tensed his neck. He clenched it, testing the best way to combat the rope.

Maybe he's right. Maybe I can hold out. Maybe—

He rounded the corner and there was the noose.

All hope abandoned him.

He would rather have jumped from the edge of the Institute than move closer to that hateful rope. A ray of morning light shone on the fibers, making the noose glow. From here, it was a portal to another world. The one Rooker had tried to avoid his entire life.

He believed in an afterlife, that the Lord of Sea and Sky weighed a man's sins upon the scale and pronounced the final sentence. Rooker Flynn believed in heaven and hell. And he knew where he was bound.

He could tighten his neck for a bit, sure. Maybe he'd stay alive for a swing or two. He could try not to kick or twitch, try not to pull the noose tighter, try to keep the air in his lungs. But even if he made it thirteen bells, he was still at the end of his rope.

Hell was inevitable.

Rooker swallowed.

His eyes fell to the hanging platform. The simple structure was only as tall as his shoulder, a flimsy wooden box held together by a single belaying pin slathered in grease. Pull the pin, and down it went.

A step-up ladder waited for him.

He stood frozen. *I don't want to die.*

The hangman wore a white hood. Rooker looked into his killer's dark brown eyes. The man was surprisingly small, his arms thin as saplings. A shock of grey hair stuck out from beneath the executioner's hood and flapped in the breeze. "Step forward," came his toneless voice.

Rooker's toes clenched inside his boots, trying to dig through the floor. Someone shoved his back. He resisted, then felt another pair of hands on him. His leg moved without his permission, and he arrived at the little ladder.

"Step up."

Rooker held his breath. It was the last step he would ever take.

And he couldn't take it.

"Test it out for me."

Rooker felt something sharp at his back. The hangman stepped toward him and spoke in a quiet, even voice. "Step up or they'll gut you now and show you your intestines while you swing."

He stepped up.

Standing at the zenith of the scaffold, he felt the box wobble beneath him. He clutched his toes again, looking for something to hold on to, but the world was far below. All that separated him from his fall were a few shaky planks and a greased hinge.

He eyed the noose as it swung in the breeze. It touched his nose, tasting its prey.

Rooker appreciated good ropecraft, and the executioner did excellent work. Wound six times, the hangman's knot was bigger than both of Rooker's fists, heavy and tight.

He was dimly aware that Gerba spoke somewhere below, continuing her pronouncement, expelling him from the Institute, but the words were meaningless. All Rooker could concentrate on was the way the platform shifted as the executioner climbed up after him. Reaching the top, the hangman gripped the noose and placed it over Rooker's head. Rooker twitched away as it passed over his eye. He felt the weight of it land on his collarbone, the prickly feel of hemp on his skin. Moving behind him, the executioner pulled the knot tight. Coarse fibers bit into his neck.

Moving around him, the hangman adjusted the noose and pulled the knot down to Rooker's ear. As he tightened it, he leaned in and whispered, "I'm putting the knot a bit forward, under your jaw. When you drop, it should jerk your head back and sever your spine." He cleared his throat, not looking Rooker in the eyes. "There's no point in drawing it out. I'll get you dead as quick as I can."

Rooker stared at him. Such was an executioner's kindness.

Descending, the hangman disappeared from view. Rooker was left standing at the pinnacle of the world, alone.

He swallowed. He had never been more aware of his Adam's apple in his life. The noose scratched against his freshly shorn neck. The platform wobbled again. Rooker grimaced and blew air through his nose, trying not to tremble.

He couldn't focus on anything, but his eyes found the horizon. The Irridin. That vast expanse of infinite blue. Home.

And there, far out beyond the pier, stood a single witness to his death. His only true love from the time he'd been a boy. The *Venture Brigand*.

The dawn sun crested her topmast, an angel in silhouette.

He let out a breath.

O girl. Half his grimace became a smile. *I never wanted anyone but you. I took yer name; I wore yer rings. I'm yers forever. I just wish I coulda stuck around a little longer.* She couldn't hear him, he knew that. Their bond was gone. "I'll miss ya, girl."

She did not reply. The *Venture Brigand* was silent. He was utterly alone.

Her silence was replaced by the maddening din of the convicts below. Shouting and stamping thundered from the assembly yard. *"Boo!"* the prisoners hollered at the top of their lungs, their faces red, furious. Bellowing at the Institute, all of them stood together, defying his execution.

Gerba Whipmarples was no longer in control of the crowd. As they screamed at her, she dropped her shoulders and gave up, then flicked her fingers at the hangman.

In one smooth movement, the executioner pulled the long metal pin from the hinges.

The crowd fell silent. Rooker was suddenly balanced above the world on a platform that wouldn't survive a stiff breeze.

The platform creaked, held together by nothing but prayer.

Rooker didn't move, didn't breathe. Every fiber of his body resisted the inevitability of his fall. Out of the corner of his eye, he saw the executioner reach for the mallet to knock the platform apart. A sudden wash of desperation flooded his veins, surging through his blood, his brain, his beating heart, the limitless power of a man with nothing left to lose.

"Fight her, ya wasteka sonsabitches!" Rooker bellowed his final command to the throng. *"Fight!"*

Silence burst to cheers and Rooker had one last instant of satisfaction before the executioner struck.

The mallet head went through the platform.

Rooker dropped.

He felt air beneath his feet. Smelled the ocean. Cursed his luck.

The rope jerked tight—

N—

His head snapped back. Something at the base of his skull cracked with an immense stab of pain, then he was nothing below the neck. His legs, his arms, his chest, all of them were gone, severed from his spine. For a fleeting instant, all he could feel was the noose clutched around his neck. Every other part of him was already dead. Alienated from his own body, he heard the constricted gag of his throat as if it came from someone else, somewhere else, somewhere far away. Panicked, shocked, terrified, he watched stars explode in his vision as the noose tightened its grip, taking him down into the dark. Nothing remained but pain and fear, the sensation of plummeting into the jaws of the abyss.

Black.

Nothing.

Silence.

An infinite void. A vast, hollow emptiness so lonely and desolate it swallowed eternity. He felt it all around him, the nothingness, the absence of love, hope, desire, comfort, all destroyed. It burned his soul like a lake of fire.

Somewhere in the forever black, a bell tolled.

Vitality surged back into him, a calamitous joy that jangled his senses alive as the Agrat-ban-Haifa's healing majik flooded his body. Hope seared through his flesh as he felt the bones in his neck unbreak with a sick thok. He rose, lifting into the air. Restored by the bell, his reinvigorated body bucked, only drawing the noose tighter.

Fight!

Suffocating, he kicked at the end of the rope, fighting for life as the noose crushed his windpipe; he felt it collapse, felt blood in his throat as ecstasy turned black.

Once more, the bell tolled.

Despair and hope became one as his larynx opened again. He felt his missing eye grow back while he strangled to death, healing and dying at the same moment. His bucking body kicked like an animal, utterly beyond his control. A moaning wail of terror escaped his lips before his spinal cord broke again.

Blood vessels burst in his eye, painting it with blood. Through it, he saw Gerba, hands on her hips, counting the tolls, wearing a thin smile of teeth. There was Jack, pinned to the rail and screaming.

Rooker's windpipe collapsed and this time the noose was too tight to let it open again. His vision faded.

Black.

Nothingness.

A white light.

Daylight again. He couldn't breathe, couldn't stop kicking, couldn't stop fighting.

His brain no longer worked; everything was colors. The crowd was wrong. They were going away, leaving.

Black.

Light.

Everything was tilting.

He saw sparks, flashes of light, white pixies.

No, I can't—

Black.

White.

Blood poured into his lungs, drowning him.

It's tilting, it's tilting—

No.

Rooker Flynn felt the last beat of his heart and still he kept fighting.

No.

Blood red sails on stormy seas, sun sunk halfway into the ocean, horizon coming fast.

An entire ocean before him, empty and dark.

N—

Black.

Chapter

4

Long Drop from a Short Rope

*All human wisdom
is summed up
in two words;
wait and hope.*

Alexandre Dumas

"*TILTING, IT'S TILTING, IT'S—*"

Jack watched one of the acolytes shout at the bell, yelling a warning.

Amazed eyes stared up at the pillars of the Agrat-ban-Haifa as the closest column began to lean. Wood groaned loudly as the pillar twisted off its axis, squealing, tilting like a drunk sailor.

A sharp rock in Jack's hand hacked at the webbing that pinned his wrist to the guardrail. He watched the bell tilt further, knowing he was out of time. He gritted his teeth and bore down with the newfound strength the bell's *wikk* lent him and sawed at the web.

Suddenly, Jack was free.

Tearing away from the guardrail, he sprinted to the base of the platform. Everyone was staring up at the Agrat-ban-Haifa; no one noticed him as he ran.

As the axis of the tower shifted, Jack looked up into the bell. Rooker didn't move, limp at the base of the noose. *Please don't be dead, please—*

Sweat poured into Jack's eyes as he watched the pillar buckle and come loose at the base.

He had placed the ringslug when he'd wrapped his arms around the pillar, hollering at Rooker to tense his neck. He had barely managed to clamp the ringslug onto itself before Winston had dragged him away, but it had connected. At the first ring of the bell, the ringslug had reacted to the noise, startled by the sound, and eaten into the pillar's base to escape.

It had chewed through the post, and now the entire bell tower stood on one leg, tilting toward the sea.

The clapper struck the Agrat-ban-Haifa for the thirteenth time. The sound sent another surge of *wikk* through Jack as he ran past the severed leg. He reached up his sleeve and grabbed the second ringslug he had stolen from the hammerdwarf barrels when Winston had knocked him down, while everyone had been distracted by the geas curse. Jack could feel the slug stuck to his chest, where it had crawled during the hanging. He pulled it free and dragged it down his forearm.

He skidded to the base of the second pillar and spared one glance up. The bell cantilevered in the sky, hanging at a slight angle, swaying in the breeze. He grabbed the second column and slapped the ringslug around the base.

Out of the corner of his eye, Jack saw Winston point at him. "Boss!" the attercop shouted.

Gerba Whipmarples' head snapped to Jack. She blinked, taking a half-second to realize what he was doing. Her eyes went wide, terrified. She shrieked, "Stop him!"

Winston leapt at Jack, hairy arms spread wide.

Straining, Jack pulled at the ringslug and felt it stretch in his hands like a slimy rubber band. Above, the entire bell tower continued its slow tilt, twisting on one good leg. His muscles burned as he fought to get his arms around the pillar.

"No!" Gerba ran for him.

Jack latched the slug's head to its tail and completed the ring around the second leg. Winston charged at him, fangs bared.

His face an inch away from the ringslug, Jack screamed at the top of his lungs.

Recoiling from the sound, the slug burrowed into the wood from all sides and created a razor-sharp noose that dug straight through the heart of the timber.

It severed with a faint CRACK.

The Agrat-ban-Haifa hung suspended for a moment. Jack drew a sharp intake of breath. Then the entire leg fell and toppled toward the sea, drawn by the weight of its fallen brother.

Attercops, acolytes, outlaws, and Gerba Whipmarples herself bore witness to the fall of the Agrat-ban-Haifa. Scaffolding collapsed and splintered. The tower wilted; it tilted over the edge and fell like a prizefighter who had taken a haymaker on the chin, a knockout punch.

Below, the prisoners stared in amazement. Closer to Jack, Gerba screamed in horror.

Jack watched the Great Bell fall past him and drop toward the bay, a silhouette of destruction against the dawn sun. Inside, he caught a glimpse of Rooker's body, still hanging from the noose, his limbs slack, falling. *Please don't be dead, please—*

Winston lunged for Jack, but it was too late. Jack grabbed on to the broken pillar and was hauled over the edge of the cliff. Clutching the wood, Jack was pulled away from the attercop, away from Gerba, and away from the Institute.

He trailed the bell tower on its swan dive from the rooftop of Huánghūn.

Jack sucked in a panicked breath a hundred feet over the Irridin. Wind ripped at his eyes and drew tears. Through them, he saw Rooker's limp body inside the bell, suspended in midair, the rope floating around him in useless loops. When the bell hit the water, the impact would break every bone in Rooker's body.

Jack let go of the pillar and kicked off into the air. His arms pinwheeled, his heart in his throat. Halfway between sky and sea, he watched three hundred tons of bronze smash into the sea with a thunderous splash as the bell hit the Irridin like a meteor. The Agrat-ban-Haifa, magnified by the water, rang out in an explosion of sound that was heard ten miles away and healed every living thing caught in the shockwave of its passing.

Jack didn't even feel the *wikk*. He was too terrified. Streamlining his body to a pencil-shape, he had a half-second to pray before he hit the water from a hundred-foot drop.

He blacked out on impact. There was a moment, a silence, a gap. Then he was driven awake by the thunderous power of the bell amplified by a trillion tons of water. Its power surged through him like lightning, overwhelming, and Jack snapped awake beneath the waves with the vigor of an Olympian.

Following the bubbles, Jack broke the surface with a gasp. He blinked, staring at the wreckage of the bell tower all around him. He looked back to where he had started, a hundred feet up. There, Gerba Whipmarples stood at the edge of the cliff, screaming impotent rage. As good as the power of the *wikk* felt, watching Gerba scream felt even better.

An acolyte reached the edge, gripping a longbow. Another joined her and nocked an arrow.

Around Jack the broken pillars angled; one end lifted from the water as the other followed the bell in its race to the bottom of the sea. Jack swam for a pillar and grabbed onto it as the thing sank under the surface. As he went under, an arrow penetrated the water, just a few feet away. He hauled as much air into his lungs as he could before he was dragged beneath the waves.

Please don't be dead, please—

Rooker's shattered body came alive trapped inside a deafening echo chamber of lightless metal. His afterlife was doomed to an eternity of being drowned, dragged to the bottom of the sea with a giant bell tied around his neck.

So I do deserve hell.

Dammit.

Cracking, the bones in his spine snapped into place, popping his neck in an incredibly satisfying way. Blood surged as his heart pumped like a forge fire, panicked and thrilled in the same moment. *If this is what death feels like, I fought it too hard.*

He saw a shimmer of ethereal light above him and kicked toward it. He broke through the surface to find himself inside an air pocket within the peak of the bell. His throat opened as the noose relaxed and he felt his lungs draw sweet breath. With bound hands he snatched the clapper of the bell behind his back. The air pocket held as the bell descended toward the ocean floor, but the sea was boiling around him like a cauldron, threatening to fill the void and drown him. He felt the bell tumble and saw the skull-sized skirt bells Gerba had added around the rim drag the lip of the bell downward again, leading the fall.

Three hundred tons of bronze forced him to the ocean floor. His back pressed against the clapper, Rooker watched fish dart out of the way beneath him. He felt the pressure grow violent in his ears as he gritted his teeth and waited to slam into the floor of the sea. The skirt bells hit first, billowing puffs of sand from the ocean floor. Rooker winced in anticipation of the inevitable, knowing the bell was about to bury him in a watery tomb. *Couldn't I have just stayed dead?*

The bell hit the sand and Rooker was thrown into the water. It was as if he had been struck blind, such was the blackness. Completely cut off from the sun, there was no way to tell which way was up. Rooker scrabbled against the bell, trying to find a way out, but with his hands tied behind his back, all he could find was metal and sand. After a moment, he gave up. There was air in his lungs. At least it knew which way was up. He let his body relax, buoyant in his chest, and soon he felt his head break through the surface and he took another breath. He waited for the air pocket to flood and drown him, but the water stopped rising. Trapped inside the void, he heard his ragged breath echo all around.

Then, there was light. A ring beneath his feet blossomed as sunlight reflected from the sand. The light grew stronger, billowing ribbons of color, ripples that danced around him like majik. The bell rose from the ocean floor as air strained for the surface. Around the rim, the chains of the skirt bells pulled tight and the bell stopped ascending, locked in place a few feet above the bottom.

Rooker Flynn found himself fifty feet underwater.

Breathing.

"Ha!" he barked and felt the bell reverberate around him. *"Ha!"*

A violent splash erupted beside him. Rooker reared back, startled, as something broke the surface right next to him. A head. A blond head.

Jack.

Rooker lunged at him like a bear, laughing like a maniac. They both went under, splashing and kicking. Unable to hug him with bound hands, Rooker pounded at Jack underwater like a dolphin, laughing, overjoyed. Jack whacked him right back, laughing too, big bubbles escaping a broad smile. Out of breath, they dragged themselves up to the air pocket. Rooker sucked in air and kept on laughing. It bubbled from the bottom of his soul, cascading from him like a geyser. He should be dead, hanged and buried. He had expected it, he had earned it. But here he was, swimming at the bottom of the sea, and he wasn't alone. Jack laughed with him, adding his own joy to Rooker's song in high harmony. Their noise reverberated inside the bell, and so it was that the final ring of the Agrat-ban-Haifa was not the toll of enslavement or death but the perfect echo of two friends simply laughing together.

"*That* is a long way down." Jack dug into his pocket and produced his little homemade scalpel. "Here, give me your hands." Rooker hooked his feet on the clapper and held steady as Jack sawed at the rope binding his hands.

"What the hell?" laughed Rooker, still unable to wrap his head around what had happened. "What the hell did you *do*?"

"What you told me to on our first day." Jack snorted. "Figure a way off this island."

Rooker stared at him, agog. "*This* is what you came up with?"

"It was my first day, what do you want? Back then, all I knew was the island had Gerba, a bunch of archers, and the Agrat-ban-Haifa. So the only idea I had was maybe use it as a diving bell." He cut at Rooker's ropes. "A really *bad* diving bell."

Rooker looked down at the skirt of bells and the series of dangling chains that held the Agrat-ban-Haifa at the bottom of the sea, trapping the air they breathed. "You *told* her to add those. The very first day."

"Who figured she'd listen to me?" Jack smiled.

Rooker grinned like a lunatic. For a man who'd just stood nose to nose with death, every living second was a miracle. He grabbed Jack and hugged him. He made a mess of it, half-drowning both of them, but neither man cared.

"Mph." Jack backed away, his tongue exploring his mouth. "My teeth are growing back. That's weird."

Rooker looked down to see a pink haze drifting in the water. "Hey, yer bleeding."

"Yeah, one of the arrows nicked me." Jack rubbed at his bloody shoulder. "If you were wondering, she's still trying to kill us."

"We're too deep to hit." Rooker grinned. "Besides," he knocked the bronze. "We've got killer armor." This time the metal didn't reverberate. His knuckle hit with a dull thud, and there was a sudden dull CRACK under the water.

Rooker saw the gold Caged Eight glyph welded to the wall of the bell, the source of Gerba's control over everything with eight legs, break. It snapped free as the bell wall cracked with it. The gold rune drifted to the ocean floor and buried itself in sand forever.

"All this air will be carbon dioxide before long and we'll suffocate." Jack breathed. "Plus, the moment we surface, they're going to shoot us."

"But other than that, we're fine." Rooker grinned. He couldn't help it. He was alive.

"Ahh!" Jack let out a shout, grabbed the clapper, and pulled himself up. "Something bit me."

Rooker scowled as he watched a tentacle loop casually under the bell, probing. "Razorsquid." The nasty buggers' tentacles were made of tiny needles meant to bleed their prey dry. The bay was filled with them, drawn by the power of the Caged Eight. "So we're either going to suffocate, drown, or bleed to death."

"Or get shot," added Jack.

Rooker laughed. "So we're trapped as we ever were."

"No. You're the one who saves us."

Rooker stared at Jack. The kid's face brimmed confidence, but Rooker was at a loss. *"How?"*

Jack blinked, a stupid look on his face, then glanced at Rooker's hand. "Right! I keep forgetting!" Rooker watched Jack dig in his pocket, then raise his hand above the water and unclench his fist. Rooker's eyes gleamed at what he saw in Jack's palm.

"My rings." The twin brass bands of the *Venture Brigand*'s deckwheel glistened in the light. Rooker felt his heart stop at the sight of them. He took them from Jack's palm delicately, touching them like a lover. *My girl.* "How did you—"

"I had to tear her pocket off to get them." Jack snorted. "But you *cannot* call me the worst pickpocket in Keymark anymore."

"How—" Rooker stared at Jack. "How did you *remember* to steal them?"

"The faintest ink is better than the best memory." Jack pulled down his sleeve. Rooker saw a series of markings on Jack's arm, written in the red grease pencil from the strîgoi pits.

2 Cu Zn Ring

Gerb L. Frnt Poket

Rooker couldn't read the Toshan squiggles, but he got the idea. "Ha!" Water caught in his throat and he coughed. "But those aren't gonna do us any good. The *Brigand* is anchored in iron."

"What do you think Leah and Memphis are doing right now?" Jack smiled again. "Or do you think that wasn't a big enough signal?"

Rooker felt a grin split his face in half. "I—"

"Tell me later," said Jack. "Call your lady."

Rooker slipped the rings onto his finger. He felt the familiar weight of them and the world was right again.

I'm here, girl. I'm here. He balled his hand into a fist. The grooves of his fingers gripped the rings perfectly. *Come to me.*

KUNG!

One of the chains at the bottom of the bell broke and separated from the rim. Rooker felt the Agrat-ban-Haifa tilt. Air tilted with it, crawling along the side of the bell.

Another chain snapped.

Come on, girl.

A third chain let loose. The bell tilted wildly. No longer evenly connected to the ocean floor, it canted sideways. Bubbles glugged past Rooker's nose.

Outside the bell, Rooker watched an arrow curl through the water and sink into the sand.

Please, girl.

He felt a sting on his leg. The razorsquid fled before he saw it.

Please.

The bell passed the point of no return. The air they had been breathing fled along the side of the bell, escaping past the lip in fist-sized bubbles.

"Get rid a yer boots!" Rooker kicked his off. "We're goin' swimmin'!" He took a deep breath and went under.

Pulling under the bell, Rooker kicked away from it. Razorsquid dotted the water around him. He stared out at the open sea, but there was no sign of the *Venture Brigand*. Jack swam behind him, bare feet kicking, his eyes wide.

Searing pain flashed up Rooker's leg as a razorsquid drew first blood. He ignored it and swam toward the open ocean, staring into the infinite blue.

Hear me.

Above, arrows splashed into the water, making little whirlpools of bubbles as they came.

Come to me.

Another squid lashed his arm. Another got his foot. He kept swimming.

Save me.

Yes, she answered.

Her voice was powerful, triumphant, encompassing his entire body. He felt it in his chest, reverberating through him like a familiar song. She came for him.

She came.

Rooker watched two white streaks appear in the distance, a pair of outriggers running in tandem, sprinting over the water's surface like twin stallions come to collect their master.

Kicking with all his might, Rooker swam for the *Venture Brigand*, reaching out to her. He checked to make sure Jack was with him. Behind the kid, Rooker saw the rock wall that rose to become the Institute, too close. *Yer comin' in too straight. Yer gonna hit the rocks! Thirty degrees starboard, now!*

The *Venture Brigand* listened, canting away. But now she was no longer headed straight for him. Her arc would take her just outside his reach. Rooker swam faster and cut the distance.

We're not gonna make it. Even if we grab an outrigger, we're too close. They'll fill us with holes the moment we draw air.

Not knowing what to do, Rooker kicked harder, facing death from above and below.

Another half a dozen razorsquid lashes burned his body. He felt one hang on and drag behind him.

No way we reach her. I just need another few yards.

Rooker grimaced and clenched his jaw.

Drop anchor, girl.

A splash broke the water as the *Venture Brigand*'s double-fluked anchor bubbled down from the surface and plummeted through the blue. Rooker watched the thing drop five yards, then ten. He forced himself to wait half a moment longer than he wanted to, knowing if the thing touched bottom, they were dead. *Hold anchor!*

The chain drew up short, suspended above the sand. It struck a rock outcrop, splintering stone shards in a cloud of dust, spinning as it came.

Rooker grabbed Jack's shirt and hauled him toward the anchor. It swung at the end of its chain, coming closer.

Now!

Rooker snatched the anchor and gripped it tight.

He smiled. *Hello, girl.*

He turned to see Jack reach for it, his hands outstretched.

He missed, his fingers brushing the edge.

Rooker lashed a leg around the anchor and let his body fall. He lunged for Jack's wrist and snatched it tight. He held on and dragged his brother's weight behind him.

For a moment, they flew together under the Irridin, hand in hand.

Weigh anchor, girl.

The chain clanked and reeled them up through the water, hauled by the might of the *Venture Brigand*. Rooker kept his fist clasped around Jack's wrist as the kid dangled beneath him, his eyes fluttering shut, out of air.

Hard a-starboard.

The *Venture Brigand* banked right and turned away from the Locke Institute, headed for the bay.

Blue water became blue sky in a crash of foam as Rooker broke the surface. He hauled up Jack, his arms tight around him, slung one of the kid's arms over his shoulder, and straddled the anchor hook. Barely conscious, the kid yarked up water in spasms.

As the anchor reached the ship's side, Rooker threw Jack over the deckrail like a prize swordfish. He gripped the wood and slid across the rail on one hip.

Rooker Flynn's bare feet landed on the deck of the *Venture Brigand*.

For so many months, he had dreamt of her. All that time, he'd been powerless, vulnerable, beaten. But now he stood on her deck at last and felt pride swell his chest. She had saved him. She had come for him. She and Jack.

Rooker Flynn had been dead. Executed. Hanged. Drowned. Alone, he was nothing. But standing here, now, with his ship and his brother, breathing free air on the waves of the Irridin Sea, Rooker had a glimpse of heaven.

Home.

He ripped the eyepatch off and threw it overboard, both eyes shining. "All right, girl. Let's *run*."

Chapter

5

T!CKẸT
= TỌ THẸ =
JẠMBỌRẸẸ

Being in a ship is being in a jail,
with the chance of being drowned.

Samuel Johnson

"**A** LL RIGHT, GIRL. LET'S *run*."

Jack heard Rooker whisper as he strode across the deck. Waterlogged and half-drowned, Jack tried to get to his feet, failed, and landed in a squishy heap on the deck. He retched up a bucket's worth of water, hacking it straight from his lungs. *I didn't think I could hold my breath that long.* Water dribbled from his nose, his ears, his eyes. *I don't think I did.*

A razorsquid was wrapped around his leg. He kicked the thing off and felt it squish against his naked feet. He dragged in a breath and a smile crossed his face. *Free.* For the first time in almost a year, no one had their hand on his neck. No one could tell him what to do. Gerba's hold on him was broken. He was free. It felt like waking into a dream.

Leah Archer appeared beside him. Her red hair whipped in the wind, a stunned expression on her face. "Jahk? Are you okay? You don't look... good."

Jack smiled at her, feeling his heart race. *I'm better than good. I'm free.* He put a hand on her arm. "Leah. I'm f—" His stomach seized and another jet of water lurched from his mouth.

Leah kept her composure enough to almost hide her snorting laugh. "If that's as close as I get to a thank you, you're welcome."

"Get yer hands off her, ya wasteka runt!" Jack turned to Rooker's shout. The pirate stomped toward the deckwheel of the *Venture Brigand,* where Memphis Kubiak, the trol who was, in all ways, the opposite of Gerba Whipmarples, tried to steer the ship with a look of furrowed concentration on his brown rhinoceros face.

"This is harder than it looks!" Memphis shouted back.

"Stop fighting her!" Rooker shouldered aside Memphis, who outweighed him fifty times. "Let her run."

Leah hauled Jack to his feet and shouted above the wind. "Welcome aboard, Captain Flynn."

Rooker stared at her, his face open and full of joy. "Lord and Lady, ya look fantastic."

Leah crossed her arms. "*There's* the scoundrel I remember."

"I mean the *Brigand*." Rooker seized the deckwheel with rough hands like a jockey taking a thoroughbred's reins. "Get 'round, girl."

The *Venture Brigand* burst to life. Wind ripped across the deck. Yellow sails fluttered and snapped full. The entire ship creaked like a wooden giant waking from a nap. The wind became a gale and every rope strained as the ship surged ahead, propelled by its own will. As it lunged, Jack stumbled back into Leah, who held him on his feet. "Wow," they both whispered.

Arrows thudded into the deck around them. Jack glanced up to find they were directly beneath the Institute wall. Acolytes lined up atop the butte loosed another volley. Jack felt Leah tackle him around the waist and throw him down on the far side of the cargo crates. A dozen arrows peppered them like black rain. One struck the crate a foot from her face. "We've got eight heartbeats before the next volley!" she shouted. "Four, three..."

"*Hya!*" came Rooker's shout. He did not take cover. Arrows jutted from the wood around him like giant porcupine quills. His eyes were wide, his white teeth bared. "Dig in, girl!"

Jack felt the ship shift beneath his feet. The *Venture Brigand* was shaped like a Λ, skiing over the water on two giant pontoons. But at Rooker's command the starboard legs of the ship drew in, shortened, and leaned into the turn like a speed skater. The deck tilted beneath Jack at a sharp angle as the *Brigand* took the hairpin turn, and he was forced to grab onto the deckrail to keep from falling.

"It's tilting! It's tilting!" Leah yelled, hanging on to the rail for dear life. She glanced at Rooker standing behind the wheel. "Is *he* doing that?!" Another volley of longbows twanged and hurtled toward the ship, but the best shot of the volley missed as the

Venture Brigand cut away from the Institute. "We're out of range! Jahk!"

Jack was too busy looking up the cliff. Majik signal flares lit the sky in blazes of crackling light a hundred feet above the wall. Near the center, framed by the flares, Jack saw the massive shadow of Gerba Whipmarples, framed by the stumps of her broken belltower. She stood in shock, her mouth open in horror.

Good.

Jack smiled. A mixture of revenge and relief flooded him as he watched Gerba Whipmarples, the headmistress of the Locke Institute, fade into the distance. *Goodbye, wasteka harridan!*

Something hit his chest. Jack felt pebbled skin wrap around him and looked down to find Fuji the tam embracing him with all four legs. "There you are!" Jack laughed and hugged the big gecko back.

Fuji's big yellow eyes peered up at him. **Apple?**

"I'm going to get you a *hundred* apples!"

"Quit playin' with yer lizard and get on that damn harpoon bow, Jack!" Rooker hollered. His eyes were fire, his knuckles white on the wheel. "We're not clear yet!"

Obeying captain's orders, Jack sprinted to the foredeck. Mounted near the head of the ship, he found a contraption covered by a canvas tarpaulin. Jack unclipped the tie and threw off the cover to reveal a huge mounted four-armed crossbow. Jack stared at the heavy weapon in awe. The thing was bigger than he was. Excitement crackled in his fingers. All *right.*

"Crank it back!" yelled Rooker. "The winch han—"

"I got it!" Jack shouted back. It was a simple machine: turn the crank, cock the bow, load a harpoon, and pull to fire. Eager, Jack grabbed the crank and went to work.

"You!" yelled Rooker, pointing to Leah. "*Aft* bow!"

Leah glanced at the back of the boat. "You want me covering the rear?"

"That's where the action's gonna be, Archer, and yer a better shot than him!" Rooker jerked his chin at her. "Anything comes up behind us, put a bolt in it!"

Leah was already running for the weapon. "Done!"

"Runt!" Rooker shouted at Memphis. "Get up top!"

The short trol had never liked Rooker, and he didn't start now. Memphis towered over the captain, angry. "Now look, you can't just go ordering—"

"Cram it, Kubiak!" yelled Rooker. "Get in the crow's nest! I need eyes in the sky." He yanked the wheel and angled the *Brigand* closer into the docks, where the little dinghies were moored. He grinned like a wolf. "O, it's just too tempting."

He cut toward the pier. Jack watched as the *Venture Brigand*'s gigantic ski ran straight over a rowboat, shattering it to flinders. The next boat, a little skiff, he split in half. Rooker laughed as an acolyte aboard a dinghy screamed and flung himself into the water before the *Brigand* crushed that one too. Rooker suddenly spun on Memphis. "What the hell ya still doin' down here?"

Memphis scowled. "I'm not going up top. I'm too heav—"

"She'll take yer weight. Move it!"

Memphis eyed the long climb to the nest. "Leah would be—"

"Leah's on harpoon, ya wasteka runt!" screamed Rooker, loud as a hundred hardened captains. He kicked Memphis in the ass. "Get up there and call out positions!"

"Of what?" yelled Memphis.

"Of *that*!"

Jack turned and realized that Gerba's little fireworks display hadn't been just for show.

Every ship in the harbor weighed anchor. Sails rose, hauled into position. Shouts echoed across the water as every sailor in the bay—acolytes and yellowjackets alike—went into action to cut off their escape. Jack suddenly realized how many ships stood between them and the open sea. More than a dozen were aligned against them, including the corvette Rooker had always admired. Suddenly freedom didn't seem so certain.

"Fine, I'll go!" Memphis disappeared in a *whuff* of majik and a brown lizard took his place. It scuttled up the mainmast in a huff.

Jack cranked the deadly harpoon bow tight as a violin string and felt it lock into position. He grabbed a harpoon from a barrel and slammed the long steel dart into the slot. He glanced at the barrel, now empty. "I only have one harpoon!"

"Then don't miss!" Rooker barked. "What color is it?"

Jack glanced at the fletching of the harpoon, wondering what possible difference it could make. "Orange!"

"Dammit!" Rooker jerked the wheel; the *Brigand* leaned north. Jack felt the ship turn away from the pier and cut into the bay. Behind, their wake cut tracks of foaming white as the ship picked up speed. Jack felt his heart thrill with excitement as wind whipped his hair.

The *Venture Brigand* was the biggest ship in the harbor; it dwarfed the other boats, a Goliath among Davids. Several nearby ships made an intercept course, looking to cut off her escape route. Rooker rode a straight line, refusing to turn. Jack heard the pirate growl under his breath. "That's it. Take the bait..." He cut hard port and left the boats chasing a phantom trajectory. The *Brigand* curled past, leaving them behind. "Call out, damn ya!"

"Two ahead!" came Memphis's booming *basso profundo* from the crow's nest. "Three scattered north, lots more spread outside!"

Jack stared up at Memphis. *Lots more?* Rooker grimaced and shouted at the crow's nest. "Where's that damn corvette?"

"In the middle! Coming for us!"

Rooker buttonhooked south. As Jack felt the *Brigand* lean into the turn, he watched Rooker stand shirtless, shoeless, spread-legged at the helm, mimicking the tilt of his ship's legs. His black hair whipped behind him like a flag, the picture of a pirate king. "Try and catch me, ya wasteka yellowbellies!"

Two yellowjacket ships loomed ahead. Rooker peeled away from the larger vessel, but the smaller one cut straight toward the *Brigand*, close. A volley of arrows arced through the air. Jack grabbed Fuji and threw himself under the deckrail as arrows bit into the wood around him. The yellowjacket ship steered hard into the *Venture Brigand* and slammed into her outrigger. Jack felt the collision shudder the ship.

As the yellowjacket boat rattled alongside the *Brigand*'s huge pontoon, a dozen men leapt across the watery divide. Several missed their footing and instantly disappeared into the Irridin, but others found handholds on the pontoon. They climbed the *Venture Brigand*'s legs, knives between their teeth.

Jack spun the harpoon bow on them but it wouldn't target anything that close. He grabbed a barge pole and darted toward them. "Get back to yer damn post!" barked Rooker. "Give 'em hell, girl!"

Jack felt himself almost vomit as the ship heaved upward. The *Venture Brigand*'s legs suddenly pulled together, making the ship rise a dozen feet in a few seconds. As her legs straightened, the yellowjackets' climb became steeper. Two slid backward and lost their grip. Screaming, they bounced off the outrigger and splashed into the drink. The remaining three held on, dragging themselves forward like spiders.

"Leah!" Rooker shouted. "Slaver bow! Compartment on your left!" Jack watched Leah flip up a hatch and pull out a work-scarred longbow and a brace of arrows. The arrowheads were cylindrical, rounded and blunt at the tip. As fast as Jack's eyes could follow, Leah drew and loosed an arrow at the closest yellowjacket. The blunted arrow broke his nose with a wet crunch and he fell screaming. Before the man could hit the waves below, she fired a second shot that nailed the next yellowjacket right between his eyes with an audible *tok*. The man blinked, fell backward, and disappeared into the white wake.

Leah drew a third arrow and the bowstring snapped, leaving a slash of blood on her cheek.

A dirk between his teeth, the last yellowjacket pawed his way across the top of the leg and slapped one meaty hand on the deckrail.

Jack grit his teeth, knowing the man would be aboard in seconds, but followed his orders and stuck to his post. *There's nothing she can d—*

Rooker reached for a colorful display of feathers embedded on the console near the wheel. He plucked one like a flower, and Jack saw sharp metal gleam at its base. Rooker flicked the dart and the air of the *Brigand* carried it through the air to pierce the yellowjacket's hand.

That was all it took. The yellowjacket lost his grip and toppled off the side, gone. Grinning, Rooker jammed a dart between his teeth. "Settle in, girl." The *Venture Brigand* spread her legs wide as falcon's wings and took a low, predatory stance above the surface.

"Two more inbound!" Memphis shouted from the top of the mainmast. Jack looked up to realize two schooners were almost on top of them.

"Jack!" Rooker pointed at the nearest of the two. "Punch that one!"

Jack wheeled the giant harpoon bow toward the closest ship. "Shoot it *where*?"

"Low!" hollered Rooker. "Just above the waterline! Don't miss!"

Jack scowled. His target was as wide as a barn. *Even I can hit that.*

He loosed his harpoon. The bolt didn't drop nearly as much as he'd expected; the exquisite force of the bowstring launched it like a bullet. Even this close, Jack's shot nearly went wide. His long steel dart bit into the wood of the ship just above the waterline. Useless, it stuck out of the boat like a twig.

"What the hell was the point of th—" Jack's words were cut off as the harpoon shattered. Something fell from it into the water and suddenly blossomed into a sailcloth shaped like a parachute. Underwater, it swallowed the sea like a whale, billowing full, heavy and slow. The schooner creaked and the wood around Jack's harpoon ripped away, tearing a hole into the boat.

Foundering, the schooner tilted sideways, taking on hundreds of gallons of water. The *Brigand* skirted past her, leaving her to sink.

"That corvette is catching up! East northeast!" shouted Leah.

Jack turned to see the lean two-master closing in behind them. The corvette was smaller than the *Brigand*, but its speed was astonishing. It barreled for them like a shark out for blood. Jack yelled at Rooker over the wind. "I thought you said you could outrun that thing!"

"Not when I gotta dodge a bay full of ships!" Rooker shouted and straightened the wheel. "Run now, girl! *Hyah!*"

Jack grabbed the rail as the *Brigand* ran in a straight line and picked up speed. The corvette still gained, hounding them. "A dozen ships!" Jack looked up to see the big trol in the crow's nest pointing dead ahead. "Making a... what is it... a *flotilla*!" Jack turned to see the remaining ships gathered like soldiers standing in a row on the outside edge of the bay.

"They're forming up." Jack barely heard Rooker's quiet voice over the wind. "Side by side." The thrill in Rooker's voice was gone. A hollow whisper had replaced it and a haunted look stole the gleam in his eye. Jack realized what Rooker already knew: They were trapped.

The corvette pursued them like a foxhound, driving them into the waiting net of ships. If they turned, the corvette had them. If they didn't, every other ship in the harbor waited for them in a solid wall.

Fuji crawled into Jack's arms and held him tight. He felt the tam lick his cheek, whimpering. Jack knew how it felt. After a taste of freedom, the prospect of being put in chains again was unthinkable. He and Rooker shared a look.

Jack abandoned his bow. He was out of harpoons anyway. Holding Fuji, he ran up the steps to the bridge next to Rooker. His voice sounded more nervous than he wanted. "What do we do?"

"Run the blockade," the captain growled. "Straight up their wasteka noses."

Deafening wind gusted at their backs and the *Venture Brigand* picked up speed, headed straight for the wall of ships. "Are you crazy?" Jack screamed. "It's suicide!"

"Ya wanna go back to prison?" Rooker's dark eyes were sharp, deadly. Jack didn't have a response. Rooker nodded. "Me neither."

Water hissed in the catamaran's tracks as their speed increased. Ahead, the blockade held its position, tightening up. None of the ships were as big as the *Brigand*, but together, they formed an immovable obstacle on the water. Behind, the corvette cut the *Venture Brigand*'s wake, closing fast.

"Hey!" Rooker barked at Jack. "Belly dome! Ya remember how to get there?"

"Yeah!" Jack shouted over the wind, watching the blockade grow ever closer.

"There's a footlocker!" Rooker snapped. "Left side of the catwalk! Inside that, there's a wooden box, red with a gold clasp!" He winked at Jack. "Grab that for me real quick, woodja?"

Jack took off running, Fuji protected under one arm.

"Archer!" Jack heard Rooker shout behind him. "When we close, punch a 'poon in whoever's on our starboard!"

"Got it!" Leah shouted. Jack glanced over his shoulder to see her jam the bow's stock into her shoulder and take steely aim.

"Runt!"

"What?" hollered Memphis, hanging on to the ropes in the crow's nest for dear life.

"Ya got fightin' majik, right?" Rooker spat. "Those little fireballs?"

"Yeah!" Memphis screamed.

"Torch their sails!"

Jack took one look over his shoulder to see Rooker Flynn produce a giant purple pirate hat with a broken feather. He popped the thing on his head, cocked it at a jaunty angle, and sang with the feathered dart still in his teeth:

> *O, I got a gal who's always rotten!*
> *Stuffs her shirt with a bale of cotton!*

Rooker Flynn leaned in, daring the barricade to stop him, displaying that daredevil grin.

> *Six foot tall, eight feet of hair!*
> *Poked holes in a barrel for her underwear!*
> *Don't know Liza, don't know me!*
> *We got a ticket to the jam-bo-ree!*

Jack ducked into the cabin and disappeared into the dark.

Making his way from memory, he tumbled down the ladder, hooked right, slid down the pole, and flipped open the trapdoor and thundered through the passageway to find himself inside the glass bowl of the *Venture Brigand*'s belly.

From the catwalk, he had a panoramic view of his impending death.

The blockade was almost on top of the *Brigand,* close enough to launch a volley of arrows. One shot flew low and bounced off the glass in front him. Behind, Jack saw the corvette ride the *Brigand*'s wake, drawing closer. Mounted at the head of the ship, a harpoon bow took aim. Through the grating in the deck above, he heard Rooker's frenzied song continue; Jack could almost hear the dart clenched between the pirate's teeth.

A mule kicked her, she kicked right back!
Made her bed out of an old haystack!

Red box!
Jack sprinted around the catwalk and found a series of foot-lockers. He threw one open and discovered it empty. Tossing the second, he found nothing red. Angry, he threw open the third and found a glossy crimson box with golden hinges.

"Finally!" Clutching the box, he realized he'd lost Fuji. Jack glanced around and found the tam clinging to one of the beams over the dome. "Come on, Fuji. I—" But Fuji wasn't looking at him. The gecko's big yellow eyes stared forward, terrified.

Jack turned to find himself on a head-on collision course with a double-masted frigate.

The ship was big as the corvette, an immovable wooden fortress directly in front of him. *There's nowhere to turn!*

Rooker's voice thundered over the chaos, louder than every-thing.

Sung last weekend in a bass quartet!
Y'ain't seen nothin' like her yet!

Jack clutched the red box, knowing there was no way to get it to Rooker in time. Only yards in front of him, the men of the blockade loosed their arrows, shouting, bracing for impact.

Above the screaming din, he heard Rooker suddenly stop singing to holler sharply, *"Get up, girl!"*

Gravity dipped. Jack's feet went out beneath him. He bounced over the edge of the catwalk, fell into the dome, and skidded to the bottom, cracking his head against the glass. "Ahh!"

Stunned, Jack had nothing left to do but watch.

Leah's harpoon sank into the hull of the starboard ship, exploding to pieces. On the opposite side, green jets of light sizzled the air, setting sails ablaze in emerald flame. Below, the *Venture Brigand*'s skis drew together and the ship rose. It straddled the frigate, one pontoon on either side.

Inside the dome, Jack was lifted over the ship's deck.

Surprised faces stared up at him. The *Venture Brigand*'s nose struck the frigate's mainmast and it shattered like kindling. As it exploded, the second mast collided and sheared off, broken in half. Through the glass of the dome, Jack watched the two masts tilt backward and fall below him. Sails billowed like fallen angel's wings as they descended. The spar smacked into the deck with a *crack* and sailors were flung overboard, screaming.

The *Venture Brigand* passed over the ship and left its broken wreckage in her wake.

Fuji crawled up on Jack's shoulder as he watched the corvette try to shoot the narrow gap between the blockade ships. Jack almost believed the corvette was going to make it through until he heard wood screech against wood. The gap was too narrow. The corvette ground to a halt, wedged between the broken frigate and a burning ship.

Jack cried out, laughing at the smoking carnage behind him. He felt the *Venture Brigand* crouch closer to the water as she picked up speed, racing into the open sea as Rooker belted out his victory.

Don't know Liza, don't know me!
We got a ticket to the jam-bo-ree!

"Free!" Jack hugged Fuji. *"Free!"* He danced around the bottom of the belly dome, slipping and falling and laughing like a lunatic. Somewhere inside him, the invisible load he had carried since he'd arrived in Keymark disintegrated in an emotional cascade of blessed relief. He took his first free breath in months. The little tam licked his cheek, excited at the commotion. Jack snatched the red box, scrambled up the incline of the dome, and pelted down the hall.

Abovedeck, Rooker leaned against the wheel, watching the corvette, the blockade, and Huánghūn fade behind them. One hand on the wheel, the ridiculous purple hat on his head, the feathered dart clutched between his teeth, Jack thought he had never seen a happier man.

Rooker Flynn was finally home.

Jack hit him in a hug that was half a tackle. "You wasteka sonofabitch! You did it!"

Rooker pounded his back, laughing. "I told you she was the best ship in the world." Rooker plucked the red box from Jack's fingers, his sparkling eyes on Jack. "Plus a bit of clever seamanship." He flicked the gold clasp and opened the box, revealing, perfectly packaged in red silk, two bottles of Roi-Tan añejo.

"You sent..." Jack laughed, snorting. "You sent me running all the way down there for *booze?*"

Rooker plucked the dart out of his mouth and flicked it away. "I died today. I'd say that's worth a belt of hooch." He thrust a bottle into Jack's hand and took one for himself. He thumbed out the cork with a pop and raised the bottle. "To you and me."

They clinked and drank. Jack felt the sting of it on his lips, the warmth in his belly. And in that moment, he had never been happier.

"Now." Rooker squinted at him, grinning. "Cigars."

= NEXT TO =
GODLINESS

Looking good is the best revenge.
Tony Curtis

CIGARS, THE GOOD CORONAS that Captain Saltz had kept hidden under the bridge rail, were still there. Rooker smiled as he opened the waterproof pouch and smelled dark, rich tobacco. He snipped a tip, popped it between his teeth, and snapped his fingers. His flame lit the cigar and he puffed it to life until the tip burned a merry cherry. Satisfied, he clipped the second cigar, the last corona, and popped it in Jack's mouth. He snapped his fingers again and lit it for the kid. "Take your time," Rooker said through his teeth. "Let it burn. And don't inhale."

He watched Jack puff the corona to life, getting the hang of it. Once it was fully lit, Rooker snapped out his flame, winked at Jack, and turned to face the sea. For a moment, they just stood, lords of the Irridin, together. Cigar smoke spiraled away from them in the breeze and curled along the bridge, over the aft deck, and into the air behind them, pointing the way toward the fading shadow of the life they'd left behind. Rooker drew deeper, feeling smoke muster behind his teeth. He took a shot of Roi-Tan and exhaled, feeling the fumes of the booze mix with the tang of the cigar. He raised the bottle in a toast and rapped his rings against the glass. *Here's to ya, girl.*

Home, she sighed.

Rooker Flynn felt more content than he had ever been. He was alive and free, the *Brigand* beneath his feet and Jack at his side. It was an unfamiliar experience; he'd never felt utter satisfaction before. He was determined to make it last. All his life, he had been running toward something or away from something. Now, for the first time ever, he felt whole, a complete man. *Maybe death was the best thing for me.*

He tipped back the bottle, took a liberal swig, and felt a needle of pain under his jaw. He reached up and found something stuck in his neck. He plucked it out and squinted at the tiny thing: a splinter of rope from the hangman's noose.

Rooker flicked it away. The rope splinter spun past Leah, flickered out into the ocean breeze, and was gone.

"Rooker, that was..." Leah Archer looked stunned, wide-eyed. She was usually so composed, so sure of herself. It was fun to watch her struggle for words. "That was..."

"The most amazing bit of captaining ya ever saw," Rooker said around his cigar. "I know."

"It was." Leah nodded. "The most amazing bit of captaining I ever saw."

"That's right." Rooker could live a week on a good compliment, even if he had to manufacture it himself. It was a shame more people hadn't witnessed his escape, although the sailors in the bay would certainly spread the story once they'd overcome their defeat. *Might even be worth a song.* Rooker blew smoke, making sure not to get any on Leah. She looked too pretty to muss up. "Good shooting."

"Ta." She nodded, and he watched her shoulders move, saw the slope of her neck. And that nose.

Rooker suddenly felt flushed. It had been a long time since anyone beautiful had smiled at him. He felt something stir in him he hadn't felt in a long time. He leaned in to Jack and said the quiet part out loud. "Bubba, you ain't kiddin'. She looks *gorgeous.*"

Jack choked on the cigar. Leah's eyes flashed surprise. Caught between laughing and coughing, Jack made apologetic gestures to Leah. "I didn't... I *did* say that. You do. Look great. I mean."

"So great." Rooker nodded.

"*So* great," Jack echoed.

Leah maintained more self-control than either of them. "Neither of you has seen a healthy woman in nearly a year." She hooked an eyebrow. "I'll give you a moment to adjust."

"Give me a year," Jack murmured.

Rooker and Leah both snorted a laugh, then she hugged Jack tight. "I'm just happy you're okay." He watched the pair embrace, grinning around his cigar. Jack was suddenly the shy kid Rooker had first met, unsure what to do with his body, straining overmuch to keep his hips away from hers. *Ol' Chicken Legs.*

Leah broke from Jack and moved toward him, but Rooker instantly held up his hand to stop her. The kid was already in enough trouble as it was; he didn't need to worry about a third wheel. "Not a hugger."

She cocked her head. "You hugged *him*."

Rooker glanced at Jack. "He's family."

A little brown lizard crawled across the bridge and abruptly metamorphosed into the massive shape of Memphis Kubiak. The runty trol towered over him, his deep voice soft and awestruck. "That was the most amazing bit of captaining I ever saw."

Jack and Leah laughed at the same time. Rooker hated trols but couldn't help but be mollified by the brownbelly's praise. "It was *much* better than ya think."

"That was... I don't..." Memphis looked even more dumbfounded than Leah. "How did you two pull that off?"

He glanced at Jack. The kid winked at him. "It was easy," Jack answered. "We just had to get Rooker hung."

The giggles hit them like a freighter. Rooker snorted, Jack laughed, and from there, they were off to the races. Each new laugh gave rise to a bigger one, and round and round it went until they were cackling. In Rooker Flynn's experience, the best feeling in the world was not being able to *stop* laughing, that sense of falling, of being hilariously out of control. It was the only thing better than sailing the *Brigand*. And it always came easiest with Jack. Rooker surrendered to the giggles, unable to stop himself, doubling over, laughing at nothing at all.

He felt the Locke Institute fade behind him, buried beneath their shared joy.

Memphis watched them like they were a pair of lunatics. The trol shook his head and chuckled. "You two are just so proud of yourselves, aren't you?"

"*Yeah!*" Jack shouted through hysterics.

Rooker's chest hurt from trying to catch his breath. "O. Stop. Stop." He got himself under control, taking deep gulps of air. "*Ahh.*"

"*Ahh.*"

Rooker found his eyes on Jack. It was like looking in a mirror. Both of them came down from the hysteria, but neither wanted to let it go. They breathed, eyes locked. Rooker nodded. "Yeah."

Leah barely contained her own laugh and folded her arms, feigning impatience. "I have a dozen questions. How did you make the bell fall? And how the hell did you stay underwater for so long? We thought you both *drowned*."

Jack opened his mouth, but Rooker punched him in the shoulder. "Later." There were more important things to attend to. Rooker stuck the purple hat on the deckwheel and rubbed a hand over his filthy, sweat-smeared, bare chest. "Strip."

Leah frowned.

"Not you. Him." Rooker pointed at Jack. Despite being recently healed by the bell and dragged through the sea, the kid was covered in dried blood and scum, caked in grime from his sticky hair to his filthy feet. He looked like a half-drowned blond rat. "We can't go belowdecks like this."

Jack spread his hands, still suffering from the giggles. "I kind of already did."

"Don't make it a habit," Rooker growled. "This ship isn't a pigsty."

He flicked a lever. Water cascaded down from a pipe in a forceful spray. Captain Saltz had installed the deck-shower almost three years ago, and it had cost a small fortune for the mage to make it.

As far as Rooker was concerned, it was the only good Saltz had ever done.

Jack hauled his shirt over his head, slapped the filthy thing to the deck, and stepped into the brisk spray, smiling.

Rooker hauled off his pants. He heard Leah chuckle behind him. "You want me to turn my head?"

Rooker shrugged, not caring if he had an audience or not. "This is where the shower is." Leah hid a smile and politely turned away. Rooker glanced at Jack. The kid looked embarrassed, still wearing his pants. "Are *all* Toshans prudes or is it just you?"

Jack spat water at him. Rooker spat back. As Jack hauled off his nasty denims, Rooker took their prison clothes and slung them overboard. *I'm never wearing denim again.* He dunked a sponge in the wash bucket, soaped it heavily, and lathered up. He scrubbed at his flesh, scouring away months of abuse. Chunks of dried blood, mud, and grime fell away from his skin.

After putting in some work, Rooker almost felt clean. Almost. He dragged a wooden comb through his hair and yanked out the snags. Finished, he handed the comb to Jack and snatched the cocoba oil from the locker. Rooker lathered it into his hair, enjoying the spicy scent as he dug his fingers in, rubbing his scalp. Now the gunk really started to come out. His hair was so filthy the shower water turned grey as it splashed at his feet. He whipped his head back and forth, thrilled at the feel of clean hair. *Ahh.* "You good?" Rooker turned to Jack.

The kid had his eyes closed, letting the water run over him, motionless. His shoulders and back were bundled tight with prison muscle, but his face was utterly relaxed. "I'm good."

Rooker flicked off the shower and threw Jack a towel. Both men rubbed down their bodies and hair. As he dried his face off, Jack blew out a loud sigh and made a burbling, happy *"Whalubab!"* sound into the towel.

Rooker mimicked him, relishing how good it felt to be clean. *"Whalubab!"*

They started laughing again.

Rooker slung the towel around his hips. "Clothes." He took a step and halted. *Might as well get it over with.* "Before I forget, thank ya."

He waited for Leah and Memphis to realize he was talking to them. Both their heads cocked at the same surprised angle.

Rooker hated saying thank you. It was a sign of weakness. It felt almost as wrong as apologizing or asking forgiveness. *But we'd be at the bottom of the bay without them.* Rooker cleared his throat, uncomfortable. "For rescuing us."

Leah and the trol glanced at each other. Memphis nodded. "You're w—"

"Clothes!" Rooker barked before more words came. Anything anyone said at this point would sound stupid anyway. "If ya got meat or bread, grab it. We're hungry."

He descended to the foredeck and disappeared down the stairs. As superstition demanded, Rooker kissed his fingers and touched the female figurine carved into the inside of the doorway as he passed. *No sense jinxing my luck now.*

The Naysayer Brothers had repositioned every stick of furniture in the captain's quarters, and all of it was wrong. Three large chairs, one built for that ogre Wont, dominated the room in a circle next to the fireplace. The desk was in the wrong place, the bookshelf was by the door, and the map racks were jammed in a corner. Only the conch shell Rooker had brought aboard months ago, when he had been arrested by the Naysayers, was still in its place on the mantle. The place looked even worse than it had during Captain Shai's brief stint as boss of the *Brigand*. Rooker scowled at the new art on the walls, wondering which Naysayer had bought this atrocious trash. There was even an oil painting of a pony. *A pony, for God's sake*. Rooker flicked open the porthole and hucked the art into the wind.

Wearing only a towel, Rooker dragged the desk into its proper position facing the door. He pulled the captain's chair behind it and sat down, feeling completely at ease. *Finally*.

"Captain." Jack entered the room, saluting.

"Mate." Rooker spun in his chair. He rubbed the arms, feeling green leather padding the wood. He had served a decade aboard the *Brigand* without the power of command, a groveling pilot to one bad captain after another as a kind of mascot, a dog, only kept alive because he could awaken the majik inside the ship. Almost two years ago, his mutiny against Saltz had earned him the captain's title, but his conquest had only lasted for one day. Then he had pursued his ship to the edge of the world, and on Huánghūn, he'd thought he'd lost her for good. During all that time he had called himself captain, but secretly he'd known he hadn't been man enough for the title, a boy playing dress-up in someone else's clothes. Today, Rooker Flynn knew he had finally earned his rightful seat on the throne.

Jack brushed a few black feathers aside as he slumped into Shant's chair. "Is this how we're spending the day? Lounging around naked?"

Rooker kept rubbing the chair, lost in thought, then realized what Jack was saying. "Clothes! Right!" Rooker leapt to his feet and walked to the captain's dresser. He threw open the doors to discover a collection of colorless dusters and one of Cant's stupid gambler hats. Rooker hurled all of the bounty hunter's clothes into the fireplace.

Jack eyed the empty armoire. "So just towels, then."

"One thing I'll never be caught without as a free man is a tailor." Rooker flicked the concealed catch inside the armoire. The hidden door in the wall opened, revealing the secret entrance to the pilot's closet. He'd stolen costumes from every captain the *Brigand* ever had.

At least two hundred suits of tailored clothes awaited him. Most were reds and honeyed tans, with half a wall of blacks, a dozen greens, and a scattering of yellows and oranges. Expensive hats, boots, gloves, jackets, and cloaks lined the pegs in addition to an armory of bladed weapons, large and small. Rooker had learned a long time ago, if you're going to play pirate, it was best to look the part.

"Yer almost my size now." Rooker thumbed through the shirts and picked out a cross-stitched midnight black shirt with articulated cuffs. He added a pair of sable pants that had been too small on him but too stylish to give up. "Those should do."

Jack slipped on the black shirt and admired the stitching. "Hey, this is nice."

"Course it's nice, it's mine."

Jack laughed and hauled on the black pants. Rooker tossed him a pair of knee-high buckle boots and finally found what he was looking for. *There you are.* His fingers plucked his favorite burgundy shirt from the peg and he slid it on. Smooth as silk, the cloth had been tailored in Rimmy's Cull, fitted across his stomach, wide at the shoulders, open at the chest, and tight in all the right places. As he dressed, he noticed how much his body had changed in prison. He'd always been lean, and he was thinner than ever, but he'd never been so muscular. His chest and biceps pulled the fabric tight. Nodding, he slipped into the honey brown suede pants Molly had made and checked his ass in the mirror. *High and tight. Not bad.*

He reached into the apothecary jar, snatched a pinch of ground attar root, and rubbed some into his neck. He took a moment to breathe it in, savoring the aroma of blended spices, rose, and sandalwood. He thrust some attar root at Jack. "Here. It'll make yer gal go nuts."

Jack snorted. "She's not my—"

"Rub it in anyway. And..." Rooker flicked through the hatboxes and found what he was looking for. He popped the top, revealing a black tricorn. He settled it on Jack's head, tilted it slightly, and flicked the brim. "Good. One that fits ya." He folded his arms and appraised the man. *Bubba finally looks as he should. Ol' Black Jack, through and through.*

Rooker grabbed a pair of shears from a drawer and slapped Jack on the back. "Come on, bubba. One last thing to do."

Feeling more like himself every moment, Rooker flicked some lint from his shoulder as he passed into the sunlight on deck. A tray of salami and grapes had been set out for them. Rooker popped one of each in his mouth, pulled up a stool, and slapped the top. "Sit."

Jack sat. Rooker tossed a sheet over him, wrapped it around his neck, and produced the shears. Jack chuckled. "An actual barber. Nice."

"Gotta keep that new getup clean." Rooker hung Jack's hat on a peg and flexed the shears, *snip-snip*. "Long or short?"

Jack chuckled. "Anything but shaved."

"Long then." His scissors went to work, trimming Jack's damp hair. Between the cocoba oil and the attar root, bubba almost smelled human. Rooker got rid of the tangles, trimmed the edges, and cut the mop out of Jack's face, nothing fancy but a big improvement. His comb gave the kid's blond hair one final flick to make the front stick up, and he slapped Jack on the shoulder. "Yer done. Me now."

They swapped spots. Jack didn't ask any questions. He just went to work. Rooker felt the *snip-snip-snip* of the shears trimming his clean hair and closed his eyes.

For a moment, he just breathed. It had been so long since he had done nothing, he'd almost forgotten what it was like. Eyes closed, he heard the gentle snip of the scissors, the roll of the waves, finally at peace.

He opened his eyes to find Leah and Memphis staring at him.

Rooker's hand flashed up to his head. "What did ya do to my hair?"

"Nothing," Jack said, startled.

Rooker eyed his rescuers. "Then what are ya staring at?"

Memphis eyed them, his voice soft. "Are you two all right?"

Rooker glanced at Jack. The kid looked back at him, no help at all. "We're fine. What?"

Leah cocked her head. "You have both been sitting there with your eyes closed... for a really long time."

Rooker blinked. He turned to Jack. *Did you fall asleep?*

The kid looked back at him. *Did you?*

They broke up laughing. Leah and Memphis looked at them like they were crazy, which made them laugh harder. Rooker's eyes stayed on Jack. He felt like he couldn't let the kid out of his sight, a lifeline he would never let go. "Did ya finish my hair?"

"It looks pretty good."

"It's supposed to look *really* good."

Memphis leaned in, his eyes concerned. "Are you two going to just skip over what happened to you?" He spread his gigantic hands. "Are you going to... talk?"

Rooker blinked. "About what?"

"About Huánghūn!" snapped Leah, exasperated. "About *prison*!"

"It's not a prison," chirped Jack.

"It's a *school*," Rooker replied. They burst into another fit of laughing. Rooker glanced at the girl and the trol. Neither saw the humor of the situation.

Rooker spread his hands. "Okay, what? What do ya *want* us to say?"

"I don't know!" yelled Leah. "You just spent nine months captive on a secret penal colony as slaves to the most sadistic bitch I've ever even heard of." She spread her hands. "Don't you have anything to"—she gestured, trying to come up with the word—*"say?"*

Jack exchanged a look with Rooker. They had lived through Huánghūn together. Rooker saw the truth in Jack's eyes, the shared reality of two survivors. Talking about it would only make it worse. At the same time, both men said, "No."

Leah stared at them, then suddenly snorted. "Okay then."

Good. She gets it. Rooker ran his fingers through his hair. If he never thought of the Locke Institute again, it would be too soon. Memphis made as if to protest, but Leah held up her hand. "Do we want to at least talk about where we're going? Get a heading? Figure out what's next?"

"There is no next." Rooker stood, pulled off the sheet, and jammed the stub of the cigar into his mouth. "We're cleaning ourselves up so we can feel like men again." He slung an arm over Jack's shoulder; Jack slung an arm over his. "And I'll tell ya, little sister, we gettin' there." Jack thumped him on the back. Rooker eyed him. "You good?"

"Good," answered Jack. "You?"

"Shipshape. Now." Rooker turned his gaze to the *Venture Brigand*. "Her turn."

From the moment he had stepped aboard, Rooker had taken note of every fault aboard his ship. The Naysayer Brothers had taken possession almost two years ago and all but abandoned her for most of that time. For some reason they had taken out the jib winch on the aft deck, the belowdecks cargo was inexplicably stacked far forward, and there were entirely too many slave nets hanging from the rigging and strewn about the deck. *It's like picking up after children.*

But above all those crimes, one unforgivable sin stood out beyond all others. Rooker glared up at the disgusting yellow canvas posing as the sails of the *Venture Brigand*. "Let's get her dressed."

Red silk billowed forth from the sail locker and streamed across the deck. Rooker had carefully packed the backup sails himself five years ago, an extensive expanse of glorious, scintillating crimson.

Jack grinned at the sight of the red sails. "It's Superman's cape."

Rooker didn't know what that meant, but it sounded right. As he pulled the weight of the sails out onto the deck, his eyes gleamed. *Wasteka Naysayers, ya can't dress her in yellowjacket canvas.* His lips curled into a smile. *My girl only sails under silk.*

"We swap out one sail at a time!" announced Rooker. "We don't want anyone to catch her with her pants down! Foremast first! Get to work!" As Jack, Leah, and Memphis leapt to the task, Rooker smiled. It felt good to have a crew work her decks again. It felt good shouting orders, making sure his ship was attended to the way she deserved.

Since Memphis hated working high up in the rigging, Rooker allowed the trol to manage the winches on deck. Leah handled the lower sails while he and Jack wrangled the upper spars. Wind whipping through freshly shorn hair, Rooker barked at Jack, "Hey! Get yer tam up here!"

Jack whistled, and Fuji crawled up the sail, its yellow eyes eager. "How's he going to help?" asked Jack. "He's really tiny!"

"Hanging sails!" Rooker grinned. "That's what tams are for!" As they worked, Rooker found a familiar joy in watching Fuji scurry back and forth, the little tam tying knots and tightening lines. For the first time in months, Rooker forgot about jungles and spiders and drained blood and lost himself in the simple pleasure of dressing the ship just the way it should be.

As the sun rose higher, the first yellow sail fell, replaced with shimmering red. The mainmast came next, followed by the mizzen and the jibs. When the work was done, Rooker wound up in the crow's nest with Jack. From the highest point on the ship, Rooker Flynn surveyed the *Venture Brigand* in all her glory. Laid out below him was glorious freedom, an ocean of it, made manifest in elven wood and scarlet sails. He felt the ship fly beneath him, everything exactly the way it should be, perfect.

Jack slipped a bottle of Roi-Tan from beneath his black shirt and handed it to Rooker. They drank, high above the vast Irridin. Fuji settled on Jack's shoulder, bobbing its head, agreeing with everything.

"Mm." Rooker wiped his mouth with a sleeve. He raised the bottle at the vast Irridin and grinned. "The world's ours, bubba."

Jack toasted him with an imaginary glass. He stared off into the blue horizon. "Where should we go?"

Over the last year, Rooker had imagined the sparse islands in the Deep Blue South so many times he could draw a map with his eyes closed. "The Bowery." He nodded. "It's a backwater port, closer than Javernis Twist. Small enough not to attract much attention, big enough to trade for whatever we need. Clean beds." He heard Jack make a *mmm* sound. "Good beefsteak. And Keymark's second-best strawberry cake."

"Sounds perfect." Jack nodded. "When do we land?"

"Before dusk. We can slee—"

Rooker's body went ramrod-straight, staring at the horizon behind them.

No.

"You okay?" Jack chuckled. "You're staring again."

Rooker pointed toward the horizon behind them. "What is that?"

A speck.

That's all it was.

A dot on the horizon.

Jack stared out to sea, confused. "What is *what*?"

No.

"That." Rooker pointed his finger.

He and Jack stood side by side, watching. Even Fuji stopped moving.

After a moment, Jack shook his head. "I don't see anything."

I do.

Rooker slipped the rings off his finger and put one to his eye. Magnified, the speck became a dark smudge against the horizon. "Something's there."

There was a long pause of nothing but the wind. Jack spoke first, his voice hopeful. "Nobody's following us. You said it yourself, we can outrun any ship on the Irridin."

Rooker scowled. "We *can*."

Jack stared into the vastness. "Then what *is* it?"

Rooker adjusted the spyglass rings and brought the smudge into focus. Six miles out, the shape took form. The first thing he saw was the gap, the hint of daylight that separated the thing from the sea. Next he saw wings, flapping with a monstrous strength, stretched between eight enormous spider legs. All sense of peace suddenly fled.

"Xeusia."

He heard Jack gasp. Rooker lowered the spyglass as cold fingers closed around his heart. The *Venture Brigand* was the fastest ship on the Irridin Sea, no question.

But even she couldn't outrun a dragon.

And it was catching up.

Rooker hollered with all his might. "*Dragon ahoy!*"

Chapter

7

WORLD'S
═END═

Give me liberty or give me death.
Patrick Henry

"*D* RAGON AHOY!" ROOKER SHOUTED again, louder. He slung a hip over the edge of the crow's nest and stepped outside the basket.

Suspended in the air over the *Brigand*, his body stretched toward the flying shape, Rooker glared at the horizon. With his unaided eye, the beast was still a blur in the distance, but he could see the rhythmic movement of its eight-legged wings.

Rooker scowled. *Damn. For a second I thought I was gonna get out of today alive.*

Jack stood in the crow's nest, dumbfounded, still trying to comprehend the words still hanging in the air. "I... what?" Rooker extended his hand and offered the rings. Jack put them to his eye and took a stutter-step backward. "No."

"Yeah." Rooker stared at the dark shape and spat. "Xeusia."

He had run into wyverns all his life. The horse-sized dragonets were littered all over the islands, most of them feeding on oxen, aurochs, and sharks. They'd kill a sailor or five at times, but they could be dealt with. The medium-sized ones, the ones that could sink a ship, were called jabberwocks, or drakes in the north. He'd run into two of those and had been lucky to get out with his skin both times. But a true dragon, one of the great bull wyrms... well. That was something else.

He swallowed. *Might as well face down the dragon that carries the world on its back.*

In all his travels, Rooker Flynn had never once seen a true dragon, not until Xeusia. The bull wyrms were the stuff of legend, of stories. Some sailors didn't believe they existed or thought they were all dead, just leftover dreams of fire-breathing devils bigger than a galleon with wings. Like everyone in Keymark, Rooker had heard epic poems and songs of heroes who had bested a bull wyrm, but they were few, far between, and made of pretty lies. Now he was about to face one on the empty sea.

Rooker couldn't help but grin. *Now* that *would be something to write a song about.* He watched Xeusia close the distance between them, growing ever larger. *If there's anyone left to sing it.*

"Move," he growled at Jack. "We got work." He jumped out of the crow's nest.

Snatching the transit-line, Rooker descended, spiraling toward the deck. As he dropped, he glanced at the red silk all around him. *We're in for it now, girl. Time to toughen up.*

Her mast bobbed, uncertain, as her wood made worried creaks.

Well, buck up, hon. This is all on you and me. Her sails were stretched tight, tense with wind, and there wasn't much more he could coax out of her. *Full ahead. Buy me some time.*

Yes. She strained to pick up speed.

He landed on the deck. Leah and Memphis waited for him. "What's the big joke?" asked Leah. "There's nothing out there."

"Inbound aft, northeasterly." He blew on his palms, cooling the rope burn. "Trust me, it's coming."

Memphis scowled. "What's a jabberwock doing all the way out here?"

"Make me repeat myself, brownbelly, and I'll throw you in the hold as cargo!" Rooker barked. "*Dragon!*"

Leah's eyes sharpened. "That thing from the Steel Trials?"

"That's the one." Rooker felt a mad grin split his lips. "Gerba's flying spider."

Leah went a whiter shade of pale. So did the trol, which made Rooker feel better, for what it was worth. Memphis's eyes went wide. "Xeusia? Not—"

"Gerba couldn't have sent it after us!" Jack's voice came from up in the rigging. He descended from the mast via the rope ladder, his tam following on nimble feet. "If she hurts me, the geas curse will kill her. I saw it."

"Geas curses are tricky." Rooker eyed the dragon's growing shadow. "Maybe she told it to kill the rest of us and leave you alone.

Or maybe just sink the *Brigand* and play fetch." Rooker squinted one eye and turned to Jack. "Or maybe she hates us so much, she's willing to die."

Jack scowled. "I'm almost ready to oblige her."

Rooker slipped his rings back on and muttered a curse. "Jump in its mouth." He shot a wicked grin at Jack. "That'll show her."

"I see it." Leah's voice had a hard edge. She didn't look frightened, only determined. Rooker had to admire her for that, naive as it was. "What do we do?"

"Only one thing *to* do." Rooker grimaced. "Run." He searched the map in his head. They were out on the edge of the world; his options were scant. The Bowery and Javernis Twist were too far. The dragon would rip the *Venture Brigand* to flotsam before they could get to either port. And there was nothing else this far down in the Deep Blue South but Huánghūn, Bounty, and—

"The Old Maid's Stitch."

"What's that?" asked Leah.

Rooker scratched his chin. "Bunch of little atolls. Cliffs, all close together. There's nothing there but seals and sea harpies. I might be able to lose Xeusia in the Stitch if I'm clever."

"So be clever." Jack grinned.

Rooker took a breath and imagined darting between unfamiliar cliffs and fjords, outfoxing the spider-dragon, trying to find an overhang big enough to shield the *Brigand*. He shook his head. "It ends one of two ways. As soon as we break cover, Xeusia catches up and torches us, or we hide in the rocks until it finds us... and torches us." Rooker set his jaw and glared at the trol. "You damn brownbellies worship dragons. Is there any way to kill it?"

Memphis had not stopped staring at the great beast pursuing them. His voice was soft and awed. "That is Xeusia ul-Styx Hakáti, of the Old World, before Keymark ever existed." Memphis's eyes were wide and reverent. "It was the mount of the Dæmon Crownéd RākṢhasa, Lord of Strîgoi. It is said Xeusia ul-Styx

Hakáti had eight legs because it killed eight hundred men a day to provide fodder for its master's army. At the end of the Extinction War, when the Old World was destroyed, their battle with Kos the Maker destroyed half of creation. Lord Kos only survived by trapping RākŞhasa within the earth itself." Memphis stared at the flying, eight-legged monstrosity. "Xeusia has never known defeat."

"Ya coulda just skipped to the last part." Rooker scowled.

"Not all trols worship dragons." Memphis scowled back. "My majik is elvish, not dæmonic." He pointed a meaty finger. "That abomination is my mortal enemy."

"So kill it with majik."

Memphis shook his head. "Even if I drew on every bit of the *wikk* from the *Venture Brigand*, my skill would be no match for true dragonfire." The trol stared at the approaching beast with desperate eyes. "Xeusia will burn this ship before I take a third shot."

A silence followed, broken by Leah's voice. "What about harpoons?"

"Won't pierce its scales," said Rooker, chewing his lip. "Might as well throw coconuts."

Leah set her jaw. "We have to do *something*."

"Ya could talk it into committing suicide, but I wouldn't count on it," Rooker growled and looked at the sea ahead to the west. Blue skies. No wind. No rain. Under normal circumstances, this was where the *Venture Brigand's* speed had the edge. But it didn't matter against a dragon. Their goose was cooked.

Tell me what to do, girl.

"Rooker," came Leah's voice, far away. "Seriously. We can't just sit here and do nothing. There has to be a way."

Jack's voice cut in, soft. "Give him a second."

Rooker closed his eyes and felt the wind in his hair. There was nothing to do but run for as long as they could. Maybe they could make a heroic end of it, try to take Xeusia down with them, but it would all end in fire, blood, and the blackness of the bottom of the sea. No matter how nobly they fought, they would die here at the nadir of the Deep Blue South where every direction was north. If he could somehow harness the cyclones that haunted the edge of the map, maybe he could pull ahead, but even then, he would never escape. Xeusia would pursue them to—

—the very end of the world.

Rooker's eyes flashed open and he glanced south, where the winds of the deadly Waste darkened the sky.

He turned to Jack and took a deep breath. "Ya trust me?"

Jack didn't need words to reply. *Always.*

"Arright." Rooker set his jaw and spun the wheel. "South."

"What's south?" asked Leah.

"Nothing." Rooker grinned. "Nothing but the Lord of Sea and Sky."

Howling wind kicked up as Rooker raced due south at top speed, driving into the tempest, piercing through it. The *Venture Brigand* kicked twin sprays of white wake three yards high as the shadow of Xeusia ul-Styx Hakáti grew larger. Rooker adjusted course and put the tremendous wind at his back, speeding faster than his ship had ever sailed. The color of the Irridin Sea changed as they flew over the waves, shifting from blue to white to an iridescent indigo. Within moments, the driving wind around them grew to the shrieking wail of a typhoon. It ripped one of the *Brigand's* pennant flags off and pulled it twisting into the darkening sky ahead.

"You're out of your mind!" yelled Memphis over the howling wind. "That's the South Waste out there!"

Rooker ignored him, focusing on Leah. "Broadhead harpoons! Blue markings!"

Leah didn't ask questions, she just bolted for the aft locker at a sprint. As she did, Jack leaned in, yelling in Rooker's ear, "You said harpoons can't pierce its scales!"

"Grab one and take yer damn post!" Rooker yelled. "And leave me some of that luck o' yers!" Jack kissed his palm, slapped it on the deckwheel, and ran for the forward harpoon bow.

"Where do you want me?" asked Memphis, eyeing the spider-dragon closing in behind them.

"At my side!" hollered Rooker. "Praying this works!"

Gale-force wind tore around them like an armada of banshees. For the first time in his life, Rooker heard the mainmast of the *Venture Brigand* creak as it leaned further than it ever had. *Hunker down, girl.* Widening her legs, the ship crouched forward and sizzled white spray from her skis.

Xeusia was sped by the wind as much as the *Brigand* and hurtled at them like an arrow. The spider-dragon stopped beating its wings and spread them wide, all eight legs splayed out like a gigantic sail that blotted out what remained of the sun. Twice the size of the *Brigand*, the dark wings caught double the air and closed the distance. Rooker saw the dragon's freakish spider head twist forward on its long neck, eight flaming eyes glowing eight red pits within its stygian skull.

It would be on them before long.

Rooker pressed the ship as hard as he could, heart pounding. *Run!*

Ahead, the color of the sky changed with the Irridin. Sea blue became navy, then faded to pure black. Rooker watched Leah, Memphis, and Jack gaze up at the sky, blinking astonishment. Blue horizon fell behind them; only inky blackness lay ahead. It was as if the vast firmament was a work of art portraying dawn to midnight, an entire day in a single tapestry. But in the midnight sky of the Waste, of course, there were no stars.

"What the hell is this?" yelled Jack from the forward harpoon bow.

Rooker stared up at the blackness and listened to the rushing wind. "I been tellin' ya since we arrived on Huánghūn! We're close!"

"Close to *what*?!"

It came into view. Rooker had never seen it, not with his own eyes, but he'd pictured it from the tales of the crazy old sailors, the ones who'd claimed they'd been there. But Rooker knew the truth: No one came back from the deep Waste. It was the end of everything, and it was terrifying.

Rooker's eyes went wide. "The edge of the world."

Half a mile ahead, the sea ended. Instead of land, only a jagged, boiling rush of water marked the horizon where white foam became black void as the Irridin disappeared over the rim of the world, a waterfall into emptiness. Beyond the edge, there was nothing. The inky maw of infinity drifted beyond, empty and cold. As the *Venture Brigand* rushed toward the void, Rooker could see colors within the emptiness that separated themselves into drifting constellations of every hue, emerald to indigo, as if light itself came to an end and its remains were broken, swirling in the maelstrom beyond, an empty mouth opened wide as a galaxy.

"It's beautiful," said Rooker as his heart drummed against his ribs.

"It's... nothing," whispered Leah.

"It's impossible!" hollered Jack.

"This is where Keymark ends!" replied Memphis. "As much as the elves could salvage from the Old World, this is where it stopped! The final border of our sphere!" His voice was loud, frightened. "Beyond this place, there *is* no Keymark!"

They stared at the edge of the world, hearing the roar of the wind, the rush of falling water, and the howl of nothing in the infinite beyond.

Rooker turned to find Xeusia. The spider-dragon's wings blotted out the remains of the blue horizon they'd left behind. *I'm gonna need all that luck right about now.* He tapped his rings against the deckwheel. "Cut speed, girl."

Memphis turned to him. "What?!"

"We're gonna let it catch us."

Memphis's eyes went wide. "Captain—"

He ignored the trol and shouted at Jack and Leah. "This is gonna happen fast!" Rooker warned. "When it comes, it's gonna blow dragonfire all over, so find some cover!"

"Cover?" Leah shouted. "The whole ship's made of wood!"

"Then make it good cover!" yelled Rooker. "We're only gonna get one chance at this. If either of you shoot early, we're dead! Do *not* fire until my order!" He raised his voice, hollering full throat, *"Do not fire until what?"*

"Your order!" Jack and Leah shouted at the same moment.

"Then take cover."

They abandoned their harpoon bows and looked for a place to hide.

"This is crazy," the trol murmured. "We're going to die."

"Quit yer bitchin'." Rooker's grin was fierce. "If I screw this up, it'll be over before ya know it."

The trol sighed, resigning himself to his fate. "Where do you want me?"

"Starboard skid." Rooker pointed down at the pontoon skimming the water, where the yellowjackets had tried to board them. "The outrigger. And don't fall off."

Memphis scowled. "You better know what you're doing, Captain Flynn." The trol ran for the deckrail of the *Venture Brigand* and threw himself over the side. In midair, he transformed into his lizard shape, landed on one of the *Brigand*'s legs, and scuttled down toward the starboard skid.

Rooker kissed his rings and gripped the wheel. *All right, girl. Here we go.*

Xeusia's massive body closed with the ship, huge spider legs splayed wide as it rode the hurricane that pushed them all toward the edge of the world. It closed the final distance, and Rooker realized how much bigger the dragon was than his ship.

It took every bit of courage he had to slow the *Brigand* even further. *Half-sail, girl!* As the ship lost speed, Rooker eyed the dragon behind him, the empty void ahead. *Have to time this right...*

But it was too late. The dragon was on him.

Its long serpentine neck stretched toward the *Brigand* and inhaled deeply, its breath more intense than the gale that bore it aloft. Eight crimson eyes burned like lava, roaring hotter as it sucked in more air. Rooker heard breath drawn into lungs the size of yachts as flame roiled between the cracks of the dragon's expanding scales and blazed like a forge fire.

"Take cover!" shouted Rooker.

Closest to the dragon, Leah had hidden near the harpoon bow, but upon hearing the enormity of the coming inferno, she realized she was too exposed. She hesitated one moment too long, her lone form silhouetted against Xeusia like an ant before a tarantula. Leah threw herself through a grate and fell belowdecks.

Xeusia breathed dragonfire.

A hundred feet long, the black gout of flame seared the deck as it broke over the ship like a rogue wave. Midnight fire spilled over her boards, charring her wood black as the flame itself. Rooker heard Leah Archer screaming belowdecks, trapped by the blaze.

Then came the ear-splitting shriek of the *Venture Brigand*. She squealed agony as her timbers roasted and split. Rooker watched, horrified, as her elegant aft deck was consumed by dragonfire. Flames billowed across her like a flood, roiling and writhing plumes of midnight-black holocaust. The jet of dragonfire ended, leaving dancing licks of turquoise and indigo as the *Venture Brigand* ignited.

Rooker felt his girl's keening wail in his bones as she screamed in torment.

—*no*—

Her perfect body was mutilated, blistered, scorched, destroyed. Rooker screamed his throat raw.

Xeusia ul-Styx Hakáti shrieked a barbaric, cacophonous roar of victory. The sound shuddered Rooker's skull, deafening him. Paralyzed with fear, he gripped the wheel with white knuckles.

No! Rooker reached out for the *Brigand* but heard nothing but her shuddering agony.

Everything burned. Jack screamed. Memphis screamed. Leah was gone, buried beneath the flames.

On fire, the *Venture Brigand* hurtled straight at the edge of the world.

No. Rooker Flynn wiped smoke away from his blazing eyes. *Not yet.*

Xeusia let fly a thunderous shriek and beat its wings. Moving faster than the *Brigand*, the massive dragon passed over the smoking wreckage of the aft deck, eight-legged wings beating mightily. Rooker watched the dragon fly directly above him; its belly brushed the crow's nest. It stared down at him. Eight lifeless eyes burned red, boring into him with pure malevolence.

Xeusia breathed in again. Thunderous, dark *wikk* blossomed in its chest, preparing to hurl a second blast of dragonfire directly down the *Venture Brigand*'s throat and core a hole straight through her hull.

Rooker glanced ahead to find the end of the world coming fast. They were nearly at the rim, all that was left was to plummet into the empty chasm of the maelstrom.

Not yet...

Above, Xeusia opened its fanged jaws, exposing boiling black majik that burned vengeful wrath. Dragonfire exploded from its mouth.

Now.

"Hard starboard!" Rooker hollered at the top of his lungs.

He spun the deckwheel with everything he had and sent it whirling like the tornado around them. The entire ship yanked right, cutting hard. Rooker wrapped his hand in a rope and hung on as the *Venture Brigand* tilted madly. He saw Jack tossed against the rail, smashing into it with a shout of pain. Out on the pontoon, Memphis screamed, his meaty fists clutched at the outrigger as his skid lifted from the water.

For a moment, everything hung suspended. Skimming along the edge of the world, the *Venture Brigand* balanced on one leg. His heart in his throat, Rooker peered down into the vast nothingness and saw a foaming cascade of the Irridin disappearing over the edge to the infinite chasm below, an impossible white curtain descending into the Waste that threatened to swallow them all.

Xeusia did not match the *Brigand*'s turn. Rooker watched the bull wyrm fly over the cliff, off the edge of the world. It hung there for a moment, black on black, then beat its wings and flew toward them.

Kick out, girl!

Skating on one leg, the *Brigand* leaned away from the edge. But the ship was caught in the wind that had forced them here, blown back toward the precipice, toward the dragon. Rooker heard screaming from everyone on board as the ship threatened to tip into the void.

"Jack!" Rooker screamed into the wind. The kid was still at his post, hanging on for dear life. *"Shoot the wing!"*

Jack fought the tilt of the ship, one leg wrapped around the base of the harpoon bow. He lined up his shot, screamed, and pulled the trigger. Taut bowstrings launched the harpoon with a furious *thrum*.

The broadhead was made of four bladed razors that formed an X like a hunter's arrow. The tip passed harmlessly through the dragon's wing. The harpoon fell silently into the void behind Xeusia, useless. Uninjured, the spider-dragon roared and drove toward them. Rooker saw Xeusia inhale, summoning its dragonfire.

Jack stood directly in its path.

Please.

Wings beating, Xeusia suddenly dipped. The broadhead's X had torn four sharp slits into the dragon's wing, and the gale force of the wind pulled the slashes wider. Abruptly, the rents split open, tearing from one leg to the next, leaving the dragon with a gaping, fluttering hole where one wing used to be.

"Memphis!" thundered Rooker. The trol hung over the edge of the airborne outrigger, leveraging his considerable weight to combat their tilt into the abyss. "Now!"

The brownbelly shouted and shot emerald elvish flame at the dragon. Jets of sizzling *wikk* punched through Xeusia's wings. They didn't tear the membrane as Jack's broadhead had but peppered its remaining wings with burning holes.

And still Xeusia came.

Fighting the wind, resisting the vacuum of the void, the great wyrm struggled mightily toward them. Its wings were too strong, its instinct too vehement, its hatred too vast to ever let the *Brigand* escape.

Rooker fought the hurricane winds, hanging on by a fingernail to the edge of the world. He couldn't pull away from the dragon. If he cut any harder, the ship would tip over the edge.

He watched Xeusia close with them, gathering its breath for a final gout of dragonflame.

I can't beat it. Rooker let a breath go. *I'm sorry, girl.*

Something punched the dragon's wing.

Turning, Rooker saw Leah Archer. Blackened and burned, the woman gripped the smoking harpoon bow, her one shot spent.

Rooker watched the hole her broadhead had punched through Xeusia's wing. It slowly tore wider. The membrane flickered, then billowed, then tore end to end. Xeusia flapped, screeching, but its tattered wings were no longer a match for the *Venture Brigand*'s sails, and certainly not for the hurricane of the South Waste.

It shrieked as the cyclone forced it over the edge. It reached for the ship with spidery claws, but the dragon could not reach them. It beat its wings, trying to fight the inevitable, but little by little the monstrosity lost its battle to remain part of Keymark. The spider-dragon shrieked impotent rage. Pulled by the wind, Xeusia ul-Styx Hakáti receded farther and farther away, drawn into the maelstrom.

Rooker watched the dragon fade into the distance, its cries growing fainter, until it was gone altogether, nothing more than a black speck in the endless void.

The *Venture Brigand* completed her long turn and finally came back down on two legs. Rooker tacked against the wind and steered them back toward the world.

He collapsed against the deckwheel and wrapped his arms around her, breathing in heaving gasps.

Good girl. He pressed himself into her wood, sobbing tears of relief. *Good girl.*

PART 2

DAY

Chapter

8

TODAY
IS
THE DAY

*You just can't beat the person
who never gives up.*
Babe Ruth

G ERBA WHIPMARPLES STOOD ABOVE the remains of the Agrat-ban-Haifa. The Great Bell lay at the bottom of the Irridin, a bronze ruin. She could see its shape clearly in the glassy water below, tipped sideways, cracked halfway up the rim, silent forevermore. Staring at the majestic bell, the headmistress felt like a mourner at the funeral of a faithful partner.

It was impossible to calculate her loss.

The Agrat-ban-Haifa had been the heart of her life on Huánghūn. Not only had the bell kept her students healthy, but it had also been the source of power for the Caged Eight. Without that majik, Gerba's iron control over the eight-legged creatures on the island would quickly erode. Every spider on Huánghūn, the attercops, the shiq, and her arachnid mount, Iktomi, would be free of her influence by dusk. One by one, her defenses would fall, and the home she had spent so long building would be overrun by animals.

The Locke Institute would be dead by sunset.

It simply is not fair.

Xeusia would be the first to shake its bonds. Over the last two years, Gerba Whipmarples had grown accustomed to having a dragon at her beck and call. Such power was difficult to abandon. But without the Caged Eight, Xeusia would take its revenge on her the moment the spell broke, and so she had sent the dragon south and from there to the far corners of the world. That, at least, would buy her some time before it returned. If the bull wyrm happened to destroy the *Venture Brigand* on its journey, she could not be blamed; she had not given it any final orders. She would be safe from the geas curse.

In her heart, however, Gerba Whipmarples hoped Xeusia tore the *Brigand* to tinder.

She stared at the broken bell, cursing the villains that had destroyed it. *I hope they burn.*

Well. She took one last look at the Agrat-ban-Haifa and took a deep breath. *What's done is done.*

Gerba tried to speak but found her mouth dry as a bone. She shut her lips and moistened her tongue. *Control, dearie. Control.* "Winnifred."

"Yes, headmistress." Gerba considered the woman behind the niqab. Winnifred was frightened, no doubt, but obedient. By dusk, Gerba's only remaining allies would be the acolytes, the men and women who worshipped Rākṣhasa. The Caged Eight did not control them; they were loyal to Gerba because she had made the island safe for them, and because she had promised to unearth their dæmonic master. *A promise I intend to keep.*

"Alert the staff. We are evacuating the island."

Without hesitation, Winnifred replied, "Yes, headmistress."

"I want my office packed up and moved to the *Hup Two*, starting with the vault." She eyed Winnifred. "I want every coin you can fit on that boat. Anything left behind stays locked in the vault, where it will be safe until we return." *If we return.* "On my personal yacht, I want my library, letters, and wardrobe."

"And the stone seat, headmistress?"

Gerba sighed. The interrogation chair had been designed to her specifications, a true work of masonic art. But the stone chair had also been fueled by the Caged Eight. Soon enough it would be an odd, eight-legged lump of rock. "No, thank you, Winnifred. I believe the chair is best left where it is. Attend to those items now please."

A nod, and Winnifred was gone, taking the other acolytes with her.

"Headmistress, what are we supposed to do?" Niko, her hammerdwarf foreman, looked like he was still in shock. He lingered by the broken bell, staring up at the shattered beams that had once held it aloft.

"You and your craftsmen may go, Niko. Your work at the Institute is complete."

The grey-skinned architect turned to her, his eyes haunted and empty. "But, headmistress, we were buildin–"

"I said your work is complete," she snapped. "Your services are no longer required, Niko. Please leave the island." Niko blinked, then hung his head in defeat. Silently, he led the hammerdwarves from the rooftop, abandoning the ruin of the once-great bell.

Gerba was left alone with the roaring celebration of the students.

She folded her arms behind her back, walked to the edge, and gazed over the assembly. The animals had not stopped cheering since the bell had collapsed into the sea. Since then, the throng had devolved to a raucous celebration, reveling in her humiliation, rejoicing in her loss. Screaming and hollering, they screeched their delight at the destruction of one of the founding artifacts of Keymark.

Reprehensible vermin.

Unbidden, Gerba Whipmarples felt a slow smile cross her lips. *Let them laugh.* To her, the destruction of the Great Bell meant the end of the Locke Institute. To the students, it meant doom. Even if these vulgar outlaws survived the night, their death sentence was signed. Without the bell to shield them, they would all perish from disease and starvation.

Tsk-tsk. She cocked her head. *Such a pity to let all that livestock go to waste.*

Gerba Whipmarples straightened, stiffening her spine. *No. Today is the day. Today, I will finally possess the Heart of Huánghūn. And when RākṢhasa wakes...*

She smiled over the mob of doomed convicts.

It will be hungry.

Word of the Locke Institute's evacuation spread quickly. By the time Gerba descended to her office, it was filled with faceless acolytes, each carrying something large and heavy, some of them at a dead run. Gerba moved swiftly to the secret compartment in the wall behind her desk, opened the hidden catch, and removed the Book of Kos. She could not leave it behind. The book had been her only guide for so long, it had become almost a part of her. But Nepenthe would take her the rest of the way.

She threw the red curtain aside and exposed the bamboo staff, pinned to the wall by seven hammerdwarf locks. Gerba admired the elven majik light moving among the carvings in the bamboo. The staff was complete now, all seven pieces gathered at last. At full strength, Nepenthe could not fail to find the treasure she had sought for so long.

She slipped on her tenasi glove to prevent the fabled staff from escaping her grip, took firm hold of Nepenthe, and released the first of the seven locks binding it to the wall.

"Boss?"

Gerba turned to find Winston looming behind her. For a moment, she thought the giant attercop was here to kill her. *No. The majik of the Caged Eight has not faded yet.* Steadying herself, she straightened her back and adopted an imperious posture. "What is it, Winston?"

"The prisoners, uh... the students." Winston flicked his fangs together nervously. "They're out of their heads, crazy. It's getting violent."

As far as Gerba was concerned, every student at the Locke Institute could spend the rest of their lives dying horribly. "Do not hold back, Winston. Restrain them. Bite them." She leaned toward the spider. "Just make sure none of them get inside these walls."

Half of Winston's eyes turned as some of the acolytes moved through Gerba's office, carrying several large trunks. "You goin' somewhere, boss?"

"Just a precaution." Gerba smiled. "Everything is fine."

"You're leaving." Winston looked agitated. "What about us?"

"I beg your pardon?"

"What's going to happen to us? If you leave, we go with you, right?"

Gerba frowned. In truth, she had not given a thought to what would happen to the attercops. They'd be slaughtered by the shiq, most likely. "Of *course*, Winston." She gave her sweetest smile. "The *Hup Two* is big enough for your entire cluster. Once dusk falls, we will all head back to Pell Isle together, and I will give you the biggest stack of khef you've ever seen. Now go take care of those students."

"I don't know." The attercop rubbed his legs. "There are a *lot* of convicts down there. Way more than when we first started this."

In two years, Winston had never dared question her. The domination majik of the Caged Eight was coming to an end quicker than she had feared. But Gerba Whipmarples didn't need majik to manipulate a fool. She put a hand on one of Winston's many shoulders. "You are such a big, strong attercop, Winston," she purred in his ear. "Those petty criminals down there cannot challenge you." She leaned in. "You have weapons, Winston. Use them."

The big spider perked up. "Yeah?"

"Absolutely." Under most circumstances, Gerba forbade the attercops to wield their lances because the giant spiders enjoyed using them too much, like a pack of savage children. But now it didn't matter if a few students got slaughtered. If a dozen attercops happened to perish in the fray, so much the better. "Kill them if you must."

Winston's fangs scissored in what she had come to know as a bloodthirsty grin. "Yeah, you got it, boss." Gigantic legs carried his massive body over the balcony and the spider descended the wall toward the yard, hollering to his fellow guards. With any luck, it would be the last time she saw Winston alive.

Gerba sighed. The attercops had always been a disgusting means to an end, but they had served their purpose. If any of them made it to the harbor before dusk, she would convince them to take one of the larger ships as their own, then burn them alive in the harbor.

They do not matter, she reminded herself. *The students do not matter.* She gripped the Book of Kos in her hands. *Only one thing has ever mattered.*

She unlocked the remaining six clamps and removed Nepenthe from the wall mount. The seven-jointed bamboo stave was exponentially more powerful now that it was complete, and she felt an overwhelming surge of vigor sizzle up her arm.

She grinned. *Today is the day.*

Descending the long stair, Gerba became part of a hive of activity that made its nexus in the central shaft. Acolytes raced up and down, ferrying boxes and bags. Some utilized the weblines as a pulley system to lower the heavier goods. The robed figures moved quickly, their steps furtive, a sense of unease thick in the air.

"Headmistress," Sun Hee interrupted Gerba on the spiral staircase. "What would you like done with these?" She gestured through a doorway into one of the staging rooms, where Gerba discovered a group of filthy and ragged students, each stuffed inside a series of squat cages that forced them to crouch. Gerba peered inside the first cage at a young jaelin who was so dark she was difficult to see. Gerba lifted Nepenthe to cast some light on her. The girl stared back with frightened round eyes.

"Who is this?"

"Farah Ibis, headmistress," Sun Hee reminded her. "She was part of the escape attempt last night."

"Ah, yes, the forger. I had forgotten all about her." Gerba squinted at the girl. "You were Fancy Nan's old assistant, yes? It seems you are doomed to low company, young lady. I have several reports that say you were the one who burned one of my atter-cops."

Farah ducked her head and Gerba peeked into the next squat cage. "And you are the one who made the unfortunate decision to stab me last night."

The muscular alpha llystra barely fit in the cage, bulging between the bars, but still showed a hint of a smile between crocodilian teeth. "Give me second chance."

"Copper Dave Feng, the Hammer of Bego." Gerba reached out and fingered the necklace around the croc's throat. It was made of some kind of hollow pasta and covered in sloppy glue, something a child would create at a craft fair. "What is this?"

"Is gift. From daughter."

Gerba was impressed. The Hammer of Bego had been captured eighteen months ago, yet the fragile child's necklace was still intact. *He must have had to re-string the thing a hundred times.* "How charming. What is her name?"

"Nina."

"Well. I am certain Nina has a much better life without you in it. But you should feel some comfort in knowing you are not the worst excuse for a parent..." She turned to the next cage. "That honor belongs to Miss Picaroon."

The jinx-cat pirate who had been so stunning at the Steel Trials glared up at her with an ugly face. In Patch's paws was a small feline baby, her moggie, suckling at her teat. "You elected to fornicate with a mass murderer and produced his bastard infant, all while serving a life sentence in a labor camp." Gerba tilted her head, enjoying Patch's bitter face. "You will be happy to know your baby has been sold to the Inquisition, where it will be brought up properly as an upstanding citizen, which is more, I dare say, than *you* would have been able to accomplish."

"Eat shit and die."

"You make my point. Take the infant." Gerba watched four acolytes open the cage to separate the babe from its mother. Patch fought them tooth and nail, a frenzy of refusal. "No! *Stop!*"

As Patch screamed, Gerba turned to Sun Hee. "Put it in one of the transport cages. And find sturdy cells for the rest of them."

"You don't want to send the students back down to the yard, headmistress?"

"No, Sun Hee, I may still have use of them today."

Patch screamed, banging against the cage as her newborn was torn from her arms. Gerba made for the door and heard a voice from the dark, next to her head. "I'm gonna kill you."

She stopped and saw a gap-toothed dwarf inside a stacked cage. His face was a livid crimson masked in black smears of cave soot. His one eye burned pure hate. "You killed my brother, you bitch."

She turned to face him. "As if anyone would miss one more Red Dwarf."

"I'm going to kill you." Yenrab Bialik's voice was cold and sharp as a winter knife. "I'm going to break these chains, get out of here, and kill you."

I don't have time for this. Gerba exited through the door and left him behind. "By the time the day is done, Mister Bialik, you shall join your twin in the grave."

When she arrived at the great stone door that opened onto the assembly yard, she peered through it, curious. The entire stone was majiked to be transparent from inside, a one-way window that spied out on the yard. She could see the students clearly on the other side. Gathered in rioting groups, their faces were ugly and furious, a pack of apes flinging rocks at a future they had no hope of stopping. As she watched, an attercop's long spear hurtled from the wall above and pierced one in the shoulder. *Good. Keep each other busy.*

Descending past the third fork, Gerba inhaled the sharp tang of sulfur below. Nepenthe's light cut through the blackness of the caves, blue elvish majik a sharp contrast to the dæmonic red of the glowing lava. She rounded the final corner and her skin drew taut from heat as the stench of brimstone hit her like a wave. She had arrived in the strîgoi pit.

Even here, the anxiety was evident. The two acolytes on guard stood well away from the cage wall, tense and nervous. Within the enclosure, four pale strîgoi prowled the edge of the lava pools, agitated, growling hungrily at them. There was no live prey in the cages, only a scattering of shattered blood vials.

Gerba addressed the acolytes. "Have they been fed?"

"No, ma'am," said the taller guard. "We haven't had a new blood sacrifice in three days. They're getting a little…" He looked past the bars at the stalking dæmons. Their red eyes shone hate as smoke issued from their fanged mouths. He swallowed. "Should we collect a few prisoners and put them in?"

"No." She waved a hand over her shoulder and left the acolyte behind. "They will feed soon enough." She disappeared into her special tunnel.

Gerba concentrated on the staff, using it to seek RākṢhasa. Immediately, Nepenthe nearly jumped out of her gloved hand, leading the way. Eager, it hummed with majik as it pulled her past all her former dead ends with the urgency of a bloodhound on the hunt straining at the leash. Near the terminus of her private excavation, the bamboo suddenly yanked to the side and jammed into the wall with a sharp *tak.*

Today. She drew back her fist and drove Nepenthe into the rock. Blue light flashed like lightning and ignited the blackened cave with starlight refracting off thousands of black diamonds as they fell to the floor. She felt Nepenthe hum, eager to strike once more, wielding the might of twenty pickaxes.

Again she struck, again and again, summoning the rhythm of a blacksmith at the anvil. One blow after the next, she hammered into the volcanic wall with the majik of Nepenthe. Stroke by stroke, she drove a hole into the rock, exercising her will upon it.

Today.

(KANG)

is

(KANG)

the day.

Her pace was slow, steady, unrelenting. Long years of self-control took over as she locked herself into the rhythm. She was unbreakable, immutable, unstoppable. Nothing could stand in her way. She was Gerba Whipmarples, a poor gypsy girl who had started life without a copper penny and by sheer will alone had risen from a stable hand to build the Locke Institute out of nothing. No one had helped her. No one had given it to her. She had created it by the power of her arm and the strength of her mind, the mistress of her own destiny.

Control. It was the reason she rose every morning at dawn, the reason her diction was precise, her manners perfect, her temper even, and her patience inexhaustible. It was the reason she dressed like a lady, exercised every morning, and read every night. She met each day's challenges with the certainty that each obstacle could and would be overcome.

Mastering oneself, after all, was the first step to mastering others.

Relentless as a golem, Gerba Whipmarples continued to strike at the rock, patiently forcing her way inch by stubborn inch through the mountain. As she dug, a spiral of copper veins embedded in the wall grew tighter, twisting inward, drawing her toward a singularity from which they all erupted. The eye of the storm. Her prize.

Nepenthe thundered into the wall with an unrelenting beat, the slow march of an army. Her brow dripped sweat, her arm ached, and yet she persisted, never once breaking tempo, thinking of an old Toshan fable.

Slow

(KANG)

and steady

(KANG)

wins

(KANG)

the race.

Her methodical chipping passed into the next hour, and then the next. Deep beneath the Locke Institute, a new earthquake suddenly gripped the island in a seizure. The rumbles shook the cave, scattering dust from the millions of tons of rock above. Trapped in the shuddering dark, illuminated only by the flickering light of Nepenthe, Gerba Whipmarples did not miss a beat, her thoughts only of the future.

Huánghūn was gone. The incessant heat and stink of it, gone. Now there was nothing but the snow and freezing wind of her ancestral home in the high mountains. Crisp air, icy caves, trol zithers and bass drums drifted through the air, familiar sounds and smells stuck in her mind like pinpricks. Baba Jana's stew, the tink of Saban's forge, each sensation a stab of cherished childhood memory. But today she was no longer an outcast, no longer spat on in the street for her family's sins. Today she had returned to walk among the Juttlanders once again, a heroine of the Horde.

All because an untouchable outcast stable girl had delivered, as a gift, an army of dæmons to the King of Trol.

Gerba Whipmarples was met with cheers, her triumphant homecoming a celebration the likes of which the Jutts had not seen in a hundred years. She was lauded, praised, revered. Feasts were held in her honor, dances, parades, revelry. She could see it all. Commoners begged her blessing; the royal family sought her council. Even the witcher-women knelt before her, offering their allegiance, pledging their fealty. She ignored them all, leaving them, fawning and begging, behind as she mounted the steps of the Sacrum Cabal. Shamed at their incompetence, the rulers of the Juttlander kingdom offered her, humbly, a seat at the high table. She could feel the blackflame crown atop her head. After so long, she was part of a tribe.

No longer rejected. No longer scorned. No longer alone.

Gerba Whipmarples was the apex predator on Huánghūn, a rank she had earned over a decade. Here in the Deep Blue South, at the edge of the world, she was without equal. Her world was made of mindless animals who obeyed her every command. Only Cant Naysayer could offer her a challenge, and the bounty hunter was anything but a friend. Their talk was limited to business and bodies, contract and coin, an unequal relation of mistress and man. No one claimed friendship with her. The nobles looked down on her, the students despised her, and the attercops and acolytes were nothing but followers, mindless as the shiq. She had been without a companion, a peer, for so long. But after today, she would be lonesome no more.

And I will do it with my own

(KANG)

two

(KANG)

hands.

The dread of being alone another day overwhelmed her. Her steady rhythm broke. Faster and faster, Nepenthe smashed at the rock. The drumbeat of her measured efforts became uneven, labored, frenetic. Black diamonds sprayed into the air, cutting little slices into her hands, her arms, her face. She felt none of it, beating at the endless mountain with a mounting desperation until there was nothing but wild, frenzied havoc left in her fists.

Dropping Nepenthe, Gerba Whipmarples beat at the wall with her bare hands, wild and rabid. She screamed at the top of her voice, buried at the bottom of the earth.

Her lungs empty, she stopped, panting, her breath loud in her ears. After a long moment, she calmed herself, picked up Nepenthe, and raised her fist to start the rhythm anew.

From the wall in front of her, a thick copper chunk fell away, spilling black diamonds all over the cave floor.

Inside the hollow of stone, an eye stared back at her.

Gerba Whipmarples stopped breathing.

The eye did not blink. It watched her, burning, red, malevolent. She felt a thrill in her chest as her heart skipped a beat.

RākṢhasa.

At last.

"Hello, my darling." A smile split across her lips. "I'm here. I'm here."

Chapter

9

=LAST=
ONE
=IN=

The sea! The sea! The open sea!
The blue, the fresh, the ever free!
Barry Cornwall

"**I**'M HERE." JACK CRADLED Leah's head. "I'm here."

Even hidden under the deck of the *Venture Brigand*, shielded by three inches of elven timber, Xeusia's dragonflame had reached Leah Archer and set her copper-colored hair ablaze. The strands felt crisp in his hands as charred ends fell away in ash.

At the moment of Xeusia's attack, Leah had turned her back. Her neck, shoulders, and arms had gotten the worst of it. Her palms, too, were burned from putting out the fire on her head. Her flesh was crimson with dragonfire burns, the skin dotted white in growing pustules beginning to blister. Parts of her shirt had caught fire and the charred edges were roasted to her back. Jack swallowed. *Time to be a doktar.* "We need to get this off and treat the burns."

"*Nnn,*" she agreed through gritted teeth. Gingerly, Jack tried to remove one arm from her shirt, but she gasped in pain every time he tried. Giving up, Jack snatched his scalpel and cut through the holes in the back of her shirt. As he peeled away the fabric, it stuck to her flesh, fused with the skin. Leah screamed. "*Ahh!* I'll do it myself!" She bunched the fabric in her fists and tore the shirt off with a jerk. She sucked air sharply through her nose but did not cry out. "There."

Jack knew everything there was to know about treating burns, but most of it involved silver sulfadiazine, oxandrolone, and antiseptics. The only problem was the nearest drugstore was in another universe. "Memphis, do you still have your bag?" Long ago, Memphis had carried a hundred pounds of modern medicine, stolen from Chicago, in his giant satchel.

"No, it's long gone." Memphis stood over them, wringing his hands. "What do we do?"

Jack stared at Leah's back, his mind racing. The best thing that could be said about her burns was they were not white. She still had sensation, which meant the nerve endings were still intact. Still, even a second-degree burn could turn septic. Jack found a clean rag, wet it in a bucket, and applied it to her back as a cold compress. It was the best he could do. "Get us some more water and some rags. Clean ones." Memphis obeyed as Jack applied another compress to Leah's neck.

"You know what would be good about now?" she muttered. "A Great Bell."

Jack almost laughed. "I shouldn't have knocked it down."

Leah forced a smile through gritted teeth. "Remember that for next time."

"Hey." Jack smiled back. "You killed a dragon. That ought to make you feel pretty good."

"Yeah, I'll celebrate later." She winced. "Don't worry about me. This is just a sunburn."

She's tougher than I am. "Hang on, I'll ask if we've got something on board." Jack got to his feet and made for Rooker Flynn.

The captain stood on the aft deck, his face grim. At his feet, the blackened timbers of the *Venture Brigand* still smoked, her elegant hindquarters charred from dragonfire. He sprayed the deck with a pump-hose, dousing out the worst of the hot spots, but it would be hours before the *Brigand* would stop smoldering. Rooker's jaw was locked tight, his eyes hard. He looked like a man attending his wife's funeral.

Jack approached him, cautious. He knew Rooker could sense the ship's feelings in his head. Right now, the *Brigand* was in agony, and he shared every pain with her. "Hey?"

"Hey." Rooker stared at the scorched deck.

"You okay?"

Rooker frowned and shook his head. "She's mutilated."

Jack didn't know what to say. It was true. "I'm sorry, Rooker."

"We're all still alive. Including her. That's a good start. Besides"—Rooker let out half a grin—"chicks dig scars, right?"

Jack chuckled. "So they say."

"How's the dragonslayer?"

"Burned pretty badly but better than she should be." Jack glanced at Leah over his shoulder. *She comes from a sturdy bloodline. Her father is a Border Knight, after all.* That identity, however, was Leah's secret to keep. "You got any aloe vera plant on board? Or honey?"

"Galley. Port side, third shelf."

Jack made to go, then stopped. "Are you sure you're okay? The two of you?"

Rooker jerked his chin. "You take care of yer girl, I'll take care of mine."

Jack returned from the galley with a sealed jar of aloe vera leaves, but he needed to disinfect the wound first. He took a bar of soap, selected a rag, and went to work on Leah's back.

"Ow! Hey!"

Jack frowned. "Sorry. I've got to clean this up, then I can apply the aloe—"

"I *know* how to clean a wound," she growled.

Jack thrust his fists into his hips. "Leah, you cannot clean your own *back*."

"I told you I'm fine. Would you *please* stop looking so down in the mouth?" Leah raised her voice, hollering at Rooker. "Both of you!" The captain frowned, staring back at her. "We're lucky to be alive right now. And in case you forget"—Leah smiled—"we *won*."

A moment passed between the four of them, a feeling of victory. Jack allowed himself a smile, but still, he needed to care for her. She had, after all, just saved their lives. "Leah, we need to cool you off, make sure you don't get inf—"

"O, for God's sake! I can cool off just fine."

Leah got to her feet, marched to the side of the ship, and launched herself overboard.

The *Brigand*'s stance was wide and the drop wasn't far, just enough for Leah to arc into a dive before she hit with a splash. Jack reflexively winced, thinking how much salt water would sting, but the Irridin was a freshwater sea. *That's not bad. And the Irridin is clean enough to drink.* Bubbles billowed as Leah's arc bent underwater. She swam under the outrigger and curled back to the top. She broke the surface with an *ahh* as she flicked away a hunk of burned, wet hair and hollered up at the ship. "Last one in's a rotten egg!"

Jack glanced at Rooker. *Well?* Rooker glanced back. *Well?* They both took off running at the same instant.

They jostled each other for position as they sprinted for the edge of the ship. Both of their feet hit the deckrail at the same time and they leapt into the air together. Not to be outdone, Rooker arced into a backflip in midair. Jack settled for a dive and hit the water with a splash. He felt Rooker hit behind him and bubbles danced all around. Laughing underwater, Jack kicked back to the surface next to Leah. She looked fine, smiling. Rooker emerged beside him and the three of them bobbed in the water, just a bunch of laughing heads.

"Look out below!" came a shout from above, and the massive shadow of Memphis Kubiak blotted out the sun. The giant trol hit the water like a bomb, spraying water in a geyser thirty feet high. The sea lurched beneath Jack, catching him in the swell as the spray hit. He felt his stomach go up and drop back down, tickling from inside. Rooker and Leah laughed as the same happened to them.

Jack watched Memphis's little brown lizard shape bob to the surface and paddle for the outrigger. He could swear it had an impish smile.

Jack let free another laugh, realizing he hadn't felt this good in a long, long time.

It was delightful, just swimming together.

They ducked around in the water like sea otters for a good long while. Fuji crawled out to the pontoon and jumped in after Jack, paddling to him like an underweight dog. The tam pawed at him with its tree-frog toes, trying to perch on his head. It turned into a game and they chased each other through the water. All of them splashed and hooted like kids at a swimmin' hole. Rooker moved easily in the water, a dolphin. Leah moved much more slowly, protecting her burns, the cool of the water a blessed relief. Trols cannot swim, of course, but Memphis joined them in his lizard form. When the game became too vigorous for him, he climbed back onto the outrigger and sang joyful tavern songs in his resonant voice. Soon enough, they all tired of swimming. Rooker produced three long, skinny, inflated bladders from a hidden compartment in the outrigger and passed them around. The long float bent in a U under Jack like a sea-saddle and kept him afloat without effort. He watched Leah wince as she struggled into hers.

"You okay?" Jack asked.

"Stop asking or I'll tie a rock to your ankle," Leah groused as she adjusted her bandages. "Uh. This is going to hurt for a while, isn't it?" *Three weeks or more*, Jack thought. That bit of medical trivia he decided to keep to himself. Leah got herself situated then snorted. "Somebody better write a song about how that damn dragon died."

"Heh." Rooker chuckled. "I know just the man for the job." Jack glanced at him. Rooker met his gaze and they shared a look. *Billy Pilgrim would do it justice.*

It was a shared thought, word for word, beat for beat. Without speaking, both men knew it. Jack suddenly realized what Rooker meant when he talked about hearing the *Venture Brigand* in his head.

He chuckled, enjoying the sensation. Rooker did too.

Memphis thumped his hand against the outrigger in a beat and sang:

There once was a dragon
As big as a cabin—

"Kubiak!" Rooker cut him off. "Yer hurting my ears!" He pointed a finger at Jack. "How are ya getting him back to the Tosh?"

Memphis glanced at Jack, his eyes surprised. "You told him where you're from?"

Jack chuckled. "After nine months in prison together, I think we're out of secrets."

Rooker glanced at him and Jack half-heard his thought. *Too right.*

"We can take him home any time." Leah spat a fountain of water. "All we have to do is get to the wreck of the *Círdan*—"

"The *Círdan*?" Rooker's eyes flashed wide. "Ya know where she is?"

Memphis looked surprised. "*You* know about that?"

"Why is everybody surprised when I know things?" Rooker shouted. Jack stifled a laugh. "Yeah, I know about the *Círdan*, ya big-nosed runt! It's the *Brigand*'s sister ship, the only other aräs windjammer ever found. She was sunk a hundred and twenty-two years ago by a brownbelly man-o'-war called the *Khŭk*. Lies a quarter day north-northwest." Rooker arched an eyebrow. "That *Círdan*?"

"Okay, okay, I get it, I get it." Memphis raised his palms and cracked a smile. "I was going to use the elvish majik in the wreck to open a jaunt gate a few days ago, but..."

The pirate turned to Jack, confused. Jack chuckled. *Right. I hadn't told him that part yet.* Rooker squinted at him. "The brownbelly opened a hole to Chegago... and ya *still* came back?"

Jack shrugged, saying nothing. In that moment, however, he felt a shimmer of pride well up inside his chest. He spoke to Rooker with his eyes. *You're damn right I did.*

Rooker snorted, laughing. "Ya made the wrong choice, bubba. Shoulda bailed."

"Too right." Jack spat water at Rooker. Rooker spat back.

"But!" Memphis spread his massive fingers. "I don't need the *Círdan*. I have everything I need right here."

Rooker nodded. "Ya can use the *wikk* of the *Venture Brigand* the same way?"

"If you'll let me." The trol cocked his head. "The majik will grow back, but it will take time and she's already injured."

"She?" Rooker lifted an eyebrow. "Memphis Kubiak. You called the *Brigand* a 'she.'"

"This ship is alive," Memphis stated as if it was plain as the nose on his face. "Of course she's a she."

Rooker glanced at Jack. "So ya can get him outta Keymark any time ya want. Right now, even."

"Well, not *right* now." Memphis chuckled. "We have a font of *wikk* and all the water we need, but opening a jaunt gate is exhausting and I'm spent." The trol shrugged. "Not to mention if I get the spell wrong, we both die."

"Let's give it a day or two," said Jack.

"In the meantime"—Memphis clapped his hands and turned to Leah—"I think we should get *you* out of the water before you turn into a prune, young lady."

Leah frowned and her face turned sour. "It's better in here."

"Let Jack do his doktaring, Leah." Memphis folded his arms and stood his ground. "I need to return you to your father... *without* scorch marks."

Jack knew his cue. "Don't worry about the climb, Leah. We'll lower down a harness."

"I told you, I'm fine." She swam to the outrigger and climbed up, hissing from the pain.

"Yer *burned*, baby sister," Rooker chided. "Ya can't—"

"*Leah!*" She thrust a dripping finger at Rooker. Jack jerked back, startled by her sudden anger. *She must be in more pain than I thought.* "Leah. Not baby sister, not honey, not darlin'. You call me by my name or nothing at all, get me, Rooker? You may be his friend, but I didn't pull your ass out of prison to be called *baby*." She grabbed a peg and climbed up the ladder, ignoring her burns as she left them behind.

Jack blinked at the outburst. Rooker suddenly snorted, laughing. He glanced at Jack. *She remind you of someone?*

Patch. Jack nodded. *All that fire.*

They stared at each other. They said nothing, but each man knew the other man's mind.

Neither liked what they found.

Memphis's voice came from far away. "You two coming up?"

The noonday sun shone overhead in a glorious sea-blue sky while they toweled themselves off and got themselves dry. As they did, Fuji jumped and skipped about the deck, rolling a tangerine and chasing after it like a ball. Jack helped apply aloe and a new set of bandages to prevent Leah's burns from suppurating. Memphis returned from the galley with a large charcuterie board and a fat pitcher of iced lemonade. Rooker produced a new tunic for Leah, all linen, light as air, in a shade of Lincoln green that complemented her eyes.

Jack glanced at Rooker. *You did that on purpose, didn't you?*

What ya want? I should give her a burlap sack?

As they ate, Memphis asked a thousand questions about Jack and Rooker's escape, marveling at each step of the way. Leah was amazed at how many ways Jack had used Toshan science to survive. Even Fuji seemed impressed. Finally, the conversation fell to Gerba Whipmarples.

"I remember hearing about her when she served the Summer Mage, a long time ago," Memphis said. "An animal trainer, basic

manipulation majik, nothing special. Just another gypsy, really."
He tilted his head, his long horn tilting with it. "But combining
a command glyph with the Great Bell, then using blood majik
to pervert the *wikk*?" The trol shook his head. "No one has ever
done that. No one in their right mind would even *think* of it.
The moment she attached the glyph, she doomed the bell itself.
Nothing can be bent so far from its purpose without breaking."

"The crack." Rooker nodded. "The bell was cracked on the
inside, beneath the rune."

Jack let out a sigh of relief. He had secretly felt guilty for destroying something so majestic as the Agrat-ban-Haifa. But if Memphis
was right, he'd only sped up the inevitable. "So what happens now
that the bell is at the bottom of the Irridin?"

Leah shrugged. "Healthy fish."

"No, with the Caged Eight." Jack leaned in. "She'll lose control
over the spiders, right?"

"Absolutely." Memphis nodded. "And the strîgoi."

Jack felt his skin prickle. "What?"

Memphis shook his head. "If she's too busy fighting off shiq to
give the strîgoi prey or blood, they'll go feral. Once that happens,
that iron wall won't stop them. They'll kill everything on the
island."

Jack glanced at Rooker. Both their expressions were dark. Rooker watched Jack for a long moment, his face blank. Finally, one
eyebrow curled. *I see ya thinkin' there, bubba. Knock it off.*

Jack exhaled. *You're thinking the same thing I'm thinking.*

No.

Yes, you are.

Well, stop thinkin' it. Rooker stood up with a scowl. He left Jack
behind and stared at the sea, squinting at the horizon.

"There's an old legend about the island of Huánghūn," said
Memphis, who hadn't noticed their silent conversation. "The lord

of the strîgoi, RākŞhasa, was believed to have had his final battle with Kos right on th—"

"Shut up." Rooker's voice was sharp. "We got inbound."

Jack blinked, then took his meaning. The infinite ocean seemed empty, but he knew better than to doubt Rooker's eye. He imagined a fleet of pursuit vessels, all flying yellowjacket sails. "Are we in trouble?"

Rooker grinned. "Just the opposite."

Jack squinted and the thing came into view. He realized why he had trouble spotting it. The boat was tiny, a four-man fishing skiff sailing under plain canvas. The *Venture Brigand* could crush it without a thought.

"Anglers. Probably looking for yellowfin." Rooker turned to Jack, his face stoic. *Here's our chance. If we're doing this, it has to be now.*

We have to.

Rooker let out a long breath. *I know.*

"All right," he announced. "Let's pay these hooksetters a visit."

Leah cocked her head. "Why?"

Jack shrugged. "Because we have to rob them."

Leah's head snapped to him. "Wait, what? We're not *robbing* them!"

"We can't help ourselves, Leah." Jack tried to keep the smile off his face. "We're hardened criminals."

Half an hour later, two frightened fishermen stared up at the *Venture Brigand*, their mouths open in an identical O as the giant ship straddled their little boat like a whale passing over a minnow. Rooker popped the hatch in the belly turret and called down to them. "Ahoy the skiff!" He swung out of the turret, stepped onto the top of their mast, grabbed a handhold, and descended gently toward their deck. "Prepare to be boarded."

In the belly dome, Jack watched. Leah and Memphis stood beside him. Leah put her hands on her hips. "Seriously, what the hell is he doing?"

"Let him have his fun." Jack smiled.

"Look at them," said Memphis. "They're terrified."

Dumbfounded, the fishermen looked on as Rooker engaged them in conversation, making much use of his hands. He took command of their boat and steered her to touch the port outrigger of the *Venture Brigand*. As he lashed the boats together, Rooker opened a hidden hatch in the big pontoon, revealing a skinny longboat the size of a big canoe hidden within. Jack blinked. *That's a good trick.*

Gesturing further, Rooker handed one of the sailors something. A moment of debate followed, but it was short-lived. The fishermen quickly got into the canoe and pushed off, leaving their skiff lashed to the *Brigand*. Paddling, the frightened fishermen made for open water. "North by northwest!" Rooker hollered after the canoe. "Put the sun on your starboard, ya'll be there before ya know it."

Leah eyed him and the now empty skiff. "You stole their boat?"

"*Traded* for it." Rooker grinned. "They got twenty gold marks of the Naysayers' money, a longboat, and the coordinates of the cave where Old Captain Kote kept most of his treasure. Personally, I think I overpaid."

"But we have the best boat in Keymark!" Leah shouted. "What do we need a lousy skiff for?"

"So I can dump you three."

"*What?*"

"I don't think ya understand my position, Archer." Rooker jammed a fist to his hip and wagged a finger at her. "Every yellow-jacket in the Deep Blue South is gonna be looking for my ship. I don't have time to wait around for ya to rest up, and the *Venture Brigand* can't afford to get her strength sapped so ya can open some damn majik portal to Chegago." He pointed at the skiff. "Take that to the Círdan. Cast yer big majik spell. And get Jack home." He grinned. "Which means get yer gear and get off my ship."

Jack frowned, folding his arms. "Rooker—"

"Don't argue with me, bubba." Rooker thrust the finger at Jack. "We're still wanted men, in case ya were wonderin'. Safer to go with them. Now get crackin'. Daylight's wastin'."

Memphis scowled at the pirate. "You selfish little—"

"*Move!*"

Leah and Memphis had very little gear remaining from the *Kestrel*, and Jack, of course, had nothing at all, so in minutes they had transferred their meager possessions to the fishing boat. Memphis scuttled down the mast in lizard form while Jack helped Leah down the rungs. Fuji followed, confused. The little tam crawled up into Jack's arms and licked his face.

Patting Fuji on the back, Jack tried to keep his true feelings under wraps. This wasn't the way he had imagined things would end, but it was the only course he had. "Let's go, let's go." Rooker clapped from the outrigger. "Ya can keep the shirt."

"Thanks a lot," Leah growled. "Wasteka *pirate*."

With everyone aboard, Rooker untied the rear cleat. Only one line still connected the fishing boat to the *Brigand*. Jack stood at the bow and felt a wave of dread ripple through him. *This is the end of the line.*

Rooker extended a hand to him. "Come up here and gimme a proper fare-thee-well, bubba."

Jack stepped off the skiff. As he did, Leah scowled. "I thought you were in a hurr—"

Jack slipped the rope from the cleat and let it go.

The skiff drifted away with Leah, Memphis, and Fuji falling behind.

Leah's eyes went wide. "Wait!"

Jack stood with Rooker on the *Venture Brigand's* outrigger and watched them go.

"Stop—" Memphis lunged to grab the *Brigand* but it was beyond the trol's reach. There was nothing he could do but watch as the two ships drifted apart. Fuji ran back and forth on the skiff, trying to figure out why his master was leaving him.

"You can't come with us, Leah. You're injured." Jack straightened. "Memphis, change those bandages every few hours. Keep her safe."

Leah's face went white. "Jahk, don't—"

"I'm sorry," Jack said, standing with Rooker. "But we can't just let them die." He stared at Leah, his heart aching. All he wanted was to be close to her, but right now all he could think about were Patch and her moggie. About Copper Dave. Yenrab. Farah. Billy Pilgrim. The people they had left behind. Jack and Rooker owed them a debt, and both men meant to pay it. "Maybe we'll get another time. In another land."

"High noon tomorrow," Rooker shouted. The skiff fell further away as Leah, Memphis, and Fuji passed out of the shadow of the *Brigand* into open sea. "The Bowery."

"And if we don't show up..." Jack felt his throat well up. "Forgive us if you can."

Jack watched his rescuers, the people he loved, drift away, dropping further and further behind. He swallowed, his throat dry, knowing he probably was never going to see them again. But at least Leah would be safe.

And Rooker was by his side.

Memphis raised one giant arm, his palm a wide goodbye. Leah stood straight, calling out to them. "Noon! Tomorrow! You better be there!" She leaned against a rope, staring at Jack. "And good luck!"

Rooker's voice was sharp. "Run, girl."

Jack watched the wake kick white behind the outriggers as the *Brigand* picked up speed. The little fishing boat faded into the distance. Both men watched it go.

"She said good luck." Rooker cocked his jaw. "When a pretty woman wishes you good luck, it always works."

"We'll need it." Jack squinted at the sky. The sun had passed its zenith and begun its long descent toward the sea ahead. Once it sank, they would not be able to set foot on Huánghūn. Everyone on the island, including Patch and her moggie, would be trapped between the shiq and the strîgoi, and there was no surviving that.

"Get up, girl," growled Rooker. "We're racing the sun."

Chapter

10

PUDDLE JUMPER

Freedom is what you do
with what's been done to you.

Jean-Paul Sartre

R ACING THE SUN, ROOKER urged the *Venture Brigand* to fly like a diving falcon, low and fast over the Irridin, skidding between sea and sky. His girl was injured just as much as Leah was. He could feel the pain of her burns as if they were on his own skin. But his girl was bigger, stronger. She would hold out long enough. *Because yer the best ol' girl in the world.*

No, she answered.

Rooker couldn't help but grin. *Then because I love you.*

Yes. She increased her speed.

Jack Swift stood beside him. Neither man said a thing. Normally, Rooker hated silence and tried to fill it with as many words as possible. But for the first time in his life, he realized what old married couples meant when they said they were so close they didn't have to talk to know what the other was thinking. It was bizarre, this comfortable quiet.

Neither he nor Jack had spoken of the necessity to protect Leah, their injured savior. Neither had questioned whether Memphis should stay with her. Neither had needed to point out that tricking the woman and the trol would be necessary. The decision to go back to Huánghūn had not required a voice. All of these things had passed between them without a sound. They had simply known what was needed and done their part to make it so.

Each man knew the other's mind as if it were his own.

A unity of purpose had crystalized between them, a determination neither man needed to announce. They both knew the futility of the path they had chosen. They both knew the impossibility of success, the certainty of death. United, they strode the sea toward whatever end.

They rode the sea as one.

Rooker eyed the sun. He did not have to wonder how long until their time ran out. Like every prisoner on Huánghūn, he had become an expert at measuring the day. An hourglass ran in his mind, constantly calculating the moment the sun would drop below the surface and bring on the horrors of night. He feared the sunset the way a beaten dog fears the club. That fear would stay with him for the rest of his life, short as it might be.

As the full heat of the day settled in, they both sweated profusely enough to remove their shirts and let the wind dry them. They made a meal of a rustic rye loaf with rosemary butter and a canning jar of wiristi olives. Rooker enjoyed the bite of garlic and peppers in the oil. So did Jack. They sipped from a chilled canteen, passing it back and forth, sharing ice-cold water.

Still, they said nothing.

As the sun continued its slow descent, the red sails of the *Brigand* continued to strain as the ship sped toward the Locke Institute. At long last, one of them spoke. Rooker was surprised to discover it was him. "How we gonna find them?"

Jack didn't need to say it. The answer was plain. *I don't know.*

They stared at the empty sea ahead.

The sails billowed in the breeze, flickering the shadow of the sun across the fly deck. Dark clouds came into view on the north horizon, a storm that threatened the far distance. The clouds grew larger before Rooker spoke again.

"She'll run."

"To Bounty." Jack nodded. "She'll regroup."

"There's nothing left on Bounty," Rooker disagreed. "The nobles aren't coming back and neither is she."

Jack glanced at him, skeptical. "She won't leave empty-handed."

"What more does she need? Coin, diamonds, artifacts... Nepenthe." Rooker snorted. "I'd *retire.*"

Jack conceded, having no argument for that. The kid stared at the horizon ahead. "You think she'll take prisoners with her?"

"No." Rooker popped his neck. "Everyone's a liability now. She'll burn the boats and maroon the survivors."

Survivors would be few and far between. If the shiq didn't get the outlaws, the strîgoi would. Even if the students of the Locke

Institute somehow managed to survive both, Huánghūn had a million ways to kill them. Without the Great Bell, they didn't stand a chance. In a tenday, the four camps would be down to a few dozen cannibals.

Another long silence passed, both men thinking of familiar faces. Rooker saw their eyes in the shiq caves, lit by whitefire flame. Copper Dave. Yenrab. Farah. Patch.

Her baby.

Rooker repeated his question. "How we gonna find 'em?"

Jack repeated his answer. *I don't know.*

Rooker leaned against the bridge rail and felt a wave of fatigue wash over him. He met Jack's eyes.

Whatever plan we come up with, it better be fast.

As it turns out, being executed is exhausting.

Rooker found himself half asleep at the wheel, dreaming of a future that consisted of cold añejo, big women, and red strawberry cake. He was in the middle of kissing white icing off Lauren Eberlee's lips when his eyes opened and he spotted a shadow on the horizon.

"Ship ahoy," he called sleepily. He knew he'd been caught napping; the other vessel was closer than he liked but still far enough away to outmaneuver. Yawning, he put the rings to his eye.

He heard Jack approach from behind. "More fishermen?" Rooker peered through the spyglass. Black sails. He recognized her markings. The *Hydra*. A cold fist squeezed his guts.

He sucked air between his teeth. "Naysayers."

"No." Jack stared at the ship, unbelieving. "It can't be. They left."

"Well, they're back now," grumbled Rooker. He brushed his eye, remembering how Cant Naysayer's stiletto had felt inside it.

Jack leaned in. "Can they catch us?"

"No," Rooker stated. The *Venture Brigand* could outmatch any ship on the sea. Of that he was certain. "Not a chance."

"You sure?" The kid watched as the *Hydra* turned toward the *Brigand* and attempted an intercept course. "How did they even find us?"

"Cant has a nose on him." The Naysayer was all too well acquainted with the intoxicating elvish perfume of the *Venture Brigand*. The bounty hunter could likely smell her anywhere in the Deep Blue South. Rooker grinned, enjoying the thought of outrunning Cant Naysayer again and again. "He's gonna get used to sniffing my wake."

"Okay." Jack exhaled and leaned against the rail. "For a moment there, I thought we were in trouble."

As he spoke, Rooker watched the *Hydra* disappear. Only a shimmer of indigo remained where the ship had been.

Rooker blinked. "Um..."

"What?"

Closer, another shimmer of indigo appeared. The *Hydra* emerged from the majik light, bearing down on them.

"We're in trouble." Rooker leaned forward. "Get on the harpoon bow."

"We're *out* of harpoons."

"Then grab a slaver bow. They're gonna board us!" Rooker shouted.

Jack ran to the foredeck and dug in the locker for a slaver bow as Rooker eyed the *Hydra*. "We could take one of them. Wont maybe. Or Shant. But we can't take all three. I'd rather fight a strîgoi."

Jack found a long triple-barbed arrow, nocked it to the string, and took cover behind the deckrail. The kid was no good with a longbow; he'd be lucky to hit the side of the boat, and both men knew it. They were defenseless.

Jack looked at Rooker. *So what's the plan?*

You come up with yers, I'll come up with mine!

Now Rooker felt the tingle of the *wikk*. The front of the *Hydra* shimmered like a mirage. The three-masted clipper, half the size of the *Brigand*, disappeared in a wink of majik and was gone.

Jack stared at the empty spot, his mouth open. "How the..."

Directly next to the *Brigand*, the *Hydra* appeared, emerging from a flickering pool of light in the air.

Rooker scowled.

"...hell."

He took a step back as the clipper emerged from the shimmering majik. At the rear deck of the vessel stood the tall, gaunt shape of Cant Naysayer. Focused on his portal spell, the warlock's body was rigid, his hat drawn over his eyes, wind whipping his duster. Beside him stood the grey goliath, his brute of a brother Wont, his curled horns painted in amber. A crooked grin played over the Steel Trial gladiator trainer's mouth. "You didn't think you could outrun us, did you, Flynn?"

"O, hi, Wont. I didn't see ya." Rooker adopted a casual stance and folded his arms. "Where's yer other brother? The sneaky bird with the feathers?"

"Stayed in Javernis Twist," replied Wont. "New contract. But I think Cant and I can handle you."

Rooker eyed the *Hydra*, steering clear. If he kept his distance, Wont would never be able to jump the divide. But what really worried Rooker was Cant's levitation majik. The warlock could cross the air between the ships as easily as strolling down a boardwalk. *Maybe he can't hold two spells at once. It looks like he needs everything he's got for this one.* The *Hydra* was already falling behind, unable to match the *Brigand*'s raw speed.

"Why don't ya hop over here before we pull ahead, Wont?" Rooker gripped the deckwheel, preparing a hard turn away. "I bet ya a thousand marks you make it."

The hulking Naysayer snarled at him. As the *Hydra* fell behind, Rooker experienced a moment of hope that died as another blossom of majik light appeared in his periphery. Rooker turned and had a stomach-twisting moment as he watched the *Hydra*'s aft deck appear ahead. The ship was split in two, half ahead, half behind, and in the wrong order.

Rooker held the deckwheel in numb fingers, not quite believing what he was seeing.

As the *Hydra* continued its portal loop beside the *Brigand*, Cant Naysayer passed through the shimmering majik and appeared ahead. The thin man finally lifted his head, revealing his half-mask and those icy blue eyes. "Hello, Flynn." His voice purred like a rattlesnake. "Where's the dog?"

Rooker opened his mouth to insult the bastard but a voice cut him off.

"I'm right here." Jack Swift stood. The longbow string was drawn tight to his cheek, a three-barbed arrow ready to fly. "Wanna see if I bite?"

Cant slowly turned his hard eyes to Jack. "Careful, Toshan. Unless you want a mouth full of spiders again."

Rooker eased forward and gripped the handbow hidden under the deckwheel. He glanced at Jack. *He's still talking. Which means he's not sure he can win. Keep him off-balance.* "'Lo, Cant. Last time I saw ya, ya were owner of a better ship."

"Last time I saw you, you only had one eye." Cant breathed deep. "Is that Memphis Kubiak I smell?"

Rooker scowled. The tracker's senses were unnerving. He glanced at Jack. They both shared the same thought: *Wish we'd kept him here. We could use a wizard about now.*

Rooker's mind raced. He had no way to outrun them and no great weapons. A lie was the only defense he had. "I was hopin' ya wouldn't notice."

Cant leaned forward. "Is he on board?"

"C'mon over and find out."

The bounty hunter sniffed and his body suddenly relaxed. "Bluff and bluster. Pity." Cant clicked his tongue. "I would have enjoyed the opportunity to test myself against him." As the *Hydra* dropped back, Rooker found himself eye to eye with Cant, each man staring the other down.

"Ya look dog-tired, Cant." Rooker eyed the majik portals. "How long ya think ya can keep this dance up? Yer usin' a lot of majik but I ain't runnin' out of wind."

"I can do this all day," Cant said.

"Enough!" Wont shouted, breaking the illusion of civility. "You two should be at the Institute!" The bounty hunter thumped a muscled fist into a muscled palm. "Gerba doesn't like it when students play hooky. How'd you get out?"

Rooker glanced at Jack. *They don't know.*

"I'll tell you what I think." Cant cocked a finger at Rooker. "You escaped with the help of Kubiak and a woman. She smells lovely, by the way. Cherry blossoms have such a faint scent. You ran, Gerba sent Xeusia after you, the dragon found you and roasted my ship."

"*Yer* shi—"

"Yet somehow, you're still alive." Cant's eyes narrowed. "Kubiak is gone. The woman is gone. And for some inexplicable reason, the two of you are headed back to Huánghūn."

Rooker looked at Jack. *What do we tell them?*

Jack jerked his chin, the bowstring pulled taut against his cheek. *Whatever you have to do to keep them off this boat.*

"Here's a better story," Rooker growled. "We *broke* the Agrat-ban-Haifa. We *killed* Xeusia." He drew himself up to his full height. "And we're headed back to finish the job on Whipmarples."

Cant Naysayer laughed. Actually laughed at him. *Arrogant wasteka bastard.* "You're slipping, Flynn. Your lies are usually better."

Rooker looked to the sky and searched the clouds. "Ya see Xeusia ul-Styx Hakáti flappin' around anywhere up there? Ya think a dragon would just give up?" Cant's blue eyes grew narrow. "We killed the damned thing." Rooker felt a sense of pride swell his chest. "We killed a full-sized bull wyrm, Cant. And came out without a scratch." He bared his teeth. "Tell me I'm lyin'."

He watched Cant's eyes. *Yeah. Now yer wondering.*

Cant considered him a moment. "Then answer me one question." He folded his arms. "How?"

Rooker wanted to tell him. He wanted to rub the Naysayer's nose in the truth that he'd blown the dragon off the map. But the edge of the world was a long way off, and he had nothing to threaten the Naysayer with here. Rooker grasped for a lie and found his hands empty. *Think!*

"Toshan majik." Jack's voice was sharp. Cant's head snapped to the kid, his eyes narrow. "Memphis brought me weapons. From *my* world." Jack stepped forward, aiming the three-barbed arrow at the warlock. "And I bet you know what *those* can do." Rooker thought of Jack's whitefire burning hotter than the sun. He'd seen Toshan majik in action. He knew it was crazy. Apparently Cant knew it too. The bounty hunter's grey face paled considerably.

Jack took another step. "Memphis Kubiak isn't here because we don't *need* him anymore. We tore Xeusia to shreds with a few of these." The kid's barbed arrow stared down the bounty hunter. Jack's face contorted in a wicked grin. "Just imagine what we can do to *you.*"

It was a stone-cold bluff.

Jack didn't blink once.

Wont glanced at his brother, rubbing meaty hands. Cant tilted his head, silent. As the quiet drew out, all Rooker could hear was the hiss of the sea and the sound of his heartbeat. The ship passed through the rear portal, disappearing and reappearing in front of them. Ringed in majik, Cant spoke. "You know I can set fire to the *Brigand* any time I want."

"We been on fire once today," growled Rooker. "Once more won't make a difference."

Cant chuckled and fingered the key ring on his belt. "Perhaps we should discuss this further. I don't suppose you would mind—"

Quick as a snake, Rooker snapped his handbow up and fired. The bolt cut the air between the two ships and buried its head into the *Hydra*'s spar an inch from the third Naysayer Brother's hand.

The black-feathered bounty hunter, the one that looked like a big raven, had been creeping through the rigging, moving into position to attack from above. Rooker shouted, *"Ya think I ain't lookin' for you, sneaky bird?!"*

Shant Naysayer glanced at his black feathers pinned to the mast and blinked at Rooker down its black beak. Rooker brought up the other handbow. "Get back down with yer brothers or I'll put the next one in yer wasteka *eye*."

Shant's raven-black head snapped to Cant, who nodded. Cowed, the raptor assassin crawled swiftly through the sails and dropped on his talons to the deck between Cant and Wont. Shant glared at Rooker. "You got lucky."

"Fool me once, Shant. No one gets two." Rooker liked the feeling of staring down all three Naysayer Brothers when he had the upper hand. It felt good. Rooker turned to the warlock and unfurled a satisfied smile. "Now. What we got here is a—whatchamacallit?"

"Mexican standoff." Jack took a step forward with his bow drawn fully. His hands did not shake.

"An impasse." Cant lowered one eyebrow. "Until we call your bluff."

Rooker straightened. For once, the truth was all he needed. "The bell is gone. The Locke Institute is dead. Gerba's running scared. You know what they say about rats and a sinking ship." Rooker knew the Naysayer Brothers operated on only one true motivation: greed. And that's where Rooker dug in the knife. "If you arrest us, what are the chances she actually *pays* you?"

An unsettled look crossed Cant's blue eyes. Rooker pressed his advantage. "She's going to cut and run, Cant. And if she doesn't pay you, who will? Is there a contract out on us? A warrant? A bounty? Anything?"

"Not *yet*," Cant hissed. "But there will be. You killed half a dozen nobles."

"So no contract. Which means yer willin' to get killed arresting two escaped outlaws who aren't worth a red penny." Rooker cocked a grin. "I thought you boys were professionals."

The Naysayer Brothers scowled as one man. They considered his words. Cant put his arms behind his back. "I take it you have a proposal?"

"No. I have a contract." Rooker straightened. "Between *us*. Stay out of our way until dawn. Tomorrow morning, the Institute is yours for the picking. The vault, the mines, all of it. Yours. There won't be anyone left to stop you, including us. You can have it all." Rooker spread his hands. "If Gerba dies, you win. If we die, you win."

"Everything in the Institute." Rooker saw a flash of greed in Cant's eyes. "Including what's buried there."

Rooker wasn't sure what Cant meant, but whatever it was, it seemed to whet the warlock's appetite. Rooker held his breath, knowing if the Naysayers rejected the bargain, they'd be dead in seconds.

After a long moment, the warlock's gaze fell on Jack. "Including Nepenthe."

"Over my dead body," came Jack's growl.

"That might be preferable." Silence followed, broken only by the rushing of the wind and the sizzle of Cant's portal majik. The bounty hunter finally spoke. "The odds say you'll both be dead by morning."

Rooker nodded, knowing it was likely true. He imagined the bounty hunters picking over his and Jack's corpses at dawn. "Sounds like we have a contract."

Cant raised his outstretched hand. "Cross my palm with silver."

If ya think I'm getting close enough to touch ya, yer out of yer head.

Rooker felt in his old shirt pocket and found the ugliest copper penny he'd ever seen. He hooked the coin on his thumb and flicked it into the expanse. "Here ya go." The air caught the penny, spun it in the wind, and flipped it right into Cant's raised palm. "One red cent."

Cant nodded and spat in his palm. "Dawn."

Rooker did the same. "Dawn."

The forward portal closed. The *Hydra* drifted backward into the majik in her wake. As she shimmered away into nothingness, all three bounty hunters watched the *Brigand* as one man.

"Pleasure doing business with you," came Cant's rattlesnake growl, then the Naysayer Brothers disappeared into the indigo light.

Just like that, the *Hydra* disappeared into the sizzling air. Majik flickered and bent as the portal snapped shut. Rooker found himself facing nothing but an empty sea.

Jack finally released his pull on the bow and let out a long breath. Rooker leaned against the bridge rail. They caught each other's eyes and grinned, happy to still be alive.

"'We tore Xeusia to shreds,'" Rooker mimicked Jack's tough-guy voice. *"'What do you think we'll do to you?'"*

Jack snorted a laugh. "I learned bluffing from the master."

Rooker shot him a grin. *Keep it up, bubba. We'll make a pirate of ya yet.*

Jack chuckled. The kid looked particularly satisfied with himself, and Rooker had to admit he'd come a long way from the scrawny, naïve boy he'd first met two years ago. But the truth was Jack Swift looked exhausted. Dark circles rimmed his eyes, his movements were weary, and there were too many furrows for the brow of a sixteen-year-old kid. Jack's fire was nearly exhausted. He was down to embers, about to burn out. *Can't say I blame him.*

Rooker again thought of the Naysayers picking through their corpses tomorrow morning. He saw Jack's body, cold and limp, and felt an icicle in his heart. Rooker didn't want to die, but he'd come to accept the inevitability of it at the end of a noose.

But the thought of Jack dead...

"Get some sleep." Rooker thumped the kid on the shoulder. "We'll be there s—" His head came up and he took a sharp breath. "Land ho."

"What?"

Rooker Flynn laid eyes on the rock where he'd died. "We're home."

Chapter

11

=PINWHEEL=
GAMBIT

Good men must not obey the laws too well.
Ralph Waldo Emerson

*H*OME. JACK HAD FORGOTTEN the meaning of the word. Chicago seemed like a faded dream now, just smudged memories of another life that belonged to someone else. He hadn't even thought of his dad in a month. He barely remembered what it was like to have a textbook in his hand, or electricity, or air conditioning. Rooker, Patch, Copper Dave, and the other outlaws seemed more real to him than America. There *was* no such thing as home. There was only Huánghūn.

Jack blinked and realized he'd been dozing. The *Venture Brigand* had come to a halt. The sails hung slack, curling in long, lazy ripples. She floated at the mercy of the gentle waves, bobbing like a water strider waiting for something to eat. The ship was far enough from the Institute to not be seen from anywhere but atop the wall, and even then *Brigand* would only be a speck, a harmless bit of nothing on the horizon.

Jack shook his head and came awake, trying to focus. In his dreams, he had found the Institute empty. There was nothing left of Gerba, the acolytes, or the attercops. Only a mass exodus of ships on the horizon. In his dreams, the Locke Institute was abandoned.

"Morning, sunshine." Rooker handed him a steaming tin cup of black coffee.

Jack grunted and took it. "How long was I out?"

"Dunno. While." Rooker looked tired, but the pirate still had a sparkle to his eye.

"Am I dreaming or did it take longer to get back here than it took to get out to..." Jack paused, remembering the waterfall into infinity at the edge of the world. That, too, seemed like a dream. "...wherever we were? Was the wind against us?"

"Nope. Huánghūn moved."

Jack snorted. "Okay. Right."

"*All* the islands move, bubba."

Jack shook his head. "Stop. I'm too tired for jokes."

"Who's joking? They move," Rooker said. "That's why navigating them is so tricky. Huánghūn is five nautical miles further east than when we started this little run. Ya never noticed how it drifts?" He chuckled. "And I thought ya were so smart."

Jack started to argue but gave up. *After everything I've seen, that's what I'm going to argue with?* He shrugged. "Okay."

"Take a look." Rooker handed over his rings. Jack put them to his eye and the Institute grew closer in the majik spyglass. There was the wall, up close and personal. Half the ships that had been there this morning were littered around the bay. The dock bustled with activity, a dozen acolytes loading boats. *So it's not abandoned. Just a dream.* Jack sighed, suddenly exhausted to his bones. *All that work to break out. How do we break back in?*

Seeing the island lent no inspiration. His mind felt like a blank sheet of paper, a hollowed-out egg containing no ideas. Jack suddenly felt bankrupt without a strategy. Tension crawled up his spine, demanding he think harder. *Come up with something.* "If we head into the bay, they'll be all over us. We can fight them off from the *Brigand* but once we're on foot, they'll have us. If we charge through the dock gate, they'll bottleneck the entrance with attercops."

"Great work." Rooker snorted. "Ya just pointed out all the obvious problems of a siege." Rooker picked up a big conch shell, brought the thing to his lips, and blew it like a trumpet, sounding a long, loud note. "Attack!"

Jack looked at him, unimpressed. *I don't think that was as funny as you think it was.*

Killjoy.

Jack frowned. "We can't get in from the prisoner side of the wall, we can't go through the shiq tunnels without phosphorus."

"We could fly in." Rooker tossed him an apple.

Jack caught it and scowled. "Will you stop screwing around? We can't *fly* in! We might as well just walk up to the gate and say, 'Open Sesame'!"

Rooker hooked an eyebrow. "What's *opensaysame*?"

"Magic word. Opened the door to Ali Baba's treasure cave." Jack frowned, frustrated. "It's just a stupid story. Forget it."

"'Open says me.'" Rooker harrumphed. "Dumbest password I ever heard. Eat yer apple."

Jack ignored him and worked the puzzle in his mind, unable to solve it, growing more discouraged.

"Ya know what I *want* to do." Rooker made a blade of his hand and thrust it forward. "Straddle the whole pier. Just run straight down it and crush every skiff on either side."

Jack almost smiled. "That would be a pretty sight. Wouldn't do us any good."

"Wait, I've got it." Rooker snapped his fingers, igniting a spark of flame. "We sneak in under cover of darkness."

The laugh hit Jack before he knew it was coming. He imagined the two of them in robber's masks and caps like a bad cartoon, creeping quietly into a moonlit swarm of fanged shiq.

As Jack laughed, Rooker nodded. "There ya go."

"Will you..." Jack laughed. "*Please* stop screwing around."

"Eat yer apple."

Jack leaned back, shut his eyes, and bit into the apple. Unbidden, a song came to him. An old one, from before his mom had died, back when Jack had loved memorizing lists. She had put it to the tune of 'Yankee Doodle Dandy.' Dreamily, he sang:

> *With on for after at by in*
> *Against because of near between*
> *Beside from under down below*
> *Through over up within without*
> *About above among around*

Before behind between and off
Are prepositions, every one,
When followed by a noun.

Rooker eyeballed him like he'd just eaten a raw razorsquid. "What the hell was *that*?"

"Old Toshan song." Jack felt woozy, like he was half in a daydream. "Ways to get in. On. Over. Up." Jack eyed the top of the Institute wall. Another fantasy flitted before Jack's eyes. "I would love to see what the *Brigand* could do with a paraglider."

"A pair of what?"

Jack chuckled. "It's like a big kite. Wings you strap to your back. Extend a rope off the back of the *Brigand*, full speed, quick start, pulls the kite up into the sky." He'd seen paragliders in Mexico with his dad. With the right tools, the *Brigand* could make him fly. Catch the right draft, let go at the right moment, and he could land right on top of the Locke Institute.

Rooker snorted. "So ya *can* fly."

"Glide." Jack shook off the idea. "If I had time to build a glider. And test it. And figure out how to fly it." Jack dropped his chin. "Maybe."

"Are all Toshans like this?" Rooker shook his head. "How do ya know all this stuff?"

"Encyclopedias mostly. Books," Jack said. "Wikipedia. Lots of how-to videos."

"Videos." Rooker folded his arms. "Is that like the... moving picture of you and yer da?"

Jack remembered Gerba had shown Rooker a video of him in Chicago. That seemed like a million years ago. "Yeah. Like that."

"I like those mountains made of mirrors," Rooker said. "I'd look pretty good on one of those."

Jack chuckled. "Yeah."

A long pause passed, the luffing of the sail the only sound as they stared at the Locke Institute, hoping for inspiration to strike. Little by little, Jack felt his conscience, his own little Jimmy Cricket, gnawing at his stomach. *If you don't come up with something, they're all going to die.* A bead of sweat trickled down his neck.

Jack found himself speaking without meaning to. "I keep thinking about Patch."

"Yeah," said Rooker. "Me too."

"And her baby. Her moggie." Jack's brow furrowed. "Why's it called a moggie?"

"I don't know. That's just what it's called." Rooker glanced at him. "No jinx-cats in the Tosh, eh?"

"I wish." Jack shook his head, hoping he could come up with a solution, but the truth was he didn't even know if Patch and the others were still alive. Even if they were, he didn't know how to find them. They could be anywhere, inside the Institute, in the camps, fed to the strîgoi, fed to the shiq, dumped in the sea, or simply dead. When he'd last seen them, Copper Dave had been gravely injured, struck down by Gerba. Yenrab had been out cold. And Farah... Jack's mind drifted to a stop. The nebbish little alchemist reminded Jack so much of himself. Both of them, given their preference, would probably just sit and read together, hunkered in some comfy chairs under some blankets with some hot cocoa. But Farah was probably dead by now. He could do nothing to save her, or any of them. He was helpless. He couldn't do anything at all. They deserved better from him. And he had failed them.

I'm sorry...

He felt a sob hitch in his chest.

"Hey, *knock it off.*"

Jack's head snapped up to see Rooker scowling at him. "What?" His sadness ignited into anger like gasoline, burning the last of the fuel he had left. "Are you going to tell me I need to toughen up?"

"No. *Lighten* up, Jack." Rooker blew out a breath. "I been trying to get ya to unclench yer ass the whole time we've been sittin' here. It's like yer immune. Ya keep twisting yerself in knots." He spread his arms. "Ya can't fix every problem."

Jack hung his head. "I have to fix *this* one."

"No. Ya don't. Yer not alone, remember?" Rooker leaned in. "The world ain't all on yer shoulders."

Jack squinted an eye at him. "What does that mean?"

"It means eat the wasteka apple."

Jack crunched into the apple and felt the sweet juice on his tongue.

"Now shut up." Rooker pointed at the Institute. "She's a trol wizard with fifty attercops, twice as many acolytes, and a baby spider-dragon. There's no way we're getting Patch without a fight, and our only shot of winning a fight is *with Nepenthe*."

"I don't—"

Rooker ignored him. "The fastest way to your whomping stick is straight up the wall. The climb isn't that bad. I did a third of it when I stole that Caged Eight rune we used in the caves. It's fine as long as ya don't fall." He spoke like it was the simplest thing in the world. "So that's what we do."

"But I—"

"Climb the wall, get yer stick, find our mates." He turned to Jack. "Ya got a better plan than that?"

Jack took one last search around his brain for ideas and came up empty. "No."

Rooker nodded once. "Then that's the plan. No more thinking. Yer done."

Jack blinked. Something let go inside him, an anxious set of talons that had gripped him since sunup. Rooker's words had set him free. There were a million problems with the plan, not the least of which was how to get to the wall in the first place. But Jack didn't need to fix it; Rooker had the wheel. "Okay." Jack felt his body uncoil and sagged against the deck like a soldier relieved of duty. "Okay."

"*Finally.*" Rooker blew through his lips. "Sheesh. Yer like a dog with a bone." He stood. "I'm gonna get us some bacon. Ya want bacon?"

"I'm not making any more decisions."

"Then bacon."

Rooker returned with an entire rasher of bacon thick as his arm. "Cooker's over here." He flipped up a hatch in the deckrail, revealing a hidden griddle installed into the rail. "Get that goin' for me, would ya?" Jack searched for a way to light a fire in the ashy tin box beneath the griddle but found nothing, not even a heat source. Rooker's voice came over his shoulder. "Snap yer fingers."

Jack obeyed. On his snap, the underside of the griddle *whumphed* into a low carpet of fire as steady as a Viking stovetop. Jack grinned and watched the blue flame dance. "See?" said Rooker. "Yer a damn wizard. Get cookin'."

Jack threw the bacon on the griddle. He found a set of cooking tongs and went to work keeping the slabs flat against the griddle as it sizzled pork fat. It felt good, a simple series of tasks, a slow, easy problem he could solve. He inhaled the scent of cooking bacon and suddenly felt much better. Bacon solves most problems.

"Hey?" said Rooker.

"Hey?"

"Ya think Billy Pilgrim might write a song about me? About us?"

Jack chuckled and handed Rooker a slice of bacon with the tongs. "I think if we live past sunset, you'll get all the songs you want."

"Pilgrim's would be the best." Rooker refilled Jack's tin cup with coffee. "Load up on that." He sat next to Jack and settled back into a slouch. "Lord of Sea and Sky, that boy can sing."

Yes, he can. Jack swallowed the coffee, feeling the heat and the caffeine combine for a good old-fashioned pick-me-up. An idea came with the next sip. "*Bessie.* Your singing saber. Is that on board?"

Rooker blinked, impressed. "I'm surprised ya remember the ol' girl."

"You thought I wouldn't remember your majik saber?" Jack snorted. "I'm not *that* tired."

Rooker sipped coffee and hooked a thumb through his belt. "Ol' Bessie. Mm. Best sword I ever touched. Stung like a bee." He shrugged. "Gerba took her. Long gone." He raised his mug, toasting his fallen blade.

They sat in silence. Rooker stirred his coffee with his bacon, sucked it dry, ate it, then burped. "Ya ever hear of a pinwheel gambit?"

"No."

"Pickpocketing scam." Rooker propped a foot against the mast. "The beggar kids in Chult would sell these cute little pinwheels, real shiny pink ones. Aggressive little bastards. 'Mister, mister, look how pretty! Five pennies!' They'd shove it right in yer face. Tell ya all about the pinwheel, how it would make a super gift for yer daughter or yer wife, haggle ya on the price, all while three other kids lifted your purse. They forced the mark to focus on a feint. Watch the right hand while the left hand picks ya clean." He drained his coffee. "That's what we need. A pink pinwheel."

Jack shrugged. "I'm sorry to say I don't have one up my sleeve right now."

"So tell me something else." Rooker hooked another slice of bacon. "Tell me about the mountains of mirrors. Yer skyscratchers."

Jack was suddenly transported back home. He imagined the Loop, Streeterville, the Magnificent Mile, the Gold Coast. He could feel the wind off of Lake Michigan and longed for the familiar skyline. "Skyscrapers are everywhere in Chicago. Willis. Hancock. The Trib. A hundred and thirty-eight mountains made of mirrors, stacked one after another, each one engineered to perfection." Jack chuckled. It was a rose-colored view of Chicago, but a touch of homesickness will do that. "Glorious."

"Tell me more," Rooker murmured, half-napping. "What about those horseless carriages?"

"Hondas. Teslas. Audis. Lamborghinis." Jack leaned back, shutting his eyes. "They make all kinds, all colors, all sizes. And some of them you wouldn't believe..." Jack felt his mind drifting. "There are car races. There's one called the Indy 500 with cars that go so fast you can barely see them go by. Airplanes. Computers. Satellites. You can find out anything in five seconds. Anything. A world-size library in your pocket."

"So that's why ya know so much." Rooker chuckled. "I just need better pockets."

Jack barely heard him. "Anybody can know what I know. Anybody. Copernicus to Curie, Archimedes to Oppenheimer, we can know everything in the universe. How to travel in space, how to harness the atom, when it's going to rain next. We know everything." He opened his eyes and stared at the griddle, aware of the exhaustion breaking over him. "I used to think that knowing everything would somehow... fix me. Make me better. But all that... knowing... and I was still alone. There wasn't a code or a formula to make people *like* me... How to make friends. I tried. I really, really tried. But there was always something else pulling them away. Nobody was like you."

Jack looked up at Rooker. "When I'm with you, I'm just... *with* you. You're never waiting to move on to someone else."

Rooker said nothing, keeping his mouth shut for once.

Jack closed his eyes and just rested for a while. The words escaped before he knew they were coming. "You know Shadow?"

Rooker nodded. "Yeah, I know yer wolf. Shows up when yer spooked."

"You haven't seen him today, right?"

"Come to think of it, no." Rooker chuckled under his breath. "Not even when we were up against Xeusia. Ya run him off?"

"No. You did." Jack opened his eyes to find Rooker looking at him, curious. "He doesn't come around when you're with me." Jack looked his brother in the eye. "I'm not scared when I'm with you."

A long silence. "Yeah," Rooker said quietly. "Jasper is usually two steps behind me, waiting to stick a knife in my back. But I ain't heard his voice since ya saved my neck. And my guess is I ain't gonna hear from him again. Not while yer around."

Jack closed his eyes. "In my world, there's a Japanese tradition called kintsugi. When an important piece of pottery shatters, a tea set or a family heirloom, they don't throw it away. They don't give up on it. They fuse it back together with gold. The craftsmen don't try to hide the cracks or pretend the damage didn't happen, they accentuate it. You can still see the fracture, but now the artistry is better and more beautiful than it was before. The vase survives, stronger for having broken." He turned to Rooker. "I think that's us."

The pirate eyed Jack and allowed himself a slow smile. "Maybe you and me are just what you and me need."

Both men nodded. Nothing more needed to be said.

Jack Swift let the wind riffle his hair and sat in peace with his brother.

"No point savin' bacon." Rooker scooped the last piece of sizzling pork off the skillet and placed it next to Jack. "You take that one." He got to his feet. "Ya want anything else before we go?"

Jack closed his eyes, unable to come up with a response. He was tired. *So tired.*

"What the hell do you want?"

Jack's eyes snapped open. The shout was not Rooker's.

It was a woman's voice, sharp and biting. Jack shot Rooker a look, eyes wide. "What was that?"

Rooker showed entirely too many teeth, like a smiling dog. He slung one elbow over the deckrail and looked over the side of the ship. "Heya, Cora."

Jack got to his feet and went to the edge. In the water below was a stunning blonde woman with aquamarine eyes staring up at them. In the crystal-clear sea below, Jack saw a massive tail curl beneath her body.

It's a mermaid.

She did not look happy. "Hello yourself, you lying son of a bitch."

Jack had never seen a mermaid before, never even imagined one outside of cartoons, and Cora wasn't quite what he'd expected. Her long sinuous body was four times the length of a man, porpoise-thin at the hips with a tail that ended in translucent flukes big as a killer whale. She sparkled blue and green scales, but her flesh was pale. Her nose was virtually nonexistent, and Jack saw the inside of her mouth was ringed not with teeth, but needles.

"I was hopin' it would be you." Rooker chuckled. "Out of all the daughters, yer still the prettiest."

"Choke on it," she snapped back. "I came because I have to. You know that."

"No reason we can't be friendly. Cora, meet Jack. Jack, meet Cora." The mermaid jerked her chin at him. Jack raised a numb hand in response. "How'd it go with the Naysayers?"

"I'm not apologizing for that." Cora crossed her arms, pouting prettily. "They offered a lot of coin for you. I completed your task. It just happened to be theirs as well. It was all very above board."

"Did ya at least get paid well?"

"Stiffed me on the bonus."

"Ain't it a shame."

Cora lowered a pretty eyebrow. "Where's the conch?"

Rooker held up the large pink shell he'd used as a trumpet earlier. "Right here."

"Well, throw it overboard." She smiled vindictively. "You've used up your third favor with Daddy."

Rooker chucked the conch over the side and brushed his hands. Jack watched it sink, wondering what, exactly, the hell was going on. *Am I dreaming?*

"I just need a quick favor, darlin'. Won't take a moment, then yer free." Rooker leaned in. "Could ya *not* stab me in the back this time?"

"That costs extra." Cora tilted her blonde head. "What's the offer?"

"Ya can spend the night in my cabin."

The mermaid scowled at him. "Some reward."

Rooker buffed his fingernails. "Remember when Saltz ransomed the Marchioness Rahira?"

Cora blinked, then her aquamarine eyes sparkled. "That gold lamé dress of hers? The one she wore to the Winter Ball?"

"It's in my cabin." Rooker grinned. "If ya keep yer trap shut until nightfall, it's all yours."

The prettiest smile Jack had ever seen crossed Cora's pink lips. "Honey, you got yourself a deal."

Minutes later, Jack was certain this was no dream. He, Rooker, and Cora knelt on the starboard outrigger of the *Venture Brigand*, close to the water. At some point, Rooker had fitted him with a shoulder belt that had a staff jammed through two loops in the back, along with a sheathed hawkbill knife and a heavy rope. The pirate carried another rope with a grappling hook and wore a katana. The ship was no longer still. It raced straight at Huánghūn. Water splashed in Jack's face, nearly blinding him as they sped dead ahead.

There was no attempt at subtlety.

The *Venture Brigand* cut through the water like a missile launched straight at the Locke Institute. She entered the bay like an opera singer walking on stage, arms wide, belting a high C.

Squinting through the sea spray, Jack watched Institute ships weigh anchor and move to attack position. Yellowjacket sailors mounted their harpoon bows, yelling. Jack clapped his tricorn hat against his head as the wind tried to take it. *This is crazy, this is crazy, this is—*

"*This is not a plan!*" Jack shouted over the wind.

Rooker crouched on the outrigger beside him, a wicked grin on his face. "I told ya, yer too uptight! Just relax!" Jack peeked at Cora, who was crouched beside him on the outrigger. Her mer-tail was gone, replaced by long, pale legs. Completely nude, she guzzled at a bottle of Roi-Tan. Jack averted his eyes, feeling the furthest thing from relaxed.

Chugging the bottle, Cora handed Jack a rope with a loop tied into it. She took a break from the booze just long enough to utter four words. "Hand through the loop."

As the *Venture Brigand* hit the middle of the bay, Rooker tapped his rings against the outrigger. "Okay, girl, come about. Not too quick. Give 'em some hope." Jack felt the ship shift beneath him, turning.

Jack looked at Rooker, confused. "I don't unders—"

Rooker threw him in.

Jack hit the water with a smack. He felt the impact in his bones, the sudden shock of it, the rush of the water, then felt himself yanked suddenly by his wrist. Wondering if Rooker had tied him to the boat, Jack looked up to see the *Venture Brigand*'s skis from below, a billowing shear of foam. They turned away from him, departing for open sea. Jack was pulled in another direction.

He twisted sideways, bludgeoned in the wake of a giant fin. A boot clocked him in the face and Jack saw Rooker twisting on the rope ahead of him. Jack felt another thrust of water batter him and realized they were both being dragged by the mermaid.

Cora shot through the water, towing them like a speedboat hauling a pair of tuna. Jack felt his body spin, twisting on the line in an uncontrolled spiral of bubbles. He'd never felt anything so quick in his life; it was like being dragged behind an atomic submarine. He felt his eyelids joggle, battered by the speed of the water. He had not had a chance to draw breath before he'd hit, and his lungs screamed for air.

I'm gonna... pass out...

Suddenly the line went slack. Jack drifted to a near stop, levitating forty feet under the water like an astronaut in space. Close by, Cora circled lazily. Her sinewy body moved close to his, passed between his legs, and brushed up against his belly. Crawling up his chest, Cora placed webbed fingers against his cheeks and moved her face close to his. She kissed him.

As their mouths moved together, Jack felt oxygen travel into his throat, fresh and sweet. As he breathed her air like a respirator, he did not think about how impossible it was or marvel at the tiny bubbles that joined their mouths or wonder why her breath tasted like peppermint. All he could think was how good her lips felt on his. That kiss alone was better than a good night's sleep.

She flicked her tongue and broke the connection. She moved to Rooker. Jack saw them kiss and averted his eyes to watch several

Institute ships soar by above him, chasing the escaping *Brigand*. Cora let go of Rooker and kicked away, pulling the tow line tight. Jack saw Rooker smile at him underwater, then they were underway again.

As the water grew shallow, Jack looked for the shore. Arcing over a rock spire, he realized they were already there. Cora's speed was astounding. As the water came to an end, Cora halted, letting the men drift past her. Jack pawed at the rock and pulled himself above the surface. Some part of him was surprised to find his hat still clenched in his fist.

Gasping for air, he tumbled onto the narrow beach at the base of the Institute wall. He wiped water out of his eyes to discover Rooker already running for cover. Jack followed. They ducked behind a rock shelf and spun to check the bay. Every boat in the harbor pursued the *Venture Brigand* as she sailed breezily away, the biggest pink pinwheel in the world.

Cora floated in the water, a bobbing head.

"Thanks, darlin'," Rooker whispered. "See ya on the ship."

Jack leaned on a rock and stared at the mermaid, panting. "Th at... that was the most incredible experience of my life."

"Get bent." Cora flicked her tail and was gone.

Jack stayed where he was, catching his breath. The sudden exhilaration of speeding underwater stuck with him, his body still humming with the tingle of Cora's lips on his.

"Hey?" Rooker looked at him. *Feelin' better? Can ya do this?*

As long as you're with me... Jack placed his dripping hat firmly on his head and pulled down the brim. *...I can do anything.* "Hey."

SEILSCHAFT

The proper function of man is to live,
not to exist.
I shall not waste my days
in trying to prolong them.

Jack London

"**H**EY!" ROOKER HEARD A shout from the dock and ducked for cover, sure they'd been spotted. He grabbed Jack's bandolier and yanked him to the sand. *Stay down.*

On the docks, half a dozen acolytes yelled to each other, but their eyes were on the *Venture Brigand*. The pink pinwheel was working; no one had noticed they'd come ashore. As the yellowjacket ships gave chase, Rooker wondered if Cora was already back on board and looting his closet. Another shout rose from the dock gate. Rooker couldn't see who was yelling, but it must have been a boss because the scattered acolytes moved quickly toward the dock gate in the wall. *They're bottlenecking the doorway, just like Jack said.*

Rooker held his breath and waited, but no further alarm was raised. *Good.* He spared a glance for the *Venture Brigand*; she was cruising just slow enough to lure the ships after her, waving red sails like a matador to a herd of bulls. *If I don't come back, just keep goin', girl. Find a good man this time.*

No, she sighed.

Rooker chuckled and glanced at the wall above him. As bad as the climb had been from the assembly yard to steal the Caged Eight, the sea side of the wall was worse. The cliff was just as steep here and, thanks to the continuous ocean spray, the bottom section looked slippery as a snot otter.

Rooker checked the docks one last time and spared a glance at Jack. The kid was still mooning over Cora, staring at the spot she'd gone under. "She's amazing."

Mermaids had a majik seductiveness to them, but Rooker knew the truth; they'd kill and eat a sailor for fun. "She's just a bandit with a great rack." Rooker checked his gear, realizing he'd somehow lost his rope on their dash to shore. *Dammit, there goes the grappling hook.* He repositioned the katana slung over his back. It was his original blade, the one he'd carried as a pilot for years before he'd won Bessie in the duel with Captain Saltz. Next to the singing saber the katana was as ugly as a mungfish, but plenty sharp. It would serve just fine. He flicked the little catch over the tsuba, the handguard disc, and affixed the sword to the sheath. *No sense losing it halfway up the wall.*

He hauled Jack to his feet and repositioned bubba's bandolero. A six-foot staff was a stupid weapon, but it was the only thing the kid was any good with. "All right, all we have to do is climb to the top. It's gonna be eas—"

The world shook. For a moment, Rooker thought he had been struck with palsy; the rock jiggled around him as he stood on unsteady feet. After a moment, he realized it wasn't his body; it was the island.

Earthquakes were common enough on Huánghūn, but this was the strongest tremor Rooker had ever felt. He managed to keep his feet but suffered the sudden, humbling understanding that the island was very, very big and he was very, very small. Each moment the quake continued, Rooker expected the world would suddenly lurch sideways and knock him into the sea. After a moment, the trembling stopped, started again, then finally ground to a halt. Rooker eyed Jack.

The kid breathed, distressed. "You were saying?"

Rooker swore. He hadn't felt the earthquakes on the *Brigand*, and he certainly hadn't been able to see them from the sea. He watched little pebbles fall from the cliff, shaken loose by the tremor. He had a sickening feeling he was about to find out how the pebbles felt. "Bad luck." He gritted his teeth and strode for the wall. "Nothing for it."

"Wait." Jack snatched his elbow. The kid unslung the rope from his shoulder and unspooled thirty feet of sturdy, braided jute. "We've got it. We might as well use it."

"I lost the grapple on the way in." Rooker glanced up the rock face, trying to pick out a route. *The whole thing looks like a wall of green snot.* He scowled, wondering how they were going to pull this off. "Keep it. We might need it later."

"No, we tie off to each other like mountain climbers." Jack raised the jute rope, a smile on his face. "A seilschaft, a rope team."

Rooker blinked. "Why?"

"If I fall, you stop me."

Ol' Black Jack had had some dumb ideas in his time, but this one took the cake. "Or you pull me off the wall."

Jack cocked his head. "Do you really wanna live without me?"

Rooker snorted. "Ya serious, bubba?" He eyed the rope and imagined Jack's weight jerking him off the wall and pulling them both to their doom. "Seems like a good way to get killed."

"*All* of this is a good way to get killed. Who are you gonna listen to?" Jack went about fastening the rope around his waist.

Rooker blew air through his nose. "That's not the right knot." He took the thing and tied it into a proper double figure eight, then bound another around his own waist. Secure, he double-checked the ropes were tight. "Happy?"

"Not particularly." Jack chuckled and repositioned the loop around his waist.

Rooker checked the wall again. For the first time, he noticed it was almost entirely in shadow; the sun had already abandoned this half of the butte. They were running out of time.

Jack stared up the cliff face and let out a long breath. "There is almost no chance I could have done this a year ago."

"There's almost no chance ya can do it now." Rooker slapped him on the back. "Five gold marks say I beat you to the top."

"You're on."

Rooker found his first handhold and began to climb.

Moss was the biggest problem. It was easy to mistake the big clumps for rocks. When Rooker took hold of one, it crumbled like tissue paper and left him scrambling for balance. Nearly the whole bottom quarter of the wall was dotted with treacherous lichen, and Rooker had to pick his way slowly and carefully, removing little green booby traps as he went. In addition, the spray of the water made every surface slippery and wet, so he could only go for the deepest handholds. Somehow, Jack was already ahead of him. Rooker scurried up another section, looking for a path to catch up and finding one. He spotted a nice handhold and slid his way toward it. Reaching with outstretched fingers, he strained to grip the rock, but it was just a fraction too far. He stretched himself further, balanced on one wet boot, and his foot slipped into the air.

He fell. Shouting, his arms pinwheeled in midair. A sickening, plummeting sense of sheer panic overwhelmed him. Falling. He hit the rocky beach flat on his back, narrowly avoiding a sharp rock that would have skewered him through. Pain hit him and his lungs shot out a painful *whuff* of air. He blinked. *Still alive.* He dragged one elbow beneath him, propped himself up on it, and blinked up at Jack.

"You okay?" Jack called from fifteen feet up. Rooker realized his fall had been so short the rope hadn't even reached its full length; it hung slack along the wall. *Damn sailshaft didn't do a thing to stop me. Useless idea.*

"I'm fine." Rooker got to his feet and felt a sharp stab in his kidney. *Oww.* "Perfect."

"Well, get moving. I don't wanna wait for you all day."

Rooker snarled and attacked the wall. Quickly, he fought his way back to the section he'd just traversed, letting anger and fear fuel his climb. Near where he had slipped, he changed course and followed Jack's path. The distance between them grew shorter, but Jack ascended like a monkey. *Kid's always been a good climber.*

Rooker ripped a hunk of moss out of his way and struggled to catch up. He put his back into it and hauled himself up one outcrop after another. In minutes, he was sweating through his shirt. He paused, wiped his brow on a forearm, and looked down to find the beach was much farther away. If he slipped now, he would not get back up again.

Swallowing, he focused on the next handhold.

Breathing harder, Rooker felt his fingers sing in pain with the effort. He switched his weight to his toes, reminding himself there was a long way to go and his hands couldn't take him the whole way. *Save 'em for when ya need 'em.*

Leaving the slippery wetness behind, Rooker found his speed increase as reliable steps became easier to find. The loop of jute rope grew slack as he moved closer to Jack. He caught up, and the two of them labored side by side up the cliff, the rope hanging in a long U between them. As both men moved faster, a sense of competition grew, each trying to outwork the other. Rooker's need to pass the kid became more urgent than the pain in his fingertips. He dug in and pushed harder. *I'm not gonna let him beat me to the top.*

"Stop." Jack's harsh whisper cut the air.

Rooker went still, his weight frozen on one foot. Clutching to the wall, he saw Jack jerk his chin toward the docks. Rooker turned to see two white-robed acolytes returning from the far end of the pier, their faces masked by niqabs. He had no idea if the Institute workers could see him on the cliff face. It was impossible to tell. The acolytes were a long way off, but Rooker doubted his crimson shirt helped him blend in. If he and Jack were spotted, it was all over.

Lord of Sea and Sky, gimmie some luck one time. Just one time.

The acolytes moved closer, tromping steadily down the pier. Rooker felt like they had to be staring right at him, they had to be, but the masked figures just kept on walking, their pace unbroken. Finally, the acolytes passed into the dock gate without any outward sign they had seen the men hanging from the wall. Rooker waited for a shout, knowing the robed figures must have played it clever, that they'd waited to sound the alarm until they'd made it back to the dock gate. But nothing came. *Or maybe it's hard to see outta those hoods. Lucky.*

"Okay," Rooker breathed out. "Let's g—"

Another earthquake hit. Rooker seized the wall and clutched at it with all his strength as the mountain jerked, yanking him back and forth. The world went side to side, up and down, all at the same time. Dust fell around him, got in his mouth and hair. Flattening his body against the rock, Rooker jammed his eyes shut and put everything he had into holding on. He listened for Jack's scream, knowing if he heard it, he was about to get yanked into thin air. His grip wasn't strong enough. The earthquake trembled one hand free and Rooker slapped it against the rock, trying to find another handhold. And just like that, it was over.

Ah. Ah. He panted. *Don't. Let. Go.*

He pressed his forehead against the wall and felt cool rock against his skin, his breathing shallow and rapid. He could feel his heartbeat in his fingertips. Rooker forced his eyes open to find Jack staring at him, his face white as a sheet.

Rooker exhaled through his nose, trying to get himself under control. He glanced at Jack and forced one word from his dry throat. "Nepenthe."

Jack nodded. "Nepenthe."

They climbed.

Fear drove him like a whip. He scrambled past Jack, who struggled with his footing. *He's too worried about falling. The longer we stay on this rock, the more likely we die.* Rooker glanced at the kid and saw sweat pour down his face, the tendons in his hands standing out like ropes.

Both of them were breathing too heavily to speak. Rooker jerked his chin. *You okay?*

No, but what else am I gonna do? Jack pulled himself up another foot.

Rooker kept moving and left Jack behind. As he passed the halfway mark, his arms felt tight as violin strings; his shoulders strained with every clawed movement. The wind picked up, pushing against him as if it were trying to pull him loose like an autumn leaf. As Rooker held on, he felt a new wetness in the handhold and realized his fingers were bleeding.

"Hey?" came Jack's voice below. It was frightened, tremulous. "Hey?"

"Incoming."

Rooker scowled. *Incoming? We're on the middle of a cliff—*

He saw it.

Nearly a quarter mile away, a shape moved toward them on the cliff face, quick and nimble, tucked in tight against the wall. From here it was nothing but a lumpy shadow. A lumpy, eight-legged shadow.

"*Attercop,*" he spat. "Son of a bitch."

"I thought they were all—"

"I told ya to stop thinkin'! *Go!*" Rooker redoubled his efforts and hauled himself up the wall. A rock slipped out from under his foot and he found himself hanging by one hand. Scrabbling for purchase, he got his boots back on the wall and kept climbing.

A third of the wall remained between him and the top.

Jack scratched against the rock, trying to keep up, but the slack in the rope grew tight. Rooker looked up. The top was only ten yards away. He could see the roots of a bush growing on top of the wall, its green leaves flickering in the wind. *So close.*

Might as well be a mile. The attercop was covering the distance too quickly. Rooker could see the big spider's orange and black markings and a familiar skull pattern. It sped at them sideways, running full tilt. There was no way they would reach the top before the 'cop was on them.

Jack was closest. It would attack him first, and the kid knew it. He struggled for a handhold, straining. *He'll never make it in time.*

"Move!" Rooker yelled.

Jack's voice was quiet. "It's Winston."

Rooker recognized the markings now. He didn't know if the Caged Eight still controlled the attercops, but Winston had his own reasons to want them dead. As the big spider raced toward them, Rooker saw Winston's fangs flicker against each other, hungry.

Jack's voice was almost a whisper. "He's gonna rip me right off the wall."

Rooker flicked the catch free and drew his katana. "Get ready."

Jack unslung his quarterstaff and the two men watched Winston come at them like a charging bull galloping along the side of the wall.

There's no way to win. He's too fast, too big, too sticky. He'll slaughter us.

Rooker grit his teeth and wished for a harpoon bow.

Unless we get to him first.

"Anchor that stick," he commanded and crawled the opposite way from Jack and Winston. "Both ends." The kid obeyed and jammed his staff into a crack, wedging it in tight. Rooker climbed, stretching the rope to its limit as the attercop galloped closer.

"Ya wedged in good?"

"Yeah."

"*Sailshaft* good?"

Jack's voice was shrill as Winston closed in on him. *"Yes!"*

"Then hold on tight, bubba."

Rooker gauged the distance. *Wait.* He saw venom drip from Winston's eager fangs. *Wait.*

"Don't let go," Rooker said, taking a deep breath. "Please."

"I won't!"

Trust him.

Rooker dropped off the cliff.

Terror seized him. A white jolt of lightning shot through his brain as he fell. His feet skidded against the wall as he dropped. Screaming, Rooker forced his legs to run, his boots skipping against the rock. The rope pulled tight and Rooker felt the jute cord cut into his belly and jerk the wind out of him. He heard Jack scream as his full weight hit. Jack hung on to the staff for both their lives.

Don't let go.

Rooker's boots found purchase and ran sideways against the wall, his body horizontal. As he reached the bottom of the arc, he put his thighs into it. The rope swung him like a pendulum up the far side. As he swung upward, Rooker felt himself losing momentum.

Dig! Dig!

His feet thundered against the rock, forcing him upward. He found an edge to push off and launched himself toward the sky. Just as Winston lunged at Jack, Rooker arrived at the zenith of his arc and drove his katana into the attercop's gut.

Winston screamed.

Rooker snatched a fistful of Winston's fur and hung on for dear life. He cut off one of the attercop's legs, then another, watching them tumble, twitching, into thin air. Hooking a leg over Winston's abdomen, he grabbed the spider's neck. The big attercop writhed beneath him, screaming, trying to get away. "Stop! Let me go!"

"Whatever you say, boss."

Rooker drove the katana through the attercop's head.

Winston shuddered and fell. Rooker fell with him, riding the body. He felt the rope clench his waist tight and his fall came to a sudden end. The katana was jerked out of his hand, the blade stuck inside Winston's head. The boss attercop's six remaining legs flailed wildly, and Winston squealed like a pig as he smashed into the rocks in an explosion of green snot.

Hanging, Rooker spit on Winston. He snatched the wall and got a foothold. Looking up, he saw Jack's face. The kid looked terrified and elated at the same time, one arm hooked around the staff. He let out a breath, and a drop of his sweat fell past Rooker's shoulder.

"Okay, I'll admit it," Rooker panted. "The rope was a good idea."

Jack laughed, hanging on the staff. "That was... one hell... of a trust fall."

Rooker climbed to him. The kid's forehead was beaded in sweat and his arms shook. "Can ya climb?"

Jack shook his head, panting. "It's all I can do... to hold on."

"Hang tight." He climbed. Rooker was in the best shape of his life but it almost wasn't enough. Jittery fingers clasped the rock. He forced himself to hang on with each new handhold, gripping with all his failing strength. His arms shivered, quaking from the strain.

Suddenly there were plant roots in front of his eyes. Grabbing them, Rooker pulled himself over the top of the cliff and rolled onto flat ground. Quickly, he wrapped the rope around a rock, anchoring it, then let out a breath. *Safe.* He flicked his fingers, trying to get blood back into them. He glanced around the rooftop of the Institute to see if anyone had spotted him. The place was deserted, but what Rooker saw stopped him cold.

He was face to face with the site of his execution.

Brutalized and broken, the scaffold was laid to waste. Jack had destroyed the thing completely. The two pillars of the bell tower were sheared off like severed fingers. The stone dais of the Agrat-ban-Haifa now held no more importance than an empty stage.

The rooftop of the Institute was abandoned, but Rooker wouldn't have noticed a hundred acolytes. All he heard was the creak of the noose, the snap of his neck. His hand darted to his throat as he felt the rope dig in. He remembered dying, again and again, right there.

But now the site of his execution was only a memory, an empty, invisible space above the Institute, only sky.

Rooker took a breath and turned his attention to the rope. He moved to the edge to find Jack had dropped his staff and dangled limp in midair, hanging from the jute rope. *I got you, bubba.*

Rooker set his feet and hauled Jack up the rest of the way. As he came over the edge, Jack threw himself on his back in much the same way Rooker had, panting.

"Thank... you..."

Rooker dragged him to his feet. "Don't stop. We need Nepenthe. My sword's gone, yer staff's gone, and we're not gonna win a fight with harsh language." Jack nodded and followed.

Rooker passed a scattering of tools and barrels, some empty tables, and Gerba's morning announcement stage. Her hourglass lay dormant, never to be turned again. The pirate made for the steps down into the Institute itself when Jack whispered, "Do you hear that?"

The sound was like the ocean, a low roar that ebbed and flowed, but it came from the wrong side of the rock. Curious, Rooker stepped to the edge and peered down into the yard.

The assembly looked like a castle siege. Shouting and violent, the throng of prisoners fought toe to toe with the giant spiders. Two attercops lay dead, sprawled out in eight-pointed stars on the hardpack. One had been trampled to paste. Trapped prisoners screamed, bound in webbing, unable to flee or fight. Dozens more lay bleeding or dead.

Several 'cops occupied the wall, crawling over each other, hurling rocks down on the prisoners, who hurled them right back. Convicts attempted to climb the wall. Attercops threw them off, but the students of the Locke Institute were not giving in. Jackal, Hyena, Vulture, and Buzzard were united in open rebellion.

Jack and Rooker stared down at the prison riot.

"Looks like your execution had an effect," Jack murmured.

"As long as it keeps 'em distracted." Rooker grabbed Jack's shoulder. "Let's move while our luck's holdin'." He covered one eye and crept silently down the steps into the dark.

Gerba's office was half-empty. Hundreds of books were missing, as was most of the furniture. All that was left was her mahogany desk and her hateful rock torture-chair gathering dust in the corner. Rooker paused in the shadows, scanning for attercops or acolytes. Convinced the room was empty, he sprinted toward the hanging curtain that covered Nepenthe.

He heard a noise and took cover behind one of the pillars. He scanned the room but saw nothing. He gestured to Jack and he came, keeping low. Rooker grinned. "Time to get the upper hand."

Rooker slipped the steel lockpick case from his belt, the best set he'd ever owned. There had been six clasps locking Nepenthe to the wall last time he'd seen it; he could only imagine Gerba had added a seventh. *This will take some work.* "Watch my back."

Rooker flung the curtain aside, revealing seven empty locks upon a blank wall.

He felt a painful breath of air escape him, and it felt like he was falling from the wall once more. Only this time there was no rope to hold him up.

Nepenthe was gone.

Chapter

13

HEART
=OF=
HUÁNGHŪN

I find that the harder I work,
the more luck I seem to have.
Thomas Jefferson

NEPENTHE WAS GONE. DISCARDED in a corner of the tunnel, the staff's only purpose now was the illumination it provided, nothing more than a lantern. The elvish blue light was pierced by a single slash of crimson, a flaming eye trapped within the heart of the mountain. That dæmonic eye flared brightly, burning malevolent hatred at Gerba Whipmarples.

The headmistress chipped away at the stone with her tiny rock hammer, careful not to strike too near to any part of RākShasa. She did her best to keep her breath under control, betraying neither exhaustion nor fear. Her position was precarious. One wrong step could kill her, which would be a tragedy so close to accomplishing her goal.

In her exploration of the rock adjacent to the dæmon's eye, she had found a bony chin, part of a pale white bicep, an edged hunk of shoulder. Then she discovered the dæmon's rib cage, and she had her path. Her cautious excavation revealed the Dæmon Crownéd had been trapped in the earth as it had lunged at the mighty Kos, frozen forever in an outstretched attack like a leaping panther. The dæmon was massive, nearly double Gerba's considerable size. Now she was wedged almost directly beneath the beast, inches away as her hammer chiseled a path down the great dæmon's body more carefully than an archaeologist unearthing a pharaoh's tomb.

She forced herself to hum a tune as she worked.

RākShasa radiated darker and more malignant *wikk* than Gerba Whipmarples had dreamt possible. Only the toll of the Agrat-ban-Haifa had come close, but this was nothing like the clean majik of the Great Bell, even after it had been perverted with the Caged Eight. This was the dark, sadistic malice of a Dæmon Crownéd. Waves of fury and loathing poured over her like a bloody river over a waterfall, again and again, each pulse more powerful and vengeful than the last. *So much power.*

She dared not chip away too much. If she loosed RākŞhasa's arm from its rocky tomb, the beast would savage her to bloody strips in the time it took to take her last breath.

It watched her with that one red eye, waiting for her to make a mistake.

But I have control.

"I see that look in your eye, dearie." Gerba chiseled her way down the entombed dæmon's chest. "But you must understand that I hold you in the highest regard. I have, in fact, spent the last decade trying to find you. To release you. To free you. I have spared no cost in the pursuit of serving you. Millions of marks spent for hundreds of slaves to muster thousands of man-hours of labor, all to excavate you. Thanks to me, your centuries of imprisonment have finally come to an end. It would, perhaps, be only wise to consider how grateful you might be."

RākŞhasa's single exposed eye tracked her the same way a tiger tracks a wounded lamb. Another wave of merciless sadism radiated from it, a diabolical corruption, and Gerba Whipmarples felt the desire of the dæmon was nothing more than to tear off her head and feast on her blood.

Now is the time for caution.

"I fear your emotions may blind you to the merits of my attention." She chipped her way down to where the thing's stomach should be, careful not to get too close. "But I feel confident that a creature of your nearly deific significance will eventually comprehend. You are seasoned enough, ancient enough, to summon your wisdom in this moment. I have the utmost faith that you will come to see things the correct way."

She paused, feeling at the stone. *Here. It must be here.*

"In fact, I know in my deepest heart, my darling, that we shall grow, in time, to become the closest of companions." Gerba drove the hammer into the rock three times, each stroke precise. Black diamonds fell away to reveal RākŞhasa's belly.

Bone-white skin stretched tight over thick muscle beneath bladed ribs. As she watched, a drop of moisture beaded upon the Crownéd's milky flesh and fell directly onto her horn. It hissed smoke as it burned into the chitin, leaving a permanent mark.

Gerba smiled.

"Not to worry, dearest." She reached into her pocket and withdrew the tiny silver knife she had carried for years. RakShasa's one eye bored into her like an acidic needle, a slash of rage burning inside a pale cavity of hate. "This will all be over in a moment. And then, I promise, you will feel *so* much better."

She slit the Dæmon Crownéd's belly open.

Her stroke continued downward, revealing the midnight pit of its guts. Sawing through the dæmon's stomach, the thing's raw intestines were exposed; they twisted like a nest of black adders, writhing above her.

RākŞhasa did not blink.

Gerba forced her hand into the thing's guts.

As her fingers went inside, she stared at the dæmon's single eye. Neither of them blinked, locked in a standoff. A low growl escaped the beast's chest. Gerba pursed her lips and whispered, "*Shh*. I am here now."

Performing her dark surgery, Gerba Whipmarples drove her hand past the blackened guts and into RākŞhasa's ribcage. She explored the cavity for a moment, then felt her fingers close around something hard and sharp.

A joyful gasp split her brown lips.

Dæmons do not have souls. They surrender them to the Deceiver in exchange for their power. It is written that the most nonpareil dæmons, the Crownéd, are gifted a black diamond as a proxy for a heart, a burning rock that houses the shrunken void of their immortal soul, the source of all their agony, their malevolence, their fury, their damnation. Their true name is inscribed upon it in flaming gold to burn for all eternity.

A satisfied smile spilled over Gerba Whipmarples' face.

My prize.

She gripped the shard and pulled it loose with a jerk. Her hand slid through the dæmon's black guts, her arm covered in inky ichor. She opened her fingers to reveal a jet-black diamond big as a man's head, a shard of purest black, spiked on eight sides.

The Heart of Huánghūn.

By Nepenthe's azure light, Gerba Whipmarples gazed upon her prize. As she watched, the shard pulsed once and changed. Like frost on a window, the black of the diamond slowly melted away, revealing the fiery core within. Veins of carnelian curled up within the heart, beating magma, translucent, darkling, unholy.

Gerba laughed. At long last, she abandoned caution, abandoned control. In a giddy frenzy she bashed furiously at the rock, smashing it away, freeing RākṢhasa's legs, its arms, its head, until it dropped on its hands and knees directly on top of her, crouched like an animal ready to feed.

Its bony, corpselike body was thirty feet long, white as a murdered ghost. Each pale hand ended in eight clawed fingers. Eight fanged tentacles ringed its mouth, flickering like bladed limbs. Black smoke issued from its throat, fouling the air around her with toxins. Free of its stone prison for the first time in centuries, RākṢhasa could now murder her in a dozen bloody ways.

It wanted to. With all its hatred, it wanted to.

But Gerba Whipmarples held its heart.

As long as she possessed the shard, she possessed the dæmon.

It crouched over her and hissed but did not attack; the flame in its eyes reflected the Heart of Huánghūn. Gerba did not move, forcing her body to relax. "Now. We are going to get a few things straight." Gerba clenched the dæmon's heart in her fist and stared into its blazing eyes, adopting the same voice she had first used with her horses so very long ago. "The first rule." She smiled. "Obey your betters."

It hissed and lowered its head.

Absently, Gerba reached for Nepenthe and held it up for illumination. RākṢhasa growled low in its bony chest, abhorring the hated elvish majik. And yet as she brought the staff closer, almost touching its flesh, the dæmon did nothing, suffering without revolt.

"Ah!" Something stung her. Gerba glanced down to find a trickle of lava emerging from the stone above. A droplet had landed on her leg and burned into her flesh. Scrabbling back, Gerba watched hot magma seep from the cracks in the rock around RākṢhasa as if the cave were leaking blood. Her eyes landed on the Dæmon Crownéd.

"Carry me."

It glowered at her, burning eyes rimmed with hate.

She felt the dæmon's claws on her back as its fingers wrapped around her, sharp nails on her skin. Then she was lifted and in its arms. RākṢhasa bore her weight easily, like she was a damsel in an old story. Cradling her, it took a lurching step out of its tomb. The thing barely fit inside the cave, mammoth, jagged, and grotesque. One taloned foot settled into the newly formed pool of lava where Gerba had lain and took another step.

The tunnel bucked. An earthquake, a large one, rocked the cavern. Buried under a million tons of stone, black diamonds fell from the ceiling as it shook violently, threatening to bury her under the mountain.

But Gerba Whipmarples was not frightened. Borne in the arms of her magnificent minion, she had nothing left to fear.

Gerba listened to the acolytes cry out as RākṢhasa entered the strîgoi pit. The clamor of the acolytes was not a fearful noise, but a joyful one. Both guards dropped to their knees, bowing before the Dæmon Crownéd, murmuring prayers of thanksgiving in dæmonic tongues. Three other acolytes who had come in search of the headmistress did the same, prostrating themselves before the beast. At the same moment, within the lava pits, the strîgoi threw themselves against the iron cage, heedless of the searing pain iron inflicted upon them, reaching pale, bony arms through the lattice, striving for their master, shrieking an otherworldly wail that split Gerba's skull like an icicle.

Gerba took a moment to savor the scene, watching strîgoi flesh burn and hiss against the iron, watching as acolytes bowed in supplication. Finally, she spoke. "Portia, you may open the cage door."

The acolyte removed her niqab, revealing a pretty face, her eyes sparkling a dark delight. Without hesitation, Portia keyed open the lock to the lava pits and threw the door wide, leaving nothing between her and the dæmons haunting the molten rock beyond. Strîgoi screeched past her, ruffling her robes as they passed. The white devils galloped straight at Gerba, howling bloody fury, ready to tear her apart.

"I have freed you"—she raised the Heart of Huánghūn in her fist—"so that you may kneel."

The strîgoi slowed, black smoke curling from fanged lips. RākṢhasa hissed, then its mighty head lowered and the dæmon bent to one knee. Slowly, it lowered the other leg and bowed before Gerba Whipmarples. It lowered its head and lay flat like a dog. Prostrate on the floor in the universal language of submission, the Dæmon Crownéd groveled at her feet.

Watching, wary, the strîgoi slowly did the same, a pack of wolves following their alpha. Their bodies were rigid and tight with fury, hissing hatred.

But they knelt.

Gerba Whipmarples stood above them, sovereign over all. Her prize was won: domination over every creature in her world. She took a long breath and her heart, at long last, was full.

An enterprising woman, she heard Cant Naysayer's words in her mind, *could become a queen.*

"Headmistress." Portia stared at her with eager eyes. Her hand clenched the niqab she had sworn not to remove until she had lain eyes upon her true master. "May I have the honor?"

O, you do not understand what you are asking, my dear girl. You are the best of them. Gerba shook her head. "Patience, Portia." She turned. "Winnifred." One of the acolytes turned, breathless. Gerba Whipmarples had never seen Winnifred's face. She had imagined it in exquisite detail, the almond eyes, the sharp nose, the high cheekbones, informed by a hundred little clues over the last five years. But still, Gerba felt as if she looked upon a stranger. *I forgot your hair was blonde.* She gave a tender smile to Winnifred, her original acolyte, the girl who had shown her what the promise of immortality could do. "You have been with me the longest. You may be first."

A tear of joy ran down Winnifred's cheek. Her hands folded, head bowed in supplication, the woman walked forward into the writhing mound of strîgoi. They parted before her. Standing at the feet of the great beast, Winnifred finally raised her head. Her eyes shone bright and hopeful as twin stars. "Lord RākṢhasa, Dæmon Crownéd, scion of the Deceiver's Flame, I give to you everything I am, my body, my sou—"

Gerba did not see RākṢhasa's claws move. In one moment, Winnifred stood before it; the next, she was in its massive hands, torn in half at the waist. The beast poured her blood down its throat like a king emptying two cups, guzzling her life to slake its insatiable thirst. It sucked her dry and flung Winnifred's sundered remains against the bars of the cage. Strîgoi lapped up her remaining blood as it dripped onto the beast's taloned feet. RakShasa's eyes met Gerba's.

With a voice like a settling mountain, it spoke one word: *"Unworthy."*

Gerba turned her gaze upon the acolytes. All of them had their niqabs off, their true faces shining and hopeful. To a one, they watched the Dæmon Crownéd with rapt, eager expressions, their mouths open with the ecstasy that only religion could claim, the passion of the devout. Their faith had led them here. Any one of them would gladly sacrifice themselves at the feet of the dæmon for a chance to join with their dark master, to become one of RākṢhasa's own, to become strîgoi.

Gerba Whipmarples had read the Book of Kos closely. She knew the beast would need to sate itself with blood before it could infect others with its infernal damnation. There would be no new strîgoi until it had consumed enough life. And even then, RākṢhasa would only choose the strongest, both in body and in soul, to become its familiars. Such was written in the Book of Kos. Portia, Sun Hee, and Marguerite were Gerba's most promising candidates, and she would not risk them until the beast had drunk its fill. "Portia."

"Headmistress."

"How many students currently occupy the cells?"

"Nine, headmistress."

"And the oubliettes?"

"Eight."

"Take Sun Hee and fetch seven students. The largest seven." She eyed RākṢhasa's towering form. "Make that eight." If eight were not enough, Gerba would sacrifice all seventeen. And if that were not enough, there were so many more. She had an entire island of livestock for RākṢhasa to feast upon. "After that, you will return to your duties."

"But, headmistress..." Portia's face contorted. She stifled tears, on the verge of sobbing. It was strange to be able to see Portia's face. In this light, crying, the girl was not nearly as pretty as Gerba had imagined, her face sharp and bony. Such a strange new face that she would know for only a short time before the girl would transform forever.

"Your time will come, dearie." *And when it does, I intend to have you with me the rest of my days.* Gerba looked down at the burgundy wetness on the cave floor where Winnifred's blood pooled. She ran her toe through it, wetting it with Winnifred. Extending her foot, she placed it into the pack of strîgoi and watched them lick the blood off her foot like dogs. Gerba smiled to herself. "Do as you are told."

Summoning the obedience Gerba had driven into her, Portia took Sun Hee and left the cavern.

Gerba Whipmarples gazed up at RākṢhasa. A decade of patience and control had yielded such majestic fruit. There were one thousand one hundred and sixty-six souls on Huánghūn. Even if only one in twenty were chosen by the great dæmon lord to be its slaves, she would have an entire legion of strîgoi at her command. After all these long years, she would finally return to her tribe, triumphant, respected, feared. She would provide the Horde with the army they needed, the gates of the Juttland Trol would open wide before her, and a place would be made for her within the Sacrum Cabal, a crown of blackflame upon her head.

At long last, she could go home.

Gerba Whipmarples took a long breath. *But the task is great and the day is short.*

"Gita." The girl, younger than Gerba had imagined, blinked with hopeful eyes. Gerba smiled her brightest smile. "You may approach."

———— ❧❧ ————

Gerba Whipmarples' head was light, almost dizzy, as she ascended toward her office. Every step of her way up the winding staircase felt as if she walked in a blissful dream. She barely noticed the climb; her mind was in the strîgoi pits. As with everything on Huánghūn, eight had been the magic number. Eight sacrifices. Then, at long last, a new strîgoi, a true strîgoi, worshipped at its master's feet. Nearly every acolyte on the island had gathered in rapture at the transformation, eagerly awaiting their moment to be judged worthy.

At the top of the staircase stood Sun Hee, waiting for her with a warm towel over her forearm and a hand mirror. Gerba blinked. She had never imagined the girl's nose could be so small. It wrinkled when she handed Gerba the towel. *Ah. The reek of brimstone.* Gerba realized she must look a terrible fright, covered in soot and blood. She wiped her face with the towel and peered into the mirror to realize she had only smeared the filth, leaving her face a putrid black. *What does it matter? I can look however I like.*

Sun Hee bowed. "Would you like me to take that down to the *Hup Two* for you, headmistress?"

It took a moment for Gerba to realize what the girl was talking about. She looked down and realized she still carried Nepenthe in her tenasi glove. The elvish majik seemed silly now, almost a joke. She would keep the bamboo stick, of course, but at best Nepenthe would become nothing but a trophy for the King of Trol, a fallen enemy's weapon to hang in his hall. Gerba felt a sudden giggle well up within her. "No, no, no, dearie. I will take it." She took a deep breath. She could see the eagerness in the young girl's eyes. "O, all right. Go on down. I will be with you shortly."

The girl grinned, ecstatic, and made a beeline for the stairs. "And, Sun Hee?" Gerba turned. "Good luck."

Sun Hee smiled and descended to her fate.

As the girl's footsteps disappeared, Gerba entered her office, drew the red curtain aside, and buckled Nepenthe into its cage, seven locks snapped tight. Finished, she turned to the remains of her library. An assortment of knickknacks and bric-a-brac remained on the shelves, and it didn't take long to find what she was looking for.

Reaching onto a high shelf, she selected an ornamented silver birdcage meant for a pikacheep and hung from a slim chain. She placed the Heart of Huánghūn inside, clasped the door shut, and lowered the chain over her head like a necklace. She admired herself in the looking glass, entranced by the shard of RākŞhasa's soul glowing on her chest.

Another quake rocked the island. Gerba barely noticed it, gazing into the depths of her black heart.

Her reflection jumped as the mirror shook with the Institute. The quake hit in one giant wallop and jerked the room three feet sideways. Gerba grabbed the wall, barely keeping her feet. The mirror fell and shattered against the floor, showering glass in a jarring spray that skittered and bounced with the earth like peas on a drumhead. After a moment, everything stood still again.

Well. Gerba put her hand to her new necklace. *I may have less time than I had hoped.*

Turning, she saw a shadowy figure standing in the stairwell.

His silhouette was lean and dark, a man, a mystery. His black shirt riffled in the breeze, a familiar hat upon his head. She knew his blue eyes. He smelled of sand, and water, and blood.

Gerba stared at the villain who had destroyed the Great Bell. *"You."*

Chapter

14

DOUBLE -TAKE-

The whole world is run on bluff.
Marcus Garvey

"**Y**ou."

Jack Swift swallowed. He flexed empty fingers, staring down Gerba Whipmarples with narrowed eyes.

With the window behind him, he knew how he must appear: a mysterious silhouette, a specter, the grim reaper come to collect. It was the only weapon he had, so he used it. Still as a statue, Jack refused to move, refused to speak. He let the silence draw out. *Don't say a word.*

His only chance was to play for time. He had nothing else.

Gerba looked wrong. She still wore her suit of funereal sable from Rooker's execution, but the black fabric had been plunged into midnight darkness by soot and stains, clawed to bitter shreds. Her walnut-brown hide was blackened by the sulfuric nightmare beneath the Institute, and her sea-green eyes gleamed a pale shade of red.

Around her neck, she wore a hideous contraption. It appeared to be some kind of lavish silvered cage. Locked within it was a black, jagged shard of diamond the size of Jack's head. He found his eyes drawn to the stone and watched a curling flicker of scarlet lick the edges, like a flame burned deep within the dark. Gerba Whipmarples stood transformed, transfigured, distorted, the prudish schoolmarm replaced with a dark shadow of herself, one that trailed tatters of dark sulfur into the world around her.

Jack remained frozen. Strapped to his leg in a gunslinger's rig, the hawkbill blade awaited his hand, useless against Gerba's leathery hide. His only defense was the geas curse. It prevented her from harming him directly, but he knew from the bottom of his soul that every moment he spent with Gerba Whipmarples, he was in mortal danger.

Pretend to be brave.

Jack let one hip shift slightly forward, a stance he'd learned from Billy Pilgrim during the Steel Trials, a commedia dell'arte pose that displayed relaxed confidence. Gerba blinked, recovering from the shock. Jack needed her to stay off balance if he was going to survive the next few minutes. *I'm gonna have to say* something.

As she opened her mouth, Jack lifted one finger and slowly ran it along the edge of his tricorn hat, a long, slow salute. "Headmistress." His voice was deeper than he'd expected. "New jewelry?"

Gerba's red eyes grew suddenly distant. Thick fingers clasped the silver cage around her neck and for a moment it was almost like she wasn't in the room, just a vapor of someone who once had been. "Yes." Her voice was breathless. "Something I have wanted for a long time." Her eyes sharpened, focused, and the hint of a grin crossed her lips. "And *you* have a lovely new hat. But, as always, you are missing one last piece of Black Jack's costume."

Jack's eyes fell on Nepenthe. All seven pieces were locked against the wall, bound tight in iron. His hand twitched. Gerba saw it. Jack forced his body to relax. *Don't give her the upper hand. Keep her off balance.*

Jack did the most unexpected thing he could think of. He walked straight at her.

He moved as slowly as he could, letting each step ring out, and kept his eyes cold. Gerba's head tilted as she watched him. As Jack closed on her, he refused to speak or blink, summoning an intimidating presence, drawing out the silence until it wouldn't hold a second longer.

"I don't need Nepenthe to ruin you." Jack's words came without thinking. "As you learned this morning."

If it was possible for the cloud around the headmistress to grow blacker, it did. After so many months under her thumb, Jack relished the pleasure of watching Gerba Whipmarples squirm.

Her hand clutched the cage around her neck and the smile returned to her face too quickly. "I may not be able to cause you harm, doktar." Her voice was frigid as a glacier. "But I can still make you suffer."

Jack swallowed, hoping she couldn't see it. Now he was the one off balance, and Gerba pressed her advantage. "Where is your partner in crime?"

"Never can tell," was the first thing out of his mouth, too quick to be clever. Jack stepped closer, his back straight, realizing exactly how he could irritate her further. "It's just you and me."

Gerba sighed and the old headmistress rose to the surface. "You and I, dearie," she corrected. "It is just you and *I*." The trol shook her head. "You were supposed to be so intelligent, my pet, yet you are *such* a poor student." She moved slowly toward her desk. As she did, Jack knew he was going to need more than words, and soon. Keeping his eyes locked on Gerba, he used his perfect memory to review the office inventory. The only potential weapon was the pike in the gauntleted fist of one of the statues, probably ceremonial. Having no other choices, Jack angled toward it, trying not to be obvious. *Time, I need time.*

"Where are your spiders?" Jack worked a taunt into his voice. "I know Winston isn't coming." Gerba stopped, her face wrinkled into a frown. Before she could utter a word, Jack dropped the other boot. "Or Xeusia."

Shocked silence from Gerba. Her eyes went wide. "That's impossible."

"That *is* impossible, dearie." Jack smiled. "And still, it's true." He had her. Gerba's two best servants were dead. In that moment, he watched her feel it like a blade in her gut. Gaining courage, Jack took another step toward the pike. He hated to ask the next question, knowing Gerba would recognize how important it was to him, but Jack knew he might not get another chance. "Where is Patch?" He took another step. "Where's Copper Dave? And Yenrab? And Farah?"

The smug expression on her face told him he had asked too soon. "I had forgotten their names." Gerba cocked her head. "What makes you think they are still alive?"

"Because you're too cruel to let them die."

Gerba snorted. "Rest assured, they have paid for their crimes."

Jack's voice was sharp. *"Where?"*

Gerba stepped toward him, suddenly in control of the conversation. "I am terribly sorry, my dear boy, but school is *out* for the summer." Gerba's dead eyes stared at him, cold. Her relaxed calm unnerved him. "No more answers today."

A rumble sounded from every inch of the room. The quake rattled the entire butte, shaking it, experimenting. Jack managed to keep his feet, but only just. His cool masquerade vanished.

Even before the room stopped moving, Gerba spoke. "Do you hear that? That is the sound of the Locke Institute destroying itself. The sound of Huánghūn dying." She spread her hands. "All this will soon be a memory, and this magnificent edifice to enlightenment will cease to stand." The headmistress stood before the fireplace, flames flickering behind her. "And you will be buried along with it." She turned away, dismissing him. "There is no escape."

"LOOK AT ME!" Jack's voice snapped loud and sharp. Slowly, Gerba's horn turned toward him, her eyes glistening red, angry. Holding her gaze, Jack took one final step and arrived at the statue. "I killed Xeusia." His bloody fingers gripped the pike. "I killed Winston." Slowly, he drew the weapon out of the statue's hand. He flipped it, getting a feel for the weight of the weapon. "And now I'm going to kill you."

He kept his breathing shallow, his weight on the balls of his feet, watching. The huge trol's narrow eyes burned hatred. *Good. Stay with me.*

Gerba raised her hand to the collar of her blackened funeral dress. Jack hesitated, uncertain, and watched her fingers close around something at her breast. She tore it free and held it aloft. From beneath the filth, he saw the faint golden glow of her brooch flickering the symbol of the Caged Eight. A cruel smile split her thin lips. "Subdue him."

Jack spun, expecting a host of attercops behind him, but there was nothing. The hall beyond was empty. He heard the rap of stone colliding with stone behind him and turned to discover Gerba's torture-chair had lurched to life.

It skittered toward him like a giant stone spider, eight legs clicking against the floor. It sprinted straight at him, bent in half, and launched itself through the air. Jack threw himself out of its trajectory. As the thing flew by, he saw a Caged Eight embedded in one of the torture device's stone pseudopods. The chair clattered to a stop a few feet away, balanced on eight legs of liquid stone. It hunched, leaning toward him, circling.

Gerba tittered, her voice dark. "Have a seat, dearie."

Shifting, the chair distributed its weight onto its hind legs. The other four flickered, stone tentacles grasping for him. Jack gripped the pike, backing away. There was nothing he could do to fight stone. Out of options, he fled for the door to escape.

From the corner of his eye, Jack watched Gerba Whipmarples seize her massive mahogany desk and hurl it at him. Tumbling through the air, the car-sized desk whipped past Jack and struck the doorway like a bomb, shattering to broken shards. Jack threw up his hands, protecting his eyes, and jerked backward. He hit the ground as a billion splinters of wood clattered around him.

Now the torture-chair was on him and wrapped a rock tendril around his leg. He struck it with the pike. The blade bounced off, useless. Jack struggled away as the stone spider gripped his shirt and ripped the sleeve, revealing the metal brand seared into his arm. More tentacles wrapped around his arm, his waist, his legs. Struggling, Jack was hauled into the air. The chair situated itself around him, grappled his limbs and throat, and bent his body to its will. Jack suddenly found himself in the same position he had been in on his first day here, and just as helpless.

His heart pounded in his chest, a prisoner once again. "Do not misunderstand me, Jack. The geas curse prevents me from harming you. And to be honest, I do not want to hurt you." Gerba walked slowly toward him, her eyes cold and merciless. "I just want to hold you down while you die."

Jack glanced over Gerba's shoulder then focused on her, keeping her eyes locked on him. He gritted his teeth, forcing a wolfish grin that would make Shadow proud. "Before you shut me up for good, Gerba, I've got one last thing to say to you."

Gerba halted, cocking an eyebrow. "And what, pray tell, is that, dearie?"

Jack paused, holding her in suspense for one final moment, praying for a miracle.

"Where is your partner in crime?"

"Never can tell," came Jack's voice, calm as a farmer discussing the weather.

Rooker hid, frozen against the wall behind the red curtain, knowing that the toes of his boots peeked out from beneath the drape. Gerba Whipmarples had stood within inches of his hiding place just a few heartbeats ago, and he hadn't drawn breath since.

When Jack had gestured someone was coming, Rooker had barely made it behind the curtain. He thanked lady luck Gerba hadn't seen him do it. If she caught him now, that would be the end of them.

Jack diverted her attention away from Nepenthe, dismissing it as unnecessary. It was a good rook, and Gerba fell for Jack's bluff.

Go.

Barely three steps from Gerba, Rooker slipped from behind the curtain, quiet as a cat. Moving to Nepenthe, he crouched and set his lockpicks to work on the bottom clamp. The seven locks were new and hammerdwarf-made, the best money could buy. He had the first one unlocked in five breaths.

One down.

"Where are your spiders?" Rooker heard Jack from across the room. The kid's voice sounded like it belonged to someone else, someone older, someone in control. Rooker licked his lips, moving to the second lock. *That's right, bubba, keep her talkin'.* As his tools slipped inside the keyhole, Rooker risked a glance over his shoulder. Gerba's massive back was to him, all her focus on Jack. Without looking, Rooker flicked his fingers and shimmied the second pick into place with a quiet *snick.*

Two.

Rooker leaned into the third lock, making each move count. Gerba stepped away from him. "Where is Patch?" came Jack's voice as Rooker felt the headmistress easing toward her desk. He ignored both of them, focused on applying pressure with the second pick. He tripped the tumbler.

Three.

An earthquake hit, a big one. Rooker was thrown to the floor and a *whuff* of air escaped him, too loud. It didn't matter. Gerba couldn't hear him over the entire mountain snapping sideways. Stone ground against stone, loud and sharp. As the tremor stopped, Rooker lashed out a hand, pulled himself back into position, and jammed his pick into the keyhole. His heartbeat drummed in his ears, knowing he was running out of time.

Four.

More words, meaningless in his ears. He wiped sweat away with his shoulder and glanced over it just in time to see Gerba turn away from Jack. *Toward me.*

Rooker's heart froze.

He could see her sea-green eye, tinged with flickering red, turning inevitably his way. There was no chance of remaining hidden.

He was exposed. She would spot him in the next heartbeat, and Rooker could do nothing about it but stare.

"LOOK AT ME!" Jack's voice came sharp as a spear tip. Gerba snapped her head away, staring at the kid. Frozen, Rooker watched Jack face her down as he pulled a pike from a statue's hands. The kid knew he didn't stand a chance against her. He was only stealing Rooker more time. Taking a gulp of air, Rooker set his fingers to work on the next lock up and felt the tumblers fall.

Five.

The last two locks were too high. They were within easy reach for a trol, but even the sixth lock was at the absolute limit of Rooker's height. He stood on tiptoe to get a fingertip on it, barely able to reach the damn thing. Picking a lock from this angle was impossible but he tried. The pins fought him, denying him entry. Grimacing, he applied more force.

His lockpick snapped.

Swearing under his breath, Rooker heard a panicked shout and glanced over his shoulder. Gerba's torture-chair had come alive, crawling toward Jack like a rock spider. *I solve this or he dies. Toughen up.*

Rooker flicked the broken pick into his mouth and replaced it with another, quick as blinking. Balancing on one toe, Rooker's clever fingers worked the lock, fighting the wobble of his body. Something large and wooden smashed into the doorway across the room. Rooker didn't blink as he felt the pins turn.

Six.

The torture-chair latched itself onto Jack, wrapping him up like a cocoon. The kid screamed, fighting it, but he couldn't win against rock. Jack's eyes landed on Rooker, wide and terrified. *Now. It's got to be now.*

Stretched to his limit, Rooker strained for the seventh lock, the last thing keeping Nepenthe bolted to the wall, but he could not reach it. Gritting his teeth, Rooker leapt up the wall and snatched the topmost rod of Nepenthe, clinging to it like a vertical ladder rung. He hung there for a moment, feeling the thrum of Nepenthe's *wikk* in his fist. Flexing, he pulled himself up and slipped the first pick into the lock, searching for the tumbler. He found it but realized he had no way to finish the job. He needed the second pick.

One hand. I can't do this with one hand. His arm strained, one bicep holding all his weight. *It's impossible.*

Pleading for a miracle, Rooker glanced at Jack and found the kid looking him right in the eye. Trapped in the torture-chair, immobile, helpless, Jack's voice came loud and strong, brimming with confidence, an unshakable faith that Rooker would save him. "I've got one last thing to say to you."

Gerba tilted her head. "And what, pray tell, is that, dearie?"

Impossible.

Sweat poured down his brow. Rooker watched Jack's lips break into a grin. "Nepenthe."

Rooker jammed the pick between his teeth into the keyhole. He twisted his neck, felt the pins click, and the lock snapped open.

Free, Nepenthe shot across the room. Rooker felt it escape his hand as he fell to the ground in a heap. Lying on his back, he watched seven streaks of blue light rocket through the air toward Jack with the urgency of an uncaged child running for its father.

"*No!*" Gerba screeched, realizing she'd been played.

Jack caught the first bamboo rod of Nepenthe in his fist. Two more joined it, attaching end-to-end. *Tak-a-tak-a-tak—*

As the last piece shot past her head, Gerba snatched out a quick hand and seized the rod from the air. It bucked in her gloved fist, but she did not let go.

—atakatak! Jack brought six feet of blazing blue bamboo down upon the torture-chair and shattered the stone tentacles that bound him. He tore himself away from the liquid stone and crushed the hated chair to shattered shards in a hail of azure *wikk*.

As it crumbled to rubble, Jack stood at his full height, a free man, his figure illuminated in eldritch majik.

"Ha!" Rooker shouted. *"Finally!"*

Gerba spun on him, glaring. *"You!"*

Rooker grinned like a hyena. "Back to teach you a lesson."

———— ✦ ————

Jack experienced the hum of Nepenthe for the first time in a year and rejoiced in the sensation.

The *wikk* coursed up his arm, singing like a choir, flowing like a mighty river, filling him with energy and power. The emotion flooding his chest was like a homecoming, as if his heart had finally been returned to him. With Nepenthe in his hands, he suddenly remembered why he had been so pig-headed as to refuse to let Gerba claim it in his early days at the Locke Institute. It wasn't because he would be nothing without the staff, it wasn't because he craved majik for himself, and it wasn't because he gave a damn about being Black Jack. He had refused to surrender Nepenthe because nothing else in the world *felt so good.* Laughter bubbled in his chest. He gripped the bamboo, feeling the divine elvish majik cradled in the palm of his hand, proud that Nepenthe had chosen him as master.

He watched Rooker, his brother, triumphant. Picking himself up off the floor, the captain leered at the headmistress, giddy with victory. "Boot's on the other foot now, bitch." A wild grin split Rooker's teeth as he winked at Jack. "Give her hell."

Damn straight. Jack spun Nepenthe. Her tips left contrails of vapor blue in sizzling arcs as she spun. The stave was a marvelous weapon, alive and elegant; Nepenthe led Jack in every movement, doing what he wanted before he knew he wanted it. Moving with

Nepenthe felt like dancing with Fred Astaire and Ginger Rogers; all he had to do was try and keep up.

Gerba straightened. She eyed the whirling ovals of blue light Nepenthe slashed through the air. Her eyes went wide, shocked, and she retreated a step. For a fleeting moment, Jack knew he had her cornered, that he had the upper hand. He was, at last, the dominant player in their long-standing game. Then, she spoke.

"You are still missing something, doktar." The headmistress held up her fist, revealing the seventh piece of Nepenthe trapped in her majik glove. She arched an eyebrow and glanced at Nepenthe. "It simply does not feel right with only six, does it?" The trol's eyes narrowed, her lips pursed to a thin smile. "That last one is the real kicker."

She's right. Nepenthe felt magnificent but incomplete. *No. She's just manipulating you. Making you doubt.* Jack shook his head. Even with only six pieces, Nepenthe sizzled a vigorous high-octane *wikk* that set fire to his blood. She could minimize the azure majik all she wanted, but Jack had no doubt that, for the first time since landing on Huánghūn, he could do the headmistress real and lasting damage.

And I mean to do just that.

No doubt Gerba knew it too, and that was what made Jack uneasy. She was too confident, too serene, given her precarious position. The geas curse prevented her from injuring or killing him, and with the spider-chair broken to bits, Gerba had no more defenses against him. But even with Nepenthe humming in Jack's hands, she seemed no more concerned than she had been a few minutes before. *What does she know that I don't?*

"Six will do the job," said Jack and stepped toward her. "Where are our friends?" He was done talking. He would beat the head-mistress within an inch of her life to get the answer. Part of him was looking forward to it. "Where are they?"

A cruel smile curled over Gerba's lips. "I do not know that you have any friends *left*, dearie. Although I have made some new ones. See for yourself."

Jack half turned, expecting a bluff, keeping Gerba in his sights. From the stairwell came a breathy press of air, the whisper of a tea kettle just before it boils. A low sound. A hissing, wicked sound. Something lurked in the dark.

Jack's head snapped back to Gerba and he found her smile had unfurled wide. "You see, doktar, you are not the only one who can play for time."

Jack heard the scrape of the broken mahogany desk as it slid aside, pushed away by a milky-white hand. Around the corner came a pale head. Its eyes burned crimson fire. The thing's mouth hung open, issuing black smoke between white fangs.

The strîgoi emerged, gaunt and deadly. Jack felt a shudder run through his body even as Nepenthe grew more powerful, sensing the thing's presence. He retreated from the dæmon, taking several steps back. He remembered the Steel Trials, how the dæmon had torn open a dozen nobles in minutes, how it had decapitated the Baronetess Ket without a second thought, how it had disemboweled Rooker Flynn.

The beast stalked slowly into the room, dragging black claws on the floor. As the strîgoi passed through the entryway, another bleached dæmon appeared behind it. *Two.*

Jack backed toward Rooker. The captain grabbed his arm, staring wide-eyed at the pair of strîgoi emerging from the stairwell.

Gerba strode into their midst, unafraid. Jack's flesh crawled as the headmistress reached out and touched one, expecting the thing to tear her to bloody shreds. Instead of attacking, the dæmons parted before her like the Red Sea, hissing malevolence as she walked between them. Gerba ran thick fingers down one strîgoi's back like a housecat. She passed beyond them and turned, now guarded by two devils. From her protected position, Gerba eyed him. "So shameful, threatening a woman who is honor-bound not to strike back. It simply is not fair play." She settled one foot forward, mimicking Billy Pilgrim's pose of relaxed confidence. "Then again, what's the point in fair?"

Jack backed into Rooker. They found themselves retreating as the pair of dæmons moved forward, sniffing the heat Jack's body had left behind. Gerba stayed where she was, watching. "I have given them no command to harm either one of you. But I am curious to discover what will happen."

Jack retreated. *They'll rip us to shreds is what will happen.*

"Who knows?" Gerba Whipmarples cast a baleful eye on Jack. "You may even join us."

Jack's skin stood up in gooseflesh, prickling cold as some new, more terrible sensation locked his heart in its claws.

Something large darkened the doorway. Long, pale hands groped the door jamb. Black nails etched scratches into the rock. A third strîgoi entered, but this one was different from the rest. It had a saurian shape, thick with slabs of muscle in its neck and biceps, dragging a powerful crocodilian tail. The strîgoi had once been of the llystra race, but its scales had become fleshy, white as milk, spears of bone jutting from its ribs and shoulders. As the strîgoi lurched forward through the doorway, Jack saw that the top of the croc's head had been nearly ripped off. The upper half of its jaw hung loose, sagging to one side. The result was a permanently wide-open maw of fangs.

Around the strîgoi's corded neck hung a necklace made of macaroni shells, painted pink with a heart in the center. A necklace made by a five-year-old girl for her imprisoned father.

Jack stared open-mouthed at the horror that had once been Copper Dave.

The strîgoi stared back at him with dead eyes, hissing softly, its breath reeking the brimstone stench of hell.

PART 3

DUSK

Chapter

15

=LAST=
STAND

My God, my Father, and my Friend,
Do not forsake me at my end.

Wentworth Dillon

A SENSE OF EXISTENTIAL dread hung over Huánghūn like a burial shroud. You could feel it in the air as the too-bright sun blurred against the horizon, descending into the sea. You could hear it in the panicked cries of the raiptar birds, strangely awake in their nests, shrieking to each other with cries that sounded like a baby being strangled. You could smell it in the acrid odor of fire, the coppery scent of blood, and the decayed reek of sulfur. You could see it in the rumblings of the earth that shook the gigantic yingcao trees and trembled the butte as the island sloughed off its old skin, transforming into some darker, more alien creature. Even the cloudless sky bore witness, bruised purple in the fading gold of a dying day. Darkness marched across Huánghūn, counting down the minutes until she could unfurl her cloak and consume them all.

Gooseflesh crawled up Rooker's neck, across his arms, down his fingertips, frozen in shock by the bloodless ghoul that had once been Copper Dave. The thing took a step toward him with a predatory glide that was nothing at all like his friend. Rooker remembered when he'd recruited the big legbreaker as their first ally, the day the Big Six had stolen enough galt for Boss Mamba, way back in the beginning. Copper Dave had always had a joke and a smile to lighten the mood, a man Rooker had eaten with, laughed with, and very nearly escaped with.

But Copper Dave was gone. There was nothing left of him.

A burbling hiss scraped the croc's throat where his top jaw wagged open, hanging from a desiccated strip of tendons like a limp rag. No man could survive such an injury, but Copper Dave was no longer a man. Possessed by the dæmon that crawled within, the llystra's body transformed as Rooker watched. Bony spikes calcified upon Copper Dave's shoulders and face, his arms too long, his body stretched too thin for the thing that wore his flesh. His deadly claws lengthened and blackened, dragging on the stone floor as the tip of his tail flicked, eager, predatory, its dead eyes locked on Rooker like an albino gator stalking prey.

Rooker's stomach dropped, his bowels cold. Copper Dave was worse than dead; he was a meat puppet for the strîgoi creeping inside his skin. Horror shuddered through Rooker as he realized what the croc's transformation meant for the others. Was Yenrab a mask for a dæmon now? Was Farah?

Or Patch?

"Dave?" Rooker heard Jack's plea. "Dave! Please!"

Rooker forced himself out of his paralysis and hooked Jack behind his arm. He drew backward, retreating before the trio of strîgoi. "Dave's gone, bubba."

Jack brought up Nepenthe, the staff shining bright. Rooker felt naked without a weapon, but even with his katana, the strîgoi would tear him apart. Without silver or majik, he was helpless against dæmons. His hand grasped at the place his belly had been torn open by the strîgoi after the Steel Trial, feeling the lash of phantom claws.

Retreating, Rooker watched the triptych of pale dæmons spread out around them, hissing. Both stairways were cut off; the only remaining option was a thick door. Rooker pulled Jack toward it, but the kid shook his head. "I've been down there. It's a dead end."

The devil inside Copper Dave stared at him with red eyes and sniffed where he had been. Rooker watched rows of bony spines run up its arms, saw its shoulders bunch in grotesque knots of muscle. Rooker's skin crawled in revulsion. The strîgoi reared its head back and *rarked*, an inhuman vocalization that sent a shiver of terror through him.

The thing that had been Copper Dave shrieked like a panther and leapt at Jack to tear him into bloody chunks.

Nepenthe spun through the air and struck it in the face like a thunderclap. An explosion of azure light half-blinded Rooker. The force of the blow sent the strîgoi staggering. It clutched the broken bones in its neck and squealed in pain.

The other two dæmons hunched at the explosion of elvish majik and glared at Nepenthe with eyes that simmered volcanic hatred. As one, they hissed.

"Get behind me!" Jack thrust out an arm, forcing Rooker back as the dæmons loosed a shrieking wail and set upon them. Rooker saw Jack's eyes go wide as they attacked, mouths open and slavering. Nepenthe came up, blocking claws and fangs. The dæmons hurled themselves at him, all mindless rage. Humming contrails of vapor blue, Nepenthe slammed one strîgoi into another, both shrieking at the touch of the elvish *wikk*. Jack smashed at them, cracking bones, crushing ribs, and the strîgoi were forced to retreat.

Yes. Nepen–

Copper Dave reared up from the floor, his neck unbreaking in a series of wet snaps.

Jack froze just long enough for the strîgoi's claws to lash at him. Jack's chest blossomed into four bloody stripes. Rooker watched his face turn from shock to agony. Nepenthe struck back with a mind of its own, smashing Copper Dave's arm to bloodless splinters. Jack's pain followed Nepenthe's lead and transformed into a barbaric fury. Screaming, Jack hammered at the strîgoi, breaking a dozen bones in a blind berserker rage.

Rooker watched the thing that had been Copper Dave collapse, broken. He had a half-moment to think Jack had won...

...before a new quartet of strîgoi emerged through the doorway.

Ya gotta be kiddin' me.

Jack Swift didn't hesitate; he charged at the dæmons, his eyes sharp as diamonds.

He struck one in the face and brought Nepenthe around to uppercut another under its chin. A third lunged at him and Jack sprang backward, narrowly escaping its claws. He broke off the top piece of Nepenthe with a *tak* and flung the bamboo rod like a missile. It hit the strîgoi's chest with an explosion of blue majik that knocked the beast to the floor. Jack jerked his chin and the missile flew back to rejoin Nepenthe with a *tak*. The last strîgoi leapt at him. Jack spun the staff and tore free the other end, unsheathing twin spear-tip blades. They flashed azure majik and skewered the strîgoi in the air.

Bubba.

Jack Swift's face shone, bathed in elvish light, the blue of his eyes a perfect match for Nepenthe, made for each other.

The battle had taken Jack across the room, and one of the strîgoi circled toward Rooker, prowling, sensing weakness. Jack was busy defending against the others, and with no weapon, Rooker was armed with nothing but his teeth. "Jack!" He snatched a hunk of the broken torture-chair and brought it up like a club. Snarling, he reared back, ready to go down swinging. "Help!"

It came at him, all claws and fangs.

Out of the corner of his eye, Rooker saw Jack crack Nepenthe over his knee and break the staff in half. "Help yourself!" Jack hurled one half at Rooker.

Rooker seized Nepenthe from the air.

He felt a vibrant sizzle of thunderous eldritch power run up his arm and thrum through his body as though he'd been set alight. It was as if he held all the elvish majik of the *Venture Brigand* concentrated in the palm of his hand, more power than he had ever known.

Yes.

Rooker reared Nepenthe back and swung with all his might. Blue *wikk* cut the air with more force than a ship's swinging boom as Rooker crushed Nepenthe down on the strîgoi's head. The dæmon shrieked, but Rooker cut off the cry as he clubbed it in the throat. He struck its arm, its leg, its chest, again and again and again, thrilling with the thunderous power in his fists. His final strike caved in the dæmon's skull; the fiend dropped like a cut marionette.

Rooker straightened, eyes blazing in the light of the elvish majik. He looked at Jack, and for a moment, they seemed like a single man in a looking glass, each bearing twin halves of Nepenthe.

Some of the dæmons returned to their feet, bones cracking back into place with sickening pops. As they rose, another pair of strîgoi slunk through the door, hissing black smoke.

Rooker grinned like a madman. "Let's *go*."

Side by side they fought. Rooker hacked at a strîgoi's thigh and broke its femur like kindling. Jack smashed another white devil, then ripped off a piece of Nepenthe and hurled it at a third. It clocked the thing in the face and returned home with a sharp *tak*. Rooker did the same, *tak*, and felt the strange push and pull of the majik in his belly, *tak*. Mirror images, they fought back. *Wikk* threaded azure arches all around them, ripping contrails in the air until the pair was blanketed in crisscrossing streams of rippling light. Moving with the symmetry they had fostered in the Steel Trials, their dancing silhouettes blistered the very air. Strîgoi fell before them, collapsing to the ground as battered, wounded, fearful animals. Rooker felt the thrill of victory, side by side, back to back, brothers in arms.

A roar split the room.

Rooker spun to find a giant in the doorway. Twice the size of Gerba Whipmarples, the monstrosity hunched through the opening, and still, its pale head scraped along the top of the doorway. The beast didn't make sense. It was too gargantuan, too obscene, something that would devour his worst nightmare. Eight appendages lined its mouth, each flickering with its own fang. The creature's jaw hung wide open, revealing a second set of needle-sharp teeth ringed within. It lurched forward, all sharp angles and bone, reeking a sulfurous stench, white flesh against black rock. As the thing emerged into the study, more strîgoi scurried in behind it like dogs following their master.

Rooker heard Memphis's voice in his head. *The lord of the strî-goi, RākŞhasa.*

The dæmon-king hissed, dripping saliva onto the strîgoi at its feet, and gestured for its pets to finish what they'd started. Rooker watched the pale strîgoi, no longer the most dangerous things in the room, spread out like a pack of hyenas.

Another earthquake hit the Institute. For a moment, the world was drowned out by a deafening roar. Wincing, he looked up to find the sound came not from the mountain, but from RākŞhasa. It bellowed insensate rage that buckled the room. Rooker staggered backward, struck nearly deaf. Only one thought remained in his mind. *Run.*

The massive dæmon abandoned the doorway and charged right for him.

Rooker felt a hand snap around his collar and yank him out of the way as the giant lunged through the space he had just been in. Crashing into the wall, RākŞhasa spun like a cat, hissing volcanic fury. Rooker could barely hear Jack shouting in his ear. "Through the door!"

"Ya said it's a dead end!" Rooker screamed back.

"Better than here!" Jack grabbed him and threw him at the door. Rooker heard RākŞhasa roar as he yanked the door open and charged inside. He spun in time to see Jack running toward him; the dæmon-king filled the space behind him. As Jack flew through the doorway, Rooker slammed it shut and threw the heavy crossbar just as the dæmon hit like a charging bull. The door buckled so hard one of the hinge bolts flew off and shot past Rooker's ear.

Jack threw himself against the door, adding his weight to the blockade. *"Ha!"* His laugh was a shattered bark, his eyes wide. "Not fighting that!"

Rooker growled. "I thought we were winning!"

"Tell him!"

"What's the plan?!"

"No idea!"

Jack hadn't been lying; this was a *very* dead end. The hall was only a few strides long and terminated abruptly in a metal wall. Embedded in the metal Rooker saw a circular vault door taller than he was. There were no visible handles or hinges, just a huge flat immovable disc-shield of polished metal.

The door bucked again and a hinge split off the frame. As Rooker winced, Jack bared his teeth and shouted a manic panic. "This isn't going to hold it long!"

"*That* will." Rooker thrust his finger at the vault door. "It's all cold iron." Rooker stared at the bizarre metal disc-door. It had no locks or bolts but embedded in one side where a handle should have been was a glowing emerald the size of a fist. "I know a majik lock when I see one."

"Then lockpick us out of here!" Jack shouted as sweat poured down his face. "Unless you want to become one of those things!" The two men shared a desperate glance. The door thudded again; Rooker heard thick oak crack.

Dammit.

He pressed his half of Nepenthe into Jack's hand. "You might need this."

"Yeah!" Jack turned his eyes to Rooker and set a defiant jaw. "I'll hold him as long as I can!"

Rooker darted to the end of the hall and skidded to a stop, confronted with the most inscrutable vault door he'd ever seen. With no lock or keyhole to beat, he examined the emerald embedded in the side. He touched his fingers to it and felt *wikk* radiating within. *How am I supposed to beat majik?*

Rooker grimaced. The emerald was some kind of ward barrier. Even with time to prepare, it would take him a tenday and a team of wizards to break into that iron monster. Desperate, he tried to rotate the emerald, push it, pull it, trying to figure out how the thing worked. It didn't budge an inch. Rooker leaned in, getting a good look at the detail work, searching for symbols, a source of light, a pattern, *anything* that would give a hint about how to open it.

The gem was flawless, unmarked, and immobile.

Rooker heard Rākṣhasa hit the oak door again and this time the dæmon won. The upper quarter of the door splintered and caved in, burst by a horned white shoulder the size of a boar.

Rooker forced the dæmon out of his thoughts and puzzled at the lock, flummoxed. He'd spent a decade tumbling keyholes for fun; there were few better safe crackers in Keymark, but this vault door was something beyond his ken. The gem didn't move, didn't have holes, and didn't give him a seam to work with. *How the hell do you unlock a rock?*

A bellow of rage assaulted Rooker's ears as an eight-clawed hand lunged through the crack and grabbed for Jack. The kid dodged away and used Nepenthe to crack knuckles, forcing the hand to retreat.

Rooker pressed his forehead to the emerald. He felt the tingle of bright *wikk* against his brow, cool and hard. *Elvish majik. Not dæmonic majik, not ward majik, not a knack. Elvish.* Memphis Kubiak was the only trol Rooker had ever met who used elvish majik. Trols are law-bound to destroy elves and only use their rivals' majik if they're forced. Why would Gerba Whipmarples use elvish majik for her vault? *It doesn't make sense,* Rooker thought, his mind racing. *Elves are crap at locks. They don't close barriers. Hell, their entire kingdom is an open door. Who uses elvish majik on a damned lock?*

Rooker heard another giant slab of the oak door rip off. Jack shouted something but Rooker couldn't hear him over the idea that hit. *It's not a vault.*

"It's not a vault!" he shouted. "It's an inner keep!" Dæmons cannot break elvish majik. Even a tin hasp with an elvish spell would keep RākṢhasa out. The headmistress might store her treasures within, but the vault's real purpose was to protect only one thing: her.

"Jack! Give me Nepenthe!"

"*What?*" screamed Jack. He smashed at RākṢhasa's clawed hands as it tore the door to shreds.

"Trust me!"

Jack ripped the top piece from Nepenthe and hurled it down the hall. Rooker snatched the bamboo from the air and pressed it to the emerald. He felt the tingle of the *wikk* run up his arms. He saw Nepenthe hum blue and the lock glowed in response to the elvish majik. Smiling, Rooker pushed on the vault door.

Nothing.

RākṢhasa tore the last of the oak door away and hurled it at Jack. Five pieces of Nepenthe defended him from the worst of it, but the kid went down on his back as the dæmon snarled. Panicking, out of ideas, Rooker jammed the only other elvish majik he had, the *Venture Brigand*'s brass rings, in contact with Nepenthe and the emerald. He felt a circuit run through his fingers, connecting all three. And still, the lock held fast.

"Dammit!" he screamed. "*How does she open this?!*"

"*She whispered something!*" Jack struggled to his feet and faced the hideous thing looming over him. Nepenthe struck once, twice, thrice, and still RākṢhasa came. "*Open it!*"

Rooker shot air through his nose. He had no idea what Gerba would use as a password, probably some kind of complex Horde incantation or a scholarly proverb or some weird Toshan fable that would—

He blinked, his mind clear.

Rooker Flynn licked his lips and whispered the only Chegago spell he knew. "Open Sesame."

The emerald shone bright, emitted a single *KUNK*, and the vault door opened. Exhilaration swept through Rooker as he spun to Jack. *"Run!"*

The kid didn't need to be told twice. Abandoning his fight with RākŞhasa, Jack sprinted for the vault. The dæmon clawed at him and sheared shreds of black cloth from his shirt. Fleeing at a dead run, Jack threw himself headlong into the vault. Rooker leapt inside and turned to see the colossal dæmon thundering toward him. He hauled the door almost closed before the dæmon hit and slammed shut two feet of cold iron between them.

Then, impossibly, there was silence.

Rooker breathed, waiting for the thing to somehow get through, but even the screams of the Dæmon Crownéd could not penetrate Gerba Whipmarples' inner keep. Lying on a pile of coins where he'd landed, Jack stared at the door, terrified. Holding his breath, Rooker waited until he couldn't any longer, then let out a breath.

He turned to see Jack staring at him.

Rooker cricked his neck. "For once I'm glad to be locked in a cage."

Jack's injuries were not deep, but blood matted the kid's torn shirt to his chest. There wasn't much Rooker could do for the kid that he couldn't do for himself, so he investigated their little stone cage. Their situation had not improved much. They were trapped inside a box until Gerba came to open it. Jack and Nepenthe might be able to fight off the strîgoi, but RākŞhasa would paint the vault with their blood.

He extended a hand to Jack and hauled the kid to his feet. The kid leaned on the staff, still staring at the door, breathing hard. *He's not all here yet.*

Illuminated by Nepenthe's light, Rooker scanned the vault for something useful. The stone room was half-filled with discarded treasures, ancient books, bizarre figurines, and a passel of strange relics from Jack's sphere, including an empty pile of colorful backpacks, all of it stacked on spilled piles of pennies, but no weapons or majik. Desperate, he dug bloody hands through the coins and searched through piles of cut-rate treasure, hoping some incredible dæmon-stopping talisman might be buried beneath. As he dug, Rooker realized the cold truth: He was looking through Gerba's castoffs. There was nothing here. Anything valuable was already gone, probably stashed on a getaway ship. After a few moments of fruitless searching, Rooker spat. "Nothing." Frustrated, he hurled a fistful of coins. "Dammit!"

He heard Jack's low chuckle. Rooker spun on him, angry. "What?"

Covered in his own blood, Jack snorted. "I never thought I'd see you disappointed in a room full of money."

"Ya call this full? All that's left is copper and junk!" Rooker kicked a spray of coins.

Jack coughed. Rooker eyed him, worried. The slashes in the kid's chest were still bleeding and his face had taken on a pale color he didn't like. The Great Bell was gone. They were working without a net, and Jack was already half-dead. "Ya got a needle and gut? I could stitch ya up."

"It's not as bad as it looks," Jack lied. "Not to ask a stupid question, but that *was* RākṢhasa, yeah?"

"Yer right. That *is* a stupid question."

"Just checking." Jack sat back down, collapsing on a pile of coins. "Big fella." Rooker watched the kid prop himself up on Nepenthe, his eyes on the door. "Looking forward to round two."

"What about this Toshan junk?" Rooker gestured at the colorful artifacts. "Anything we can use?"

Jack shook his head and leaned against the wall, bleeding. "Walter Payton High School supplies. Textbooks, binders, a pocket watch, a few screens, a very dead drone... oh, and a Norelco."

Rooker scowled at the foreign words. "Is that a no?"

"Yes. No."

"So what do we do?"

Jack snorted. "Ya can't fix everything."

Rooker smiled and jerked his chin. *Nice.*

Nice.

Rooker gave up and leaned against the wall beside Jack. He turned to him and wiped some of the blood off the kid's brow. *We're gettin' out of this, right?*

She hasn't killed us yet.

Always a first time.

Jack nodded. They stared at the door, waiting.

After a long silence, Jack suddenly cackled a gallows laugh. Rooker turned to him. "What?"

"Butch Cassidy and the Sundance Kid."

Rooker didn't understand one word. "Hah?"

"It's an old movie." Jack glanced at him. "Like a play. Dad took me to see it last year. Music Box Theater. Good fun."

"A Chegago play, eh?" Rooker leaned back next to him and closed his eyes. "Did it have those skyscratcher things in it?"

"No skyscrapers. It's a western... an old story. A *true* story." Jack spat blood onto silver coins. "Heh. Two outlaws in one desperate last stand against impossible odds."

"Yeah?" Rooker smiled. "How do they win?"

"They get killed." Jack chuckled. "Slaughtered, really."

"Inspirational." Rooker glared at him. "Glad ya shared that, bubba."

Jack giggled and tipped his tricorn hat.

Rooker got back up and paced the room, unable to keep his agitation at bay. He paused at the door and put his fingertips to it, trying to steady himself. He pressed his forehead against the door, not wanting to ask the question, then closed his eyes. "Did you see the last strîgoi that came in at the end? The one that looked like it used to be a jinx-cat?"

A long silence. "I saw it."

Rooker glanced at Jack and knew the kid was thinking the same thing. "Was that Patch?"

Jack shook his head. "I don't know."

Rooker shot air through his nose and kicked a pile of coins. *Well, hell. What was it all for then?* He paced, not knowing what to do with his body. "Just do me one favor."

"Okay."

"If it gets me first, kill me." Rooker hung his head and felt his lip twitch. "I... I don't want to wind up like..." He let his breath run out, unable to say the rest.

Jack leaned against the wall and nodded. "As long as you promise me the same."

"It's a deal." Rooker stared at the iron door. *At least that's settled.*

"We could wait her out." Jack held up the little gold medallion on a chain, the thing he'd called a pocket watch. "Use this to keep track of time, hole up until sunrise, try and escape then."

Rooker grimaced, staring into the dark. "And save nobody."

"And save nobody."

Rooker turned to Jack. They locked eyes. *We came to get them out.* He straightened and rubbed his bloody knuckles. *Let's not waste the trip.*

Jack cracked Nepenthe and handed half to him.

Rooker gripped Jack's hand and pulled him to his feet. The kid winced and let out a sharp hiss of pain. Rooker scowled. "Ya okay?"

"Ask me again in a minute." Jack took a deep breath. "You ready?"

Rooker gripped Nepenthe, summoning his courage. "Yer whomping stick packs a wallop. No wonder ya didn't want to give her up." He sighed. "But I gotta admit, and ya know, no offense, but pound for pound I still prefer Bes..." Rooker looked up as Nepenthe illuminated the top of the vault door. Lying flat along the keystone, he glimpsed a familiar sharkskin scabbard. "...sie."

The acolytes had missed it in the evacuation. It was easy to see how; Gerba had placed the sword on top of the vault door; an easy reach for her, but barely visible to a normal-sized person. Rooker felt his face break into a ravenous grin. He crawled up the round vault doorframe, snatched the pommel, and yanked the sword down. Gripping the sharkskin sheath, he drew the singing saber.

Bessie sung furiously, angry at him for leaving her for so long, a vindictive chord in an unknown key. The sensation in his hand was utterly different from Jack's staff, a choir of angels compared to a string of curses. Nepenthe felt fast and fluid. Bessie felt like a nest of wasps stinging his fist with sweet pain.

Rooker gripped the sharkskin pommel and felt his blood stain the grip. Satisfied, the singing saber warmed in his fist. *Hello again, you nasty witch.*

Jack assessed him, approving. "*Now* you look like ya should. The Captain Rooker Flynn."

Rooker snorted and tapped Nepenthe with Bessie. The *wikk* reverberated from the iron vault walls, feeding on itself, growing louder. Together, the two sounds made a dangerous harmony.

Rooker faced the door and took a breath, preparing himself for what lay beyond. "I open the door, you hit the gap swinging. I get past RākŞhasa, and we hit him front and back." He wiped sweat from his brow. "At least that way one of us might get in a lucky shot."

But Rooker knew they'd used up all their luck. They wouldn't last ten heartbeats against RākŞhasa. *So much for that song.*

Rooker took hold of the door, preparing to open it as quickly as he could. He gripped the handle and breathed faster, gulping air into his lungs. "Ready?"

Jack bounced on his toes like a boxer and gripped Nepenthe. "Set."

"Go." Rooker ripped open the door and Jack charged into the hallway, whipping the stave to strike—

Nothing.

The hall was empty.

Rooker blinked. He reset his feet, waiting. "It's a trap."

The sound of their breathing echoed in the dark stone corridor. He waited, expecting strîgoi to pour through the broken oak door like a pack of dogs at any moment. But there was nothing. Even the smell of brimstone was gone. Rooker frowned. "I don't—"

He slammed into the ceiling as the Institute lurched downward. The quake was unhinged, as if the island itself was having a seizure. Rooker hit the floor and the Institute lurched him into the air again. He landed halfway on top of Jack in a corner along with a shower of falling rock. Shaken like a rat in a dog's mouth, Rooker felt as if a giant had picked up the Locke Institute and shook it. He was certain he was going to die in a world gone mad.

The quake stopped as suddenly as it had begun.

Breathless, Rooker waited a moment and then glanced up.

The hallway was wrong. Its left side was higher than its right, warped, off kilter. The corridor was a tilted, shattered carnival funhouse.

The quake had twisted the entire mountain.

Another rumble reverberated at his feet.

Rooker swallowed. "Move."

Quickly, he pelted up the hallway, expecting an ambush with every step. He went through the broken door to find Gerba's office ruined. The floor was cracked in a jagged tear half a foot wide. One side of the room drooped slightly toward the assembly yard. The earthquake had broken the Institute itself.

Rooker spun at the sound of a bubbling hiss. He glanced over a pile of stone to find the remains of Copper Dave Feng, the Hammer of Bego, crawling toward him.

A rock had crushed him in the quake. Several ribs stuck through the skin in his back. Still the dæmon inside the croc heaved the broken body forward, trying to kill them all. Rooker heard Jack make a strangled sound, almost a cry. The thing reached out for him with one claw, hissing.

Rooker drove Bessie through Copper Dave's chest. Whatever was inside him squealed with the singing saber's song. The pale body locked up then collapsed as the dæmon fled back to hell. A final hiss escaped Copper Dave's broken jaw and he finally rested in peace.

Flicking the ichor off his blade, Rooker knelt. His hands trembled as he gazed upon the pasta shell necklace around his friend's neck and thought of Copper Dave's little girl, Nina, who would never see her daddy again. In that moment, Rooker Flynn felt compelled to say the two words he'd never uttered in his life. "I'm sorry."

A strange sound issued from the broken balcony, a roiling, rushing burr of noise. Wary, Rooker stepped onto Gerba's veranda and discovered the stone was cracked nearly in half. It leaned outward drunkenly. He stepped to the edge, looked down, and his stomach dropped. "Hey?"

"Hey?"

"I found the strîgoi." Rooker gazed down at the assembly yard and watched a thousand prisoners scream in panic. A coven of dæmons cut through the crowd, pale wolves in a herd of sheep, led by their alpha. Rooker watched RākŞhasa slash a woman in half, then tear the head off an attercop. As the Dæmon Crownéd waded into the throng, its dogs tore through the prisoners, unchained beasts feasting on a banquet of blood.

Chapter

16

MOVABLE
=FEAST=

The flash and outbreak of a fiery mind,
A savageness in unreclaimed blood.

William Shakespeare

A PERFECT BANQUET FOR a noble house is a nearly impossible event to manage, but Hugo Dubois had perfected his portion of it. His specialty was wedding cakes, towering structures nine tiers high dressed in crème frosting. A mere pastry chef, Hugo was only a small part of Chef Kai's brigade of cooks, carvers, and sauciers, but Hugo was a standout. They'd nicknamed him Sugar because the brides loved him and, more often than not, he ended the night with lipstick on his cheek. Houses throughout the Deep Blue South commissioned Chef for their daughters' weddings, debutante celebrations, and fancy year-end feasts. Hugo Dubois had once shaken the hand of the Sultan of Thaj, at the coming-out party for his dangerously wicked daughter Shehzadi. All in all, Hugo had a good life and never would have been sentenced to prison had it not been for the gambling.

Dice were his weakness. Playing after work with the other cooks, rolling twelves in the alley. It was all fun and games, but every so often one of the young emirs would wander by, drunk and flashing platinum crowns like they were pennies. Hugo spent too much time with noble families not to want every coin they had. Deep down, he loathed the nobles and their easy, vacuous lives. If some lordling was too drunk to notice when Hugo switched to loaded dice, that was his fault. It's not like they would miss the money in the morning.

In the last game of twelves Hugo ever played, the emir's father showed up at the wrong moment, completely sober, curious, and wary. Hugo couldn't swap out the dice and, left to the uncertain hand of lady luck, lost more than his life was worth.

The only way to pay a rich man's debt is with a rich man's money, and Hugo knew plenty of rich men. He waited until the next party was in full swing before he slipped away into a duchess's bedroom, searching for easy coin. Instead, he found her having sex with Chef Kai. She screamed and Hugo was captured on the spot while the Chef escaped unseen. The nobles ensured the Inquisition made an example of him, and Hugo was sent to the Locke Institute to pay for his crime.

The execution of Rooker Flynn and the spectacular disaster that had followed had ignited a spark among the prisoners. The pent-up anger of a thousand men had been unleashed, and suddenly their fury could not be contained. Hugo threw rocks at attercops while the prisoners with weapons did the real damage, chopping off legs, even killing a few. After a few dozen flaming bottles of moonshine, the 'cops were scared, confused, and retreating. As the battle raged on, Hugo began to think the prisoners had a chance. They might even break out of the Institute and make it to the boats. He swore that if he got free, he would never touch a pair of dice again.

Hugo blinked as he saw something pale crawl down the wall toward him. It moved like a spider but wasn't nearly so big as an attercop. Screams suddenly erupted from the crowd, and Hugo saw a dozen more albino creatures descending the wall toward the assembly. Far above he spied a much larger grotesquerie, a pale giant. It shrieked a cry that made Hugo's balls retreat into his stomach.

Hugo ran.

Breathing heavily, his bare feet pounded dirt. Hugo crossed half the yard in moments. He'd been chubby before Huánghūn, most pastry chefs were, but now his prison-thin body was quick enough to outrun any—

Red spray misted the air before his eyes. Something stung his back as he found himself lifted off his feet into the air. Twisting, he saw a pale pit of teeth and smoke beneath him.

Hugo didn't scream, unable to comprehend what was happening. He felt himself hit the ground like a broken egg. Raising his head, he realized his belly was open, exposed to the jungle air. He did not scream as he watched a chewed piece of galt he had eaten this morning slip out onto the ground in a red puddle. A scarlet-eyed fiend crouched over him, claws wet and red. Its jaw unhinged like a python's, and Hugo smelled the reek of black smoke on its breath as its needle teeth bit down on his face.

Only then did he scream.

Yolanda Frost liked things simple. She was not a smart woman; she had long since come to terms with that. Her value was in her fists. Jailed after a cartel robbery gone wrong, Yolanda had suffered since the first day of the Locke Institute, the only surviving member of the original coterie of women convicts. She had been instrumental in enforcing the "all for one" mentality that had kept them all alive and unmolested. During the Steel Trials, when Black Jack and Patch went missing, she and Copper Dave shared the boss duties of Hyena, he of the men, she of the women, like two oxen in the same yoke. But neither of them was well suited for command. Strength and fearlessness made for good fighters, not good bosses. For Yolanda, it was too complicated; the bickering, the galt wars, the growing population of delinquent women who were none too obedient under the best of circumstances.

But when Copper Dave had approached her two days ago, just before the sit-down riot, and given her an axe, things had become simple once again.

Someone had smuggled the axe-head out of the Steel Trials. It'd been blunt and chipped, but Yolanda had lovingly sharpened it for hours and constructed a long, thick handle for the weapon. She had killed two attercops in the riot, the first by burying the axe-head in its brains. The second she'd lit on fire.

There was a simplistic truth in violence that appealed to Yolanda Frost. In Rimmy's Cull, it had been this simplicity that had made her so effective as an enforcer. A man refused to pay the cartel;

Yolanda broke their arm. A man failed again; she broke their leg. Very few men dared to miss a third payment, but those who did found themselves a sticky mess. Simple.

Boss Flynn's botched hanging this morning had made everything simple once again. The bell was gone, and any prisoner with half a brain knew they wouldn't survive long without it. Yolanda's only chance at staying alive was to get into the Institute, now or never. Simple.

She had enjoyed the initial battle with the attercops this afternoon, taking delight in injuring as many as she could, but the 'cops had retreated to the walls like cowards. The spider wardens had grown too used to guarding half-naked slaves; 'cops didn't know what to do when faced with armed opponents.

But now there was a new threat, and things were simple no more.

Yolanda knew the strîgoi. She had grown up in the southern Midlands, where they still told ghost stories to children about boogeymen who wore white flesh. Two hundred years ago, the Frost clan had barely survived the Highway of the Nomads; only one member of their bloodline had escaped alive to the Gemini Lakes. No descendant of Hercule Frost would ever forget the strîgoi.

Frozen, Yolanda watched the white dæmon tear Sugar Dubois apart. Every childhood fear she'd ever experienced was made real, right in front of her. Paralyzed with terror, Yolanda stared, her axe forgotten in her hand. More strîgoi descended the walls and tore into the assembled convicts. Wide-eyed, Yolanda watched them slaughter twenty men in less time than it took to count them.

Then the boogeyman went after a group of women.

Yolanda's fear evaporated. Simplicity reigned again. Her girls were in trouble; only she could stand between them and danger. Yolanda gripped her axe and ran straight at the strîgoi. Screaming at the top of her lungs, she charged into the dæmon and smashed into its side. It stumbled, snarling bloody fangs as the women fled. It spun on Yolanda and hissed like a snake.

She buried her axe in its skull.

The thing twisted and shrieked. She hit it again, bashing its head into the ground. Prone, it tried to regain its feet, but Yolanda brought the axe down on its neck.

The blow was hard enough to fell a tree, yet its spine did not break. She saw a long arm lash out at her and the earth shook.

Suddenly the world was too complex. It was dizzying, roiling, a complicated jumble of colors and sounds, a cacophony of sensations that made no sense.

The last thing she saw was her own boot as her head struck it and bounced away.

"Buh-buh-buh-*buh*," came the steady rhythm in Billy Pilgrim's head. It was comforting, reliable, dependable as C Major. As long as he kept the rhythm, Billy knew everything would be all right. Something snarled, a wet spray hit Billy's hand, and a bloody corpse fell to the ground beside him. He looked away, ignoring it. "Buh-buh-buh-*buh*."

He did not run. There was no point. Many terrible songs had been sung about the strîgoi, and none ended well. He'd seen the dæmon at the Steel Trials and what it had done to the nobles. He had no silver, iron, or salt. He was helpless.

Billy's only choice remaining was the last song he would ever sing.

Huánghūn had taught him to hide within the shifting confines of madness, his only escape from the horrors of the Institute. Billy had been safe within his lunacy for so long, an invisible shield erected between him and the terrifying shiq that consumed each night. But Black Jack's majik music box had reminded him of the sanctuary of song. It, too, provided a shield. Music transformed fear to courage, misery to humor, hatred to love. Pilgrim still needed the madness to protect him from the insanity of Huánghūn, and the madness had demanded his power of speech as sacrifice. But Black Jack had given him back his voice, and that music was his only remaining escape.

In that moment, Billy Pilgrim chose his swan song.

Fly away.
Together it's you and I.
Floating away through skies, it's just we two.
Holding your hand and knowing it's me and you.

Billy kept his footsteps at a steady pace, keeping time with the peaceful song in his head. He strolled as if he were walking in a city park, immune to the carnage around him.

A strîgoi raced past him and brushed against his elbow. Billy stumbled forward, forcing his feet to keep the beat. He straightened to watch one of the fleeing prisoners be cut in half by a strîgoi's claws. Blood sprayed over the crowd as the bag of guts that had just been an outlaw emptied onto the assembly yard.

Billy Pilgrim kept the rhythm. Across the yard, a dæmon tore two Vultures to pieces. Billy's madness turned blood to confetti, a flying cascade of red party streamers. He turned the monsters into white-painted clowns, but the pale jesters did not soothe his mind, so he decided to turn them into white show ponies instead. Streamers flew and ponies danced as his madness turned carnage to carnival.

He could not see the slaughter. There was no point in seeing it. There was nothing he could do to help, nothing he could do to escape, nothing he could do but replace the reality around him with something better. All he could do was keep the beat.

A woman fell, screaming, but Pilgrim knew she wasn't really screaming. She was harmonizing along with him, performing their love song in a duet. Billy bent at the knee and scooped the woman off the ground. He held her in his arms, walking away from the carnival, neither of them alone any longer.

Billy Pilgrim sang sweetly to the woman, looking deep into her eyes as he carried her gently, letting the music guide his steps.

And someday...
We'll marry and settle down.
Answer our prayer so, together we both know
We'll have a good life and watch all our children grow.

One of the white show ponies drew closer, drawn by the music they made together. Out of the corner of his eye, he saw it prance toward them, smiling white teeth. Billy Pilgrim fixed his eyes lovingly on the woman in his arms, singing only for her.

When we're old
We'll walk slowly hand in hand.
My darling, now don't cry, we'll never say good bye.
I shake my head, oh no, it can't be our time to—

The beat ended.
Billy Pilgrim never finished the verse.

Nepenthe lit Jack's way through the darkness of the Locke Institute's central spire. His chest burned from the slashes, his head pounded, exhausted from the lack of sleep. His mind, his best asset, was spent, empty, barely able to keep him on his feet. When he and

Rooker had silently agreed to return to Huánghūn, neither had imagined taking on a coven of strîgoi or witnessing the wholesale slaughter of Gerba's prisoners. Jack could not absorb everything that was happening around him, barely able to string one moment together with the next. All he knew was one thing: He had to find Patch. *Alive or dead, I have to find her.*

Another quake hit and buckled the stone beneath him. The stairwell that cored through the center of the Institute bent a half-turn, twisting like a colossal snake. There was no chance of keeping his feet; Jack tumbled onto his chin down the stairs, skidding, and fell face-first into a corpse.

The dead acolyte had been ripped open in half a dozen places, her belly slit open like an overripe tomato. One severed arm lay on the staircase, stiff as a broomstick. As Jack stared at the dead woman's face inches from his own, he felt a rough hand seize his arm. Rooker dragged him to his feet and stared him in the eye. *Ya okay?*

No. I'm not. Copper Dave is dead. We're never going to find Patch, and strîgoi are—

"Look out!" hollered Rooker, and Jack saw a giant shadow crawling up the stairs at them. As he watched, the darkness formed eight gigantic legs. Iktomi, Gerba's spider mount, spawn of Xeusia, appeared around the corner, big as a box truck. Its fangs searched the air, sensing prey.

Rooker shouted and ran straight at it. He cocked Bessie over his shoulder like Babe Ruth with a Louisville Slugger, ready to smash the thing out of the park.

The baby spider-dragon leapt into the central hollow of the stairwell. It snatched a web line, swung in the air, and hissed at them. Four legs took on a menacing posture, filling the entire gap, while the other four legs continued their ascent toward the summit. Still threatening Rooker, Iktomi ascended, leaving them behind without a fight.

Jack watched Iktomi go, rising into the darkness above. Rooker stared after it. "What the hell?"

"It's running." Jack stared after it. "Iktomi, the acolytes, the attercops, it's all falling ap—"

Huánghūn dropped. Jack hung in the air, floating, separate from the earth. He fell into gravity's undeniable grip and hit the ground a full yard below where he'd started. Rooker hit somewhere nearby, shouting painful curses. *Apart.*

Jack watched as the wall cracked and crumbled around him. Gaps broke through carefully shaped hammerdwarf stone and split a spiderweb of cracks into its surface. Tremendous chunks of rock fell away to reveal a dying orange sky over Huánghūn. Jack stumbled and grabbed the wall that had become a picture window. Below, he saw the lower parts of the Institute wept lava. As Jack watched, a sudden gush of magma blossomed in the assembly yard. Helpless, he saw three prisoners caught in the geyser of molten rock. Jack jerked his eyes up, not wanting to see what happened next, but he heard their agonized screams.

At the far edge of the assembly yard, a jet of lava burst into the air, followed by another and another. Further out in the jungle, steam escaped from old pyroclastic vents as they flooded with magma. He could see the outline of Tom, the shiq tunnel they had used to enter the Institute, become a trail of smoke and fire, boiling red all the way into Hyena camp and the clique they had called home. Lava boiled beneath it. One leg succumbed and the hut slowly keeled over, burning.

Forced out of their tunnels, shiq flooded the jungle. Yellow bodies scurried into the sunlight to flee the magma, escaping one death to suffer another. Ultraviolet radiation from the waning sun crippled them; their legs twitched in pain as their bodies melted in the light.

"Lord of Sea and Sky, look." Rooker pointed. In the middle of Hyena camp, smoke rose from between the roots of the big yingcao tree, curling up around the massive trunk. As Jack watched, the first lick of flame danced around its roots. Come nightfall, there would be no camp left to return to, no yingcao pods to shelter inside.

The sun was almost down. The last rays of daylight cut through the burning smoke, reaching for the Institute.

"At sunset, they'll be dead," Jack whispered. "Everyone on the island." *Everyone.*

"If they don't get killed by the strîgoi first," Rooker growled. "Move."

Jack descended the stairs two at a time. His head swam, dizzy with the thought of the sheer scale of slaughter rolling over Huánghūn. It seemed impossible to save *anyone* out of this mess, including himself or Rooker. Gritting his teeth, Jack forced himself to concentrate. He had no good way to find Patch or his friends. Gerba could have done anything with them and had most likely fed them to the strîgoi. Even if they were alive, they could be in any one of a dozen places, including the assembly yard being butchered right now. Swearing, Jack cursed himself. *Come on, you wasteka idiot! Come up with something! Anything!* But his brain felt like tapioca, exhausted, used up.

He stumbled over his own feet and hit the floor. Jack felt the bloody slashes in his chest open wider, forcing him to shout in pain. Rooker dragged him to his feet, his face a mass of dirt and worry lines. "Jack. Do we just get out of here? Make for the docks?"

"I don't—" Jack panted. He was losing his grip, he couldn't think, couldn't breathe. "I don't—"

A tiny wail split the air. At first, Jack thought it came from his own lips, a howl of despair, but the keening whine came from below, further down the stairs, an anguished cry.

The cry of a baby.

Jack's heart leapt into his throat.

Patch's moggie.

He traded a look with Rooker.

She's alive.

Jack leapt to his feet and sprinted down the stairs. The chamber below was empty, the acolytes gone. He skidded around a corner to find himself in a long hallway. Frantically, Jack followed the sound of the screaming baby, his heart pounding in his chest. The wail grew louder as he burst through the door.

The room was filled with rows of small cages, all empty save one. Inside, the screaming moggie lay on its back, kicking and screaming, clutching the air with tiny, furry paws.

Alone.

Jack felt something inside of him break.

Rooker entered the room behind him. *"Patch?!"*

Jack didn't say anything. He simply opened the cage. It wasn't even latched. Rooker arrived beside him but Jack couldn't meet his eyes. "Hey," panted Rooker. "Where's Patch?"

Gently, Jack picked up the baby. It screamed louder, twisting toward him. He let out a breath and held the moggie against his chest. He turned to find Rooker staring at him, his eyes white and wide.

"Jack?" Rooker clutched his shirt. *"Where's Patch?"*

Jack hung his head and held the baby close.

"Patch!" Rooker hollered as he felt a chill creep up his guts. Patch would never leave her moggie. Not willingly. She'd fight tooth and nail. If she was gone, it meant they had been separated by force. Either that or she was—

Don't think it.

"Patch!" Rooker screamed, not caring if everyone in the Institute heard him. He sprinted past the cages down the hall. Bessie picked up and amplified his shout until his ears rang. He found a narrow chamber that curved into a cul-de-sac of stone peppered with iron grates in the floor. It took Rooker a moment to realize he'd been here before. *The oubliettes.*

He went to the nearest grate and looked down into the blackness below. "Patch!" As his eyes adjusted to the dark, all he saw was a face-down corpse at the bottom.

"Rooker!?" came a shrill woman's voice from the next grate. Rooker leapt to it and saw nothing but darkness. He blinked and realized two eyes were staring up at him from the dark, followed by a flash of white teeth. *Farah. Little mouse.* "Help me!"

Alive.

Rooker fumbled with the flood-chain and yanked it down. He heard the sudden rush of water pour into the oubliette below. Farah could swim up to him, but it would take time. "Farah! Where's Patch?"

"I don't know!" she hollered from below. As Jack entered the room, Rooker looked at him, hopeful for the first time.

"Lord of Sea and Sky, git me outta here, ijit!" came a roar from the next oubliette tube. Rooker looked down inside to see the furious crimson face of Yenrab Bialik. The Red Dwarf stared up at him with one baleful eye. "What in tarnation you waitin' fer, bucko? Pull the damn chain!"

"Dwarves can't swim!" Rooker yelled. "You'll drown!"

"I'll take my goldurn *chances*!"

A scream, high and panicked, erupted within the cul-de-sac and ricocheted off the stone walls. Rooker followed the sound to a grate across the room. He peered into it and his heart missed a beat.

Lava bubbled at the foot of the oubliette; it filled the bottom of the cage. Silhouetted against the glowing magma, wedged into the stone tube, was a jinx trying to flee up the chimney and escape the fire below. Her arms and legs trembled, suspended over molten fury.

Patch Picaroon looked up at him, terror in her golden eyes. *"Rooker!"*

"Hang on!" Rooker yanked the chain and flooded the oubliette. Water slashed down over Patch, almost jarring loose her grip on the wall. *"Agih!"* she screamed as the cold water hit her. It splashed down into the lava and turned into a sizzling steam that billowed to fill the tube. Rooker coughed as smoke and ash curled up into his lungs, and Patch was lost from sight.

"Dammit!" Rooker slung his upper body into the hole and clung to the edge, reaching down, searching. "Patch! Take my—" He broke off, coughing as acrid steam overwhelmed his lungs. Still he clung to the wall, trying to reach her, but she was too far down.

Jack gripped Rooker's ankles. Gritting his teeth, the kid lowered Rooker further than he could reach by himself. He grasped down for Patch, searching blindly. Steam bathed the walls, making them slick and hot. For a moment, the smoke cleared and he saw the grimace on Patch's face, her slit belly seeping blood. But he could not find her hand.

Rooker heard Jack grunt as the kid tried to lower him further. Suddenly Yenrab and Farah were at his side, lending their strength. Rooker descended a few scant inches and felt Patch's furry paw at his fingertips. She reached for him, lost her grip, and fell.

Rooker snatched her wrist, gripping with all his strength. He braced his feet against the wall and strained to support both their weight. His muscles grew tense, every sinew standing out against his skin. "Pull!" he hollered and felt Jack and the others drag him back over the edge. Gripping her wrist with white knuckles, Rooker hauled Patch Picaroon out of the hole.

Gasping, they lay in a heap together, a tangled mass of legs and arms. Patch struggled to one elbow and stared at him, amazed. Rooker grinned and opened his mouth to say something, but her eyes snapped to the sound of her moggie crying. Before Rooker could blink, Patch took her baby from Jack and pulled it to her breast. "O. O, you." Tears spilled down the singed fur of her cheeks. "O, you."

Jack hauled Rooker to his feet. Rooker held his grip longer than he needed to. They locked eyes and shared a quiet moment of satisfaction, knowing that no matter what happened next, they had made the right choice to come back.

Damn right.

Rooker moved to Patch and slipped one arm beneath her. He lifted her and her moggie into his arms and held them against his chest, surprised at how light they were. "Rooker..." She looked at him, her eyes moist, almost beginning to cry. "Rook—"

"I'm here, Patch. We both are. We're here now." He sniffed and wiped his cheek against his shirt. He glanced at ugly old Yenrab and the nebbish Farah. "Let's all get the hell out of here."

Bessie hummed in Rooker's hand, ready for a fight.

She didn't get one.

Every step down the spiral stair showed more evidence of the evacuation: broken items, discarded scraps of paper, a few scattered coins, all littered among the collapsed stone of the Institute. The stairwell itself was eerily silent, abandoned, as they descended to the ground level and reached the huge entryway and the great stone door.

This was where the work camps entered from the assembly yard to the mines, the space from which the galt appeared every afternoon. Rooker had seen it a hundred times, but never once had it been completely deserted. Not an acolyte or a hammerdwarf remained in the Institute. The place was barren.

Empty but not silent.

A dull roar thundered against the walls. As Rooker watched, lava seeped from the fresh cracks in the stone walls, illuminating the room in a bloody firelight. The island quaked, a rumbling volcano about to erupt.

And yet this sound was something more. Something worse.

Rooker lit a torch and saw the great stone door flicker in a twisting mass of shadows. They writhed within the stone like tortured souls, wailing an anguished, muted moan. Staring at it, Rooker didn't understand what he was looking at. Some new dæmon, a legion of them.

Farah said a word he didn't understand, something majik, and the amethyst crystals in the cave suddenly gleamed with an eldritch light and revealed the tableau beyond.

The great stone door was transparent from this side. Rooker had forgotten that. Outside the door he could see throngs of prisoners who had thrown themselves against the stone, trying to combine their strength in a desperate attempt to force it open. Silent shouts came from open mouths as the outlaws struggled in vain against the impossible lock that held them trapped.

Behind them, pale figures, huge and clawed, cut through living men and women like farmers threshing wheat, one wide stroke after another. Beyond the strîgoi, yingcao trees blazed a hundred feet into the air like giant torches lit against the dying sky.

Rooker Flynn realized he was witnessing the last gasp of Huánghūn.

Beyond the jungle, beyond the island, beyond the sea, the sun itself finally gave up the ghost. It winked to darkness and was no more. As beams of amber left the sky, their golden glow reappeared within the jungle. Moving silently among the palms, the shiq flooded the island with their own shade of yellow.

=OPEN=
SESAME

*Let us advance and advance
on Chaos and the Dark.*

Ralph Waldo Emerson

Y ELLOW BODIES FLOODED THE island in a shiq swarm so large it covered every plant, every tree, every square inch of dirt. The green of the jungle disappeared, buried beneath moving yellow legs. No shiq cluster so large had ever massed on the surface of Huánghūn. Their numbers dwarfed even the late summer dry season when every healthy adult arachnid fought for mates. The moment the last ray of sunlight fell, billions of spiders erupted from their hiding places, fleeing the caves they called home during daylight. Driven to a kill-crazy frenzy by the quakes and eruptions, they fell upon each other, fighting for dominance over whatever was happening to their home. Civil war broke out as millions of arachnids tore at each other in a useless effort to combat the quake. As they destroyed each other, opportunistic raiptar birds fed on them two at a time, dragging twitching spidery bodies into the sky. Half a million shiq died in the first bloody minutes of nightfall. Too soon, the spiders gave off destroying themselves and turned their attention to the source of the disturbance, the Locke Institute, with one single animalistic thought: *kill*.

Jack Swift knew none of this. All he knew was that the prisoners were being slaughtered like cattle.

He stood at the great stone door with a sickening pit in his stomach as he watched the tableau of suffering prisoners crush themselves against the other side, trying to escape. Blurred mouths twisted in silent screams and panicked bodies fought the unmoving door, struggling to open it. Jack stared helpless at the inhuman distortion gibbering before him, a trembling mass of living men and women in their last desperate moments.

Jack tried to say something but no words came, a silent witness.

He heard Rooker's body shift at his side, heard the captain's fist tighten on Bessie's pommel.

"We have to go!" yelled Patch. She clutched her moggie, her voice shrill with fear. Yenrab moved to her side, murmuring sounds of ascent. Farah took a step back, staring in horror at the semitransparent door. The moggie cried out, feeling its mother's panicked heart. Patch clutched it close to her breast and urged Rooker to flee to the docks. "Come on!"

Jack stood unmoving. He watched the struggling mass of humanity on the other side of the door, unable to look away. He turned his head to find Rooker's eyes. They were wide in horror, but when they locked on Jack, something changed. Rooker's expression grew hard, his brow furrowed, and despair transformed to decision. Jack felt his strength reflected in Rooker's eyes. Their shared intent lent steel to his thoughts and drove his own fear into retreat. Jack's jaw shifted. *Okay.*

Rooker put Patch down and they moved to the door as one man.

"What are you *doing*?" Patch screamed.

"Giving them a chance." Jack didn't bother looking at Patch as he spoke. Beside him, Rooker threw his weight at the spinning wheel that opened the door. It didn't budge.

"They jammed it," Rooker barked. The captain eyed the mechanism and pointed at the broken chunk of wood forced between the gears. "There."

"Good!" Patch shouted, her amber eyes wide.

Jack put his shoulder to the wheel and heaved at it. "Give us a hand, will ya?"

Patch made a furious noise as she struggled to her feet. "We have to get o—" She was cut off when Farah moved to the door. The dark girl joined Jack and put her back into turning the broken wheel. "Farah! What ar—" Now Yenrab left her, the Red Dwarf striding to the door. "Stop!" Patch screamed, clutching her one-day-old child. "Jack, please! Please. My *moggie*."

Yenrab attacked the wooden blockage with a chisel and tried to break the jam loose. Jack shot a look at Patch. "They don't have to die like this."

Jack felt Patch's eyes bore through him, a poisonous glare. He knew that she hated him in that moment; he was nothing but a threat to her newborn baby. *I don't have a choice. I'm sorry.*

Patch glanced down the passage that led to the dock gate. He knew she had to flee, she had to save her baby. Part of Jack wished she would. But Patch Picaroon turned, settled her baby in the crook of one furry arm, and limped toward them. She grimaced and set her shoulder to the wheel. "Damn you all."

Together, they strained against the weight of the door. Yenrab's chisel split the wooden wedge and the gear spun, crushing the remains to splinters. Jack felt the wheel turn as the great stone door let out a stubborn squeal. *Open Sesame.*

Jack slapped Rooker on the back and both men sprinted for the gap. As the door rolled open, the screaming became a cacophony as the closest prisoners jammed their hands through, clawing at the door. Jack turned to see Patch clutching her moggie, determinedly turning the wheel with Yenrab and Farah. He jabbed a finger at her. "If the strîgoi come, roll it shut." Jack wiped his lips. "Even if we're on the other side."

Patch scowled at him and held her moggie tight. "If a dæmon gets anywhere *near* that door, I'll shut it on all of you." Her eyes were golden fire, her jaw clenched. "You're crazy, you're both of you *wasteka* crazy!" She turned the wheel faster. "Go."

Rooker Flynn charged through the opening, grabbed the first convict he saw, and threw him through the doorway behind him. Shouldering his way into the crowd, he watched the panicked throng of prisoners grow even thicker as some realized the door was opening. A surge of humanity pushed at Rooker like a river, slowing him to a crawl, forcing him backward. *Get out of the way,*

damn ya! Rooker hurled another outlaw aside and elbowed his way into the mass. "Move, you *wasteka* bastards!" he shouted and fought his way upstream. *"Move!"*

Desperate cries for help became frenzied shouts of hope as outlaws hurled themselves at the door like drowning men grasping for a buoy. Rooker recognized the faces in the mob. Boss Mamba's old flunkies. Gladiators he'd fought with during the final Steel Trial. Some Shavers, some cartel boys. All their differences were gone. The outlaws were at last unified in a panicked struggle for survival. The crowd bunched into a mass at the door as they clawed at it, forcing it to open faster in their fight to escape.

Finally, Rooker broke through the mob and saw the battlefield clearly for the first time. The scene was set in bloody red. The dead sun, the bursting jets of lava, and the flames of the yingcao trees made a blazing crimson triptych, a vision of hell. Strîgoi hunted the perimeter of the yard in pursuit of prey and tore outlaws limb from limb. Rooker saw RākŞhasa stalk the tree line. The great beast threw prisoners aside, attacking only the strongest. Behind the Dæmon Crownéd, one of its victims suddenly lurched to its feet, its flesh pale, its eyes red, another strîgoi added to the coven.

Rooker eyed the escaping outlaws. They would need time to make it inside. *And we need to buy some.* Unless lady luck truly shone on him, Rooker knew he was probably never making it back through that door. He cricked his neck. *Hated that place anyway.*

Jack struggled through the crowd and hollered at prisoners to get through the door. Rooker cocked a grin. "Ya really think ya need to *tell* them to run?"

"I should take my own advice." Jack grimaced, holding his bloody chest.

Rooker eyed the nearest strîgoi. It feasted on a dead Jackal who was missing his face, gobbling down the blood. The dæmon hawked down a gobbet of flesh and turned to discover the mob at the door. It watched them as a wolf watches penned sheep.

Rooker gripped Bessie's sharkskin pommel. He heard the thrum of Nepenthe paired with Jack's steely voice. "What are the chances we make it out of this?"

Rooker shrugged. "I woke up expecting to die." He flicked Bessie's blade. "Still waiting."

The strîgoi ripped off a hunk of its victim and ate the meat as it prowled toward the crowd.

"You're better at this than I am." Jack flipped a piece of Nepenthe in his hand. "What's the play?"

Rooker wiped sweat from his chin. The dæmon darted at the bottleneck, ready to make a bloody feast of the fleeing mob. Rooker felt a snarling grin split his lips. "The play is to kill the everloving hell out of it."

Rooker sprinted straight at the dæmon, screaming.

The strîgoi's head snapped to him. Rooker howled like a mad dog and thundered straight at the beast, loud as ten men. Distracted from the throng, the dæmon slowed and assessed him with lifeless red eyes. It snarled, threw aside the meat hanging from its claws, and faced him.

As he closed the distance, Rooker unleashed the singing saber from its sheath; Bessie screamed loud and long. His throat hurt matching her as he made a headlong suicide rush straight at the strîgoi. Meeting his challenge, the dæmon roared and galloped right at him.

Rooker's voice cut off and Bessie mimicked him, suddenly silent. All his false rage dropped away to reveal calm expertise. His bum rush antagonized the strîgoi into a big haymaker swing that was easy to dodge. He ducked under the thing's pale arm and reared up behind it. "Don't look where I *tell* you to look."

He brought the blade down hard enough to fell a tree. Bessie cut deep into the dæmon's shoulder, split putrid flesh, and cut through two ribs. Blood fountained from the cut, black as oil.

Rooker hit it again, chopped the singing saber through the joint, and took the arm off.

Shrieking, the strîgoi snapped at him; fangs scissored at his face. Rooker jerked back, trying to get Bessie around, but the dæmon was too fast.

Blue light flashed with a thunderbolt impact. Half-blinded, Rooker watched the beast stumble, stunned. Jack spun Nepenthe around for another strike, but the dæmon leapt away. Without missing a breath, Rooker took advantage of the distraction and darted at it. He brought Bessie up and jammed it through the dæmon's chest.

It shrilled an inhuman shriek more piercing than any sound Rooker had ever heard. He felt his teeth rattle as the dæmon's back arched in agony. Rooker drove Bessie in further and the thing's scream became a gibbering garble of mindless, hellish fury. A sudden flash of glacier cold burst from the dæmon's fanged mouth and Rooker glimpsed the malevolent specter inside, wicked, dark, and red. The dark ghost wailed a damned cry of eternal torture. Sent back to the pits of hell, the specter dissipated into nothingness and left behind nothing but the echo of its scream. The pale body of the strîgoi's puppet dropped to the earth, finally a lifeless corpse.

Like that.

Rooker glanced at Jack and extended Bessie's blade. Jack tapped it with Nepenthe and the two weapons sung their strange harmony. Rooker winked. "One down."

Twenty more strîgoi eyed him as he stood over their murdered kin. The yard was dotted with dæmons; each glared infernal malice at him. They dropped their prey like discarded dolls, eager for revenge. At the edge of the yard, RākŞhasa turned.

"I'll take three of 'em." He heard Jack's dry voice. "You take the rest."

Rooker snorted. "Luck to us both."

Something moved in a pile of bodies nearby. Rooker saw a pale hand crawl weakly over the corpses. The attached body was bony, skinny, and white, its hair bright orange.

Rooker felt his heart skip a beat. "Pilgrim."

"Billy." Jack stared. The troubadour was coated red with blood, his eyes were white, rolled back into his head. In one arm he held a dead woman, most of her gone below the waist. Billy lay against her, the ragged remains of his voice whispering, "...*buh-buh-buh*-buh..."

Jack wrapped his arms around Billy. It was impossible to tell what was the balladeer's blood and what was the woman's, but Billy's forehead was slashed open and his thigh was ripped in three jagged lines. The claws hadn't hit the femoral artery, but the leg was shredded, useless. More than that, whatever scrap of sanity the singer had still possessed was long gone. Billy Pilgrim was in total shock, his eyes dead as cue balls. "...*buh-buh-buh*-buh..."

A strîgoi sprinted toward Jack at a loping gallop, moving like a pale silverback gorilla.

Jack whispered in Billy's ear. "I got you. I got you."

The strîgoi leapt. Jack whipped Nepenthe in an arc that slammed the dæmon out of the air. Roaring, Jack cracked it in the head and smashed its skull.

The dæmon's bones knitted back together as Jack watched. A new protrusion of bone grew from its head as it turned on him. This was one of the new strîgoi. One of RākṢhasa's.

It lunged at Jack, long claws bared. He felt the sizzle of the *wikk* as he brought Nepenthe around to block, but it was too late. The strîgoi was faster, and it had him.

The dæmon bent in half as Bessie landed in its gut. Rooker's sword sunk deep into its blanched body. The dæmon spun on Rooker, snatched his head, and threw him to the dirt. Jack watched Rooker bounce against the ground, dropping the singing saber.

Jack stepped away from Billy and faced it alone.

It clawed at him once, twice, thrice. Jack deflected its razor claws with blue arcs. Backing away, Jack snapped off the tip of Nepenthe and slung it. Light blasted as the bamboo rod struck the strîgoi in the eye and boomeranged home with a *tak*. Jack whipped up the other end, cracked the dæmon in the jaw, then fastballed another missile that shattered a fang. Pressing his attack, Jack pounded the thing in a barrage of cracking lightning, *tak-a-tak-a-tak!*

Claws swiped and cut his fingers to the bone. Jack screamed. His useless fingers dropped Nepenthe to the dirt, covered in his blood. The strîgoi reared to strike. He held up his bloody hand to ward off the final blow.

Bessie took its head off at the neck, wailing like an opera singer.

The headless dæmon corpse took a step forward. One arm swung blindly at nothing, then it collapsed to the ground.

Jack threw himself toward the troubadour and dragged him to his feet. "Billy."

Pilgrim's voice was a ragged whisper. "...buh-buh-billy..."

"Jack." Rooker's voice came like a snap.

Jack looked up to see the scene. All over the assembly yard, more strîgoi closed in on them. But what made Jack's heart seize up was the yellow swarm that covered the island beyond.

Huánghūn was all one color, a rolling carpet of spiders. At the edge of the tree line, Jack watched a dozen escaping prisoners buried whole beneath an amber tide. The shiq didn't give them a chance to scream. The convicts were turned into skeletons before they hit the ground. Jack saw thousands of shiq bodies slough off chunks of chitin in the dying light of the sun. Their carapaces dripped like melting wax, a misshapen mass of legs and fangs.

"Go, go, go, we have to go." Rooker hoisted Pilgrim's arm over his shoulder and together, they sprinted for the great stone door.

Two hundred convicts packed the gap, a heaving tangle of hysterical flesh trying to escape. Jack knew both shiq and strîgoi would reach them before everyone was through. As he entered the press of bodies, Jack was suddenly smothered in sweaty muscle that reeked of blind panic. "Move!" Jack watched monsters rushing toward them. *We'll never make it.*

Jack was trapped within the chaotic mess, all packed flesh to flesh like penned cattle. Someone's elbow bashed his chin and he almost let go of Billy. Rooker too was caught in the heaving bodies. Helpless to control his fate, Jack could focus only on keeping his feet and hanging on to Billy.

He heard the scrape of stone and his blood went cold.

True to her word, Patch Picaroon was closing the door.

Wait!

Above the cacophony of terror, a woman's shrill voice cried out. "Get them out!" Jack heard another voice repeat the call, followed by a third. "Get them out!" Jack felt himself shoved, this time by a dozen hands. Refusing to let go of Billy, Jack traded startled glances with Rooker as the crowd surged around them. Slowly, they were lifted into the air.

From that vantage, Jack Swift saw what would be his dying memory of Huánghūn. The horizon burned with ten thousand trees. Blood-red cracks of magma split the earth, a dæmonic miasma curled into the dusky jungle air. The strîgoi hunting pack descended upon the Institute door. Toward the rear, RākŞhasa stood on a mound of earth, raised above it all. The Dæmon Crownéd stretched one pale claw toward Jack as the yellow tide of shiq met its pale body and broke over it like the sea against a stone. Spiders flowed over the dæmon, around it, through its legs without ever stopping. Covered in shiq, RākŞhasa strode straight at Jack, building to a run.

"Get out!" The shouts of the prisoners truncated to two syllables, screamed at the top of their lungs as they packed against the closing door. Hands supported Jack and Rooker, still clutching Billy's limp body between them. Jack felt himself floating over the crowd, lifted by them, passed from one outlaw hand to the next. "Out! Out! Out!" Rough hands shoved him over the leading edge of the throng and through the crack in the door.

Rooker hit the ground inside the cave and rolled. Jack hit like a sack beside him, his hand a wet mess of blood. Billy looked mostly dead. Yenrab hauled Rooker to his feet and watched the gap in the door become too narrow to pass. Outside, hands flailed at the stone. Jaelin hands, jinx hands, llystra, razorback, dwarf. Yellow spider arms joined those hands, claws reaching through the crack like living knives. Then the door shut.

Rooker watched the shadows trapped on the other side. The last remaining prisoners of the Locke Institute were buried beneath the yellow mass of shiq like a breaking wave. Arachnid bodies washed over the door, covering everything, and the outlaws were gone.

Rooker took a step back, silent, unable to watch, unable to look away.

A pale, dæmonic shape appeared, a figure of white within a sea of shiq. The strîgoi stood at the doorway, its head cocked. Spider bodies crawled over it, ignoring the dæmon as it ignored them. Another strîgoi joined it. Another. Their shadows stood at the door, waiting. A larger silhouette appeared behind them, barely visible through the wall of spiders. RākṢhasa's gaunt figure, tall and crooked, pressed one eight-clawed hand against the door.

Rooker took a step back.

It stared at him through the rock. It could sense him. He could feel the dæmon inside his bones. *Lord of Sea and Sky.*

RākṢhasa's body lunged at the rock, sunk its claws in, and climbed. It disappeared out of sight. The coven of strîgoi followed, joined by an ocean of shiq.

"They're going over the top," Rooker heard Jack whisper. He glanced at bubba and found the kid was caked in almost as much blood as Billy. His chest was bleeding freely now, and his fingers looked like they were cut to the bone. Jack had lost too much blood, and Rooker knew his brother wasn't going to make it much further.

"Let's not be here by the time they come down." Rooker ripped the sleeve off his favorite shirt and bound crimson cloth around Jack's bloody hand. "Here. This way they won't know yer bleedin'."

Jack laughed and looked up at him, his face pale and skeletal. "Let's go home."

Chapter

18

BREAKING
TIDE

The "price of anything" is the amount of life you exchange for it.
Henry David Thoreau

*H*OME.

Gerba Whipmarples entered the trol capital city of Barŭkek in a magnificent parade flanked by legions of strîgoi. Trumpets lit the air in a glorious fanfare that echoed throughout the city-beneath-the-mountain, all for her. Dæmons marched behind Gerba in lockstep, orderly and disciplined as a colony of ants obeying their queen. Cheers rose from the streets, praising her, lauding her. Every voice in the city called her name. On a slim golden chain no thicker than a kite string she led RākŞhasa through the grand thoroughfare, her control on display for all to witness. Drinking in the crowd's adoration, she took a deep, satisfied breath and touched the Heart of Huánghūn, trapped in a golden cage upon her breast, beating in perfect rhythm with her own heart.

She had not been prepared for the power of the dæmon shard. Not at first.

The sensation of the dark *wikk* was an intoxicating, glorious power that dwarfed her greatest expectations. She had joined with the dark *wikk*, become part of it, a powerful, incessant throb of raw dæmonic fire that made her blood pulse with its blazing cadence. The Heart of Huanghún gave her the strength to reign supreme, a power unknown by any mortal since the Fell Prince of Keymark. That power allowed Gerba Whipmarples to see her future with perfect clarity, real as here and now.

Eyes closed, she turned her thoughts away from Barŭkek and bent the dark *wikk* to focus upon the island she would never call home again.

Gerba Whipmarples was protected from the shiq upon her little yacht, the *Intelligentsia*. It was moored away from the cargo wharf, and the spiders would not reach her when they came. All the same, she longed to see her new legion of strîgoi with her own eyes. After the dæmons concluded their feast, they would seek her out and bow in supplication before their queen. Gerba's mind drifted back to Barůkek; she heard the cheers, the sea a susurrus of praise in her ears.

She felt the infernal energy of the black diamond shard at her breast and peered through the eyes of her strîgoi as they feasted upon the Institute. She witnessed glimpses of bloodletting and felt the thrill of the kill. At moments, she felt she was one of them, her own claws sundering flesh and bone, the satisfying taste of blood on her tongue.

But best of all was when a new strîgoi rose. Gerba Whipmarples understood it now, the desire for the strongest blood. She had been a fool to collect so many weaklings. They were useless, discarded, nothing more than food to slake her hunger, and the world was full of weak men. Only the strong could drink from RākŞhasa's blackened fury. Physical strength, intellectual fortitude, unbreakable faith, a spirited heart, all these things made a soul worth seizing. When death came to escort it to the other side, that departed soul was like an empty room, and the larger the room, the stronger the dæmon that could occupy it.

She felt another strîgoi rise.

Mistakenly, Gerba had believed many of her acolytes would be well-suited to become strîgoi. It only made sense after their years of devotion and service to RākŞhasa. But it was not to be. Nearly a hundred acolytes had sacrificed themselves to their dæmon-king today. Only two had been deemed worthy. *Two.*

Gerba opened her eyes and glanced at Portia and Sun Hee. More loyal than ever, the acolytes flanked her like guard dogs, their scarlet eyes glittering hatred, their white robes exchanged for white flesh. Their bone spurs continued to grow as Gerba watched, stretching to suit the shape of the strîgoi inside. As she considered them, Gerba felt the Heart of Huánghūn pulse as one more dæmonic heartbeat joined the bloody jewel around her neck. Another dæmon in the coven.

Today was the Locke Institute's Graduation Day, when the students became who they were always meant to be. More than two dozen convicted criminals had joined Gerba's dæmonic ranks in the last hour.

Far fewer than she had hoped.

Twenty-six. Gerba felt her savage children race through the Institute, seeing through each of their eyes. They moved with a purpose, heeding her call, and would arrive at the docks before the mindless shiq. *Twenty-seven.*

"What do you think, Portia?"

The thing that had once been Portia glared at her with hellfire in its eyes. It hissed, hating her. Gerba looked into those eyes and saw her future in a new light. Her homecoming parade now seemed a minor curiosity, disregarded on the silent streets of Barůkek. She led RākŞhasa on a slim chain, yes, but twenty-seven strîgoi were no army. In the eyes of the Horde, Gerba Whipmarples appeared small. Weak. Not enough.

"Not enough." Gerba nodded to Portia. "I think so too, dearie." *No. It simply will not do.* Gerba Whipmarples had a reputation to forge. She needed to make an indelible impression, a triumphant return that would force the Horde to forget forever the outcast gypsy girl she had once been and see her only as an Arch Witch of the Sacrum Cabal. "We can do better."

Gerba stepped off the boat.

The seaside structure that welcomed merchant vessels, yellow-jackets, and nobles alike to the Locke Institute was divided into two gigantic sections: the cargo wharf, where shipments and students were unloaded directly from the boats, and the warehouse, where they were placed behind lock and key, waiting within to be assigned a destination. The cargo bay and the warehouse were divided by the gigantic dock gate, a floor-to-ceiling iron cage wall built by the same hammerdwarf crew that had built the cage wall in the strîgoi pits.

It had only one purpose: to keep things locked inside.

Gerba smelled the sulfuric stench of Portia and Sun Hee as they followed her past one of the reinforced beams that supported the cargo wharf ceiling. Together, the trio arrived at the dock gate door. It stood open, as it had during the evacuation, a yawning mouth that led to the warehouse and the Institute beyond. Gerba heard stone crack as a rock fell from the ceiling and shattered apart on the floor of the warehouse. Beyond, in the dark Institute hallways, Gerba heard the throng of students coming; their panicked, animalistic noises echoed against the cave walls. *It would be a waste to just let them go now. Who knows how many more might be turned? Perhaps there is an army here after all.*

She closed the dock gate door, locked it, and threw the key into the sea.

"Chins up, ladies." Both strîgoi snapped their heads up so quickly Gerba heard tendons snap. The girls didn't seem to mind. "Best foot forward." Both women extended their right foot. "And remember, the key to a good argument is how you present it. So let's have some smiles."

As the girls bared their new fangs, Gerba Whipmarples rubbed her meaty hands together and listened to the approaching gang of outlaws who had managed to survive to reach the final exit from the Locke Institute. *These are the ones with spirit.*

These are the ones I want.

Jack Swift led three hundred escapees through the twisting passages beneath the crumbling Locke Institute as they fled for freedom.

Ah! Ah! His chest wounds made him wince with every step, but he knew the map in his head that led to the dock gate was the only way the others could escape. He ran, leading the exodus of terrified prisoners to the sea.

Tremors shuddered the stone passage around him. The quakes grew more frequent by the minute. As Jack passed a lower path, he saw the glow of steaming lava filled it like a flaming vermillion river. The black diamond mines were already submerged in lava. Whatever remained below was entombed forever in molten stone.

"You *sure* this is the way?" Patch shouted as Rooker carried her and her moggie.

"He's sure." Rooker slapped him on the shoulder. *Yer sure, right?*

Jack glanced at him and saw hundreds of desperate outlaws behind the pirate, all following him. His mental map of the Institute was incomplete; he was only half-certain he knew how to get to the dock gate. "I better be."

He sprinted down the hall and scouted the way ahead. Skidding around a corner, he discovered a large stone-walled warehouse combined with a breath of fresh air unpolluted by sulfur. A panoramic vista of a darkening sky and pale starlight above open water. The Irridin Sea was thirty yards in front of him. And beyond that, infinite possibilities.

Between Jack and freedom, silhouetted beyond the closed gate, stood a familiar outline, her hand cocked against her hip just so. Gerba Whipmarples stood waiting. At the headmistress' side was a pair of strîgoi dressed in shredded acolyte robes that jutted with hideous bone spurs. Jack had long since memorized the idiosyncrasies of every attercop and acolyte at the Institute and knew the colorless string of beads at Portia's neck and the red sash of Sun Hee's belt.

Gerba Whipmarples stepped into the light, her eyes glittering with feral malice. "You owe me an execution."

Jack brought Nepenthe up. Rooker stepped past him, gripping Bessie. Side by side they moved directly toward Gerba and spoke in unison. "You first."

"How delightful. Let us discover who obeys whom in the next few minutes, shall we, dearies?" Gerba revealed a glowing lightchain in her fist and wrapped part of the cord around her arm. Sizzling red *wikk* illuminated her horned face. "I simply cannot wait to put you back on your leash."

Jack heard the roar as terrified convicts entered the warehouse behind him. The first of the prisoners burst from the passage, followed by a dozen more. They stared at the trol at the gate, eyes wide, but not one of them broke stride. More terrified of what was behind than what was ahead, they raced for the gate. Jack watched Gerba take an involuntary step back, surprised at the frenzy of bodies barreling straight for her.

Jack followed them, joining the tide. "You can't stop all of us."

Convicts hit the dock gate a dozen at a time. In moments, a ton of muscle threw itself against the door. More outlaws lent their strength and pushed from behind. Several prisoners crawled up the cage and rattled the bars with their combined weight, banging the iron enclosure back and forth.

Jack watched as Portia and Sun Hee slashed strîgoi claws at prisoners' fingers, forcing some to fall back, but more took their place. Heedless of danger, unable to be caged any longer, the desperados of Huánghūn would not relent until they tore their way to freedom.

Rooker leapt to the front of the throng and hacked at the metal pins that bound the cage to the wall. Bessie wailed; the singing saber fed off the screaming outlaws. Her own shriek gained strength as the pins weakened. Jack bashed Nepenthe against the opposite wall's moorings in a fusillade of blows that rang out like a cannonball barrage. More prisoners threw their united strength against the bars, their only outcome freedom or death.

The cage wall broke from its foundations and fell.

Outlaws rode it down, hollering as the dock gate collapsed. Gerba and her strîgoi were forced to retreat to avoid being crushed beneath the Institute's cage bars.

Jack raised Nepenthe over his head and shouted at the top of his lungs, *"Get to the boats!"*

Rooker took up the cry, along with Patch, Yenrab, and every other outlaw left on Huánghūn. *"Boats!"* As one, the desperados sprinted for the exit. Screaming outlaws charged through the cargo wharf. There was no way they could all make it out alive. Gerba's dæmonic acolytes would slaughter too many, but her students were long past willing to take that chance. The first wave went straight up the middle as Gerba and her strîgoi retreated, too shocked to strike. Jack watched Farah and another outlaw make it across the wharf, out onto the pier, and escape the Institute for good. They dragged Billy Pilgrim with them. The man behind her was not so lucky and fell under Sun Hee's claws.

The pair of strîgoi slashed at the crowd, spraying blood to the ceiling. More prisoners darted past, but Portia and Sun Hee took down too many, gutting them like fish. Twenty outlaws were dead in ten heartbeats and more died every second. Packed in so tight with the prisoners, the dæmons only needed to flick their claw for an easy slaughter.

Gerba Whipmarples wasted no time assisting them. She snatched two fleeing outlaws by the head and hurled them against the wall, leaving wet stains. She stepped forward and crushed an escapee's leg beneath four tons of muscle. An inhuman roar, a lion's roar, a *trol* roar, escaped her throat, and Jack finally saw her as the animal she was. Gerba brought her five-foot horn almost to the floor, bucked her neck up, and impaled an outlaw on its bejeweled tip. She jerked her head and flung him back into the crowd.

She snorted and turned to kill Rooker Flynn.

He carried Patch in both arms. The jinx-cat was nearly un-conscious, limp. Her moggie screamed against her chest. Rooker struggled to carry the woman and her baby; he had no free hand for Bessie as Gerba thundered toward him.

No...

Jack sprinted straight at Gerba. She reared back to crush Rooker under her fist.

If she hurts me, the geas curse will kill her.

Without hesitating, Jack slid under Gerba's huge arm and popped up in front of her swing. Her tremendous fist came like a wrecking ball. Jack jammed his eyes shut and leaned into her blow, driving his face at her knuckles.

Gerba flinched away as if stung by a wasp, yanking her fist back before she struck. Unable to touch him, her eyes blazed dæmon-ic red. Frustrated, furious, she bellowed the roar of an insensate beast.

Nose to nose with the headmistress, Jack stood his ground.

He eyed her down. "Not fair when you can't fight back, is it?"

Jack Swift belted Gerba Whipmarples with the thunderous might of Nepenthe. Her head snapped back like a mousetrap. A spray of saliva and lipstick misted the air. Broken pieces of her horn's jewelry scattered into the escaping outlaws. She stumbled back ten feet. A tooth clattered to the floor.

Jack had never felt anything more satisfying in his life. Here, free of the last cage, standing at the edge of a freshwater sea lit by two moons, he watched Gerba Whipmarples grimace in pain. Jack glanced down at the steel brand burned into his forearm. He would carry Gerba's metal mark for the rest of his life. He intended to leave her with a few marks of his own.

Black Jack felt a bloody smile cross his lips.

He whirled Nepenthe like a helicopter blade and brought it around to smack the stupid look off Gerba's face, but one leathery hand shot up. It caught Nepenthe. For a half-second Jack saw the seventh piece of the staff trapped in her glove. As the other six hit, his staff exploded in a blue jolt of light. Refusing to attack itself, Nepenthe shattered to useless joints, clattering against the floor like so much kindling.

Gerba eyed him; the seventh piece glowed in her fist. "I cannot attack you. You cannot attack me." She unlooped the lightchain from her wrist and began to swing the glowing red cord back and forth. One manacle swung like a pendulum at the end of the majik chain. "But there is more than one way to skin a cat."

Jack flexed his fingers but one hand was completely dead, his strîgoi-slashed knuckles bloody and nerveless. He summoned the broken Nepenthe back to his one remaining fist; she came at a gallop, *tak-a-tak-a-tak!* All around, the cargo wharf rang with the screams of dying and escaping prisoners. He saw the strîgoi rip them apart. Saw the lightchain weaving in Gerba's powerful hands. Heard the headmistress' voice in his head: *I do not want to hurt you. I just want to hold you down while you die.*

Jack struck like lightning. She fended off the blow with the glove. Nepenthe shattered again, but Jack was ready. He summoned the flying bamboo back together in midair, grabbed a piece, and slung it at Gerba's face. It struck her horn with a blinding flash. Nepenthe returned to his fist, but Jack found the lightchain wrapped around his wrist. He dropped Nepenthe and snaked his hand out of the chain just before Gerba could pull it tight as a noose. He backed away, summoning the stick. She was so quick for something so big. If she caught him with the lightchain, he would never get free; a lightknife was the only thing that could sever the chain, and who knew where she kept it. He stepped away, wishing he had two working hands.

Gerba assessed him, enjoying her victory. She tightened the lightchain between her gigantic fists. "Which one of us, do you think, will come out ahead?"

Jack's feint had lasted just long enough. He grinned. "Depends who's smarter."

The singing saber screamed as it pierced through the front of Gerba's armored skin. Bessie shrieked victory as it ran the trol through from back to belly. Rooker Flynn stood behind her, twisting the blade.

Screaming, Gerba pawed at the air. She spun and backhanded Rooker with an anvil-sized fist as both of them hit the ground hard. Gerba twisted to wrench Bessie from her back and threw the singing saber aside.

Jack hurled a piece of Nepenthe. Another. Each rod struck Gerba's belly-wound, forcing her to double over. She fell to one knee, screaming. "Portia! Sun Hee! *Come!*"

Both strîgoi leapt toward Jack. He twisted aside and forced one to miss, using his momentum to sweep the other's legs. The dæmons were back on their feet faster than he could think. Portia and Sun Hee closed between Jack and Gerba, forming a wall to protect their queen. They lunged. Jack fended off the first, but the other got too close and he felt sharp claws rake his ribs. Red slashes split his already lacerated flesh and he screamed in pain.

Jack Swift felt his head go light. Felt a numbness in his bleeding fist. Felt blood pour from his chest.

I can't.

I can't.

He staggered in retreat as dæmons closed on him.

Rooker danced out of the way just in time for Gerba's sharp horn to punch a hole through his favorite shirt. He felt his heart gallop in his chest as he marveled at how terribly strong the trol was. He'd run her through with the singing saber and she still meant to kill him for it. The trol stepped toward him, forcing him further from Jack.

This is going very wrong very fast.

Unarmed and bleeding, Rooker Flynn faced Gerba Whip-marples alone.

Bessie lay on the floor where she had fallen. Gerba spun the lightchain in a slow circle, waiting for him to go for the singing saber. Rooker saw an imperious glare flicker over the headmistress' eyes. That smug, superior stare. Those pursed, disapproving lips.

I'll still wipe that look off your ugly face.

The cargo wharf had thinned out. With Gerba and the strigoi otherwise occupied, the remaining desperados disappeared down the pier, escaping to freedom. Rooker forced himself to laugh as he sidestepped toward the singing saber. "Looky-looky, all yer students playin' hookey." He jerked his chin at the fleeing outlaws.

She turned to glance at the docks and Rooker darted for the sword. But Gerba was ready for him, quicker than a striking cobra. The lightchain lashed the air like a sizzling whip. It forced him to pull up short, away from the sword.

Rooker glanced at the strewn corpses around him, prisoners who had not managed to escape. One's fingers twitched; its flesh bleached white before Rooker's eyes. *It's turning into one of them.*

"Perhaps when you become strîgoi"—Gerba whipped the lightchain back and forth, making red trails in the air—"you will *finally* learn to obey."

Don't count on it. Rooker moved for the sword again, but a tree-stump foot stomped down and nearly crushed his hand. He feinted away, ducked back for Bessie, and felt the lightchain around his neck. Gerba wrapped him in two scarlet loops and her thick arms yanked upward.

Rooker got his arm under the lightchain just in time to save his throat from being slit as Gerba yanked the cord tight. It bit into his forearm, into his metal Institute brand, into the sides of his neck. A choking sound escaped his throat. *"Hgh."*

She pulled the chain tighter.

Choking, bleeding, Rooker saw stars pop. Gerba loomed over him. A wicked smile split her lips, her eyes gleaming emerald fury. Rooker tried to move away from her, but she wrapped her fists around the chain and pulled tighter. He felt her saccharine breath on his cheek. "It is a rare thing to see a man strangled to death twice in one day."

Losing consciousness, Rooker staggered a half-step forward. His vision narrowed. He took another half-step, felt Bessie with the tip of his boot, and kicked the saber up into his hand.

He jammed the singing saber under her arm and struck a soft spot in her armor. A painful cry escaped Gerba's throat; she fell back, releasing her grip long enough for Rooker to slip his head free of the chain.

Gasping, Rooker spared a glance at Jack. The kid fought for his life against the strîgoi, bloody, slow, and outmatched. Two on one.

Better together.

Rooker charged at Sun Hee. He barreled his shoulder into her side and knocked the strîgoi over. The dæmon sprang to its feet as Rooker brought the singing saber around and took the thing's head off.

Rooker heard Jack grunt. He flung two rods of blue majik that smashed into Portia's face. Taking advantage, Rooker lunged at the strîgoi and it spun on him, which was the opening Jack needed. He punched Nepenthe through the dæmon's chest. The elvish weapon left a jagged hole where Portia's blackened heart had been. He ripped the staff free and the dæmon collapsed to the ground.

Rooker flicked Bessie clean and stood side by side with Jack.

Hey.

Hey.

Gerba took one nervous step back as both men stared her down. "Okay, Gerba." Rooker spat. "Now *yer* the one who's alone."

He feinted. Jack feinted. Rooker was on her. He hammered Gerba with Bessie. The blade cut into her arm, then an explosion of blue light struck her face as Jack hurled another piece of Nepenthe. Rooker and Jack attacked with a single mind. Like a pair of dancers they moved, an improvised ballet of combat. One took the lead, then the other. Each man built upon the last man's move, greater together than either could be alone. Their assault grew faster and built to a marvelous crescendo, a symphony of blows that rained down upon Gerba Whipmarples like a Huánghūn rainstorm. The headmistress went to one knee, outmatched.

Rooker swung with all his might.

He decapitated the top half of Gerba Whipmarples' horn. It tumbled to the rock and bounced. Trinkets and jewelry embedded within the tip tinkled as they exploded and scattered across the ground.

Gerba screamed. She dropped the lightchain and fell to her knees. Blood spattered her face. Her lungs labored with painful breaths. Kneeling, she gripped at her broken horn, shorn blunt, just a misshapen lump on her ugly face.

Panting, the headmistress stared at him. Rooker saw despair in those hateful green eyes. She was beaten.

Rooker felt his chest fill with pride as he stood over his jailer, victorious. His black hair twisted and flew as the sea wind beckoned, drawing his eyes up. There, at the end of the pier, he saw the silhouette of the *Venture Brigand,* waiting for him to come home.

We win, girl.

An earthquake struck. Somewhere above, Rooker heard a deafening crack of stone. An instant later, he watched an impossibly gigantic section of the butte plummet from the sky. The mountain hit the bay like a meteor, an exploding geyser of water and lava.

The Locke Institute began to collapse. Another section of the butte sheared off and plummeted into the sea. Inside the cargo wharf, one wall split apart and a cascade of boiling lava poured through the crack, immolating the bodies of the fallen before it spilled into the Irridin and hissed like a gigantic snake made of fire.

Nearby, one of the corpses stood.

Rooker blinked. Another dead prisoner moved and lurched to its feet. Its bones snapped, jutting through the corpse's clothes. Black smoke hissed through growing fangs.

Now, Gerba smiled.

Rooker turned toward the destroyed dock gate. Another new strîgoi emerged from the dead bodies, another. Now more strîgoi emerged from the far passage, covered in blood from their slaughter of the assembly yard, another, another, another. Two came on the ceiling, clinging to it like white dæmon spiders.

Gerba Whipmarples leered at Rooker through the blood in her sea-green eyes. "I believe the victory is mine."

RākŞhasa emerged from the blackness and let fly a blood-curdling bellow. It stepped on the collapsed dock gate with one taloned foot and crushed it flat. More strîgoi poured out between the great beast's legs.

"RākŞhasa." A low laugh burbled from Gerba's mouth, her lips stained red with blood. "Do as you will."

A terrible shriek burst from the dæmon's bladed mouth. Rooker felt his blood go cold. The Dæmon Crownéd charged at him and Jack, followed by a legion of its pale offspring.

Rooker Flynn had felt victory for a single moment, just a single moment. But it was gone, evaporated into a forgotten dream. There was no way to beat Gerba Whipmarples and the Locke Institute. The house would always win. Fighting her was like fighting the tide itself.

I had her.

I had her.

"Rooker!" Jack shouted. "Now's our chance! We have to go!"

Gerba Whipmarples, his jailer and executioner, glared at him over her broken horn and grinned bloody teeth.

Just one more shot.

Jack grabbed him and threw him toward the pier, toward home. *"Run!"*

He ran. As he fled for freedom, Rooker Flynn heard the screeching yowls of dozens of strîgoi. But above that dæmonic cacophony, he heard only one sound that cut through it like a blade.

Her laugh, high and shrill, chasing him into the night.

Gerba laughed as Rooker and the doktar fled, her voice high and shrill.

Today is the day.

Strîgoi raced past her in a thunderous white mass. For a moment, she felt as if she stood in a herd of galloping horses. She closed her eyes and felt their fury within the Heart of Huánghūn as they rushed by. *Ten. Twenty. Fifty. Eighty-eight. And more rising.* RākŞhasa passed her last. She stroked her hand lovingly along the Dæmon Crownéd's leg as it charged past her and up the pier.

She felt the laughter come to a bitter end with one final *"Ha!"* as her dæmons passed into the moonlight to hunt down the last students of the Locke Institute.

Alone, she straightened, touched her jagged horn, and felt the uneven stump, cloven in two by Rooker Flynn's cursed blade. Her heart quailed as she realized she was hideous, malformed, a freak. A trol's horn was the symbol of its pride. Carved, decorated, painted, and bejeweled, it was the first thing by which one trol judged another.

A broken horn meant a broken person.

Gerba felt bitter laughter bubble up again, hysterical. The Horde would never accept her now. Yes, they might embrace her gift or even allow her to join the ranks of the Sacrum Cabal, but she would never be respected. They would laugh about her behind her back, make snide comments when she left the room. She would be maligned, mocked, ostracized. She would never be one of them. She would never be more than a joke.

When Rooker Flynn's corpse returned to her with his bones sharp and his eyes red, Gerba Whipmarples swore she would flay his flesh from his bones.

No. She shook her head. *I will not live as an outcast again. I did not succeed in all this just to be laughed at. No.* She raised her chin. *No.*

She would create a new horn. Cast in gold. Crafted by the most expensive hammerdwarves in Keymark. Her horn would be longer than a man, inlaid with ivory, bedecked with jewels. A legendary horn worthy of the trol queens of the Old World.

Gerba smoothed her dress and collected herself. She checked her cuts, clucking her tongue. The wounds in her chest and back were particularly deep and would take months to regenerate properly. But they would heal.

She took a breath, closed her eyes, and touched the Heart of Huánghūn on her chest. She bathed in the power within, drawing strength from the dark *wikk.*

Yes. A golden horn and a legion of unstoppable dæmons. That *is how I shall return home. A heroine and a champion.*

Finally, after a decade of trials, Gerba Whipmarples felt at peace.

Her struggle was at an end. She would have her respect. She would have her glory. Her great task, at long last, was accomplished.

Churr.

Gerba turned. A lone shiq hung from the ceiling above the far passageway.

She glanced over her shoulder at the cargo wharf dock. The *Intelligentsia* still waited for her. None of the outlaws had risked stealing a boat so close to the strîgoi. The ship rested only twenty steps away, bobbing in the dark water. The shiq could not touch her on the sea.

She felt at her breast for the brooch but stopped herself. No. There was no majik left in the Caged Eight. Not even enough to control a garden spider.

Suddenly, Gerba was ashamed of herself for ever taking pride in the Caged Eight. Now that she knew what real power was, she felt a resentful loathing toward the rune and the shiq it controlled. The yellow spiders were pointless, reprehensible, just one more herd of dumb animals she had been forced to manipulate. The Caged Eight was a child's toy compared to her legion of strîgoi.

Another shiq crawled over the ceiling. Another followed it.

Well. Gerba put her hands on her hips and allowed herself the tiniest smile. *I believe I have spent quite enough time on the island of Huánghūn.*

Now my real life begins.

She took one step toward her boat and heard a soft *klik*.

Gerba looked down to find something at her feet. It was a man, an ugly old dwarf, not tall enough to reach her knees. The dwarf's horrid red face turned up to stare into her eyes. The man grinned between gapped yellow teeth.

Yenrab Bialik.

The *klik* had been the sound of the dwarf locking the scarlet lightchain around her ankle. Following the glowing red line, Gerba realized the other end was clamped around one of the cargo wharf's huge support beams.

She was trapped like a rabbit.

Cold icicles prickled beneath her thick skin. Fear washed through her, the kind of terror she had not known since she'd been a helpless child. Gerba Whipmarples felt that little girl's keening wail rise in her chest, but she stifled the scream before it escaped.

Churr.

She spun to realize a few shiq had multiplied into hundreds. They coated the ceiling, the walls, the floor. She tried to run, but the lightchain pulled tight, locking her in place.

Gerba's thick hands fumbled to the hidden pouch in her belt and searched for her lightknife, the only thing that could sever the majik cord. *There.* She pulled it from its sheath.

She heard the ugly dwarf grunt as his filthy hand slapped the thing out of her hand. The lightknife skittered off the edge of the cargo wharf and fell into the Irridin.

No. Gerba's heart thudded as the little girl's scream threatened to break loose. A hundred shiq had become a thousand. Ten thousand. The swarm came for her. *No.* Panicked, she cast about for another solution, but she was bound as fast as any prisoner had ever been. *No.*

As she knelt to pry at the lightchain manacle, Yenrab Bialik grabbed Gerba by her broken horn. The Red Dwarf stared her right in the eyes, his face a vengeful victory. "You killed my brother, bitch."

Shiq washed over both of them in a swarm. Now Gerba Whipmarples screamed. She felt sharp yellow legs crawl over her. She crushed a shiq beneath her fist, but it was replaced by twenty more. Shiq covered her chest, her arms, her head. Her screams cut off as spiders plunged down her throat. The headmistress strained her mighty body against the lightchain, striving to break free. She flailed one arm and reached for something, anything, to help her. More shiq washed over her, biting her legs, her arms, her eyes.

Stop! She clutched the Heart of Huánghūn and summoned her strîgoi, but she knew her dæmons could not help her now. *Stop!*

Trapped by her own chain, Gerba strained for freedom. One hand stretched toward the undulating sea and the darkening sky, her body a misshapen lump buried beneath a wriggling mass of legs and fangs. *Please.*

She fell to one knee. The headmistress' massive body was buried beneath ten thousand shiq, a writhing, broken lump overwhelmed by the animals it had once controlled. The shapeless mass continued to move, slower and slower, until it finally collapsed.

At long last, Gerba Whipmarples learned to obey her betters.

Chapter

19

ROAD'S
END

Liberty is worth paying for.
Jules Verne

Two men were the last to escape Huánghūn; their shadows fled onto the long pier, lit in double moonlight. The pair ran side by side, each matching the other's stride, their footsteps a single percussive rhythm.

Ahead of them fled three hundred escaped prisoners.

Behind them pursued the snarling coven of strîgoi.

Without a word, the two men turned at the same instant. One of the dæmons caught up. It leapt for them. A sword flashed; a stave smashed. The strîgoi screamed fury, denied its prey. Razor claws lashed out at them; they fended off each blow, batting them away. The stave clubbed the side of the beast's skull and knocked it into the sea. The pale dæmon scrabbled at the dock and tried to gain purchase, but a score of razorsquid tentacles lashed at the beast. Something larger than a razorsquid arrived and dragged it beneath the waves.

Rooker and Jack breathed in unison, awaiting the rest of the coven. They glanced over their shoulders to where the dock ended surrounded by the open Irridin. At the terminus of the pier, panicked outlaws boarded the *Venture Brigand* in a rush, but they could only climb her narrow legs so fast. They needed time. Side by side, Jack and Rooker set their feet and braced their defense. A score of dæmons thundered toward them. At the rear of the throng, RākṢhasa emerged from the cargo bay. Illuminated in dual moonlight, the pale Dæmon Crownéd was a thousand devilish nightmares rolled into one.

"At least we got a choke point," Rooker growled and jerked his chin at the pier. "They can't get at us more than six at a time."

"Three each." Jack nodded. "Knock one in the water, move on to the next. Don't let 'em get behind us. Anything else?"

"Don't die."

"Easy."

They watched the onslaught come. Neither man flinched. They were both tough enough to die well.

Fifty feet away, the tide of dæmons came to a sudden halt. Ravenous, the strîgoi snarled at the pair of men but moved no closer, as if they had been pulled up short by a leash. At the back of the coven, the great beast Rākṣhasa suddenly let loose a barbaric, vengeful scream, furious as if it had been denied something precious. For a moment, its flaming eyes glared pure hate at the pair of men, wanting nothing more than to claim them as its own. Abruptly, it turned and galloped back toward the dock gate, unable to deny Gerba Whipmarples' final summons.

The strîgoi coven followed their dæmon king, hissing, and just like that the pier was empty.

"What—" Jack let out a rush of air from his nose, holding the wounds on his chest with one bloody hand. "What the hell was that?"

"I think we just used up the last of our luck."

Before the last word passed Rooker's lips, the cargo wharf flooded with spiders. A million frenzied shiq burst from the tunnel. A million more skittered over the wall of the crumbling Locke Institute. As the swarm came, a massive part of the butte face sheared off, geysering lava. It bathed ten thousand shiq in flames and drowned another ten thousand in the sea. It made no difference. They were innumerable, infinite, and they flooded onto the pier toward Rooker and Jack like a boiling yellow carpet.

Jack glanced at Rooker. "You and your big mouth."

They fled. Two pairs of boots pounded the dock at a dead run. Thundering down the path, they saw no skiffs remained tied to the pier; they had all been taken. The marina was littered with escaped prisoners bending arms to oars. The only ship remaining at the dock was the *Venture Brigand*. Two hundred outlaws lined her decks, urging them on, to run faster, to not look back.

Sprinting down the dock, Jack and Rooker heard the terrifying arachnid *churr* closing in behind them. Jack strained as hard as he could, but his breathing was labored, his step ragged and tired. He slowed to a jog, then a limping shamble. His body was spent. He'd lost too much blood and fought too hard for too long. He had nothing left to give. Jack stumbled.

Rooker hooked his arm under Jack and kept him on his feet. The shiq poured toward them, an unstoppable mass of legs. Jack could only struggle forward at a hobble, but Rooker refused to leave him behind. The shiq would overwhelm them before they ever touched the *Brigand*.

Still, they refused to give in.

Rooker panted, using the last of his strength to keep Jack upright. "Hey?"

"Hey?"

"If we don't make it, just want ya to know one thing." Rooker glanced at Jack, sweat streaming off his brow. "It was yer fault."

Jack snorted a laugh.

Huánghūn bent. The two men were thrown off their feet. The pier buckled and broke like a gigantic, fractured spine. Some of the long dock twisted in half a spiral, cracking wood and timber, spilling shiq into the sea. The swarm was cut off as beams shattered in a dozen places along the pier from tectonic torque as the island ripped itself apart.

Landing on their backsides, the pair gazed up at the Locke Institute. Boiling red pāhoehoe, long ropy strands of molten rock, spilled from the butte like bloody waterfalls. Superheated crimson poured from newly opened cracks in the face of the wall, which grew wider and more inflamed with every geothermal seizure. As they stared, a portion of the wall the size of a house jettisoned off from the main. It arced into the air almost in slow-motion, tumbling sideways until it struck the sea with a catastrophic crash that burst it into a million broken hunks of hissing magma. The gigantic hole it left behind allowed moonlight to break through from beyond, spilling through the remains of the wall and into the sea, free.

At the peak of the Institute, the broken beams that had once held the Agrat-ban-Haifa aloft danced in flames. In silence, they slid toward the assembly yard and disappeared from view.

Jack and Rooker stared, unable to move.

Neither was sure which one picked up the other, but together they got to their feet and limped their way to the end of the dock. The ship was silent, the prisoners' unblinking eyes gazing upon the destruction in shock. Rooker threw his hip upon the *Brigand*'s outrigger and pulled Jack aboard. Staring at the death of Huánghūn, he tapped his rings against her wood.

"Hard about, girl."

The *Venture Brigand*'s red silk sails snapped tight. She broke away from the pier and left the Locke Institute behind.

Three hundred escaped convicts watched Huánghūn eat itself. Black smoke wreathed moonlit darkness in a sulfuric cloud lit by red streaks of fire. Once more the wall bucked and an eruption vomited from the pinnacle of the butte and expelled slags of molten rock into the sky. A Vesuvian explosion of phreatomagmatic pressure sent flaming embers half a mile in every direction.

Jack and Rooker felt their hair blown back as the shockwave hit them. A shower of embers fell into the sea and left smoking paths in the water, bubbling and hissing as they sunk to the bottom. One huge chunk flew right through the *Brigand*'s starboard sail and left a smoking hole where it passed.

The silk lit on fire.

Rooker was on his feet in a heartbeat. He climbed like a monkey up the arcing leg that connected the outrigger to the ship. Once aboard, he bypassed the deck entirely and scrambled straight up the ratlines to the top of the mast.

Jack tried to keep up, but he was too injured to do much more than throw himself aboard. Above, Rooker mounted the spar where a water bucket awaited just such an emergency. Rooker sluiced water and wet sand down the jib sail, dousing a portion of the fire. "Form a bucket brigade, damn you all!" Rooker hollered at the outlaws on deck who stared dumbfounded at the volcano that used to be home. "We can't sail without *sails!*"

Quickly, the outlaws leapt to the task. They formed a line of men and women that traveled all the way from the outriggers to the top of the mainmast. With their help, Rooker had the flames out in minutes. Left with dozens of full buckets, Rooker shot a furious look down upon them. "Well, drench the damn deck, ya wasteka skags! She's already burned enough! We get hit again, I don't want a hole in my hull!"

As the outlaws bent to work drenching the dragonfire-burned hindquarters of the great ship, Jack slumped against the bridge deckrail. Rooker joined him and leaned against the wheel. Behind them, the black smoke of Huánghūn's burning corpse pillared into the sky. As they cruised out of the harbor, a dozen smaller boats pursued in the *Venture Brigand*'s wake, trailing the big ship like baby ducks following their mother.

Jack looked upon the survivors of the Locke Institute. Farah moved among the outlaws, helping spray the deck with water. Billy sat on the foredeck, bandaging his bleeding leg and whistling a strange, sad tune. Patch held her moggie with one arm while she shouted orders at the outlaws, demanding they move quickly or feel her claws on their backs.

Jack smiled and turned to Rooker. "Looks like you have a new crew."

Rooker spat. "*Bah.* Half of 'em are lubbers and the other half are—" He cut himself off, peering at the sea.

"What?" asked Jack.

Rooker ignored him and tapped his rings on the spar, a slow grin curling his lips. "Hard a-starboard, girl. Half sail."

The *Venture Brigand* slowed and turned in a tight arc. Rooker snatched a rope and hauled himself to his feet. "Patch!" he shouted, his voice sharp. "Assign battle stations and prepare to board."

Patch Picaroon scowled at him, holding her baby. "I'm a little busy, Rooker."

He fixed hard eyes on her. "Ya wanna be mate on the *Brigand*, yer gonna work for it."

Patch's eyes snapped to him. A smile spilled over her face. "Mate?"

"Prepare to board." Rooker jerked his chin up. "And get yer game face on."

Soon enough, the *Venture Brigand* overtook the little boat Rooker had spotted. It was the *Hup Two*, Gerba's dependable little transport. The *Brigand* loomed over the barge like a vulture. A score of hardened pirates readied to attack it from three sides, some on the skids, some waiting in the belly turret above. Dwarfed beneath the massive catamaran, the *Hup Two* slowed to a crawl. Only one figure manned the little boat, a frightened-looking woman dressed in filthy acolyte robes. She still wore her niqab, though there was a hole in one side of it.

Inside the belly dome, Rooker whispered to Jack. "Which one is that?"

"Marguerite."

"Ahoy the *Hup Two*!" Rooker shouted as he popped open the belly hatch and stared down on the little barge. Seeing the acolyte's frightened eyes, he leaned out further. "Looks like the winds have shifted, Marguerite, ol' gal. It's yer turn to give *us* some blood."

Laughter broke from the assembled pirates as they leered down at the lone acolyte. She shifted, eyes darting, trapped. "I... I don't—"

"Take that damned thing off!" Rooker shouted.

Marguerite removed her niqab. Beneath it was the face of a woman no older than twenty, covered in soot and char. She dumped her veil into the Irridin. "Please don't kill me."

"Why not?" Rooker flung out a rope and descended in one smooth movement. He landed on the deck of the little barge and eyeballed the former acolyte. "We're all in the mood for a little revenge. And lady, you sure earned it." Shouts of violence thundered from the assembled outlaws as Rooker stood nose to nose with the shivering acolyte. "Now, yer lucky, Marguerite. Because there's only two things that'll satisfy revenge. Blood..." He ripped aside the tarp covering the deck of the *Hup Two*. "Or gold."

Treasure filled the floor of the barge. Gems and diamonds, precious art, and exquisite pieces of jewelry were littered like candy among large chests bursting at the seams with the wealth of a thousand bounties. Above, outlaws let out a hoot and a holler at the sight of so much swag.

"Ya bled us dry. We should do the same." Rooker pointed the singing saber at Marguerite. "Or... ya can carry all this up to the *Brigand* for us and we'll call it square. If yer sweet, maybe there's a pirate or two who'd lend ya a hand."

Cheers broke from the *Brigand* as outlaws descended on the *Hup Two* like ants. Quickly, Marguerite grabbed the first chest and handed it to a pirate. By the tenth box, she was almost smiling.

"All right, ya skags!" Rooker hollered. "There's not enough liquor on board for all you wasteka criminals! We set sail for the Bowery! First drink's on me!"

An eruption of shouts thundered from the former prisoners, now free men and rich. *"All hail the Captain Rooker Flynn!"* shouted Patch at the top of her lungs.

"All hail the Captain Rooker Flynn!" Cheers rained down on the captain of the *Venture Brigand*, none louder than those of Black Jack himself.

Only a few citizens of the sleepy trading post called the Bowery were awake at half past midnight, and only one witnessed the pirate flotilla arrive in Bow Bay. Kettle Simms, the harbormaster, stared open-mouthed at the thirteen ships. They were led by a three-masted catamaran in the shape of a Λ that skated on the sea like a colossal water strider. She was, quite simply, the most magnificent ship Kettle had ever seen. She towered over the rest, silhouetted against two moons and a million stars.

Kettle rang the alarm bell and watched the pirate ships come, knowing there was nothing the Bowery could do against a marauding force so large. Terror rising in his throat, the harbormaster watched the big catamaran overwhelm the Manta Dock, straddling it like a jockey mounting a skinny pony. The big ship disgorged her contents. Hollering pirates streamed down the ship's legs and dropped from the strange glass dome in her belly. Manta Dock was suddenly overrun with the raggediest group of criminals Kettle had ever seen. Most were thin as a bony dog, two or three hundred of them, each covered in dirt, soot, and blood. They stared at the Bowery with ravenous eyes and white smiles. One, a lean and rangy fellow that appeared to be the captain, walked straight up to Kettle with a grin that looked like trouble. The black-haired buccaneer stunk of sulfur and sweat. Behind him, another pirate dressed up like the folk tales of ol' Black Jack leaned on a bamboo staff, his hand bandaged in fresh gauze.

The pirate captain snatched the clapper out of Kettle's hand and silenced the alarm bell. "Enough of that. Simms, right?"

Kettle blinked, not having the first clue how the captain knew his name. "Uh... ayuh."

"Keep both eyes on my girl." The captain jerked his thumb at the big catamaran. "In fact, bring down two more sets of eyes. And I want the entire aft deck watered down from here 'til morning. If one sail is out of place at sunrise, I'll keel-haul you from here to Rimmy's Cull." The captain flicked his thumb and a gold coin enough for a month's labor landed in Kettle's hand. "Get me?"

Kettle had never heard of a pirate paying a dock fee before a raid, but he slipped the coin into his bathrobe pocket, not wanting to cause any trouble. "Ayuh."

The captain made to go ashore with some of his crew, including the Black Jack fella. Uphill, Kettle watched a few scattered lanterns wink on in some of the homes. Suddenly the captain was right in his face. "I said *both* eyes."

Kettle turned to the big catamaran. As he did, a gaggle of shaggy pirates scampered up the dock, making excited noises. Most looked thin enough to keel over in a strong wind, filthy as sin, but their voices grew joyful as they approached the town. Frightened to take his eyes off the big ship, Kettle watched the sea dogs move ashore, heading for the only large tavern the Bowery boasted, the Road's End. He heard a fist pound at the tavern door. "Wheezer!" the captain shouted for the innkeeper, long since asleep in his bed. "Wake up, ya old crook! Ya got customers!"

Half an hour later, every beer bottle and barrel in the Bowery was open and frothing. Frightened but curious, the townsfolk watched the midnight revelry in curious awe. Outlaws doubled the population of the trading port and filled Road's End to bursting. The remainder of the pirates spilled out into the streets, drinking heavily and singing familiar sea shanties at the top of their lungs, howling at the novelty of the two moons.

Little by little, the citizens of the Bowery grew less fearful. The pirates' manner was rough, their language coarse, and they could not be mistaken for anything but desperate criminals. However, against all expectations, there was no sound of breaking glass, no fires, no looting. Their takeover of the Bowery was strangely civil.

Denied good food, strong drink, and the joys of the night for so long, the survivors of Huánghūn gorged themselves on everything they could get their hands on. Most gathered inside the Road's End, devouring fried chicken, spit-turned pork, pan-broiled beefsteaks, fried potatoes, watermelon, cantaloupe, and spicy noodles as fast as the tavern owner and his daughters could serve them up. They ran out of mugs for the beer, so the survivors simply grabbed the barrels and drank from those. Behind the counter, old man Wheezer effused delight as the captain slapped another fistful of platinum onto the bar, enough to pay for all the food in his larder twice over. For the first time in Keymark history, a pirate gang filled a town's pockets rather than emptying them.

One of the outlaws made a joke about ordering galt for dessert. He was forcibly removed from the tavern.

As the alcohol flowed, so did the desires of the convicts who had been pent up and caged for so long. Patch Picaroon made it known, loudly and in no uncertain terms, that any man who forced his affections upon a woman of the Bowery would find himself at the bottom of the Irridin, as would any outlaw who failed to stop an unwanted advance. With that said, many of the crew found willing partners, some among the townsfolk, some within their own ranks. Patch kept one ear open for trouble, ready to nip it in the bud, but for most of the night she simply cooed to her moggie with a motherly look on her face.

Billy Pilgrim was waited upon like royalty. The balladeer was provided with three things almost immediately upon entering the Road's End. The first was a crutch to use until his bandaged leg could heal. The second was the most comfortable chair in town, which the survivors placed on top of a grand table in the center of the room. The third was the only item stolen from the Bowery the entire night, a dented brown fiddle.

Pilgrim tucked the instrument under his chin. His bowstring moved slowly at first, but Billy's eyes seemed to focus as he found himself within the music. A series of long chords built into a few bars of a melody. He peppered the rhythm with pizzicato pinpoints, then the troubadour was off and running. The tune became a series of shanties and jigs as beautiful music, that singular art that felt so close to the power of the *wikk,* poured from his fingertips.

He sang. Most of the words were nonsensical, simply syllables sewn together into an ever-quickening string of notes. Billy's fingers blurred the violin bow over the strings, playing faster and faster, the tune an ode to joy that rose and built upon itself until every ear in the Bowery turned to listen. Pilgrim built the tune to an ebullient crescendo, held the single high note for a long moment, then sang the first bar of 'Sit Down, Sit Down.'

Enthusiastic shouts rang out as the survivors joined in. With sudden emotion, they echoed Billy's lyrics, mocking the Locke Institute, shouting more than singing the words. Their noise could be heard a mile over the water when they reached the pinnacle of the protest song with a thunderous "We'll tell her, too, what she can do, go stick it up her ass!"

Laughter bubbled through the little town as the outlaws inside and out hollered for an encore. Billy obliged them.

At the bar, Farah sipped her drink, watching the commotion unfold without saying a word. Before long, she found herself folded into a comfortable silence with a few Hyena girls who shared her love of quiet. They sat, content, a counterpoint to the brouhaha clamoring around them. After a little time, they disappeared to find out-of-the-way beds to settle in for a long and comfortable nap. To Farah's delight, she found her bedchamber filled with books and fell asleep with one in her hand.

As the party continued long into the night, two figures sat together in their own silence. Rooker and Jack had taken a large booth in the corner of the bar for themselves. They didn't drink much, didn't eat much, and did not talk at all.

They just sat together. A low, satisfied smile curled on their lips, each man a mirror of the other.

After some time, Rooker held up his single shot of Roi-Tan. Jack held up his own glass and clinked it with Rooker. Both men tapped their glasses on the table and shot it down.

Pilgrim struck up a new tune, a drinking song no one had ever heard before that night but would soon become a beer-hall favorite that was sung throughout Keymark for as long as she survived.

One pirate sailed across the sea
They locked him up, threw away the key
He picked the lock and walked out free
Now hear my violin – ho!

Old tyrants said there's no excuse
They hung him up from a hangman's noose
He said this necktie is too loose
And slipped it off his chin – ho!

Princes bow at his command
A singing blade in his red right hand
Rides the helm of the Venture Brigand
The Captain Rooker Flynn!

Xeusia ul-Styx, it had him trapped
Its dragon breath like a thunderclap
He breathed right back, blew it off the map

King of the Irridin – ho!

The trol-witch wished he'd not been born
She tricked him with cruel schemes and scorn
Our Captain chopped off her long horn
Used it to toast his win – ho!

Princes bow at his command
A singing blade in his red right hand
Rides the helm of the Venture Brigand
The Captain Rooker Flynn!

Now the greatest trick that you'll ever see
Was he up and set the prisoners free
He saved us all, both you and me
And did it with a grin – ho!

Princes bow at his command
A singing blade in his red right hand
Rides the helm of the Venture Brigand
Does Captain Rooker Flynn – ho!

Amid the rounds of applause, a half-drunk Patch searched the Road's End for the man himself. "Hah!" cried Patch as she found him in his shadowy booth. "Hey, Rooker! I guess you finally got your song! Hey! Rooker!"

Rooker Flynn leaned on Jack Swift, both of them dead asleep.

Chapter

20

=SWEET=
BYE & BYE

Friendship is the greatest of worldly goods.

C. S. Lewis

D AWN ROSE OVER THE white sandy shores of the Bowery, unnoticed by everyone in town save the milkman. Sleeping bodies lay half in and half out of beds, chairs, and doorways, snoring peacefully. Not one shop in town opened until noon, when some of the more enterprising merchants began roasting coffee to help the pirates shake off last night's bender and spend more gold. There was little left to eat in town so the children were sent to gather mangos, eggs, and chickens from outlying farms. As the outlaws woke, most found their bellies stuffed from the night before. For the residents of the Bowery, many of their pockets felt the same.

Jack's head snapped up, warding off a nightmare.

His eyes flashed open and he blinked to discover he was lying in a soft feather bed with a floral homemade quilt. His only enemy was the sunlight streaming through the window. He let loose a sigh, feeling the ache of the cuts on his chest, back, and hand. He gingerly pulled back the covers to find new stitches in his chest and remembered he had let one of the townspeople, a barber, sew him up last night. It was decent work. His fingers looked swollen and they still throbbed, but the pain was better than yesterday.

Longest day of my life. And one of the best.

He glanced sideways to see Rooker in the other bed, his face mashed down into a pillow, his back squinched up, his limbs splayed at crazy angles like a crashed two-year-old.

"Hey," Jack said.

"Hey," came the muffled response.

They didn't say more for another hour, lounging in silence.

Eventually they rose and left their room to find Farah, asleep with a book in one hand and a knife in the other, guarding their door. They let her snore on, bypassing her quietly. In the bathhouse, they showered, luxuriating in streams of sun-warmed water. Rooker found an ointment for Jack's cuts and helped re-bandage his wounds with fresh linen. As Rooker bound him up, Jack chuckled and gave him a look. *You know what would make this easier?*

Rooker snorted. *Maybe ya shouldn't have knocked the Bell into the sea.*

Maybe I shouldn't have. Jack chuckled and pulled on a shirt.

Together they stepped through the human wreckage of the Bowery. They found a bakery and shared a quiet breakfast of honeyed toast and fresh chilled milk. Not a word passed between them the entire meal.

Walking out to the Manta Dock, they discovered Patch Picaroon lounging in a giant leather chair that took up nearly the width of the dock. Parked directly in front of the *Venture Brigand,* she lounged comfortably with her moggie, nursing. Someone had set up a vast yellow umbrella to protect her from the sun. At her side, within easy reach, sat an ice bucket full of oranges.

Jack squinted, too sleepy to understand the point. "What are you doing?"

"Protecting my home." Patch bit into an orange and ate it like an apple, peel and all.

Rooker's voice was thick and slow. "Good idea."

"I *know* it's a good idea," Patch shot back. "Not everyone sleeps 'til noon." She nodded her head. "Captain."

Jack cricked his neck and stepped toward her. "I should get a look at your stitches."

"My stitches are fine." Patch waved him off. "Barber sewed me up before he carried me out here this morning." She cocked her head at him. "If it makes you feel better, more than half of your work held."

Jack shook his head, realizing he'd stitched her belly up only... *Yesterday? It feels like a month ago.* He blew out, realizing he was breathing not like a convict, not like a gladiator, not like a student of the Locke Institute. For the first time in a long time, he was just breathing like a person. He glanced at Rooker. *Okay.*

Rooker nodded. *Okay.* He climbed over Patch's giant chair and made for the ship. "Ease down, girl."

Straddling the dock, the *Venture Brigand*'s long legs stretched wide, lowering her belly dome a foot above his head. Rooker popped open the hatch and started to climb in.

"Where are you two headed?" Patch turned in her chair.

"O, just out," said Rooker. "Back before sunset."

Patch made to get up. "I should go with you."

"You can't even walk, Patch. Besides, you've got someone depending on you now." Jack gestured at her moggie. "Does she have a name yet?"

"Not yet."

Jack cocked his head. "Actually, I've got an idea. Something you could help me with while we're gone." He leaned down and whispered in Patch's ear.

She glanced at him, puzzled, then nodded.

"What the hell are you doing, bubba?" Rooker grumbled. "Come on."

Jack didn't answer but put one hand on Patch's furry shoulder. "Get some rest. We'll be back."

Under a cloudless tropical sky, the *Venture Brigand* made its way east-southeast through the Deep Blue South. White sea birds spiraled through the sky, kept effortlessly aloft by the air currents. Neither man spoke a word the entire trip, watching the smoke of a distant volcano funnel into the sky. *If I didn't know better, I'd think this was Hawaii.*

As they closed in on their destination, they found the tiny islet of Bounty deserted. The dock was empty, the colosseum was silent, smoking quietly. No one from the Institute had escaped to the little skerry lump of land. It stood abandoned, likely forever. As the *Venture Brigand* rounded the islet head, Huánghūn came into view.

Jack felt a shudder ripple through him.

A cooling blanket of black lava spiderwebbed over the remains of the Locke Institute. The center of the butte had collapsed in on itself, leaving an open view into the smoking jungle beyond. The camps were destroyed, the yingcao trees were gone, burned away. The fires had gone out, but the smoke continued to rise from the cooling earth. A few raiptar birds occupied the hazy air, searching for new nesting grounds, but apart from the birds the island was silent as a grave.

They watched it a long, long time.

When they docked, Rooker pulled a touch-and-go, sending the *Brigand* back out to sea. Jack knew Rooker would never drop anchor in this harbor, never run the risk of being trapped here again. Stepping onto the twisted pier, Jack saw the last sludgy remains of a thousand shiq bodies melted to yellow slime by the sun. Slowly, they made their way toward the wreckage of the dock gate, prepared to flee at any moment.

Halfway there, Rooker put a hand to Jack's chest and stopped him. He pointed at the ash coating the pier. Fresh tracks dotted the trail. Jack was no tracker, but he could make out a narrow pair of boots, a set of giant bird claws, and two cloven hooves.

Naysayers.

Jack remembered the deal they'd made. The bounty hunters would have arrived before dawn, waiting for the shiq to die and their promised opportunity to pillage the Locke Institute. The only problem was the Institute was destroyed and Rooker had stolen the *Hup Two* with all of Huánghūn's treasures. *If they're still here, they're not going to be in a good mood.*

Jack gripped Nepenthe and felt the stitches in his knuckles pull tight.

"Don't bother," said Rooker with cold finality. "They've come and gone."

Jack might not be able to read the tracks, but he trusted Rooker. He relaxed, letting Nepenthe slip looser in his hand. They picked their way over the twisted pier, around the blackened lava at the waterline, and made their way ashore. A few pieces of dead shiq carapace littered the cargo wharf, slowly melting in the half-sun-light.

Further up, they found what they were looking for.

A jumbled mound of remains lay on the floor, a tremendous corpse eaten down to the bone. A femur thick as a truck axle, a hollow pelvis wide as a lounge chair, a rib cage nearly as tall as Jack. All were picked clean, bone white. At the tip of the skull, what was left of the primary and secondary horns had been chewed to nubs, the keratin just as much a meal as the flesh and organs had been. As always, the shiq refused to eat the eyeballs. The skull's hollow sockets contained two sea-green eyes that stared at nothing.

Around one bone ankle, a lightchain glowed gently.

Around the other ankle clung Yenrab Bialik. The dwarf's de-nuded skeleton was wrapped around her leg; he had held her fast until the bitter end.

Jack laid out the blanket he had brought with him, and the two men slowly began moving the dwarf's remains onto it, carefully, piece by piece. Neither man said a word.

When Yenrab had been folded into his death shroud, Jack eyed the trol's body. The silver birdcage around her neck was empty, the shard of black diamond gone. Her hand, too, was empty, her lace glove in tatters, the single rod of Nepenthe nowhere to be found.

I guess the Naysayers got what they came for.

Jack gripped Nepenthe and summoned the missing stick. He felt nothing, as if the seventh piece did not exist. Wherever it was, the Naysayers had taken it beyond his reach. For a moment, he felt as if he had lost a piece of himself, one of many stolen from him here on Huánghūn.

Jack eyed the six pieces of bamboo in his hand, Nepenthe ready to serve.

And a lot of people lost a whole lot more.

He and Rooker picked up Yenrab Bialik's cloth coffin.

It took more than an hour to find a safe route over the cooling magma. They took their time, sharing the burden of the bindle that contained Yenrab's bones. Both men were prepared to flee at the first sign of movement, but the island lay still. No strîgoi shadowed them. The dæmons did not appear.

Eventually they reached the other side of the ridge that had once been the Locke Institute and arrived in the assembly yard. No one waited for them. The bodies of the dead had been carried off by the shiq. The island was empty.

Jack finally spoke, his voice quiet. "What do you think?"

Rooker looked at the cooling lava all around him. "I think the strîgoi are buried somewhere under the Institute. Right back where they came from."

"And RākŞhasa?"

Rooker took a long breath. "Wherever it is, it's not here. Not much we can do about it either way. Come on. Let's get this done."

They fetched tools. Their picks cut into the ground, one strike after another, the two men working in a steady rhythm. For the next two hours, neither man spoke as the grave grew deep enough to stand in.

Jack placed the blanket containing Yenrab Bialik inside the hollow in the earth. Rooker helped him out of the hole and together they filled in the pit. Jack crafted a marker as best he could and carved Yenrab's name into it.

Rooker leaned on his shovel and wiped the sweat off his brow. "You or me?"

Jack shook his head. He didn't have the faintest idea of what to say. "You."

Rooker took a deep breath.

"Here lies a... good man. Yenrab Bialik, an ugly, one-eyed, gap-toothed hillbilly dwarf who saved our lives and the lives of a lot of other men and women who didn't deserve to be here. He loved good moonshine. And he loved his brother." Rooker glanced at Jack. "We lay him to rest in this earth so he can share his final sleep with his twin Barney... and Copper Dave... and Major West and Fancy Nan and everybody else who died on this damned rotten island. May the Lord of Sea and Sky have mercy on all our wretched souls." Rooker jammed his shovel into the dirt, unable to say more. "Ya got anything?"

Jack knew he should say something, but he didn't know what. All he could think of was the song a church choir had sung at his mother's funeral when he'd been just a boy. He sung it as best he could.

There's a land that is fairer than day
And by faith we can see it afar
For the Father waits over the way
To prepare us a dwelling place there
In the sweet by and by
We shall meet on that beautiful shore
In the sweet by and by
We shall meet on that beautiful shore
We shall sing on that beautiful shore
The melodious songs of the blessed
And our spirit shall sorrow no more
Not a sign for the blessing of rest
In the sweet by and by
We shall meet on that beautiful shore
In the sweet by and by

We shall meet on that beautiful shore.

Rooker was not surprised to find Leah and Memphis waiting for them on the Manta Dock. He saw the fishing boat he'd purchased for them tied up nearby. Patch was gone, relieved of duty by the girl and the trol. Calling out to them, Jack quickly dropped from the belly dome and was hugging them both before Rooker reached the trapdoor. Fuji circled up Jack's leg and licked his face like an excited puppy.

One big happy family.

Rooker scratched at his stubble and watched them embrace. He felt a sharp twinge of jealousy, followed by a longer, deeper pain of regret. He knew what would come next. He didn't want to face it, but it was coming whether he wanted it or not. Rooker hesitated, waiting, then decided he looked stupid with his legs just dangling in the air, so he dropped to the dock with a thump.

"Leah. Memphis." His voice sounded darker than he'd intended.

The big brownbelly spread his hands. "I thought you two were going to try and save a few people, not the *entire prison*."

Rooker frowned. "We didn't get everybody."

Leah gestured at the bustling docks of the Bowery. "Looks like you saved quite a few."

Rooker shrugged. "Might make a half-decent crew. With some work."

"Well." Leah arched an eyebrow. "I'm glad to see you alive."

"Good to be seen." He kept his face blank.

"I've never been to a trading post this far south before," said Memphis. "Let's head up to the tavern. We'll buy you a few drinks."

"I'm not goin' up there," said Rooker. "I've spent too much time with dirt under my boots this year. Let's get on the water if ya want to drink. Or talk. Or whatever."

Jack gave him a look. "Seriously?"

A cold fish swam up Rooker's guts. It was all he could do to keep from wincing. "Seriously."

It was Jack's turn to frown. "You okay?"

"I'm fine. Let's go."

"Well, hang on, there's a few things I need to..." Jack cut himself off. "Memphis? Will you come with me real quick?"

"Sure." Jack and the trol cast a look over their shoulders at Rooker as the two of them disappeared down the docks. Rooker found himself alone with Leah.

They stood together in uncomfortable silence. Rooker leaned against the belly dome, pretending to clean his nails. She cleared her throat. "So what's—"

"Where ya headed, Leah?"

"I..." She blinked at his sudden interruption. "I'm going home. I've got responsibilities that are long overdue. Promises to keep."

"In that?" Rooker jerked his chin at the fishing boat.

Leah shrugged and smiled. "I was hoping you might give us a ride north."

"Mm. You and the trol?" Rooker nodded. "He's got responsibilities too?"

"We just want to get home." She leaned against the glass dome beside him. "How about you?"

"I *am* home."

Leah straightened. Her face changed. Finally accepting his bad temper, she adopted a scowl of her own. "Fine. What's your plan, Rooker?"

"How d'ya mean?"

She put her hands on her hips. "You've got your ship. You've got a crew. You've got your freedom. All you need now is someone to rob."

"Yer thinkin' of someone else." Rooker looked up at the pink and gold clouds that stretched across the sky. "That guy got hanged."

Leah raised an eyebrow, surprised. Rooker felt a tickle of satisfaction at that. *Nice to know she doesn't know me as well as she thinks she does.*

Leah's voice was soft. "So who are you now?"

Rooker stared at the sea. "I suppose we'll find out, won't we?"

Memphis Kubiak trundled down the dock carrying Patch Picaroon, who, in turn, carried her moggie and, nestled in her lap, a large wooden box wrapped in a pink bow. Jack followed them, a secret grin on his face.

Leah eyed Patch and offered a smile. "Who's this?"

Jack extended his hand. "Patch Picaroon, meet Leah Archer."

"I've heard about you," said the jinx-cat. She glanced at Memphis. "Both of you. It's an honor."

"For me as well." Leah leaned in and smiled at Patch's baby. "That's a beautiful moggie you have."

"Thank you."

Rooker scowled, uncomfortable with the pleasantries. "What's in the box?"

Patch shot him a look. "Ladies' undergarments." Jack and Memphis chuckled. Patch raised her eyebrows at Rooker, hopeful. "So is this a family cruise or can anyone join?"

"Just family," said Rooker. "Come on."

A few minutes later, Rooker cast off the *Venture Brigand* and returned to the sea. A sense of calm control took over once the deckwheel was back in his hands. *Come on, girl. Let's get this over with.*

Cruising out of the harbor, they found a comfortable chair for Patch and her moggie. All the while, Rooker glanced at the box with the pink ribbon, trying to figure out what it was for. Finally, he could contain his curiosity no further. "What *is* that?"

Jack shrugged. "I got you a little something."

Rooker frowned. *A farewell gift.* "What is it?"

"Hasn't anyone ever given you a present before?"

"Not willingly."

"Well, open it."

Rooker slipped out his beltknife, cut the ribbon, and looked inside.

Black and tan fur puffed out at crazy angles as the puppy rolled out of the box. Its ears were little tan triangles that matched its tiny paws. Its little brown face had a dark stripe down one side, showing off its golden-brown eyes. It unleashed a squeaking growl and bit at Rooker's boot.

Rooker stood silent, watching it. What passed over his face was not a smile. It was something more.

Something better.

Jack nodded, watching his eyes. "Next time someone asks you 'Where's the dog,' the answer's right by your side."

Rooker bent down, picked up the little guy, and cradled him in his arms. It made a tiny *ruf* sound and licked at his cheek. Rooker couldn't help but grin. He held up the darling little puppy in both hands and buried his face in its fur. "Well, hello, little fella. Who's a good boy? Who's a good boy? What's yer name, huh?"

Jack cocked his head. "I was thinking Pip."

Rooker's eyes found Jack.

He nodded, smiling.

Thank you.

"Pip."

Under the ebbing sun of the Deep Blue South, the *Venture Brigand* skated water so calm and smooth it rode like glass. They talked of small things, passing time as the world spun by. Leah cuddled with Patch's moggie. So did Memphis, the tiny baby almost disappearing between the leathery cracks in his arms. Patch idled with the boys, sharing stories, sharing time. Rooker and Jack scampered with Pip the pup, using an old bandanna to play tug-o-war.

After most of the day had passed, Rooker sniffed the air and realized he was almost at his destination. He felt an urge to ignore it, to just keep going and chase the horizon for a few more days, even another hour.

We're at the end. No point dragging it out.

Rooker cut sail. The outriggers slowed, the water without wave, the sky without wind. The *Venture Brigand* came to a stop.

Rooker's gut felt sour. "Here we go."

Jack glanced around to find nothing but ocean in every direction. "Where is here?"

"Same place ya came from." Rooker looked down into the clear water to see the mirror image of the *Venture Brigand* below. He felt separated from his body, like he was hovering above himself in another plane of existence. He never thought it would twist his stomach to see the wreck of the *Brigand*'s sister ship, still preserved in all her beauty at the bottom of the sea. But it did. It wrung him out like a wet rag. "The *Círdan*," said Rooker, feeling his voice catch in his throat.

As he watched, the pixies in the water began circling, excited. He tapped his rings on the deckwheel, anxious. "The *Venture Brigand*'s too injured, but the brownbelly can use the *wikk* in the *Círdan* to open his majik door, right?" Rooker glanced at Memphis. "Right?"

The trol opened his mouth, then shut it. "Yes, but..."

"So do it." Rooker cracked the knuckle of his thumb in his fist and turned to Jack. "Ya can finally go home." Jack stared at him, saying nothing. Rooker hated the feel of the kid's eyes on him. He was uncomfortable enough as it was. "Ya can be in Chegago before ya know it."

Jack didn't say anything. For once, Rooker couldn't read the expression on his face. The pause seemed to go on forever. Rooker jammed his fingernail into his palm and darted a glance at Memphis. "Anything else ya need?"

The trol glanced at Jack. "I was planning on waiting a few more days, but... no. We can go right now."

"So." Rooker set his jaw and forced himself to face Jack. "I guess this is it."

Jack watched him for a moment then looked down on the sunken ship. Pixies gathered speed, their green light circling in a vortex below. "I guess it is."

"Home. Back to yer da." Rooker nodded. "Back to yer... whatever. Toshan friends. Yer life. I guess." Rooker stood a little straighter, took a half-step forward, and put out a hand to shake Jack's. "I just wanted to say... thank you. Whatever our differences, we had one hell of a run." Jack took his hand. Rooker held on just a bit longer than he had to.

He almost let it out, just for a moment. He wanted to say what he meant, say what he felt. He could beg Jack to stay. Beg him to turn his back on his home, on his father, on his world, just to stay with him a little longer.

Once Jack was gone, Rooker knew he would never be whole again.

But Rooker Flynn had spent a lifetime bottling up his emotions, and he put a thick cork in this one before it could escape.

"Right." Rooker forced himself to let go of Jack's hand. "So. Time to go."

Jack's voice became soft. "Rooker."

Rooker couldn't meet his eye. "Yeah."

Jack placed one hand on Rooker's shoulder. As Rooker raised his head, he found Jack's blue eyes staring into his. "I'm not leaving you."

Rooker's breath hitched.

He had not cried since he was ten years old and he did not cry now. But his eyes were suddenly wet. He felt a warmth tremble up from his belly, something tremulous and fragile. Something he'd never felt before, an emotion he couldn't put a name to. It was sadness and joy and relief and comfort, all packed together inside his heart.

Rooker snatched Jack into his arms and held him tight.

At last, at last, at last. *Home.*

Above, the *Venture Brigand* sighed happily. *Yes.*

Pip tried to lick them both at once.

Jack and Rooker didn't let go. Their embrace went on for a long time. Longer than mere friendship would allow. They embraced as only family could.

Neither said a word. They didn't need to. They just grinned over each other's backs, content. After a moment, they broke it up.

"Well."

"Well."

"Still..." came Memphis's quiet voice.

Rooker turned, unsure what was happening.

"What?" asked Jack.

"Oh." Leah Archer nodded as a smile broke over her lips.

Memphis Kubiak shrugged. "We're already here. I mean... It seems like too good an opportunity to pass up."

Leah grinned. "O, that's brilliant."

"What?" Rooker glanced at them. "I don't get it."

"Well." Memphis spread his hands, eyeing Jack. "One way or another, he has to talk to his father. So... maybe..."

Jack smiled, getting the idea. He slapped Rooker on the shoulder. "So maybe you should see some mountains made of mirrors."

Chegago was something out of a dream. It was loud, dirty, fast, and never stopped moving. Rooker Flynn loved it from the moment he laid eyes on it.

He couldn't understand a word anyone said, including Jack, but it didn't matter. He probably wouldn't have heard the words anyway over the noise of the otherworldly metropolis. He watched the huge throngs of people, the fast carriages, the skinny boats on the Chegago Sea, all with a sense of childlike wonder he hadn't felt since he was too small to remember.

Rooker got the jist from the hand-talk Jack had taught him during the Steel Trials, but even then he could not take it all in. It was too big, too magical.

Jack's dad stopped at a little yellow cart near one of the wide streets made of flat stone. The cart-man scraped some peppers and onions off his fireless grill, along with a short brown tube of meat, and plunked it all into a little trencher of bread. Jack sprayed some yellow goo on it and handed the thing to Rooker. He sniffed it and took a cautious bite. The weird sausage was soft, warm, meaty, and tangy all at once.

Rooker ate three more.

A few hours later, Rooker found himself seated within a tremendous stone gladiator arena, larger than anything he had ever dreamt. Apparently, the entire population of Jack's world had shown up for the event; there were thousands more than he could count, all arranged in a circle around a big green lawn with white lines drawn on it. The music was loud and exciting, but Rooker couldn't find the band anywhere. Soon enough, the crowd screamed as a bunch of helmeted soldiers in blue and orange ran onto the grass, then played war with another group of soldiers wearing green and gold. It was no Steel Trial, but for a sport without bloodshed, it made for an exciting afternoon. He ate five more meat tubes and a cup of brown sugar water that, through some form of Toshan majik, made little bubbles that fizzed in his mouth like they were laughing for him.

At sunset, Rooker Flynn stood on top of the world.

Jack had taken him to a mountain made of mirrors so tall Rooker had to arch his back to see the top. They stepped inside a little room with a bunch of other doktars and when the doors opened, the room had teleported to the top. Jack took Rooker's elbow and stepped him forward into a glass room. It was similar to the belly dome of the *Venture Brigand*, except it floated a thousand feet over the city.

Beneath his feet was nothing at all, just empty air all the way down to the street. Scattered beneath him were a hundred skyscratchers, towers of mirrors that gleamed in the fading sun.

He felt like he was flying over it all, a bird, free as the air itself.

Rooker Flynn stood over the city. People bustled below like insects, wearing their strange coats and their amazing shoes, all hustling on to whatever was next in their very important lives.

He smiled at the wonder of it all.

In the reflection of the glass box, he saw Jack's face beside his own. The kid's blue eyes stared out over the city with him, standing side by side like kings of the world, and he knew in that moment that he would never be alone again.

And that, of all the amazing things before or since, was the best majik Rooker Flynn ever saw.

The End

The Black Jack Saga Continues
in
Aim of the Archer

Support My Work

PLEASE SCAN THE **QR** code to hit those **Amazon stars** before you move on. 5 stars would be great, but touch whatever number you think best. Tapping those stars is the <u>most</u> powerful thing you can do to keep me writing. More powerful than your social media, more powerful than your dollars, your stars tell Amazon this book might be a good fit for the next reader.

Tapping those stars means you get more Keymark stories. Some of us are going to escape Huánghūn together and travel on the *Venture Brigand* through a sea lit by mismatched moons. And there are so many more amazing places waiting to be explored.

Give this book to a friend. Maybe they'll come with us...

Your #1 Fan,

-Andy

Scan to Rate the
Book

Thank You

"If you want to go fast, go alone. If you want to go far, go together."

N OT NEARLY ENOUGH IS written about friendship. It's the least-lauded love, and it deserves better.

Romance gets whole aisles of stories. Family is stitched into almost every plot. But friendship? That's rarer. *Of Mice and Men, Anne of Green Gables, Butch Cassidy and the Sundance Kid,* Tom & Huck, Frodo & Sam... You can name the classics without ever taking off your socks to count on your toes.

"Lovers stand face to face; friends stand shoulder to shoulder," to paraphrase C. S. Lewis. I got lucky in friendship. My best buddy Brian and I have been shoulder to shoulder for nearly four decades. We've fought, snapped, groused, and grumbled, but our friendship—real, enduring friendship—runs on forgiveness, not perfection. I'll screw up. So will he. And when we do, we don't walk away, we dig in.

Too often we treat friendships like Kleenex: disposable, replaceable, cheap, like we'll just stumble upon a new buddy around the next corner. But turn enough corners, and you find yourself walking alone. Friends don't come easy. They're rarer than diamonds and worth twice as much.

If you've got a friend—a true friend—stand shoulder to shoulder.

And when they fail you... forgive them if you can.

Thanks to my friends Sarah Chorn, Esmay Rosalyne Borst, Isabelle Wagner, and the Red Fury, Joshua Thompson, for helping this story be better than I could make it on my own. And thanks to my pals Andrew Mattocks, Kayla Yetman, and Madison Goodyear for their steadfast encouragement.

I want to thank every reviewer, reader, and indie fan who has taken the time to discuss and promote my work—there would be no more stories without you.

As always, I want to thank my mom and dad for encouraging me to follow my own path.

William, my dear son, you are a miracle.
And yes, I love you most of all, Glo.

About the Author

A. R. Witham is a three-time Emmy-winning writer-producer and a great lover of adventure. He is the world's foremost expert on the history of Keymark. He loves to talk with young people and adults who remember what young people know. He has written for film and television, canoed to the Arctic Circle, hiked the Appalachian Trail and been inside his house while it burned down. He lives in Indianapolis, home of the greatest spectacle in racing.

If you would like a sneak peek at his upcoming work or upcoming events, please reach out to him:

Linktree: linktr.ee/arwitham
Website: arwitham.com

The Stories of A. R. Witham

Black Jack Saga

The Legend of Black Jack

Locke Institute Trilogy
The Crimes of Rooker Flynn
The Trial of Rooker Flynn
The Execution of Rooker Flynn

Upcoming
Aim of the Archer (Black Jack Saga #5)
Don't Die Dave (LitRPG)

Shorts
(available free at arwitham.com)
The Tale of the Border Knight (Novella)
Border Crossing (Short Story)

*H*E WAS AN OUTLAW, *of that there can be no doubt.*

       His eye was dark, his hair was black, and his smile was a lie.

I can smell him even now, all these decades later, a perfume of sweat, salt, and spices from far-off foreign lands. He smelled of the Irridin Sea, for it was his home.

They called him Rooker Flynn, although none knew his true name.

The stories are cryptic as to whether he summoned Black Jack from another sphere or resurrected him from the dead. Whichever tale you believe, he brought the legendary bandit and his majik staff Nepenthe back after a hundred years in the grave. Together, they defeated the Fell Prince, ended the Black Accord, and returned the healing majik to the Great Bells of Keymark. Those legends are true and survive to this day.

It is said he only gave his heart to one woman, but she never once drew breath.

They say he escaped the Winter Caverns unscathed, haggled for the soul of a sea witch, slayed a host of dæmons, and humbled the Mermen King into offering him three daughters in tribute. He talked to the sea and it talked back. Some insist he only had one eye, like a cyclops. Others claim he rode a dragon that flew from the edge of the world. They say there was no lock he could not pick, no cage he could not break, and no woman who could resist his charms. And his greatest crime was not as a pirate but as a friend.

Freedom was his only master, and he fought for it until the day of his execution.

Those are the folk tales about him.

Now you know the truth.

www.ingramcontent.com/pod-product-compliance
Lightning Source LLC
Chambersburg PA
CBHW031331020726
47499CB00005B/1218